Magus to the Hermetic Order of the Golden Sprout, 12th Dan Master of Dimac, poet, adventurer, swordsman and concert pianist; big game hunter, Best Dressed Man of 1933; mountaineer, lone yachtsman, Shakespearian actor and topless go-go dancer; Robert Rankin's hobbies include passive smoking, communicating with the dead and lying about his achievements. He lives in Sussex with his wife and family.

Robert Rankin is the author of *The Garden of Unearthly Delights*, *The Most Amazing Man Who Ever Lived*, *The Greatest Show Off Earth*, *Raiders of the Lost Car Park*, *The Book of Ultimate Truths*, *Armageddon The Musical*, *They Came and Ate Us*, *Armageddon II: The B Movie*, *The Suburban Book of the Dead*, *Armageddon III: The Remake* and the *Brentford* quartet; *The Antipope*, *The Brentford Triangle*, *East of Ealing* and *The Sprouts of Wrath*, which are all published by Corgi books. Robert Rankin's latest novel, *Nostradamus Ate My Hamster*, is now available as a Doubleday hardback.

What they say about Robert Rankin:

'One of the rare guys who can always make me laugh'
Terry Pratchett

'To the top-selling ranks of humourists such as Douglas Adams and Terry Pratchett, let us welcome Mr Rankin'
Tom Hutchinson, *The Times*

'A born writer with a taste for the occult. Robert Rankin is to Brentford what William Faulkner was to Yoknaptawpha County'
Time Out

'One of the finest living comic writers . . . a sort of drinking man's H.G. Wells'
Midweek

Also by Robert Rankin

THE ANTIPOPE
THE BRENTFORD TRIANGLE
EAST OF EALING
THE SPROUTS OF WRATH
ARMAGEDDON THE MUSICAL
THEY CAME AND ATE US,
ARMAGEDDON II: THE B MOVIE
THE SUBURBAN BOOK OF THE DEAD,
ARMAGEDDON III: THE REMAKE
THE BOOK OF ULTIMATE TRUTHS
RAIDERS OF THE LOST CAR PARK
THE MOST AMAZING MAN WHO EVER LIVED
THE GARDEN OF UNEARTHLY DELIGHTS

and published by Corgi Books

THE GREATEST SHOW OFF EARTH

Robert Rankin

CORGI BOOKS

THE GREATEST SHOW OFF EARTH
A CORGI BOOK : 0 552 13924 6

Originally published in Great Britain by Doubleday
a division of Transworld Publishers

PRINTING HISTORY
Doubleday edition published 1994
Corgi edition published 1995
Corgi edition reprinted 1995
Corgi edition reprinted 1996

Set in 10/11pt Monotype Plantin by
Phoenix Typesetting, Ilkley, West Yorkshire.

Corgi Books are published by Transworld Publishers Ltd,
61–63 Uxbridge Road, London W5 5SA,
in Australia by Transworld Publishers (Australia) Pty Ltd,
15–25 Helles Avenue, Moorebank, NSW 2170,
and in New Zealand by Transworld Publishers (NZ) Ltd,
3 William Pickering Drive, Albany, Auckland.

Printed and bound in Great Britain by
Cox & Wyman Ltd, Reading, Berkshire.

For a good friend
of mine,
Pádraig O'Méalóid

I

How Raymond came to meet the flying starfish from Uranus. And how that same flying
starfish taught him the meaning of the word
'schmuck'.

If you enter the village from the end where the common
is, turn left at the mini-roundabout that everyone drives
straight across, take the first right beside the big house
that's always being done up, then you'll find yourself in
King Neptune's Road.

Go down it for about half an old mile. Pass the
overgrown playing field, the youth club where they
play the loud music on Mondays, The Jolly Gardeners
where music is never allowed, the road where Simon
lives, and the big green corrugated workshop of Vinny
the Builder.

The-lane-that-dare-not-speak-its-name is tucked away
on the left, at the very top of the hill.

You will have to drive quite carefully down the lane,
because it is full of potholes that no-one wants to take
responsibility for. But if you do make it safely to the
bottom you'll notice several houses hiding there.

There's the horrid new one, with the satellite dish
and the three bad dogs; the proud red tile-hung job on
the corner, where the mad old major lives. And, up
on the bank, the little Victorian cottage with the cast-iron
gate.

And *that's* Raymond's house.

Of course, if you happen to come into the village from
the other direction, it can all get really complicated.

7

So the best thing would be to stop and ask at the post office. But if you do have to ask at the post office, then ask either the lady with the dyed blond hair or her assistant with the nice blue eyes. Don't ask the bald postmaster who's 'a bit of a lad', or the ancient granny who sits and knits. Because they both hate Raymond, so they'll probably give you the wrong directions.

Oh yes, and if you get there any time after six of a warm spring evening, you won't find Raymond at home anyway. He'll be at work on his allotment. And God only knows how you get *there*.

Naturally Raymond knew the route to his allotment well enough. He even knew the short cut. But then he knew his way all around the village. He'd lived in the village for all of his life so far and he knew all of the things it was necessary to know.

He knew where to go on Mondays if you wanted to hear loud music. And where to drink the rest of the week if you didn't. He knew better than to attempt the retrieval of another tennis ball from the garden of the horrid new house with the satellite dish. And he knew that the potholes in the-lane-that-dare-not-speak-its-name were not his responsibility.

Raymond was twenty-three years of age. His eyes were blue and his hair was brown. His height was a little under six feet. And his feet were a little over size nine. He worked for Vinny the Builder on the big house that was always being done up. And when he wasn't working, or listening to loud music, or drinking quietly, or disavowing responsibility for potholes, and it was after six on a warm spring evening, as it was now, he could, like as not, be found digging on his allotment.

It was mostly digging that Raymond did there. The actual planting and nurturing and harvesting aspects of allotment life were, as yet, *terra incognita* to him. He *had* sent off a postal order for a manual on the subject, but it had failed to arrive within the promised twenty-three days. Raymond had telephoned the publishers, who assured him that it *had* been sent. And later he remonstrated with the bald postmaster, who swore blind that it *had* been delivered. Voices *had* become raised and insults exchanged. And Raymond had found himself barred from the village post office.

In fact, the manual *had* been delivered, but in error to the horrid new house with the satellite dish. And the man who lived in that house hated Raymond, because Raymond had once knocked a tennis ball through his greenhouse roof and then trampled down many prize blooms whilst making good his escape from the three bad dogs after trying to retrieve it.

So the man in the horrid new house with the satellite dish had decided to keep Raymond's manual and grow some vegetables on the bare patches of land where the flowers had got trampled down.

So Raymond just dug for now. Often in his vest, and many times whistling loudly. Habits which got right up the noses of the other allotment holders. And on this particular warm spring evening, he was doing it all alone.

His fellow allotmenteers had tired quite early with the sound of his whistling and the sight of his armpits, and repaired to The Jolly Gardeners, where whistling was prohibited and singlets proscribed. Raymond was fashioning a hole in which to plant an apple tree. A Granny Smith, or perhaps a Cox's Orange Pippin. He had plenty of time to make up his mind, as apple trees are best planted in November.

His spade struck upon a light brown stone and Raymond stooped to pick it up. He was examining the stone with some interest when his best friend Simon happened by.

Simon was slightly older than Raymond, but no wiser. He found favour in the eyes of the local womenfolk and had worked, ever since he left school, for Mr Hilsavise the Gardener, whom many claimed to be in league with the devil. Simon had dark hair, dark eyes and very expensive dental work that he had saved up for.

'Evening, Ray,' said Simon, flashing his smile. 'Digging a hole?'

Raymond looked up from his digging. 'Good-evening, Simon.' said he. 'New hat?'

Simon, who never wore one, even in winter, shook his hatless head. 'I've been thinking about growing a beard. But it's only in the ideas stage yet. What is that you hold in your hand?'

Raymond drew a spittley finger over his find. 'It is either a stone that longs to become a potato, or a potato which has affected a most successful transformation into a stone.'

'Perhaps it is a fossilized potato.'

'Or a simulacrum.'

'Possibly so.' Simon made a mental note to look that one up when he got home. 'Did you read that thing in the paper the other day?' he asked.

'No,' said Raymond. 'You must have me confused with somebody else.'

'It would appear', said Simon, 'that the Russians have drilled this hole.'

'No.' Raymond gave his head a shake. '*I* dug this hole.'

'No.' Simon gave his head a shake also. 'Not the hole I'm talking about. This hole is another hole entirely. In Siberia. Russian scientists drilled it to study the movement of tectonic plates.' Simon paused in the hope that Ray would ask exactly what tectonic plates might be. But he didn't, so Simon went on. 'Twenty-three miles down they drilled. Through the solid bedrock. Then suddenly their drill broke through the roof of some kind of mighty cavern. So they pulled it up and lowered down this special microphone on a very long lead. And you'll never guess what they heard.'

Raymond leaned upon the handle of his spade which, since the arrival of Simon, had done no digging whatsoever. 'Was it the sound of millions of souls screaming in eternal agony?' he enquired.

'That's what it said in the paper.'

'I see.' Raymond pocketed his stone/potato, climbed out of his hole and began to fill it in. 'Would you care for a cup of coffee?' he asked Simon.

'Yes please.'

'Me too. But I only have tea.'

Inside his allotment hut, Raymond uncorked his Thermos flask and poured out two piping-hot cups of tea. One with sugar and one without. 'I wish it were coffee,' he said in a sorrowful tone. 'I have never cared for tea.'

'You should ask you mum to make up coffee for you, instead of tea then.'

'If only it was that easy.' Raymond sighed. 'But I always make up the flask myself.'

Simon sipped at the tea that was offered him. 'I am baffled by the Thermos flask,' he said between sippings.

'How so?'

'Well, you put something hot into it and it stays hot. And you put something cold into it and it stays cold.'

Raymond nodded thoughtfully.

'Well. How does it *know*?'

Raymond grinned the smile that he'd got on the National Health and did his best to explain the situation. 'It doesn't actually know as such. You see the Thermos flask consists of two glass bottles, one inside the other. And between these two bottles there is a quarter of an inch of vacuum. And heat cannot travel through a vacuum.'

'Get away,' said Simon. 'So heat can't travel through a vacuum?'

'You have it.'

Simon scratched at his fine dark head of hair. 'Then tell me this: if heat cannot travel through a quarter of an inch of vacuum, how can the heat from the sun travel through ninety-six million miles of vacuum and reach the earth?'

Raymond peered into the steaming glass throat of his Thermos flask. 'Perhaps it does *know* after all,' he whispered in an awestruck kind of a tone.

'Makes you think,' said Simon. 'What is that terrible smell, by the way?'

Raymond sniffed. 'You have trodden in dog pooh again, I suppose.'

'No, not that smell.'

Raymond sniffed again. 'It smells like fish. Have you trodden in fish?'

'Don't be a schmuck,' said Simon, who had come across the word in his dictionary while looking up 'tectonic', and had been hoping for an opportunity to use it.

Raymond was about to ask the meaning of the word 'schmuck', when the sound of a terrific detonation, coming from very near by, caused him instead to drop his Thermos flask and take a dive for cover.

'Whatever was that?' asked Simon, joining him at floor altitude. 'Are we at war?'

'No, we're still friends.' Raymond rolled on to his back and struck his head on half a bag of solid cement. 'Go out and see what's happened.'

Simon felt at his teeth. 'Would you do that if you were me?'

There was a second detonation, somewhat louder and nearer than the first.

'Run!' cried Raymond, leaping to his feet.

There was a good deal of undignified struggling and fighting as the two young men sought their escape through the narrow doorway. But when it was over and done with and they emerged, puffing and panting back into the warm spring evening, one thing was immediately apparent to them. And that one thing was, that nothing whatsoever appeared to have changed upon the allotments.

'I see no shell holes,' said Simon, straightening his hair and dusting down his manly denims. 'Nor any holes at all for that matter.'

'I have many down my lane,' said Raymond. 'But they are not *my* responsibility. I wonder what made those loud bangs.'

'Have you ever heard of The Barisal Guns?'

Raymond shook his head and showered his shoulders with cement dust. 'I must hear of them now, I suppose?'

'They might be pertinent to the situation.'

'Pertinent?'

'Pertinent.' Simon hooked his thumbs into the belt-loops of his jeans and began to pace about. 'I read of them in a book about unexplained phenomena that I received through the post.'

'I sent up for one of those,' said Raymond wistfully. 'But mine never arrived.'

'Shame. Well in this book there's an article about The Barisal Guns. They are sounds resembling cannon fire that are regularly heard around this little village called, coincidentally enough, Barisal. Which is somewhere in the Ganges delta. They're not cannons though and no-one knows what causes them. They're believed to be of an atmospheric nature and they go . . . Ouch my nose!'

'That would surely be a misprint in your book then.'

'No, its ouch *my* nose.' Simon staggered about, clutching at his face.

'I don't think I altogether follow that,' said Raymond.

'I just banged my bloody nose,' whined Simon, somewhat nasally.

'On what?'

'I don't know. On something. Something there.' Simon gestured in the general direction of where the nose-banging incident purportedly occurred. Raymond stepped over to see what might be seen.

But nothing was to be seen.

Although something was to be felt.

'Shiva's sheep!' cried Raymond. 'I have banged my

nose also. And stubbed my toe into the bargain.' He reached out a seeking hand and found it blocked before him by a cold, hard and quite invisible wall. 'It is glass,' said he.

'Glass?' Simon slouched over, rubbing his nose. 'How is my profile?' he enquired, and, 'Show me this glass.'

'It is here.' Raymond went tap tap tap with his knuckle.

Simon put out his hand and he too gave it a tap. 'It is very clear glass,' said he, 'as it cannot be seen at all. And very cold glass also and . . .' He put his tapping knuckle to his nose. 'It smells strongly of fish.'

Raymond sniffed at his own knuckle. 'Perhaps it is recycled glass,' said he. 'But who put it here and, for that matter,' he began to tap up and down and all around, 'how big is it?'

'Let's find out. You go that way and I will go this.'

The two set off, reaching and tapping and stooping and tapping and doing that thing with the palms of their hands that mime artistes never tire of boring their audiences with. Presently they found themselves together once more. On the other side of Raymond's hut.

'Ah,' said the allotment holder.

'Ah indeed,' said his companion. 'We would appear to be encircled. This isn't good, is it?'

Raymond scratched his head. And so did Simon.

'Kindly stop scratching my head,' said Raymond. 'And help me to smash our way out.'

'Good idea.' Simon took up Raymond's spade and Raymond sought out the pickaxe that he had once been persuaded into buying by the man with the earring who ran the ironmongers in the high street.

They swung and they smote. They pummelled and they pounded. They beat and belaboured, bashed and blackjacked, battered and bludgeoned, biffed and banged. Great ungodly oaths were sworn and knuckles grazed aplenty. But it was all to no avail. The invisible wall didn't give. Not a crack, nor a chip, nor a chaffing. It held.

Presently the end came off Raymond's pickaxe and nearly took his eye out. He flung aside the shaft and sank to his knees in the dirt. Simon dropped down beside him.

'How are you on screaming for help?' Raymond asked, when he'd got back some of his breath.

'*Help!* screamed Simon.

'Pretty good,' said Raymond. 'Heeeeeeelllp!'

The sun was just beginning to dip behind the fine old meadow oaks that bordered the allotments, and hoarseness of the throat was taking its toll of the 'help' screamers, when Simon had an idea.

'We could light a fire,' said he in the voice of Louis Armstrong. 'Stack stuff up against this invisible wall and set it ablaze. Melt our way out.'

'Do you think that would work?'

'Have you ever heard of Euclid's fifth proposition?'

'No,' said Raymond. 'Nor do I wish to hear of it now.'

'We could burn that old pickaxe handle. What else do you have?'

Raymond cast a troubled eye towards his nice wooden hut.

They got a really decent blaze going. They stood back and admired it. They warmed their hands by it and they poked at it with sticks. They threw things onto it and they generally behaved in that childish irresponsible manner that all men do when they have a bonfire.

'Do you think it's starting to melt yet?' Raymond asked at length.

'Bound to be.' Simon fanned at his face and took to a fit of coughing. 'There's an awful lot of smoke,' he observed.

'An awful lot.' Raymond joined in with the coughing. 'I say. Look up there.'

'Up where?'

'Up there.' Raymond pointed towards the vertical.

The smoke was gathering thickly and not too distantly above.

'I think I am beginning to suffocate,' said Simon.

'Stamp out the fire!' croaked Raymond.

The smoke hung captive in the great big transparent and seemingly impenetrable dome that enclosed the better part of Raymond's allotment patch. Raymond sat upon the half a bag of solid cement, on the little concrete rectangle where, until so recently, his nice wooden hut used to stand. Simon sat beside him. Both were growing somewhat short of breath.

'I don't want to be an alarmist,' said Raymond, 'but unless help comes really soon, I think we are going to die.'

Simon glowered into the concrete. 'This is all your fault. I should never have come here tonight.'

'My fault? I like that. I was quietly digging my hole and minding my own business until you turned up. It is *you* that has brought this thing upon us. I'll bet you have fallen out with Mr Hilsavise, whom many believe to be in league with the devil.'

'I have not.' Simon dabbed at his nose, which was starting to run. 'I don't want to die,' he complained. 'I am young and handsome and I paid a fortune for these teeth.'

'You and your damned teeth,' said Raymond.

'Dental hygiene is very important. You'll be all gums by the time you're thirty.'

'I shall never see twenty-four unless I get out of here. You couldn't see your way clear to chewing our way out I suppose.'

Simon rose to take a dizzy swing at Raymond. 'You schmuck,' said he, lapsing from consciousness.

Raymond sat and hugged at his knees. This really was all too upsetting. The evening, which had started out so well for him, had turned into the stuff of nightmare. It looked as if he was actually going to die.

Raymond had never given death so much as a second thought. And it now occurred to him that this might have been something of an oversight on his part. Had he stored up any riches in heaven? he wondered. Would the good Lord smile favourably upon him? Had he been a 'good' person? He was certain he'd never really been a bad person. But was that enough? Was it for him the choirs celestial or would he be despatched to join the screaming sinners of Siberia? If he was, he would certainly keep his eyes open for any sign of a dangling microphone.

Raymond's head began to spin and his thoughts began to get all jumbled about. He climbed unsteadily to his feet and stumbled about clutching at his throat and gasping for air. And then he tripped over his spade and fell flat on his face.

And then, in that final desperate moment. He had an idea.

The sun was almost gone behind the fine old meadow oaks now and the moon was climbing up to take its place. The birds of the allotments called good night to one another, as they swung in wary arcs around the big grey smoke-filled dome that smelled of fish. And as silence fell with darkness and the stars began to light up, there came a stirring of the earth. A mole perhaps?

Not a foot from the edge of the big grey smoke-filled dome, a clump of soil rose up and fell aside. And the polished head of Raymond's spade broke the surface.

There followed then a scrabbling and a struggling, a hand, an arm, a shoulder and a head. Raymond breathed in the good fresh air and dragged himself out to safety. His body left the hole with a sound not unlike that of a cork being drawn from a bottle. The night air rushed down his tunnel and flooded into the terrible dome. Raymond didn't waste a lot of time.

Minutes later he and Simon lay side by side staring up at freedom's sky. Well, Raymond was staring up at it. Simon was still out for the count.

'Phew,' said Raymond. 'Phew indeed.' He shook Simon roughly by the shoulder. 'Phew eh?'

Simon stirred fitfully. 'Unhand me, Mr Hilsavise,' he mumbled.

'It's not what you think. I hardly know your daughter.'

'Scoundrel,' said Raymond cuffing his chum.

'Aaah, oow . . . oh.' Simon came awake. 'I think I'm going to be sick,' said he.

'You are saved,' Raymond told him. 'What do you think of that?'

Simon threw up all over the place.

'Some thanks,' said Raymond.

And then.

'Congratulations, Earthman,' came a voice from on high. *'You have passed the test.'*

Raymond turned his eyes once more towards the heavens and, to his horror, saw that a goodly portion of the sky was now filled by something quite unsettling. An enormous star-shaped something. It was bulbous and bloated. Tiny coloured globes twinkled about five monstrous appendages. Light pulsed from an unwholesome middle section, all flesh-flaps and chewing mouthparts. A fishy fug, that would have challenged the fortitude of a seasoned Grimsby trawlerman, cloaked the allotment air in a healthless miasma.

Simon took the opportunity to throw up once again.

Raymond clamped his hands over his nose and did shallow-breathing exercises.

'I am Abdullah,' declared the star-shaped something. 'I represent The Divine Council of Cosmic Superfolk. And I am pleased to tell you that you have passed the initiative test set by his magnificence, The Sultan of Uranus.'

'I've chucked up all down my front.' Simon plucked at his shirt. 'That smell. That voice. What is all this?'

'Spacemen,' said Raymond through his fingers. 'From Uranus.'

'Uranus? Bugger that!' Simon jumped to his feet with a quite impressive display of agility, considering his sorry condition, took to his heels and fled the allotments.

Raymond watched sadly as his friend vanished away into the darkness.

'Some thanks,' he said, for the second time in a single evening.

Abdullah the flying starfish waggled his monstrous appendages. 'Nice teeth your mate,' spake he. 'No bottle though.'

'Eh?'

'Not like you.' The unwholesome middle section pulsed and throbbed. 'You're heroic.'

'Thanks.' Raymond struggled to his feet, a firm hold on his hooter.

'So,' said Abdullah, 'as you have now passed the initiative test, you are entitled to a seat at The Grand Interplanetary Convention. It's on Venus.'

'Venus?'

'Venus. So, what do you say?'

Raymond wasn't at all sure just what he *should* say. It was all so, well, so unexpected really. 'Could I have a few minutes to think about this?' he asked.

'No,' said Abdullah. 'You can't.'

'Oh. Well, then I suppose it's yes. All right.'

'Good man.' Abdullah's unenticing middle section bulged alarmingly and extruded an obscene-looking tentacle with a big pink suction pad on the end. This fastened itself onto the top of Raymond's head. Certain chemicals passed from it, entered him.

Raymond was aware of a popping in the ears and a metallic taste in his mouth. His eyes crossed, his sphincter tightened. Oblivion overtook him.

When he awoke, it was to find that he was no longer on the allotments. And, as his head began to clear and his senses to return, that he was no longer on the planet of his birth. Perspective seemed all wrong and the colour of the sky was a muddy green. It was cold too.

Raymond rubbed at his arms. Then he glanced down at his arms. And his legs. He wasn't wearing any clothes. He was naked.

He tried to stand, but bumped his head and sat back down. He was all sealed up again, but this time inside a hollow sphere. He had a little seat to sit on. And what was this?

Raymond turned up a label that hung on a string about his neck. He read aloud the words that were printed upon it.

GRAND INTERPLANETARY CONVENTION
CHARITY AUCTION.
LOT 23, SPECIMEN OF EARTH LIFE. MALE.

'So,' said Raymond. '*That* is the meaning of the word "schmuck".'

2

Simon lay a goodly while in the long grass beneath the fine old meadow oaks that bordered the allotments. He'd witnessed the entire affair. Overheard Raymond's conversation with Abdullah, and watched in wonder as his chum was sucked into the bowels of the flying starfish and whisked away to outer space.

And now here *he* was, all on his own, wondering just what he should do next.

He hadn't really meant to run off like that. Not without first saying thanks to Raymond for saving his life and everything. But he really hadn't had any choice in the matter.

Simon had read once in a medical magazine about this special chemical that you had inside your brain. And how, in times of grave personal crisis, such as the threat of physical violence, this special chemical weighed up the pros and cons and as quick as a flash decided whether you stood your ground and fought your corner, or clenched your buttocks and ran for your life. In Simon's case the special chemical unerringly chose the latter of the two decisions.

So, it wasn't as if he was a coward or anything like that. Oh no. It was the special chemical. Simon felt sure that Raymond wouldn't hold it against him once he'd returned in glory from Venus.

'I hope he brings me back a present,' said Simon to himself. 'I wonder what they drink on Venus.'

And wondering what they drank on Venus, made Simon remember what they drank on Earth. And how, if he just hurried, he could catch a pint or two of it at The Jolly Gardeners before closing.

'Boom Shanka,' said the lad with the teeth, rising from his grassy nest and saluting the night sky. 'Nice one, Raymond, and hope to see you soon then.'

And with that said, Simon made off for a quick change of shirt and the pub.

Now in every village, as in every town, there are pubs and there are *pubs*. These span the saloon-bar spectrum 'twixt the spit and sawdust and the slick and Spritzered.

Down at the infra-red end, there are great beer-bellied blackguards, who maintain a turbulent dominion over smoke-wreathed drinking dens, where the devotees of rival sportswear cults have at one another with billiard cues, while Faith No More play on the jukebox.

While up in the ultra violet, you have the gentile 'we're more a traveller's rest than a public house really, dear' kind of establishment. Here, short, middle-aged, well-kept ladies, with tall hair and lipgloss, divide their time between working out at the gym and artistically arranging beer-mats. They hold court from tall bar stools, while husbands named Keith or Trevor ogle the teenage barmaids, as they constantly empty the ashtrays and worry at the tabletops with fragrant J-Cloths. A tape of 'background music', that the landlady brought back from her holiday in Benidorm, nags at the nerves from secret speakers.

The Jolly Gardeners occupied a mellow middleground between these gaudy extremes. Andy the landlord served a clear pint of ample measure at an honest price, smiled upon all of his patrons and said 'jolly good', whenever he thought it appropriate. With little more than a voice of quiet authority, he had won the respect of his regulars. In fact, he had engendered such a spirit of camaraderie amongst them, that on the single occasion when violence actually erupted, the perpetrator was made instantly aware, by the appalled looks of those around him, that he had committed a most grievous *faux pas*, and slunk from the pub, never to return.

Under Andy's benign rule, The Jolly Gardeners was finally starting to flourish. For the first time in its long and colourful history, it was actually running at a profit.

The previous landlord, gone upon a midnight clear, hailed, according to local opinion, from a long line of well poisoners. And met eventually, according to local legend, with a sad accident involving cement and deep water.

The brewery had confidence in Andy. He had their trust.

He did not intend to betray it.

Now, it must be said, however, that for all the excellence of its present management, The Jolly Gardeners, as a building, was not a thing of beauty and a joy Forever Amber.

Oh no no no.

To those who hold to the unfashionable conviction that some things *are* better than other things, and to some people capable of making the distinction, the golden age of public house design apparently died with Queen Victoria.

Among the many books that will never see publication, there is one called *Great Pubs of the Twentieth Century*. This will be written by a man who has a thing about 'mock Tudor'.

Mock Tudor!

It was definitely the death of Queen Victoria that did it. History proves to us that inadequate architects, when faced with an uncertain present, inevitably take refuge in a pipedream of the past. Those of the Edwardian era, employed by the breweries certainly did.

Mock Tudor!

The Jolly Gardeners was a mock-Tudor bar. It had been given a face-lift shortly after the First World War.

This consisted of gutting out all the mahogany and etched-glass partition work and beaming the place around and about and up and down with tarred railway sleepers. There had even been talk of renaming the place, The Dick Turpin.

But that was all very long ago now. And few there were still living, who could recall the pub in its previous incarnation. The regulars merely accepted it for the thing it was, a haven of good ale, good companionship, merry converse and no music whatsoever. That was quite enough really. They didn't give a toss about the aesthetics.

Simon was a regular at The Jolly Gardeners and *he* certainly didn't give a toss about the aesthetics. He emerged from the alleyway which lead from the allotments and his house, crossed over King Neptune's Road and approached the pub in question.

Tarred railway sleepers, peely-painted stucco, knackered old coachlamps and a pub sign with only one hinge.

'Home sweet home,' said Simon.

He entered through the saloon-bar door, ducked his head beneath the-beam-that-strangers-bash-their-skulls-upon and sidled up to the bar.

Regulars, engaged in merry converse, broke off momentarily to savour Simon's sidling. And having savoured same and found it pleasing, returned to their discourses, with words to the effect that, though his teeth were sound, his stride was shifty. And a shifty stride on one so young was not, of truth, a good thing to behold.

Simon ceased his sidling and perched himself upon his favourite bar stool. Andy smiled at Simon and the lad smiled at the landlord in reply.

Andy was of medium height, whatever that may be. Smart turn-out, ironed shirt, trouser creases. The head of an old Greek god atop the body of a young British businessman. A lot of unanswered questions. And a beard.

'Evening, Simon,' said Andy. 'New hat?'

'No thanks. Just a pint of the usual, please.'

'Pint of the usual. Good idea.' Andy gazed along the row of pump handles. 'Pint of the usual, you said?'

'I did, yes.'

'Now, let me just clarify this. Would that be the usual you usually order when first you come in? The more-expensive-usual that you order when someone else is buying a round? Or the cheap "Death-by-Cider" usual that you have at the end of the evening, when your money's running low?'

'The usual that I usually order when first I come in.'

'But you don't usually come in this late.'

Simon stroked his manly chin. 'I see what you mean. Then tell you what, I think I'll go for the more-expensive-usual that I usually order when someone else is buying a round.'

'Quite sure?' Andy arched an eyebrow.

'Quite sure.'

'That one's off, I'm afraid,' said Andy.

'Cheap "Death-by-Cider" usual then.'

'That's off also.'

'What about the usual that I usually order when first I come in?'

'That one's on.'

'A pint of that then please.'

'Jolly good.' Andy placed a glass beneath the spout of a nearby beer engine and drew off a fine full measure. 'Seen Raymond tonight?' he asked Simon.

'No, not tonight.' As Simon spoke the lie he peeped at his reflection in the mirror behind the bar. Just to see if his teeth were sidling. They weren't.

'Shame.' Andy presented Simon with his pint. 'Only a parcel arrived here this morning for him by mistake. I wondered if you'd pass it on.'

'I'd be pleased to.' Simon took out a five-pound note.

Andy plucked it from his fingers. 'Good man. You see my wife accepted the delivery and there were no stamps on it and she had to pay the postman. I'll take the cost out of this and you can get it from Raymond when you give him the parcel. Cheers.'

'Cheers.' Simon sipped at his pint. 'I don't usually drink *this*,' he said.

Andy returned from the cash register with a few small coins. 'Something wrong?' he asked.

'No,' said Simon, 'everything's just fine.'

'Jolly good.' Andy sank away beneath the counter.

'Evening, Simon.' The voice came down the bar from the lips of Dick Godolphin. 'New hat?'

'I refer you to the answer I gave a moment ago,' said Simon, in a prime-ministerial tone.

Andy rose again, a large parcel in his hands. He placed it on the counter next to Simon's pint. 'There you go,' said he.

'Cheers,' said Simon once more.

'I have often wondered,' Andy said, 'why is it that members of the opposition party always waste half of Prime Minister's question time asking the PM what his appointments are for the day.'

'Ah.' Simon brought his teeth into play. 'I have a theory about that. I reckon they think that if they keep on asking him again and again, then one day he'll simply crack and say something like, "This morning I had meetings with Cabinet colleagues and others and at lunchtime I had a naked Filipino lass lowered onto my honourable member in a revolving split-cane basket. Oh damn, now what have I said? I resign."'

'You think that might be it?'

'Definitely.' Simon finished his pint.

'Same again?' Andy asked.

'I would seem to be without funds,' said Simon. 'Does Raymond still have an account here?'

'Certainly does. All paid up since last night. A twenty-five-pound credit line. This is the only pub hereabouts

26

that still affords him the privilege. A privilege he has not as yet been foolish enough to abuse.'

'Nor would he ever. I'll have a pint on his account then.'

'You certainly will not.' The landlord shook his old grey beard in a professional manner. 'The door to trust swings both ways you know.'

'Indeed I do.' Simon fell back in mock alarm. 'But am I not Raymond's best and trusted friend?'

'You are his only friend at all, I so believe.'

'And have I not just paid the postage on his parcel, as only would a best and trusted friend?'

The old grey beard went up and down.

'Then do not seek to drive a wedge between true friends. Put an IOU into the till on my behalf and same again, landlord, please.'

'Jolly good,' said Andy taking Simon's glass. 'What was it you were drinking by the way?'

'I'll have Death-by-Cider,' said Dick Godolphin, suddenly at Simon's side. 'As my good mate here's buying.'

'Would that I could,' replied the drinker with the newly acquired twenty-five-pound credit line. 'But even if I could, I bet I wouldn't.'

Godolphin muttered curses of the Romany persuasion and prepared once more to buy his own.

Dick was Bramfield's token gypsy poacher. Every village has to have one. It's a tradition, or an old charter, or a worn-out cliché. Or something. Dick was short and dark and fearsome to behold. He wore a waxed cap and a tweed jacket, which was half right and possessed a pair of eyes which, in the words of D.H. Lawrence of Arabia, "Shone out as black as pissholes in the snow."

Dick had a wife who was forever in the family way and a lurcher that forever humped his leg.

He dwelt in the vampire world between the time of pub-close and the dawn of day. During these unhallowed hours he sallied forth, his lurcher on his leg, to reap a horrid harvest in the fields of rabbitkind.

Oblivious to the season or the weather or the signs that said 'Keep Out', Dick limped across the uplands and the downs, scattering flocks of sheep before him and putting the fear of God into the corn circle makers. On a good night he would bag as many as four fat bunnies, which would fetch as much as a pound a piece from the local butcher.

To the average town dweller, this might appear an extremely difficult way of scraping a living. But what do townies know about country life?

Not a lot. That's what.

Dick was the last of a dying breed. Or one of the last, at least. And he felt it his holy destiny to continue with a fine old country way, which without the likes of him might vanish for ever, along with the hand-drawn plough, the tied cottage and the squire's right to have his pick of the village virgins whenever there was an R in the month.

And so he eked out his humble living with little to support him but a pound a bunny, the social security payments and the handsome weekly stipend awarded him by The Society for the Preservation of Rural Crafts.

God bless you, Dick Godolphin.

'Piss off, Dick,' said Simon. 'And get your dog off my leg.'

'Down, Lurcher,' said Godolphin. 'Come to heel.'

'Here you go,' said Andy, passing one more pint to Simon. 'Sign here upon this beer-mat if you will.'

'I'll sign for the entire twenty-five pounds. You don't want a lot of beer-mats cluttering up your till.'

'Jolly good,' said Andy. 'Same again, was it, Dick?'

'Same again,' said Dick.

Simon sipped his second pint and sidled with his eyes. Most of the regulars were in, gathered in their favoured corners on the mock-Tudor pews or the low stools with the reproduction Queen Anne legs. Others ranged along the bar holding forth on this thing or the other. Sex and scandal. Wars and rumours of war. Everything and nothing, as is oft the way in pubs.

28

Simon watched them at it. Long Bob the chicken farmer, headless behind the-beam-that-strangers-always-bang-their-skulls-on-when-they-come-out-of-the-Gents, laughing uproariously amidst members of the village rock band, Roman Candle (the parachute accident, not the firework); Military Dave, who was something in the refinement of engine oil, hunched above a triple vodka dreaming of Brooklands; the Scribe, who apparently wrote for a living, although none could ever find his books in the shops; two fragrant checkout girls from the supermarket in the high street. And so on and so forth.

Simon knew them all, many from as long ago as school. Same old faces. Same old jokes and, Andy willing, same old rounds of drinks.

But here sat *he*. And he was no longer the same. He had seen his best friend sucked away to Venus by a flying starfish. He could never now be quite the same again.

And so he sat and sipped and sidled mentally about the best way he could capitalize upon this knowledge that was known to him alone. It would have to be handled with care as the precious package it was. If he could persuade a Sunday newspaper to believe his story there might well be large cash payments to be had. But there was the far greater likelihood of being branded a nutcase.

Simon set in to do some serious thinking.

And then he was clouted in the ear.

'Ouch!' went he, collapsing to the floor.

The sudden silence born to this appalling breach of social etiquette died an equally sudden death as its cause became apparent. It was Liza, Simon's long-suffering girlfriend, and as she struck down the lad on a more or less regular basis, even Andy turned a Grecian-sightless to it. He drew the line at her putting the boot in though.

'Nine o'clock!' cried Liza as the regulars returned to their merry converse. 'You'd be round at nine, you said.'

In his head upon the floor Simon's memory struck a sexual chord. But as his face was now receiving the

29

unwelcome attentions of Dick's lurcher, he was a bit stuck as yet to voice an eloquent apology.

'I've been dangling in that bloody split-cane basket for an hour. My bum looks like a barbecued beefburger.'

'Get your dog off my face, Dick,' Simon spluttered.

'Up, boy,' said the poacher. 'Come to heel.'

Simon struggled to his feet. All sickly smiles. 'I thought we agreed to meet here, Liza. I wondered why you were late. I was just coming round.'

'You lying . . .' Liza tried to swing a foot. 'Get your bloody dog off my leg, Dick.'

'Listen, Liza, please.' Simon spat out pubic dog hair. 'Something unexpected came up. I'm very sorry.'

'Very sorry?' Liza flexed her nostrils. Fine young nostrils they were too. Set where nostrils should be set, beneath a pretty nose upon a pretty face, framed all about by an extravagance of fine young auburn hair. 'What is that smell?' she asked.

'Smell? What smell?' Simon began to fan at himself.

'Smell,' said Liza.

Around the bar the regulars began to sniff. Though the smiting of Simon hadn't been much of a thing in itself, the mention of the split-cane basket and the barbecued bum had drawn some interest. This latter talk of smells now had them hooked.

Hooked, as in *fish*, possibly.

'Fish!' said Liza. 'It's fish. You stink of fish.'

'Fish?' said Simon. 'No I don't.'

'It is fish,' said Andy. 'I noticed it when you came in. I was far too polite to mention it, of course.'

Sniff sniff sniff, went the regulars and, 'Fish fish fish,' they said.

'It's not me,' wailed Simon. 'It's Dick's dog.'

'It bloody *is* you, boy.' The poacher leaned all too close and savoured Simon's wang. 'You honk of fish.'

'Wet fish, not frozen,' said the landlord.

'You dirty pervert.' Liza levelled a foot at Simon's shin. A fine young foot it was too. Set where a fine young foot should be set. In a white leather shoe with a winkle-picker toe and a three-inch stiletto heel. Simon took to hopping all around and howling also.

'Perhaps it's part of Simon's act,' said Long Bob the chicken farmer, ducking his head to grin about the bar.

'Act?' The word was passed about to the accompaniment of shrugging shoulders.

'Act?' said Liza, louder than the rest. 'What *act* is this?'

'The act I saw him and Raymond rehearsing when I passed by the allotments earlier. That thing that mime artistes never tire of boring their audiences with. You know the one I mean.' Long Bob began to mime the mime in question.

'Not bad,' said one of the Roman Candles. 'Can you do the one where you seem to be walking along, but you stay in the same place?'

'Oh I can do that,' said someone else. 'That's easy.'

'I can juggle with three dead rabbits,' Dick told Liza. 'While balancing a pint of lager on the end of my wi—.'

'*Simon!*' screamed Liza. 'SIMON!'

But suddenly Simon was nowhere to be seen. The special chemical inside his brain had made another of its split-second decisions.

Raymond's parcel was missing from the bar counter and all that remained to suggest that Simon had ever been there, was a half-gone pint, an IOU, an irate girlfriend with a lurcher once more up her leg, half a dozen full-grown men trying to get out of imaginary telephone boxes and a haunting smell of fish.

Which was really quite a lot when you come to think about it.

3

Raymond was a sad and sorry schmuck.

He sat, all hunched up, in his beastly little bubble and glared at the planet Venus. He couldn't see too much of it, but all that he could see, he hated.

His bubble stood on a sturdy tripod affair at the centre of a bleak grey plaza, surrounded by low, dull, bleak and equally grey buildings of the industrial persuasion. By swivelling around on his little seat Raymond could make out a whole host of other bubbles similar to his own. These ranged in size from the teeny-tiny to the dirty-great-big and housed an amazing assortment of what can only be described as 'things'. Some whirled and thrashed about in their transparent prisons, others just sat in attitudes of desolation similar to that of Raymond.

Kidnapped by aliens! This really was about as bad as it could possibly get. Being taken hostage by Middle Eastern maniacs was a grim enough business. But at least on Earth there was always some hope of release.

Simon had a theory that when you were taken hostage in the Middle East, your kidnappers always negotiated a deal with a London publishing house for a share of the royalties on the bestselling book you would be expected to write as soon as you were released. Simon said he'd seen a 'leaked' office memo to this effect. And also that most kidnappings were only supposed to last for a month. It was all the delays with the agents getting the contracts typed out that held things up.

Raymond was of a far less cynical turn of mind than his friend. Although he had always wondered how come it was usually journalists who could write well that got kidnapped.

But this was the planet Venus. Oh dear.

Raymond sniffed. But for the bubbles, the plaza was otherwise deserted. Where were all the bidders? And what might the bidders look like? He perused once more the tag that hung from the cord round his neck. It *was* printed in English. So Venusians surely spoke the English tongue. And he *was* breathing. So they seemed to breath air also. But *what* were they? Some superior race, no doubt. He was probably going to be sold as a pet. There were possibilities there. Especially if they wanted him for breeding purposes.

Raymond's stomach made grumbling noises. The lad shivered, he was very cold indeed. They might have left him his underwear. To be put on public display in your birthday suit. The shame. The terrible shame. Must be for 'stud' purposes, Raymond told himself. Hence the no knickers. Mind you, what with it being so cold and everything. And.

And . . .

Oh dear.

Raymond suddenly clutched at himself in a shameless manner and rammed his spare fist into his face. He needed the toilet. It had been creeping up on him. And now it was here.

Oh calamity.

Perhaps the little seat concealed a commode. Raymond tore at it with his non-groin-holding hand. It didn't budge.

What to do? What to do?

Find a hole. Yes, that seemed a reasonable idea. After all, the air had to be getting in somewhere. Raymond's hands floundered about inside the bubble.

'Hold on. Hold on,' he wailed at himself. 'Just a second or two longer. Oh dear Lord. Oh dear. Oh Lord.'

A probing finger found itself in the outside world.

There was a small round hole just beneath the seat. Raymond took a careful aim.

'Oh Lord. Oh yes. Glory be.'

He slumped down onto the seat. A poor naked schmuck with a warm wet foot and a really stupid grin on his face.

'*And that's enough of that, lot twenty-three.*' It was the voice of a terrible suddenness.

'Aaaagh!' went Raymond. 'Toilet paper please.'

'Now just you calm yourself.'

Raymond cowered and peered and then found himself very much impressed. Smiling down at him was a beautiful being. It was a man, but it wasn't. It was better than a man. A sort of idealized version of what a man should be. It was well over six feet in height, dressed in a floor-length toga. It raised a calming hand.

It was completely silver.

But for the eyes. Golden eyes. Staring from a face which expressed wisdom, calmness and compassion.

An angel? An angel with a clipboard?

'How are you feeling now?' asked this vision.

Raymond tried to get his mouth into gear, but the words just wouldn't come.

'Would you mind if I just asked you a few questions?'

Raymond shook his head.

'Just nod or shake your head. Oh you did, didn't you? Splendid. Specimen of Earth life. Male. Is that correct?'

Raymond managed a mumbly, 'Yes.'

'Splendid. And a very fine specimen too, if I might say so.'

'Oh,' said Raymond.

'Name?' asked the being.

'Raymond,' said Raymond.

'George,' said the being.

'Hello, George.' Raymond waggled his fingers in foolish greeting.

'Not me George. You George,' said the being.

'Me Raymond,' said Raymond. 'I mean, I'm Raymond. My name's Raymond.'

'Well, if anyone asks, say it's George. It makes things easier all the way round.'

'But I'm Raymond.'

The being consulted his clipboard. 'I have you down as George here, I'm afraid.'

'It's a mistake then.' Raymond suddenly brightened. It was all a mistake, that had to be it.

'A mistake?' asked the being in a kindly tone.

'Yes.' Raymond bobbed up and down. 'You see I was on my allotment and there was this flying starfish called Abdullah. And I passed this initiative test set by the Sultan of Uranus for The Divine Council of Cosmic Superfolk.'

'Did you get a certificate?'

'No,' said Raymond. 'I didn't get a certificate.'

'Typical.' The being flicked through sheets of paper on his clipboard. 'Someone's really fouled up this time.'

'Then it *is* all a mistake?' Raymond began to wring his hands in a pathetic pleading fashion.

'Tell you what,' the being smiled upon Raymond in a manner that seemed to momentarily warm him from head to naked toe, 'will you trust me to sort this out for you?'

'Yes indeed.' Raymond's head bobbed up and down.

'Well, you just take a little rest now. Go to sleep for a bit and I'll get it all fixed in no time at all. What do you say?'

The golden eyes stared deeply into Raymond's. 'Go to sleep and it will all be well.'

'Go to sleep. Yes. Thank you.' The boy in the bubble smiled out at his silver saviour. His eyelids became heavy and his head began to droop. All would be well.

'Sleep well.'

And Raymond would certainly have drifted off completely into a soft and silvery slumber, had he not somehow managed to get a big toe jammed into the little airhole beneath his seat.

'Ouch!' went Raymond, leaping up to free himself.

And, 'Ouch!' went Raymond again, as his head struck the top of the bubble.

And, 'Aaaeeeiii!' went Raymond, as sudden agony informed him that he had just sat down upon two spherical portions of his anatomy, which should never ever be sat down upon.

Bent double in paroxysms of pain, his eyes starting from his head, Raymond sought help from the silver being. But the being was striding away.

And the being wasn't listening. In fact, the being was laughing. Very loudly. And between great guffaws of laughter Raymond caught just the two words. One was 'certificate' and the other was 'schmuck'.

'You dirty rotten bas . . .' Raymond made fists, but he unmade them on the instant and just stared dumb with disbelief. For something most extraordinary now occurred.

The laughing striding silver being seemed to blur and then in mid-stride, without a broken step, it underwent a stunning transformation. No longer strode the sleek and shining superman, now strode instead a thing all shaggy spines and dragging wattles. But one still carrying a clipboard.

Raymond rubbed at his eyes, his pains forgotten. He *had* seen that, hadn't he? The being had just pulled off the finest quick-change act this side of . . . where? Here obviously. Raymond looked on in redoubled awe.

The being in its new form now stopped beside another bubble. Inside this something thrashed around. Something all shaggy spines and waggling wattles. The being spoke to it and soon it quietened and sank down in a heap. And then the being strode away once more.

Raymond watched it as it changed again to mimic the thing in a further bubble. And he saw it change twice more before it went beyond his line of vision.

'Well bugger my old brown dog!' said Raymond. That was a sneaky trick and no mistake. Appear before your captive in an idealized form of himself, speak a few honied words to calm him down, then what? Hypnotize him to sleep, that was what.

Raymond nursed his tender places. If he hadn't caught his toe, he would have drifted off along with the rest of them.

'I wonder what that fellow looks like without the special effects,' Raymond wondered. 'And I wonder what I should do for the best now. Play dead and see what happens next, I suppose.'

And so that's exactly what Raymond did.

His stomach took to grumbling in a very hollow tone. He was cold and hungry and he hurt. His fellow captives slept on all around him. Perhaps they were cold and hungry too. Probably they were. Had Raymond been capable of adopting a detached attitude to the situation, he might well have felt some admiration for the ingenuity of the Venusian shape-shifter. No need to pay out on food for the lots before they were sold. And no screaming from the lots to put off the buyers. It was all very clever really.

But Raymond was in no mood to adopt anything remotely resembling a detached attitude, so he just sat and scowled and shivered.

And presently a siren sounded in the distance and a line of cars swung slowly into view. They were big and bulbous, but hardly the kind of thing Dan Dare used to drive across the front page of *The Eagle*. These had that stolid utilitarian look about them. These cars said, "We are built for use not beauty, to be driven by folk who prefer good gas mileage to the whimsy of aesthetics."

These were dull cars for dull people.

Raymond played dead and peered through his fingers as the cars swelled towards him from the foreshortened perspective.

The cars drew up to park in regimented rows.

And then their occupants alighted from them.

'Oh dear,' said Raymond to himself alone. 'So *that's* what they look like.'

They were not pleasing to behold. They walked upon two legs with feet, and had arms to an equal number with hands on the end. But as for the rest of them. Their bodies were roughly egg shaped. The bellies became the heads in a seamless, chinless join. The big broad faces were a lacklustre grey in colour.

They reminded Raymond of those Mr Potato Head outfits he used to get in his Christmas stockings. The ones that he only got to play with a couple of times before his mum got fed up with the waste of King Edwards and quietly consigned them to the dustbin.

And these weren't even good-looking potato heads, these were really evil-looking. And most of them appeared to favour what was obviously the Venusian equivalent of the shell suit.

Raymond hated them on sight. And the degree of his hatred, for which he could find no obvious cause, save the appearance of these 'people', startled even himself by its intensity.

Because Raymond wasn't a racist.

As a child he'd puzzled over racial intolerance and once broached the subject with his father, who was home for a brief spell between sessions at the turf accountants.

The old chap had laid aside his *Sporting Life* and given the matter a moment's thought.

'Son,' said he, 'there are good and bad in all races.'

And pleased with the simple purity of this, young Raymond had gone out to play.

'But what I want to know,' his father continued from behind his paper, 'is why all the bloody bad ones have to live in my street?'

The boy Raymond never caught this particular remark and so from that day to the present, held fast to the belief that his bigoted git of a father had been a great humanitarian.

But it wasn't helping now.

Raymond continued with the furtive peeping through his fingers. 'I *really* hate these bastards,' he muttered beneath his breath.

The potato heads shuffled amongst the bubbles, consulting their auction lists, pointing and nattering away to one another.

Raymond listened to them at it. English. They all spoke English. A group drew near to his personal prison. Typical family, by the look of them. Mother, father and a brace of kiddies. Little boy and little girl. Shell suits all. The Humpty Dumptys.

'What's this one?' asked the smallest of the hideous offspring, the daughter one.

Daddy Dumpty squinted at his auction list with black button eyes. 'Lot twenty-three. Specimen of Earth life. Male.'

'Yuck,' went the daughter. 'Isn't he ugly?'

Ugly? Raymond chewed upon his lip but maintained a passive pose.

'Can we wake him up?' The other little spud began to bang at Raymond's bubble.

'I'd rather you didn't, if you don't mind.' Raymond knew that voice, although he could not as yet see the speaker. It was the voice of Mr Chameleon, the silver sham with the clipboard. 'A prime specimen, don't you think, sir?'

The potato heads nodded from the big bellies up. 'Very nice,' said Daddy Dumpty.

'Does he have a name?' asked the darling daughter.

'Yes. His name is George.'

Raymond ground his teeth.

'All Earth males are called George,' Mr Chameleon went on.

'Is it a tradition, or an old charter, or something?' Daddy asked.

'No. It's just because they're stupid.'

Raymond's teeth ground a mite harder.

'So, if all the Earth males are called George,' said

Mrs Dumpty, 'what are all the females called?'

'Mildred,' came the reply.

'Mummy, I want George,' said darling daughter.

'No, dear. We've come to buy a Klingon today.'

'But I want George. I don't want a Klingon. I *must* have George.' Raymond watched the brat's face contort and the little feet began to stamp.

'How much do you think George will fetch?' asked Daddy Dumpty.

'Let me have a look.' And now Raymond could see Mr Chameleon, who had stepped into his line of vision. And lo, he was a potato head also. And a short one at that.

He leafed through papers on his clipboard with a stubby little finger. 'The reserve price is five pounds, sir,' he said.

Five pounds? With considerable difficulty Raymond kept his rage in check. Five pounds? Of course, the Venusian fiver was probably not the same as the Earth fiver. It was probably worth much much more. Bound to be. Had to be.

'Five pounds?' Daddy Dumpty shook himself. His daughter was turning purple, while repeating the phrase, 'I *must* have George,' again and again in a higher and higher register.

'Of course you must, dear. Please calm down.'

'Then I can have George?'

'Well . . .'

'See the fine young physique, sir,' said Mr Chameleon. 'This specimen is in excellent physical condition. He'll provide well.'

Provide? Raymond wondered about provide. Provide, as in working? Slavery, then? Or some other kind of provide. Provide as in offspring? Stud farm work? Yes, he'd be prepared to give stud farm work a try.

'Are the Georges always this unpleasant blue colour?' asked Mrs Dumpty.

'Oh no, madam. Not when you warm them up. They're quite pink then.'

'That's nice, pink. I like pink. What's the best way to warm them up?'

'Slow grilled over charcoal,' said Mr Chameleon. 'They're best cooked live, of course. With the mouth glued shut and a chilli pepper stuck up the bum for seasoning.'

Raymond bit right through a filling.

But he sat very quietly throughout the auction. It didn't teach him much about the Venusian way of life. It was just like any auction on Earth. Any cattle auction say, or one where porker pigs are being sold for bacon.

Mr Chameleon extolled the virtues of each specimen, the flavour, the tenderness of the special cuts. Raymond's blood ran colder and colder. He did learn that there were one million pennies in a Venusian pound, but he didn't learn what a Venusian penny was worth. And he really didn't care.

All he cared about was how to escape from this dismal planet in one piece. And preferably before the chilli pepper was inserted.

'Here you go then, sir.' Raymond peeped once more through his fingers. The auction was now over. The bloody Humpty Dumpty family *had* got him, and for the knock-down price of £4.99,999p.

'A porter will roll the containment sphere to your car for you.' Mr Chameleon was all smiles. 'Handle it with care. As you know, the spheres are virtually indestructible from within, but a sharp tap on the outside will shatter them. Wear gloves, we wouldn't want you to cut yourself.'

'Can I cut George's balls off?' asked the darling daughter.

'Of course, dear,' said her doting dad. 'But put them on the barbecue to cook with George. They won't taste very nice if they're raw.'

'I *really, really* hate these bastards,' Raymond muttered. 'And now, at least, I know just *why* I do.'

4

Simon woke early and took another shower. He'd taken two the previous night, but he felt sure that the unsavoury taint of the flying starfish still clung to him like a mildewed body-stocking.

In a curious way, however, he found the smell almost comforting. Without it he felt certain he could have quite easily convinced himself that all which had occurred with Raymond was nothing more than the product of his over-active imagination.

Simon recalled an article he had once read whilst sitting in the dentist's waiting-room. It was part of a hand-printed pamphlet affair published by an organization with the enigmatic acronym B.E.A.S.T. and it was all about how the human brain tended to filter out things that didn't fit into the everyday. For example, seeing a ghost. You saw the thing when you were stone-cold sober and you were definitely certain you'd seen it. But the next day your memory began to fade and in no time at all you'd convinced yourself that you'd never really seen it at all.

The article hinted darkly that subtle influences were at work which came from beyond the brain. Possibly emanating from the ghost itself, or the UFO, or whatever. It was all part of some evil psychic smokescreen to keep mankind from learning some terrible truth.

Simon had found the article quite fascinating, but he hadn't had time to finish it, because he'd been called into the surgery to have some new crowns fitted. And the next time he went to the dentist the pamphlet wasn't there.

Perhaps he'd just imagined it.

But he was sure he hadn't imagined Abdullah the flying starfish.

As he scrubbed away at his teeth for the umpteenth time, he wondered just what Raymond might be up to.

'Probably wining and dining at the palace of some Venusian monarch,' said Simon through the toothpaste foam. 'The lucky sod.'

His ablutions completed and aftershave liberally applied to even the most intimate of places, Simon set out to face the day ahead.

Now Simon being Simon, the evening hadn't been a complete disaster for him. Having legged it away from The Jolly Gardeners, he had chanced to bump into the landlady from The Bear Flag Inn, who was trying to clear her blocked sinuses with a late-evening jog. Her husband Keith (or possibly Trevor) was away at a bar food conference in Penge. Simon had been invited back for an after-hours Campari soda. This had led, as Simon hoped it might, to several hours of frenzied sexual athletics, culminating in an oral contract for him to tend the pub's hanging baskets throughout the summer.

It is interesting to note that when the landlady's sinuses finally cleared and her husband returned from his conference, both would be equally baffled by the strong smell of fish which led from the bar, up the staircase and into the marital bedchamber.

It was mowing all this week for Simon. Mr Hilsavise had, through many years of hard toil, and the convenient, if strangely unaccountable, collapse of all the other gardening firms in the village, built up a vast clientele; and Simon, being his only employee, was never short of work.

Today Simon had to take out the big Allen Scythe and crop the meadow below Long Bob's chicken farm.

Simon was very fond of the big Allen Scythe. It was a mighty hulking piece of 1950s farming technology, all green and shiny. Massive solid wheels with old-fashioned

43

racing-car tyres, and a giant hair-clipper arrangement on the front.

It went at a fair old lick once you'd primed it up and teased it into life. Little short of concrete posts could stand before the big Allen Scythe.

Simon reversed the Transit flat-back up to the meadow gate and switched off the engine. He swung the gate open, dropped the Transit's tail-flap, angled down a pair of scaffold boards and wheeled the Allen Scythe carefully to the ground.

The day smelt sweet. The sun shone vigorously, birds exchanged gossip, daffs held their heads up high. All those bunnies who had escaped the attention of Dick and his dog the night before, bounced around as only bunnies can.

It was all very heaven.

Simon was attending to the minutiae of carburettor tickling, prior to starter-cord tugging, when the sound of distant drumming reached his ear.

'Hello,' said Simon, as one would. 'Whatever can this be?'

Roman Candle practised in Long Bob's barn. But this wasn't your 'Rage Against the Machine' type drumming. This was more your military type drumming. The sort that marched the peasant cannon fodder into the jaws of death. It didn't seem to fit on a day like this.

Simon did shifty glancings to the left and the right of him, wiped his oily fingers on the rag which he had brought for that purpose and took to sidling once more. He did low sidling this time, ducking from one tree to another. Slinking and creeping and moving furtively in a suspicious manner (which is really 'sidling' in the true sense of the word).

He crept up the bank that fell away from the lower boundary of Long Bob's farm and peered through the tall grass he had been sent to cut. And then he wondered at what he saw.

Long Bob stood in the middle of his farmyard. And

a fine traditional farmyard it was too. Set with all the things a fine traditional farmyard should be set: a tractor lacking wheels, two wrecked cars of uncertain age, many sheets of corrugated iron far gone with the rust, and many many many plastic fertilizer bags.

And chickens.

Long Bob stood in the midst of his chickens as well a chicken farmer might. So it wasn't this that had caused Simon to wonder. It was more the manner of Long Bob's attire.

He was clad in one of those ex-army single-piece, zip-up-the-front tank suits onto which he had fastened a pair of home-made epaulettes, wrought from gold milkbottle tops and Christmas tinsel. Atop his tall cranium perched an old tin helmet. Onto this had been glued a pair of chicken wings.

The long fellow was beating on a small tin drum.

Simon watched him at it. If the farmer's strange appearance was sufficient to inspire wonder, what might be said regarding the behaviour of his chickens?

What indeed?

Now Simon knew of chickens. You could hardly live in the country and not know of chickens. Chickens and the ways of chickens are things well known to countryfolk.

The ways of chickens do not extend to much beyond pecking at grain, sitting on eggs, getting eaten by foxes in the night, and on rare occasions, running around the farmyard after their heads have been chopped off.

But there was something different here.

Long Bob's chickens weren't engaged in normal chickenly pursuits. They were standing still and quiet and they were all staring intently at Long Bob. The farmer played another roll upon his drum. 'Ten . . . shun,' went he.

The chickens didn't move.

'Ten . . . shun. Come on now, you can do it.'

If the chickens could they didn't choose to.

'Come on now. Tenshun.'

The chickens just stared on. And then in ones and twos they ceased to stare. Their heads began to bob, their claws to scratch, their beaks to peck up grain. And soon they all were bobbing, scratching, pecking and the like.

'Bugger!' Bob tore off his drum and flung it to the ground.

He shouted further words, but these were swallowed by the din of clucking hens. Simon watched him as he stalked off to his farmhouse, kicking fowl to left and right.

What a curious how-do-you-do.

Simon dropped down from his lair and returned to the Allen Scythe, shaking his head and clicking his expensive dental work. Long Bob was clearly two eggs short of a fry up. But those chickens. The way they'd really seemed to be listening. Whatever was all that about?

Simon gave his head a final shake. He would find out in good time, he felt quite sure of that. And when he did, then he would profit from the finding out. He felt quite sure of *that* also.

'Boom shanka,' said the lad. 'Boom shanka boom.'

By lunchtime he had finished with the meadow. He dragged the big Allen Scythe up onto the flat-back, flung the scaffold boards after it, locked up the tail-flap, took from his pocket a crisp white linen handkerchief, applied it to his face and wiped away the sweat of honest toil.

The sky was blue. The sun was high. The pub was calling.

But not The Jolly Gardeners.

And not The Bear Flag Inn.

Simon drove into the village and left the Transit in the customers-only car-park behind the supermarket. Today he would risk The Bramfield Arms, a Ploughbloke's Lunch and a pint of Cloudy.

He was almost halfway over the zebra crossing by the chemists when a shiny grey van pulled out unexpectedly from the kerb and nearly ran him down. Simon leapt for his life.

He rolled nimbly into the gutter, where several village

females (one of whom just happened to be called Mildred) helped him to his feet and fussed around. They spoke in righteous tones regarding the need for a bypass and traffic-calming speed ramps, whilst they felt him up and down for broken bones.

Simon thanked them for their concern and assured them that he was uninjured. He prised away the hand of one lady he'd recently known (in the biblical sense), declined the offer of a nice cup of tea, or something 'a little stronger' to steady his nerves, and slipped into The Bramfield Arms.

Now, from the sunlit street to the unlit saloon bar may just be one small step for a man, but it's a giant leap in at the deep end for the unwary stranger.

The Bramfield Arms did not extend to the traveller a warm and cheery welcome. No home fires burned in the inglenook. No apple-cheeked village lovely made sheep's eyes at you across the bar as she drew the farmhouse cider and cleaved off a slice of cherry pie. Oh no. Oh dear me no.

Here, in a subaqueous gloom, made rutilant by the depth-charge flares issuing from the games machines, Black Jack Wooler, beer-bellied blackguard and lord of the underworld, wallowed behind his bar counter like a great bloated pike.

The air had a definitely liquid quality to it. You sank into the saloon bar as you entered it. 'Orrible it were!

In the snooker room to the pub's rear end, Faith No More played on the jukebox and youthful sportswear cultists had at one another with billiard cues. But the sounds of their jollification scarcely reached the saloon bar. They went down with all hands, to vanish in the dark and icy depths. Yuck!

But for Simon, the saloon bar lacked for a customer. Which was just the way Black Jack liked it at lunchtimes. Simon blinked his eyes and squinted through the murk towards the barlord. Black Jack perused Simon with a piscine peeper and moved a mirthless maw.

'Off with that new hat in my establishment,' quoth he.

The gardener's apprentice flashed his pearly whites, lighting up a small area of bar and scratched his hatless head. 'Good morrow to you, lord of the bar. Hail fellow well met.'

Black Jack ground the blackened stumps of his teeth and hawked a frog-sized gobbet of phlegm into a distant corner. It landed unseen in the darkness, with a dull squelching plop. Simon made a mental note not to seek out a chair in that direction.

He approached the bar with a spring in his step, although inwardly he sidled. 'A pint of Cloudy and a Ploughbloke's Lunch, if you would be so kind.'

Black Jack glowered, placed a pint pot beneath the spout of the beer engine and filled it with ale. 'Pay now and I'll bring the nosebag over as soon as I can be bothered.'

'Very nice of you, thanks.' Simon paid now, took up his pint and struck off across the fag-pocked lino, bound for a window seat.

'And have a care for my sumptuous furnishings,' bawled the barlord.

'I shall treat them as if they were my own.'

'You bloody won't; this is a bar, not a knocking shop!'

'Quite so.' Simon settled down upon the kind of couch you normally associate with builders' skips and sought a glimpse of life beyond the unwashed window. A decade's grime put paid to any such folly and so he was forced to apply spittle to his finger and his finger to the glass. With no small effort he wore away a little viewing hole.

The sunlight rushed in and the lad peeped out.

The world that was Bramfield came and went as it always did. The usual lunchtime walkabout. Simon sipped his ale and appraised the female shoppers, many of whom he found pleasing to gaze upon. Simon was always among the first to admire the swelling buttocks of another's wife. And even in so small a village, there was never any lack of variety. Everybody seemed to be 'doing it' with everybody but the body they really should be 'doing it' with. The intricate love knots, extramarital flings, bits on the side, toy boys, comings and goings and goings and comings never ceased to not-amaze him at all. For, after all, he'd grown up here. This was what life was like, wasn't it? Yes, of course it was. Same everywhere, bound to be.

Black Jack suddenly loomed out of the darkness and flung a pork pie on to Simon's table.

'There you go, scumbag,' said he.

'That's not a Ploughbloke's Lunch,' said Simon.

'It bloody is if he comes in here to eat.' Black Jack made a very menacing face indeed.

'Yum yum yum,' said Simon.

'And keep your grubby fingers off my window. You're letting in the ozone layer.'

'Sorry.' Simon prodded his pie. It had an unyielding quality to it. It seemed to say, 'Just you dare.'

The bulging barlord rippled mighty jowls and drifted away to settle once more behind his counter.

Simon took another sip from his pint. Whatever had possessed him to come in here for lunch? Death wish?

Simon sighed and put his eye once more to his viewing hole. It was blocked. A shiny grey van was parked, half up on the pavement, outside.

Simon peered at the van. It looked familiar. It *was* familiar. It was the van that had nearly run him down on the zebra crossing.

And chaps were getting out of it. Dull pinched-faced chaps in dull narrow-shouldered suits. Matching suits. Matching sunglasses; grey framed, the lenses too were grey. As were the shirts and ties and shoes and socks of these chaps. Three chaps in grey. All grey. Thrice grey.

And by the looks of them, they were coming into the pub.

Simon set his pint aside and Black Jack scowled up from the nose he had been picking, as sunlight blared and three grey men strolled in.

Simon comfied himself down upon his rotten couch. He did not require the special chemical in his head to counsel caution. For although these chaps looked frail and pinched, there were still three of them and only one of him. He wouldn't be mentioning the matter of how they had nearly killed him. But he would certainly enjoy whatever horrors Black Jack chose to heap upon them. For Black Jack hated strangers. And strangers wearing suits especially. He had once thrown a rep from a potato crisp company to the other side of the zebra crossing simply on the grounds that the rep's suit clashed with the dartboard. And The Bramfield Arms didn't even have a dartboard.

'Give 'm hell, you bloated blackguard,' whispered Simon to his ale.

The three grey men strolled up to the bar. Hands in pockets. 'Shop!' said one. Simon flinched.

'Good-day, gentlemen,' said Black Jack, smiling with his stumps and wiping his big fat hands upon his apron. 'And how might I serve you?'

'Eh?' went Simon. 'Come again?'

'Three pints of your very best,' said a man in grey.

'Certainly, sir. If you and your companions would care to take a seat, I shall bring your drinks over to you directly.'

Simon scratched the head that never wore a hat. Black Jack was obviously working up to something really special. A triple drenching perhaps?

The three men in grey seated themselves at a nearby table. They were still wearing their sunglasses. Simon wondered how they could possibly see where they were walking. Black Jack pulled three pints.

Then he brought them over.

On a tray!

'Anything more, gentlemen?' he enquired in a voice of silken obsequiousness.

'Food,' said one grey man.

'Make it *good* food,' said a second.

'And make it quick or else,' the third one said.

Simon's jaw dropped open. *Make it quick or else?* Boy, were they going to get it now. Dear oh dear oh dear. He slipped his pint from the table to a place of safety beneath the couch. He didn't want it getting knocked into his lap if one or more of the grey men were thrown in his direction.

'I shall be as quick as I possibly can. Enjoy your beer.'

The barlord bowed politely, then hurried (*hurried!*) away.

Simon pocketed his pork pie. Now might well be the time for him to hurry away also. It seemed more than probable that when Black Jack did return, it would be in the company of either his shotgun or his Pit Bull terrier. It would be far better to read about the massacre in the local paper, than actually witness it at first hand.

Far preferable.

'Oi, you.' A grey man turned suddenly in Simon's direction.

'Me?' Simon pointed to his chest, the way you sometimes do.

'Yeah, you thickhead in the new hat. D'you live around here?'

'Me?' Simon shook a head that was anything but thick and *still* refused to wear a hat. 'Er, no. I'm just a tourist. Why?'

'Doesn't matter then. Go back to sleep.' The grey man turned back to his companions and they all laughed together.

On second thoughts, thought Simon, who was having second thoughts, I think I shall remain here and enjoy the bloodbath. And possibly even join in the kicking when they're down.

He sought out his pint, but it now had cobwebs in it. So he just sat back and listened to the grey men's conversation.

'I hate these jobs out in the sticks,' said the first grey man quaffing ale. 'There's always some loose end you miss.'

'How many more sites left to clear up this week?' asked the second grey man.

'Just the one here and another five miles over at Billington.'

The third grey man rubbed his hands together. 'Then I'm taking a holiday next week. I'm due some leave.'

'You won't get leave with all those extra orders coming up,' said grey man number one.

'I will. My passport's been scanned. My documents are all in order. I'm going topside for a month.'

'Going topside you?' The first man laughed. 'The only way you'll go topside is pickled.'

'Or canned,' said grey man number two, joining in a joke that escaped Simon completely.

'Or bubbled,' went the first grey man to further hilarity.

'I am going topside. I'm all booked up. I might even apply for a post there too. Be nice to see the stars again.'

Simon adjusted his hair. Now what on earth were these prats on about? Pickled, canned or bubbled? Salesmen obviously. Seeing the stars again? Holidays in Hollywood?

Were these men yuppies? Simon had always wondered what yuppies looked like. Then the nineteen eighties finished and there were no more yuppies. That had to be it. They were yuppies. That's why they were so rude. And here *he* was, just about to witness the yuppy race finally become extinct.

The door behind the bar flew open with a mighty crash.

'Grub up,' called Black Jack wading through the gloom.

Grub up? Simon cowered on his couch. Some euphemism for gut-shooting perhaps?

'Our finest local fare.' The barlord was wearing a

chef's hat. He was carrying a silver tray. 'Boiled potatoes, sprouts, spring beans, lamb chops and gravy. I trust you will find all to your liking.'

Simon's mouth stayed open. He couldn't shut it at all.

Black Jack's wife, who never ever entered the bar, carried a nice clean white linen table-cloth. His son Filth held polished knives and forks and a silver cruet set. Jack's daughter, Chubby-Behemoth Wooler clutched an ice bucket to her ample bosom. A champagne bottle stuck its golden nose out.

Within moments they grey men's table was spread. Delicious smells wreathed themselves throughout the bar. Simon's mouth slammed shut. But it soon fell open again.

'If there's anything else you need, don't hesitate to ask.' Black Jack bowed low and his hat fell off. He scooped it up and rammed it into his apron pocket.

'Three more beers,' said grey man one.

'And some HP Sauce,' said grey man two.

'And make it quick or else,' said grey man number three.

And Black Jack scuttled off, his family in his wake.

And Simon gave his head another shake. Not yuppies then? Policemen then? The Mafia then? The Mob then? Who then? Black Jack treated them like royalty. Royalty then?

Simon took his cobwebby glass up to the bar. Black Jack was labouring at the pump. And as Simon watched, he drew off a pint of stunning clarity.

'These chaps friends of yours then?' Simon asked.

'No friends of mine.' The barlord shook his big bald head and as he did so a bead of perspiration dropped from the tip of his nose and fell into the pint he was pulling. Simon smiled, that was something, at least.

The barlord stared at the pint in horror. Then he poured it straight down the sink and took up another glass in a hand that had a most definite shake on. Simon was amazed. As far as he knew, Black Jack feared no man living, but for Mr Hilsavise, whom many claimed to be in league with the devil.

'What is going on here?' Simon asked. 'Who are these dreadful sods?'

'Keep your voice down. And get out. Just get out.'

'Where's our beer? called the voice of grey man one.

'Coming, sir. Coming right up.'

Simon leaned his elbows on the bar counter and watched as Black Jack struggled with the drinks. This was all wrong. The barlord was a bad'n, everyone knew that. 'A soul so black as would obscure the darkness of hell,' was the way Andy liked to put it. But the way these grey fellows had him bowing and scraping. It was wrong. All wrong. It had to stop. Right now.

'Get a move on, fat boy,' crowed grey man number one.

Simon's right hand sneaked back over the bar counter to where he knew that Black Jack kept his big stout stick.

'We haven't got all day,' sneered grey man number two. 'Shift your great arse.'

Simon's hand alighted upon the big stout stick. Just hit one of them, he willed the barlord, I'll be right in there with you. I promise I will.

Now you should never make promises that you can't keep. But Simon felt that he really would keep this one. He felt a curious alliance to Black Jack. Almost as if he and Jack were set against a common enemy, which they sort of were, but not in the way Simon thought.

'Chop chop.' The third grey man raised a hand and made sinister wiggling motions with his fingers. 'We wouldn't want to have to tell big Abdullah that you held us up, now would we?'

'No, sir, no.' The barlord put down the beers. 'Not big Abdullah, no.'

'*Big Abdullah?*' Simon's hand left the big stout stick and gripped the bar counter. '*Big Abdullah?*' Simon's brain went click click. What had they been saying? About loose ends and sites to be cleared up. And extra 'orders'. And going 'topside'. And pickled, canned or bubbled. And seeing the stars again. *Big Abdullah!*

Simon's brain went click click click. And a special chemical sped through it.

Simon left The Bramfield Arms and lurched blinking into the sunlight, traffic roar and pushchair-wheeling mums. The lady with the nice blue eyes, who worked in the post office, smiled at Simon. Simon stumbled up the high street. Three men in grey, who cleared up after big Abdullah. Men in grey. As in *Men in Black?*

He'd read all about the Men in Black. They cleared up after UFO landings in the nineteen fifties and sixties. So these were the nineteen nineties' models. And Black Jack knew who they were and what they were.

Who else did?

Simon did furtive glancings as he stumbled along. Who else might know? Some of them? *All* of them?

The familiar faces now seemed strange. Alien.

I have to get out of here. Simon made off towards the Transit. Get away from this village and think things through.

No, not that. Not yet. Simon ceased his stumbling. He'd seen enough old science fiction films to know how this worked. If he tried to escape, it would turn into a chase movie, with him being chased. He had to be cleverer than that. The grey men didn't know that *he* knew. No-one knew that *he* knew. Only Raymond. And where was Raymond? Gone 'topside, pickled, canned or bubbled'?

'Right,' said Simon. 'What to do?' Follow *them*. That was what. Be the pursuer rather than the pursued. They had come to clear up. So they were on their way to the allotments. So, follow them there. See what they got up to.

Better still. Get there first. Lie in wait. That was far better.

Simon jogged into the customers-only car-park behind the supermarket.

And then he stopped.

And then he gaped. His mouth once more at full-down hinge.

The Transit was not quite the way he had left it.

The back flap was down. A scaffold board lay on the Tarmac.

The Allen Scythe had been stolen.

And if that wasn't all . . .

If that wasn't all . . .

The Transit had been wheel-clamped!

'Oh dear,' said Simon. 'Oh dear, oh dear, oh dear.'

'Oi, you!' called out a voice. And Simon turned. A grey man was approaching at a trot. 'Yeah, you. I want a word with you.'

'Oh my!' Simon glanced up at the empty flat-back, down at the wheel-clamp, then across towards the man in the grey suit and sunglasses.

And then Simon took to his heels and really truly fled.

5

On Venus things weren't going well for Raymond. The Humpty Dumptys had a flat-back truck. It was not altogether unlike the one that was currently wheel-clamped in the customers-only car-park behind the supermarket in Bramfield. It was slightly lower and wider and the doors were bigger. But it was the same kind of thing.

Raymond was on the back. Upside down and still in his bubble. He wasn't taking in the passing scenery to any pleasing effect. Not that the passing scenery was particularly pleasing.

It was all suburbia now. And all very earthlike also. Estates of housing, somewhat lower and squatter and with fatter doorways. They even had satellite dishes. And garden gnomes.

'I hate these bastards,' said Raymond.

The truck passed along beside a high and solid-looking brick wall, above which a gigantic hoarding flashed an impressive holographic display, announcing that the circus was in town.

Raymond wasn't impressed.

The voice of the darling daughter came back to him from the cab. 'Can we go to the circus, Daddy?' it asked.

'No dear, I don't think so.' Daddy Dumpty turned left and the truck began to rise up a long steep hill.

'Why can't we, Daddy?'

'Because,' Mrs Dumpty explained, 'the circus is for common folk. Not for well-brought-up young ladies like you.'

'But I *want* to go to the circus. I *need* to go to the circus.'

Raymond couldn't see the brat. But he could picture the face.

'*I* want to go *too*,' said Dumpty jnr.

'Please be quiet and let your father concentrate on his driving. This is a very dangerous hill.'

'But I *must* go to the circus,' screamed darling daughter. 'I *must*. I *must*. I *must*.'

'Sssh now,' went Mrs D. 'If you're very quiet all the way home, I'll let you have a special treat.'

'What treat?' asked the two little tykes.

'Well.' Mrs D. thought about it. 'You can play with George.'

'Can we get George *out* and play with him?'

'All right. But we'll have to break his ankles with a hammer. We don't want him running away, do we?'

'Can *I* break George's ankles with the hammer?' the darling daughter asked. 'Oh please, Mummy, please.'

'Stuff this.' Raymond eased himself into the upright position. 'I have to get out of here right now.'

But exactly how, that was the question.

Raymond recalled Mr Chameleon's remark to his clients.

As you know, the spheres are virtually indestructible from within, but a sharp tap on the outside will shatter them.

If I can somehow get this bubble to fall off the back of this truck, thought Raymond, it will surely break when it hits the road and then I shall be free.

Now, as to whether the dictionary definition of the word 'free' actually extends to 'running around naked on a distant hostile planet', Raymond wasn't too sure. But getting out of the beastly bubble had to be a step in the right direction.

So, how to go about it?

Well, Raymond stared thoughtfully down the hill. And the big holographic circus hoarding shone brightly back at him.

And Raymond had an idea.

It wasn't really his idea. It was something he recalled Simon telling him about, only a few days ago, in fact, although it now seemed more than a lifetime.

Simon had been reading this book about circuses and had been impressed by a Victorian performer named LaRoche. This LaRoche had originated an incredible act whereby he entered a metal sphere a mere two feet in diameter, then proceeded to manipulate it up a spiral ramp some twenty-four feet in height.

So. If a French Victorian could pull off a stunt like that . . .

Raymond wormed his finger into the little airhole now directly above his head and took a firm hold. And then he began to shift his weight about from side to side. It took a bit of starting off, and getting a steady rhythm going was anything but easy. But Raymond went about it as he went about everything.

With a will.

Raymond hammered himself from side to side. Bruising his shoulders and sorely numbing his bare behind. And the beastly bubble began to rock. Back and forwards. Back and forwards.

Raymond increased his efforts. Sweat broke out wherever it could and with his finger jammed in the airhole, breath was soon in short supply. With that mighty and supreme effort that one sometimes reads about in books of derring-do, Raymond flung himself forwards.

The bubble tumbled from the back of the truck and struck the road.

And with a single bound . . .

Our hero, wasn't free!

The bubble didn't break. It struck the road but it didn't break.

It spun around on the road's surface and continued up the hill for a few yards. But it didn't break.

Confusion now reigned within the Dumptys' truck. Daddy had seen Raymond's departure in his driving mirror. He slammed on the brakes. The truck swerved to the side of the road, spilling the family from their seats. Raymond's bubble missed the bumper by inches. And then it stopped.

Raymond clutched at his spinning head. 'I'm not free,' he observed. And then, 'Oh help!'

The Dumptys were clambering from their truck anxious to reclaim their purchase. They bumbled around him.

'Let me out of here,' cried Raymond. 'I don't want to die, set me free.'

'You naughty George.' The face of darling daughter scowled in at him. Raymond could now see just how sharp and pointed her little teeth were.

'We must roll George out of the road before something runs into him. Come on give me a hand. Oh—'

And 'Oh—' went Mummy Dumpty and the two small Dumptys too.

Because Raymond's bubble was no longer still. Raymond's bubble was yielding to a law of gravity, which obviously applied upon Venus as it did upon Earth. Raymond's bubble was starting to roll back down the hill.

'Stop,' yelled Daddy. 'Stop I say.' He clawed at the shiny sphere, but he couldn't get a grip. As Raymond began to turn head over heels once more he was overjoyed by the sight of the Humpty Dumptys going down like tenpins before a bowling ball.

'Ha ha ha ha,' went Raymond. 'Gotcha, you bastards. Oh no—'

Daddy Dumpty's remark about getting Raymond off the road before something ran into him, had not been an idle remark. There was a fair bit of traffic about. Going down the hill. And coming up.

Especially coming up. Raymond was now rolling straight down into its upward path.

'Look out belowwwwww—'

Potato faces froze above driving wheels. Trucks swerved to either side of the onrushing bubble.

'I *must* have George back!' screamed a high piping voice, but Raymond didn't hear it.

A very large lorry hung a left beside the high brick wall beneath the holographic circus hoarding and rumbled up the hill. It was a very large lorry indeed. And at the wheel of this very large lorry sat none other than Mr Chameleon himself.

His auction house always provided a special delivery service for all the posh Venusian restaurateurs who bought in bulk. And today Mr Chameleon's very large lorry had no fewer than fifty bubbles stacked up neatly on the back. The occupants of these lazed in their hypnotically induced slumbers, blissfully unaware of what fate held in store for them.

Mr Chameleon was whistling. He had had a most successful day. And one run with the clockwork precision which had distinguished the five generations of his family who had gone before, to make the auction house the most fashionable on Venus.

The auctioneer changed up, the very large lorry gathered speed and travelled up. And then the auctioneer suddenly ceased his merry whistling and a look of dire perplexity spread across his big broad face. Before him vehicles were swerving. And what was this? Something was coming down the hill towards him. Something that was accelerating at a goodly rate of Venusian knots.

And that something was—

'*GEORGE!*' shrieked the auctioneer, dragging the steering wheel to the right and hammering the brake.

Raymond didn't see the very large lorry. He was moving much too fast. He didn't see the look of horror on the face of Mr Chameleon. Which was a shame because he would really have enjoyed it. Nor did he see the dramatic manner in which the very large lorry jack-knifed and overturned, shedding its load. So he also missed the sight of all those fifty bubbles as they smashed and shattered. The screamings and roarings of the enraged beasties as they were rudely awakened were lost on him also.

Raymond just kept rolling.

As his head whirled about and his brain whirled within it, Raymond recalled something else that Simon had recently told him. It was about an experiment that had once been performed by a Frenchman (not M. LaRoche). This Frenchman had dropped a penny (or perhaps it was a franc) from the top of the Eiffel Tower and it had embedded itself a full two inches (or perhaps it was four centimetres) into the pavement (or perhaps it was the boulevard) below.

But whatever the whats, whys and wherevers, the general gist was that the further a thing fell, the more mass it gained and the bigger the smash it made when it finally hit something solid.

And Raymond now held in his dizzying mind a very strong visual image of the high, substantial-looking brick wall at the bottom of the hill. The one with the holographic sign above it. And Raymond wondered now, in a rushing tumbling sort of a way, whether he had really done the right thing in working the bubble off the back of the potato heads' truck whilst it was travelling up such a very steep hill.

He concluded that perhaps he hadn't.

'HeeeeeeeeeeeeeLLLLLLLLLLLLLLPPPPPPPPP!' went Raymond offering a practical, if unsolicited demonstration of the Doppler effect to any that might feel inclined to appreciate it.

But none apparently did. They had other things on their minds. Such as avoiding the unwelcome attentions of the howling, screaming torrent of hungry auction lots that were already on the rampage.

Jammed into the wreckage of his cab, Mr Chameleon gazed in terror towards the ferocious creature, all bristling spines and waggling wattles, that was climbing through the shattered windscreen. It looked very angry. And very hungry.

And Raymond kept on rolling. 'HeeeeeLLLLPPP, oh HeeeeLLLLP,' he went, as further cars and trucks and preposterous-looking Venusian motor scooters swerved to the left and right and crashed into one another. 'HELP!'

The great big solid brick wall rushed up (in an Einsteinian relativian sort of a way) towards Raymond. Inside his wildly whizzing bubble the poor naked schmuck tried his best to cross himself and make his recommendations to his maker, whilst bracing himself against the terrible terminal concussion to come.

And come it did. Although not in quite the manner he had expected that it would.

Although Raymond had taken a passing notice of the big brick wall, he had paid no attention whatsoever (and why would he have?) to the height of the pavement kerbstones. Now, as anyone who has made a lifetime's study of kerbstones[1] will tell you, these articles are inevitably constructed to a greater height than usual at the bottom of steep hills. Because here they usually incorporate storm drains. Raymond's speeding bubble was heading for one of these right now.

And what a sickening crash it made as it struck home.

'Ooooooooooooooh,' went Raymond continuing to travel forwards, although now in a forwards and upwards sort of direction. With shards of splintered bubble spiralling around him he cleared the raised kerbstones by inches and the top of the big brick wall by centimetres. But he didn't clear the holographic circus sign. This he struck with a vengeance.

For the benefit of any potato heads who had missed

[1] Dr Hercules Doveston of Harlech University is reckoned to be the world's leading expert on kerbstones. His twenty-three-volume work *The Kerbstone: A Deconstructionist Viewpoint on its Socio-Political Implications in the Assassination of JFK and the Sad Decline of Doo Wop Music* is now sadly out of print.

Raymond's demonstration of the Doppler effect and were not now busily engaged in either crawling from the wreckage of their crashed automobiles, or attempting to evade *The Revenge of the Bubble Creatures,* the spectacular explosion caused by the flying schmuck, as he passed through the intricate web of electronic hocus-pocus that powered the holographic circus hoarding, would provide animated conversation for many barbecue lunches yet to come.

Raymond entered the hoarding as a whirling white thing. He emerged on the other side still whirling. But now of a somewhat darker hue. And trailing smoke.

There are many exotic pleasures to be had in the sport of nudist skydiving, but Raymond did not experience any of them.

He fell from the sky screaming all the way.

And then he struck the roof of the circus tent.

And then he passed through the roof of the circus tent and continued down towards the ring.

And there, regrettably, we must leave Raymond. Held, as if at the touch of a celestial pause-button, halfway 'twixt roof and ring. Hardly the way things are usually done it is to be agreed. But at this particular moment it is necessary to return to Earth to catch up on Simon's progress. Why? Because Simon is about to make a discovery. And no small discovery. The discovery Simon is about to make is a discovery of considerable magnitude. Concerning, as it does, what happens to Raymond after he has fallen through the roof of the circus tent and how this event leads to other events, which culminate in Raymond performing a great service to mankind.

In saving it from destruction.

And everything.

Simon slammed shut his front door, threw the bolts and thrust on the security chain. Then he sank down onto his bottom and did great gaspings for breath.

He was in trouble here and he knew it. And this was not your everyday 'wronged husband out for revenge' sort of trouble. This was a different kind of trouble altogether. And what made this trouble all the worse was that it wasn't *his* fault.

It was all Raymond's fault.

The way Simon saw it, if Raymond hadn't agreed to go off with Abdullah, then Abdullah would probably have flapped away to some other village and snatched away some other schmuck. And then the grey men would never have come to Bramfield and now be chasing after him to 'clean up'.

It was definitely all Raymond's fault. Not his.

'Bloody Raymond,' said Simon.

On hands and knees he crept down his hall, into the front room and over to the window. Here he lifted a corner of the net curtain and peeped out at the street.

No grey man. He'd outrun him.

Simon did not trouble with a sigh of relief. There was no escape to be had here. Black Jack knew where he lived. It was doubtful that he would choose to withhold the information.

'I think it's time I took a holiday,' said Simon. 'New Zealand perhaps, or Tierra del Fuego.' He backed away from the window and made off up the stairs.

Now, there are always many decisions to be made when you make up your mind to take a holiday; and exactly what to pack is possibly the greatest of them all.

There is an art to it, of course, as there is with anything else. What clothes to take, which 'factor' of suntan lotion, the big lilo or the small one, should you take last year's flip-flops or splash out on a new pair?

And, of course, what are the currently fashionable sexual practices in the area you are about to visit and so which appliances should you sterilize? There's no point in turning up with a suitcase full of the usual ball weights, pressure tusks and Labret studs, only to discover that this season's taste is for flesh tunnels, nipple clamps and stirruped barbells, and you've left all yours at home in the fridge. That sort of thing can really spoil what would otherwise be a decent weekend away at Lourdes. We've all had it happen.

So, there's an art to it. You have to be thorough and you have to be precise. There's no point in going off half-cocked. It's always worth spending that extra few hours to do the job properly.

'Passport,' said Simon. 'Chequebook, credit cards, toothbrush. All packed.'

All packed?

'All packed! All packed if I can actually find my passport, of course. Now I remember putting it somewhere safe when I came back from that incredible weekend away at Lourdes. Ah yes, top left-hand drawer of the dresser, with the Rintintin vibrator and the Arab straps.'

On top of the dresser was Raymond's parcel.

Simon had not got around to opening it yet and now he glared at the thing in a manner which no parcel, other than one containing either a bomb or the torso of a young woman, deserves to be glared at. He snatched it from the dresser-top and flung it to the carpet, where it burst open disgorging its contents.

Simon took to rooting in the top left-hand drawer.

No passport was forthcoming.

'Bugger,' said Simon, starting on the right.

Still no passport. Simon cursed the dresser, tore out both drawers and flung these to the carpet. Then he began on the drawers below.

No passport.

'Bugger bugger bugger.' Simon now took to stalking around the bedroom, ripping open cupboards, tearing out their contents, kicking things in general, 'buggering' all the while.

Then he tripped heavily upon the contents of Raymond's parcel and fell to the floor.

66

'Ouch,' he said, and then, 'What's this?'

It was a book. A glossy hardback of a book. A great big glossy hardback of a book. Simon stared at the front cover. The face of Raymond stared back at him. Simon read out the title.

The Greatest Show off Earth
The Unofficial Biography
of RAYMOND
Saviour of Mankind

'Saviour of mankind?' Simon turned the book between his fingers. There was no author credited. Just the publishers, B.E.A.S.T. That rang a bell somewhere. Ah yes, the pamphlet Simon had read in the dentist's waiting-room. That had been published by B.E.A.S.T. also.

'Saviour of mankind?' Simon thumbed the book open. This had to be some form of elaborate hoax. This was Raymond having a pop at him, and Andy was probably in on it too. Mocked-up cover folded around a library book or something.

Simon examined the inside title page. *The Greatest Show off Earth.* Same business. A *very* elaborate hoax.

Simon perused the first chapter. It was a full account of what he and Raymond had been through on the allotment the previous night.

'How on earth?' Simon flicked forward a few chapters and read aloud from the book:

The Transit had been wheel-clamped!
'Oh dear,' said Simon. 'Oh dear, oh dear, oh dear.'
'Oi, you! called out a voice. And Simon turned.
A grey man was approaching at a trot.

'Shiva's sheep!' Simon stared at the page in utter disbelief. 'That happened only a few minutes ago. But I've had this parcel with me since last night. It's impossible. Unless . . .' An awesome thought entered his head. It couldn't be, could it?

He leafed back to the beginning of the book and stared at the publication date. It was a year from today. This book had been written in the future.

The future!

Simon thumbed through the pages. And yes, here he was. Right here and now, searching for his passport in order to escape to Tierra del Fuego.

Simon glanced up and down the page. There was no mention of him finding this book though. Which meant . . . Simon's thoughts became justifiably confused. Which meant what? That the author of the book never knew that Simon had found it and read it. That must be what. Found it and read it before it had even been written. Before the things in it had actually happened. This was deep.

Simon fingered his fine head of hair. This was also brilliant. Why with this book in his possession he could always be one step ahead of the grey men. He could be one step ahead of everybody. The possibilities were endless. The financial possibilities. The sexual possibilities.

'Boom shanka!' said the lad.

Knock knock knock, went his front door.

Simon looked up in horror. And then he looked down at the open page:

> A knock came at Simon's door.
> Luckily for Simon it was only
> the postman.

'Thank God for that.' Simon placed the book carefully upon his bed and gave its cover a loving pat. 'Pardon me for a moment,' he told it. 'I just have to pop down and see what the postman's brought me.'

With a considerable spring in his step and a multitude of thoughts buzzing around in his head, Simon pulled bolts, unclipped the safety chain and threw open the front door.

On the doorstep stood a man in grey.

He wasn't a postman.

'I've been looking for you, Simon,' he said.

6

A mighty finger released the celestial pause button and Raymond continued on his way towards the circus ring.

He had time for just one more brief 'Aaagh' before he struck the sawdust with a hideous bone-fracturing report.

And then with a scream he awoke.

Raymond jerked up and rubbed at his eyes. Where was he? Where?

With shock, horror and a cold sweat on, Raymond gave his immediate surroundings a fearful scrutiny.

And then he blinked, rubbed his eyes again and then went, 'Oh.'

And then he began to smile.

A real face-splitter it was. Almost to the ears.

'I'm home,' sighed Raymond. 'I'm home in my bed.'

He felt at himself for broken bones. There were none. Charring? No. Bruises? Not a one. And he was wearing his pyjamas.

'I dreamt it. I dreamt the whole thing.' Raymond dragged a pyjama sleeve across his face and raised a fist toward the ceiling. 'It was a dream. A dream. A nightmare!'

Raymond shuddered. 'Whatever was I drinking last night?' He ran a tender hand across his brow. He did have a bit of a headache. It must have been the old Death-by-Cider. He'd have to give that up. Nightmares about man-eating potatoes he did *not* need.

Mind you. Raymond made a perky face. It would make a pretty good story if it was typed up. Plenty of excitement. Bit of a cop-out ending though, having the hero fall through the roof of a circus tent and then just wake up in his own bed. Perhaps if he went back to sleep for a couple of hours he could dream the rest.

'*No thank you.*' Raymond pushed back his blankets, swung his bare feet onto the carpet. Rose, stretched, farted, sighed. Padded over to the mirror on top of the chest of drawers. Gazed into it and smiled. Repulsive. He was, as all men always are, quite repulsive first thing in the morning.

Why was that? Raymond wondered. Why was it when women always looked so very fine? All tousled and warm and puppy-smelling. Apart from the glaringly obvious, he really had no idea at all.

Raymond glanced down at the bedside clock. 7.30. He wouldn't even be late for work today. A couple of aspirins and a cup of tea and he'd be ready to rock and roll.

Raymond shuffled over to the window and drew the curtains.

Outside the planet Saturn filled three-quarters of a star-pricked sky.

Raymond yawned mightily, dropped his pyjama bottoms, kicked them into a corner and pulled open the underpants drawer.

Now what should it be today then, eh? The red lycra 'Adonis' posing pouch with the padded crotch 'for the perfect profile'? Or perhaps the black spandex botty-hugger with the velcro quick-release side straps, 'for the man in a hurry to be going places'? Whatever possessed his mother to keep buying these things for him? And why, when she did, didn't she just put them straight into his drawer. Raymond was forever finding them under his mother's bed, or in the laundry basket. Usually after he came home from an all-night angling session. And she never seemed to get his size right. Some of them were far too big.

Raymond shook his head. 'I think I'll just stick with the gingham boxer shorts.' He plucked out a pair and stepped into them.

'And do I have a clean shirt?' Raymond raked at his stubbly chin. 'And if I do, should it be a long-sleeved or a short? And, for that matter, *why is the planet Saturn outside my window?*'

'Aaaaaaaaaagh!' he continued.

'I'm terribly sorry about that, Raymond.' It was a woman's voice. And what a voice, it sent little shivers up and down his spine.

'Who said that?' Raymond glanced back at his bed. It was unoccupied. 'Who's there? Who?'

'*I'm* here. I do so apologize about Saturn, you woke up before I could finish.'

'Where are you hiding?'

'Here. I'm here.' The voice came from the chest of drawers.

'You're hiding in my chest of drawers?'

'I *am* your chest of drawers.'

Raymond rammed a knuckle into his mouth and began to shake all over. It had finally happened. He was slightly mad (oh dear).

'I've lost it,' he mumbled. 'I've gone stone bonker.'

'Of course you haven't.' The voice was sweet. And so sympathetic. Not the way you would expect a chest of drawers to sound at all. 'The professor thought that you'd feel more comfortable if you woke up in your own surroundings, after all you'd been through. So I created this room from the stored memories in your subconscious. It's what I do, you see. It's my act. And I was just about to start on the view from your window when you woke up, and then I couldn't reach your memories any more. So you see, it's all quite simple. Do you really wear the 'Adonis' by the way? It must ride up terribly when you bend down to tie your shoe laces.'

'Get a grip now, Raymond.' The lad began to rock on his heels. 'All right, so you're getting the voices. It doesn't mean you're mad just because you're getting the voices. There could be a perfectly logical explanation. Oh my God.'

Raymond fell to his knees before the chest of drawers and crossed himself over his own chest region. 'Are you the blessed Virgin Mary?' he enquired.

'The blessed who? Oh I'm most dreadfully sorry, I haven't introduced myself. I am Zephyr. Would you mind jumping up in the air please?'

'Do what?'

'I can't hold the room any longer. Just a small jump.'

'*What?*'

'Sorry. Can't hold it.'

Suddenly Raymond was no longer kneeling. He was flat on his back. The carpet yanked from beneath him. And as he gaped up the ceiling went with it, as did the walls, the window, his bed, the whole illusory shebang. The room folded in upon itself, collapsed and vanished into the underpants drawer with an unappealing plug-hole gurgle.

Leaving Raymond all alone with nothing but his chest of drawers.

All alone. But where?

Raymond glanced around and about. He was on the deck of a ship. And a fine big one by the looks of it. If a trifle ancient. The deck was all salt-bleached, pocked and barnacled. Rust around the cabin doors. Faded canvas on the lifeboats. Peely paint on the rows of steamer chairs. More of a dry dock museum-piece than an ocean-goer. On a nearby lifebelt letters spelt out the name *SS Salamander*. That rang a distant ship's bell somewhere.

And it was cold on deck. Decidedly nippy. Especially when you were only wearing your PJ top and your gingham boxer shorts. And then there was old Saturn, filling three-quarters of that star-pricked night-black sky.

'Aaaaaagh!' went Raymond. 'We're in outer space. I'll die. I'll suffocate. My eyeballs will pop out. Aaaagh!'

'Oh dear. I am so sorry. All a bit of a shock I suppose.'

'Airlock,' mumbled Raymond, clamping his hands over his face.

'You won't suffocate. There's plenty of air out here.'

'Mmmph. Ummph?'

'Of course there is. Trust me.'

'Mmmph um mmphummph mmph mm mmph?'

'I'm *not* a talking chest of drawers, I'm Zephyr. Take your hands away from your face.'

'Mm!'

'Oh go on.'

'Mm! Mm mmphing mm mmph.'

'You're *not* holding your breath. I can see your chest going in and out.'

'Mm mm!'

'You're not!'

'Oh all right!' Raymond took his hands away from his face. He *was* breathing. There *was* air. 'I am breathing,' said Raymond. 'There is air.'

'Told you.'

'Yes, but how can there be air in space?'

'Nature abhors a vacuum,' said the chest of drawers. 'And if space wasn't full of air, how could the heat from the sun reach the planets? Tell me that.'

'Well,' said Raymond. 'I suppose . . . no hang about. Hold on here.'

'What is it?'

'I get this. All this.' Raymond made expansive gestures. 'You don't fool me.'

'I don't?'

'You don't. All this. I'm still dreaming, aren't I? I'm still asleep.'

'Whatever makes you think that?'

'Little things.' Raymond made a 'little things' gesture with his thumb and forefinger. 'Such as, that I am currently conversing with a chest of drawers, on the deck of an ocean liner, in orbit around the planet Saturn.'

'And breathing air,' said the chest of drawers helpfully. 'Don't forget about breathing air.'

'And breathing air, yes, thank you.' Raymond got a smug old grin on. 'You see what must have happened is, that I *woke* up, but I didn't actually *get* up. I probably just

74

turned over and went back to sleep. So I'd best wake up now, or I'll be late for work.' Raymond closed his eyes.

'What exactly are you doing?' asked the chest of drawers.

'Waking myself up.'

'By closing your eyes?'

'I know what I'm doing. If I'm dreaming with my eyes open. Then if I shut them I'm bound to wake up.'

'What a very strange person you are.'

'*Me* strange? There's nothing strange about me.'

'I've got a top drawer full of second-hand men's knickers that wouldn't agree with you.'

'Second-hand?' Raymond almost opened his eyes. 'I'm not talking to you any more. You're only a dream.'

'And you dream about this sort of stuff often then, do you?'

'No. Mostly I dream about trains.'

'Oh come on, Raymond. Open your eyes.'

'No.' Raymond folded his arms.

'It will be worth your while. Trust me. I promise.'

'No. Leave me alone now. I'm waking myself up.'

'You'll have to open your eyes when you wake yourself up, surely.'

Raymond thought about this. 'All right. I am going to open my eyes and wake up at home in my bed. Right . . . wait for it . . . now!'

Raymond opened his eyes.

He wasn't home in his bed. He was still on the deck of the *SS Salamander* and the *SS Salamander* was still in orbit around Saturn. But there had been one or two small changes.

For one thing Raymond was no longer in his PJ top and boxer shorts. Now he was dressed in a really spivvy pale silk Giorgio Armani suit. White linen shirt, crêpe de Chine tie, posh woollen socks, brogues by Hobbs of Piccadilly. The outfit Clapton wore that time when he played at The Brighton Centre. Raymond had always dreamt of having a kit like that.

'Cor,' said Raymond. 'Well, I mean to say . . .'

And, for another thing.

The chest of drawers had vanished. But where it had been standing stood—

'Hello, Raymond, I am Zephyr. Zephyr the Miraculous.'

Raymond's jaw dropped open and the space air jammed in his lungs. Smiling up at him was the most beautiful woman he had ever seen in his life.

Now it is generally agreed, by those who generally agree upon such matters, that feminine beauty is the sum of its attendant parts. And in Western society at least, that these attendant parts are better when exaggerated or reduced in scale. The laws that determine which parts should be which are pretty rigid. Large eyes and tiny noses for example, find great favour, the reverse do not. Long legs are preferred to short ones. Slim waists to fat ones. Bums and bosoms come and go, but mouths stay always wide.

It is all highly sexist, of course, and the standards set seem inevitably to be set by men. But then they would be, wouldn't they?

Raymond had cast adoring eyes over many women in his time, seeking for that perfect being to whom he might offer his undying love. And she did exist in the village. But only in kit form. A pair of long legs here, a wide mouth over there. One girl's ears, another's fingernails. It was getting them all together on a single woman that was proving to be the problem.

It wasn't a problem shared by Simon though.

But Raymond wasn't Simon. Raymond was a Romantic and when he found Miss Right-bits-in-all-the-right-places-and-exaggerated-or-diminished-according-to-his-personal-preferences, he would love her for ever.

The sheer outrageousness of this seemed to escape Raymond completely. That one day, along would come this raving beauty, who fulfilled all of his wildest imaginings of how a woman should look; and that she would fall instantly in love with him, and that they would both live happily ever after.

But he could always dream.

And was he dreaming now?

Raymond certainly hoped he wasn't.

Zephyr stood before him. And it was *her*. She was everything, had everything, that he could ever ever have hoped for in a woman.

She had the ankles of Angela the check-out girl, the legs of the woman who taught step aerobics at the sports centre, the torso of the barmaid at The Bear Flag, the facial bone structure of Sue the solicitor's secretary; and on and on. She even had the nice blue eyes of the lady in the post office.

She had the lot. And naturally she was wearing *the little black dress.*

'I love you,' said Raymond falling at her feet.

Zephyr smiled him a wide-mouthed smile. Raymond drew back in alarm. She had Simon's teeth.

'Sorry,' she said, rapidly closing her mouth before smiling anew. This time she displayed the teeth of the headmistress at the junior school. Raymond glanced down. She had her shoes on too. Raymond jumped up.

'It's another trick,' he cried, as his heart sank all away. 'You don't look like that at all really, do you?'

'I'm so sorry. I was only trying to cheer you up.'

Raymond stared off into space. 'I really am here, aren't I? I'm not dreaming this at all.'

Zephyr shook her beautiful head. She did it just the way the lady librarian Mrs Conan did. Raymond always asked her lots of questions whenever he was in the library. He just loved the way her neck moved when she shook her head.

'Stop that!' said Raymond. 'It isn't fair.'

'Sorry,' said Zephyr. 'I couldn't help it.'

'What about this suit?' Raymond clutched his Giorgio Armani to his bosom. Forsaken in love was bad enough, but not the suit also.

'It's yours. You can keep it. You look really nice in it.'

Raymond fingered the fabric. It felt perfect. Just how he had imagined it would feel. But for how long?

'How long can I keep it?' Raymond asked.

'As long as you want to. As long as it makes you happy.'

'Thank you. Thank you very much. What do you really look like, Zephyr?'

Zephyr tossed back her hair. It was rich and auburn. A fine young head of hair. It was the fine young head of hair of Simon's girlfriend Liza. Raymond had never been aware before just how much he loved Liza's hair. 'Will you come and meet the professor now?' she asked.

'Who is the professor?'

'Professor Merlin. This is his ship, sort of. You fell through the roof of his tent. After you demolished his very expensive holographic hoarding.'

'Ah that. I did do all that, didn't I?'

'I'm afraid you did. But you can make up for it I'm sure. The professor wants to have you for dinner.'

'*For* dinner?' Within his well-cut Jekylls, Raymond's knees began to knock. 'Not that again. Not *for* dinner.'

Raymond sought somewhere to run to. If all this *was* real and not just a bad dream, then Zephyr was probably the twin sister of Mr Chameleon the auctioneer.

'Stay away from me.' Raymond raised his fists. 'No-one's having me for dinner.'

'Oh, I'm so sorry.' Zephyr put up her hands. They were the hands of Pat the papergirl. 'I didn't mean *for* dinner, I meant *to* dinner. No-one's going to eat you, Raymond. You're quite safe here.'

'Then you're not a Venusian, underneath?'

'*A Venusian?* Certainly not!'

'And you don't eat people?'

'Raymond, if we wanted to eat you, do you think we would have gone to all the trouble of fixing you up after your fall and creating the replica of your room to make you feel comfortable when you woke up?'

'I suppose not, but . . .'

'No buts, Raymond. We wouldn't. Now I'm sure you must be very hungry. So why not come with me and have dinner with the professor, he'll explain everything to you.'

'Well . . .' Raymond dithered and then he shrugged and then he nodded. He really didn't have anywhere to run to. And, although he now knew that Zephyr's appearance was nothing more than a glorious illusion, conjured somehow from the gleanings of his subconscious mind, it didn't make her any the less marvellous to gaze upon. And there was always the chance that her bottom would move when she walked, just the way that Sheila who worked at the farm shop's did.

So he followed her into the ship.

And it did.

'Just one thing,' Raymond asked. 'This Professor Merlin. *He's* not a Venusian by any chance, is he?'

Zephyr tossed her hair once more and grinned back at him. 'Of course he's not a Venusian. Professor Merlin comes from planet Earth.'

7

Simon stared at the grey man on his doorstep.

The grey man stared back at him through his greyly tinted specs.

There was that moment of silence which is known as the pregnant pause.

Simon chewed upon his lip. *This* wasn't supposed to happen! Not yet anyway. 'Can I help you?' he asked, in as steady a voice as he could manage.

The grey man smiled a crooked smile. 'That remains to be seen.'

'Are you a Jehovah's Witness? I bought a *Watchtower* from you once, I think.'

'I'm not a Jehovah's Witness.' The grey man's crooked smile became an evil grin. 'I'm more a Jehovah's Nemesis, as it happens.'

'I gave already, I think. Goodbye.' Simon started to close the front door. The grey man put his foot against it.

'You have your foot against my door, I think.'

'I do.' The grey man gave the door a mighty kick that nearly took it from its hinges. Simon tumbled backwards and came to rest at the foot of his stairs (which is where northern people often go to when taken by surprise).

The grey man took two brisk steps into the hall and slammed the door behind him. Simon struggled to his feet. 'Now just you see here,' he began.

'No, pal, just *you* see here. I've followed you all the way from The Bramfield Arms. You left in a bit of a hurry, didn't you? Overheard something you shouldn't have? Know something you shouldn't know?'

'I don't know what you mean. I have a dentist's appointment, I think.'

'I think, I think? Can't you finish any sentence without saying "I think"?' The grey man took another step forward. Simon stood his ground.

'I have a letter somewhere here, I think.'

'A letter? What are you talking about?'

'In my wallet. I think.' Simon fished the thing from his trouser pocket. 'I have a medical condition.'

'Oh yeah?' The grey man stared at him eye to eye. Simon could smell his breath. It didn't smell good.

'Let me show you.' The gardener's apprentice dug out a grubby-looking envelope with many folds in it. He held this up and the grey man snatched it from his fingers, sniffed at it suspiciously, opened it up and withdrew a crumpled piece of paper.

'What is this?' he demanded to be told.

'Read it, you'll see, I think.'

The grey man read it. '"This is to certify that Simon . . ."' He paused and looked up. 'Is this really your surname?'

Simon offered a dismal nod. 'I try not to think about it.'

'Obvious to see why. So. "This is to certify that Simon, surname as stated, has been a patient at my surgery for ten years and suffers from short-term memory loss. He is therefore excused games and must always have a seat next to the radiator in winter time." What is this?'

'It's a doctor's note. You see I forget things. All the time. Like, you just said I was in The Bramfield Arms. Perhaps I was. I don't remember.'

The grey man raised an eyebrow of a likewise hue.

'It's not my fault. I can't help it.'

'So you don't remember where you were, say, yesterday evening, for instance?'

'Yesterday evening.' Simon pursed his lips. 'Give me some time and I expect it will come back to me.'

'How much time?'

'The doctor said about fifteen years.'

'Oh yeah? And when did he say that to you?'

'About fifteen years ago, when he wrote the note. I think.'

The grey man looked Simon up and down. 'You're a bit of a prat,' said he. '*I* think.'

Simon nodded hopelessly. 'I suppose I am. What did you come in here for? Was it to read the meter?'

'Yeah, that was it. To read your meter. And I've done it now.' The grey man stalked back to the front door and swung it violently open, taking the lock-keep right out of the door frame. 'Goodbye,' he said.

'Er, just one thing.'

The grey man turned.

'Could I have my note back please?'

The grey man screwed up Simon's note and tossed it back at him. 'Prat,' said he, departing into the street.

Simon paused a moment before hurrying into the front room and once more lifting the corner of the net curtain.

The shiny grey van was parked on the corner of the street. The grey man's grey companions were lounging against it. Simon's unwelcome visitor strode up to them. Words were exchanged. The unwelcome visitor twirled his finger against his temple and then gestured back towards Simon's house. Some laughter was shared. Then all three grey men got into the shiny grey van and drove off, in the direction of the allotments.

Simon returned to his hall. Pushed the front door shut and reslotted the security chain. He picked up his 'doctor's note', smoothed out its latest creases, returned it to its envelope and the envelope to his wallet. He returned his wallet to his pocket. Which he patted. Smiling as he did so.

It had served him well had the old 'doctor's note'. Got him out of many a heavy scrape in the past and into more than a few beds also. It was remarkable how fast word could travel around a village WI that there was a handsome young man with whom a frustrated housewife might live out her most intimate sexual fantasies, secure in the knowledge that he would remember nothing about them the following day.

'Prat?' said Simon. 'I don't *think* so . . .' But then a troubled look appeared upon his face. 'That book,' said he. 'About that book.'

Simon went back upstairs, seated himself upon his bed and took up the book in question. He rapped his knuckle upon Raymond's nose. 'We haven't got off to a very good start, have we?' he asked. The book did not reply.

Simon thumbed through it once more and found his place.

> A knock came at Simon's door.
> Luckily for Simon it was only
> the postman.

Simon clicked his porcelain caps. 'Wrong,' said he, reading on.

> Or so Simon thought. Although
> exactly why he thought this
> is unclear . . .

Simon ground his porcelain caps.

> . . . Especially
> considering the remarkable,
> some might even say uncanny,
> powers of perception he was
> later to display.

'Ah,' said Simon. 'Ah.'

He read on. It was all there. His encounter with the grey man at the door. It was all there, but it wasn't quite the same. The version in the book was better, it had Simon running spectacular verbal rings about the grey man, before finally frog-marching him down the hall and tossing him into the street.

Simon chewed upon a thumbnail. Now why was that?

'Oh dear,' said Simon. 'I know why. Because that must be the way *I* tell it to whoever writes this book. It's the way I would have wanted it to have happened. Bugger.'

Simon flung the hardback to the floor. He could hardly capitalize on what was in there, if all that was in there was a load of exaggeration and half truths. What cruel and bitter irony. Hoist with his own petard. And such like.

'But hang about.' Simon picked up the book and ran his nail-chewed thumb across its glossy cover. 'I know this now. So. If I make a solemn vow right this minute, to tell the truth, the whole truth and nothing but the truth to whoever interviews me in the future about my side of the story. Then . . .' Simon thought about it.

'Then, everything in this book about me, from this moment on, *will* be correct. Yes. It must work. It must.'

And it seemed logical that it should. Well, as logical as anything so improbable could seem anyway.

Simon scratched at his head. Telling the truth, the whole truth and nothing but the truth was going to be something of a challenge. But it was something that he had to do, because then he could be absolutely certain that everything the book said that he'd do, he'd do.

And the beauty of it was, that if he was very careful and just read the book a little bit at a time, then let the events in it catch up with him, he'd be sure to make the right moves every time. Because he'd know what the right moves would be, he'd have just read about himself making them. Magic.

And the possibilities were endless.

'Now, just let me work this out,' said Simon. 'Say, for example, that I wish to back the horses tomorrow. At this present moment I do not know which ones will win. But six months from now, or whenever I'm interviewed by the writer of this book, I will know them then. So, if I tell the writer that I backed those winning horses, and I make sure that he puts down their names in this book. Then I can consult this book now, and know which horses will win tomorrow. Which means that I will have told the whole truth to the writer, because I did win on those particular horses.'

Simon's hands began rubbing themselves together as thoughts about multi-million-pound killings on the stock exchange and the world's money markets now swarmed into his head. He had struck the mother lode this time and no mistake. This book was his passport to paradise.

'Perhaps I should flick on a few chapters and see if I'm sailing on my luxury yacht, surrounded by page-three lovelies.'

The temptation was overwhelming. A quick look couldn't hurt now, could it?

'Oh yes it could.' Simon did big nods. 'That way madness lies. I will have to be extremely disciplined about this. Only work one page at a time. Now, how to begin? Hm. Well, start in a small way. First thing in the morning I will go to the bank and draw out fifty pounds. Shall I check on that?' Simon made with the furtive glancings, then leafed furiously through the book.

> Simon was the first in the queue
> outside the bank that morning.
> When it opened at nine-thirty
> he went in and drew out all of
> his savings. Precisely one
> hundred pounds.

'One hundred pounds?' Simon stroked his chin. 'Nice round figure. Yes, one hundred pounds it is then. But what do I do next?'

> Then he set off to the bookies,
> where he placed his now legendary
> four-horse accumulator bet.

'*Yes!*' Simon leapt up and made punchings at the ceiling. He kissed the cover of the book, going 'Yes yes yes' as he did so. He flung himself on to his bed and kicked his legs in the air. 'Yes!' he went, and 'yes' and 'yes'.

He'd cracked it this time and no mistake.

'Thank you, Raymond.' Simon hugged the book to his chest. '*You* did this, didn't you? Somehow you sent me this book from the future. The future where you become, what is it?' He reread the title. 'The Saviour of Mankind. Brilliant. Then it looks as if we're both going to crack it. What can stop us, eh? The grey men are off my case now. They can go clean up the allotment. And I shall clean up here. Financially speaking, of course. And you can save mankind from whatever it has to be saved from. Brilliant. Absolutely brilliant. *Yes!*'

And that, thankfully, is where we leave Simon for now. Lying on his bed, hugging Raymond's book, kicking his legs in the air and repeating the word '*Yes!*'.

Not a pretty sight. But then, watching some ruthless, callous, self-seeking bastard furthering his own ends without giving a tinker's toss for the rest of us, rarely is. And what made it all the worse in this particular case, was that the bastard in question had actually witnessed his best friend being taken into space by a flying starfish; had learned that this sort of thing happened on a regular basis and that teams of grey men were employed to cover up afterwards; *and* that this was part of a diabolical conspiracy, which existed to conceal an interplanetary trade in human beings, pickled, canned or bubbled.

And with all this terrible knowledge in his possession, what does this bastard do? Does he use the book from the future as the potent weapon it is to help save the world from the aliens who secretly prey upon its people?

Does he heck as like! He uses it to make himself rich! Bastard!

* * *

But then. Perhaps. Are we being too hard on Simon? After all, what is he actually *free* to do? He holds in his hands a book which foretells his future. A future already mapped out for him and from which it is impossible to escape. Just as Judas was destined from birth to perform his dirty deed, so too is Simon a victim of predetermined fate. Helpless and without any genuine free will of his own.

Perhaps.

Perhaps.

But then, what about the way he conned the grey man with that phoney doctor's note. No-one could ever get away with a stroke like that, could they?

But *he* did.

Bastard!

8

The grand salon of the *SS Salamander* was quite simply splendid.   A veritable tour de France in Victorian marine Moorish, it resembled nothing less than the grand harem of some grand vizier from the grand Baghdad of Scheherazade.

Twenty-three traceried columns, wrought with opulent enamels and inlaid with lapis lazuli and chrysoprase and alexandrite, offered their enthusiastic support to a richly ornamented dome of a ceiling. This was of the most gorgeous rosy tint, smothered by a confusion of erotica. Bonking big time. The walls of the grand salon were similarly frescoed. But all in the best possible taste. This wasn't the leering nastiness of the cheap pornographer. This was the jolly romping sex of Peter Fendi or Thomas Rowlandson. A kind of comic Kama Sutra.

Pierced screens of gopher-wood and sandalwood and sycamore broke the floor, which was a marvel of inter-locking mosaic.

It was a pretty swell old gaff.

And it had a bit of a history also.

When Isambard Kingdom Brunel designed the ill-fated *Great Eastern*, his avowed intention was to create a 'floating palace' on a scale which had never before been known. And indeed *The Great Eastern* was the biggest vessel to brave the waters since the now legendary ark of Noah.

Mr Brunel was a man with a vision. An engineering genius who helped shape the Victorian age. The Great Eastern was to be his triumph. It proved to be his downfall.

Isambard died, a broken man, at the age of fifty-three, within days of the big ship's launching. A launching which had been delayed for three long months, the land-locked vessel stubbornly refusing to leave its dock and enter the Thames. Ill fortune travelled with it from the first, when an engineer and his mate were sealed up alive within the double hull. On its maiden voyage one of the funnels exploded killing several crewmen. A catalogue of disasters followed which dogged the ship for thirty years until it was finally broken up in 1889. Its interior was never completed and it had caused the deaths of many men. It was a jinxed ship and a sad legacy for Isambard to leave behind.

But he left others. Amongst these his unborn son Colin. History speaks little, in fact nothing whatsoever, about young Colin. The boy who would one day build the *SS Salamander*, but would never get a commemorative medal from Queen Victoria for so doing. The *Salamander* was commissioned by an Eastern potentate. A *great Eastern* potentate. The symmetry of this pleased young Colin, who had inherited neither his father's genius nor his name.

Colin was born on the wrong side of the duvet, to a Whitechapel prostitute of his father's acquaintance. This lady of the night had managed to escape the attentions of Jack the Ripper, whom she chanced upon during his Grand Guignol farewell performance at Miller's Court. She produced a doctor's note which explained that she had short-term memory loss and so wouldn't remember in the morning that Jack was really Mr Gladstone.

Colin did not actually design the *SS Salamander*. Because, as has been said, he did not inherit his father's genius. Colin inherited his father's briefcase. The man of vision having forgotten to take it with him after the night of passion during which Colin was conceived. In the briefcase were the plans for the *SS Salamander*, a liner so magnificent as to make *The Great Eastern* look like a tugboat in comparison.

And the rest is unwritten history.

The *Salamander* was built.

But not on planet Earth.

The great Eastern potentate was a very Far Eastern potentate.

He hailed from Uranus, where he was the sultan.

Now, as none of the foregoing was as yet known to Raymond, he simply stood in the vestibule of the grand salon, eyeing all around and about him, with his jaw hanging slack and his hands adangling at his sides.

It was all a little much to take in. And if the salon was a marvel to be seen, what could be said of the banquet presently in progress?

Quite a bit actually. At the centre of the salon, beneath the mighty ornamented 'dome, stood a table of heroic proportions; and laid out upon this, a repast deserving of an ode.

There were comports of curly kale, cabbage and
cauliflower.
Bowls of bouillon, bortsch, bouillabaisse.
There were salvers of sweetmeats and soufflés and
mousses.
And truffles and crumbles and fruits *à la glace*.

There was ragout and fricassee, salmi and casserole.
Salt-water herring and freshwater trout.
Bilberries, dewberrries, gooseberries, cranberries.
A clam bake, a pot roast, a beano blow out.

It was Jaffas and mandarins
Stone fruits and tangerines.
Haggis and hotchpotch and chowder and stew.
It was waffles and whitebait.
Butterscotch shortcake.
Plum duff and dumplings. And potables too!

Red wines and white wines and rosés and sparklings.
Tawny Madeiras and twelve-year-old ports.
Champagne and Chardonnay, claret and Burgundy.
Cognac and cordials, snifters and shorts.

And so on and so forth. It was very impressive. And Raymond did have a very empty stomach.

And if the salon was a marvel to be seen, and the repast deserving of an ode, then what of the banqueters? What of those who sat about that table of heroic proportions, within this marvellous salon, and dined upon the viands aforementioned.

What indeed?

These were the artistes of Professor Merlin's Circus.

They were gorging themselves upon the fabulous spread. Laughing and joking and carrying on in that easy manner in which only true friends can. And they were the most amazing characters that Raymond had ever seen.

There were about twenty of them and they presented a singularly colourful and flamboyant display.

To Raymond it was all a riot of sequin and spangle.

Exotic women with painted faces, high-topiarized hair-dos, primped into peacock perms and hung with danglums and tassles. Bedecked with jewellery. Necklaces of sarkstone, cat's-eye and tourmaline. Bloodstone pendants, gilded noserings set with heliotrope and beryl. Torques of coral and jade.

Their costumes were of the most lavish that may be imagined, and quite the prettiest and best becoming, glamourizing the wearers with a luxuriance of frills and furbelows, decked with swathes of chiffon, which released a tantalizing glimpse or two of perfumed flesh. Here a powdered shoulder and there a dainty ankle, clenched by a circlet of black pearls.

The menfolk were robust and well knit. Big broad-shouldered types, but none the less bedecked and bejewelled. Veritable dandies all, they displayed themselves in regal fineries. Frocked coats of cloth of gold, with padded shoulders and slashed sleeves. Silk bandannas and velvet cummerbunds, moleskin pantaloons and quilted spats. And each and every bit and bob of a sparkling rainbow hue.

And at the head of the table, holding forth to the merriment of all and seated upon a throne-like chair composed of peacock plumes and ostrich feathers sat quite the most fantastic of them all.

He was tall and tapered. Long and lean and loose of limb.

A purple periwig adorned a narrow head distinguished by many a notable feature. Twinkling turquoise eyes flanked a slender sweeping shark's fin of a nose. Beneath this, waxed moustachios taut as watchsprings coiled and uncoiled, as a jolly mouth, well-to-do with golden teeth, munched upon choice snackeries and gave out with a humorous monologue which held the diners in a state of high jocularity. A chin of considerable length dipped and bobbed as if possessed of a life of its own.

Raymond noted also a curious tattoo above the right eyebrow and the large clear-glass ring which pierced the left earlobe.

Moving on down, this gentleman's get-up seemed all of the Regency period. High starched collar, rising above a white silk cravat. A waistcoat of rich red brocade, embroidered with arabesques of golden thread and dressed with an indulgence of silver watch fobs and dandy chains. A frock-coat of green velvet, the lapels peppered with emeralds and sapphires. Laced shirt cuffs flounced from beneath the ornamented sleeves.

The rest of the apparel was lost below the table and so Raymond could only guess at it. He guessed correctly, however, that it was of a similar sumptuousness.

And he was greatly taken with the gentleman's hands. These were slender, the fingers elongated, hung with elegant rings, the nails manicured and burnished. These hands were of a ghostly white, as was the gentleman's complexion. He had about him the look of an animated mummy. But one fiercely animated and not prepared to crumble into dust.

And Raymond stared on, with polo mint eyes and his mouth catching flies, and he saw as he stared, something more. Raymond took in the fantastic costume, the countless conceits and fripperies. But he knew instinctively that these were not the studied eccentricities of the vain poseur. This was the natural wear of a man who knew who he was.

And *he* was Professor Merlin.

Oh yes indeed.

'Raymondo!' Professor Merlin rose from his chair and flung wide his wonderful hands in an all-embracing gesture which embraced both one and all. 'You are restored to us. Come hither do.'

The lad from Earth gazed upon the colourwash of eager faces that were gazing unto him. And he was somewhat stuck for a reply.

'Go on,' whispered Zephyr. 'Say hello.'

Raymond waved some foolish fingers. 'Hello,' he said.

'Hello to you, Raymondo.' The professor inclined his head as one might do when taken in the company of royalty.

The banqueters broke into wild applause. Someone cast his pink peruke towards the frescoed ceiling. Another threw this head, which he again caught expertly upon his shoulders. Happily Raymond missed that.

The professor stroked his animated chin. 'I tell you truly, my Raymondo, that I dig the duds.'

'The duds?' Raymond stroked his head.

'The whistle. The Rooty-toot. The demob. The radiation-wear.'

'The suit,' whispered Zephyr. 'He's admiring your suit.'

'Oh, my suit.' Raymond preened at his natty lapels. 'It was Zephyr, she—'

'You positively pauperize us.' The professor hung

down his head and did melodramatic heart-clutchings. 'I shall have my tailor hauled from his toggery table and tossed off the starboard bow.'

'Oh no, please don't do that.'

'It's all right,' whispered Zephyr. 'He doesn't have a tailor.'

'Oh, I see. Or rather I don't.'

'Come, Raymondo, come. Sit upon my right hand and bring your beautiful wife.'

'My beautiful wife?'

'He means me.'

'But Zephyr, you're not—'

'I sort of am for now.'

'I am most perplexed,' said Raymond.

Zephyr smiled and linked his arm. 'I'll help you understand. Come on and sit with the professor.'

Raymond took a deep breath. And then *he* smiled. This really wasn't all that bad when you thought about it. Dressed up in the Giorgio Armani dream suit, with your best girl by your side and invited to dine at the captain's table. There was quite a lot going for it. At this particular moment, anyway.

Raymond straightened up his shoulders. Yes indeed. Why not?

'Shall we dine, my dear?' he asked.

'If you will kindly lead the way.'

Oh yes indeed. And Raymond did, to further wild applause.

'Raymondo to the right of me and Zephyr to my left.' Professor Merlin smiled them into their seats. Raymond sank his bottom onto the comfy chair. Having first pulled up his trouser knees of course.

'Cushioned in?' The host turned his head from side to side.

'Very nice,' said Raymond. Zephyr smiled that smile of smiles.

'Then dine. I will introduce you all around,

Raymondo, of a shortness. But as now your belly cryeth out for feastal cheering, eat your fill.'

'Well thank you very much.' Raymond took up a crisp serviette and tucked it into his shirt collar. There was no way he was going to sully the suit with spillage. But exactly *where* to start? *That* was the question. The other banqueters were once more back at banqueting. Plucking things apparently at random. But there might well be some special protocol to be observed and Raymond had no wish to make a schmuck of himself.

The professor, noting Raymond's hesitation, nudged him gently in the ribs. 'As and where you wish,' said he. 'Just bung it down your cakehole.'

'Thank you, then I will.' Raymond ladled delicacies on to his plate. A nice good-sized plate it was. White china, with a coat of arms and the words '*SS Salamander* First-Class Salon' printed upon it. Snazzy-looking cutlery too, silver, with ivory handles and a selection of exquisite drinking glasses.

Oh yes indeed.

Raymond spiked up something white and steaming, testing its fragrance under his nose. It smelt preposterously good. He opened wide his smiling mouth and prepared to 'bung it down'. But then he paused and glanced across at Zephyr.

'It's all right,' she said. 'I told you.'

'Told him what?' the professor enquired.

'About the "George".'

'The "George"?' Professor Merlin fell into hilarity. 'You mean he thought that we . . .' He gestured around at the marvellous spread and the marvellous company. 'That we eat . . .'

'Eat George, yes.'

'Eat George!' The professor rocked about in his chair. Tears of mirth ran down his mummy's face. 'Raymondo,' he croaked, when he could find his breath, 'you are a caution, so you are. We're circus folk, Raymondo. Artistes, performers, workers of wonders and makers of

95

magic. We spin dreams. We are come unto you, then we are gone. The coxcomb and the mountebank, the crooner, the contortionist, the pierrot and the merry prankster. We ain't no stinking cannibals! So kindly dig in do.'

Raymond dug in. He dug in with a will and he found all that he dug into quite superb. The professor poured him wine and served him this and that, delighting in Raymond's gasps of amazement and hiccups of pleasure.

At length the lad's belly had a rosy glow inside, as did his cheeks. He winked across at Zephyr. 'Is this great, or what?'

But Zephyr just sat with her hands in her lap. Her plate was empty and clean.

'You're not eating.' Raymond said.

'No.' Zephyr turned down her nice blue eyes. 'I don't.'

'What, not at all?'

'Raymondo,' the professor broke in, 'you haven't told me what you think of the old *Salamander*.'

'Quite incredible,' Raymond said, as he gulped down a further glass of something. 'But tell me truly, if you will. Are you *really* from Earth?'

The professor's chin bobbed up and down like a nodding dog in a Cortina rear window. 'As really from Earth as you are.'

'But how?' Raymond scratched at his head with the handle of his fork. 'How did you get up here, into space? How did you get this ship up here?'

'What makes the ship run? Is that what you're asking?'

Raymond popped a sweetmeat into his mouth. 'I think I am,' he said, between munchings.

'It's a steam ship, Raymondo. Surely you noticed the funnels.'

'But steamships don't fly through space. Spaceships fly through space, but not steamships.'

'Oh!' The professor seemed genuinely surprised. 'So what do steamships fly through? Steam?'

'Water,' said Raymond. 'I mean they—'

'Don't pull my leg.' Professor Merlin nudged again at Raymond's ribs. 'You cannot kid the kidder.'

Raymond looked bewildered. He *was* bewildered. 'I am bewildered,' he said.

Professor Merlin made a mock conspiratorial face and beckoned Raymond nearer. 'Would you believe me if I told you that I have replaced the ship's existing steam turbine engines with a revolutionary new interplanetary hyper-drive system of my own design, which powers the ship through space due to the transperambulation of pseudo-cosmic anti-matter?'

Raymond gave his head another scratch. 'Probably,' he said.

'You'd be a schmuck then. Because I haven't.'

'Thanks very much.' Raymond hunched his elegant shoulders.

'Would you believe me then if I told you it was done by magic?'

'No.' Raymond gulped some more wine. 'I would not.'

'Pity. You'd have got it right that time.'

'Get real,' said Raymond. 'Magic indeed.'

'Magic,' the professor smiled, 'has nothing whatsoever to do with "getting real". Quite the reverse, in fact. But of course if you have a better explanation for the ship being here, I'd be pleased to dismiss it out of hand for you.'

Raymond was beginning to get a sulk on. The professor refilled his glass. 'This arrack is distilled from a thousand sacred spices. Take a sipping. Tell me what you think.'

Raymond took a swigging. It was pure nectar of the gods. 'It's OK,' he said, grumpily.

'*OK?* This is the finest that Jupiter has to offer.'

'Oh, Jupiter, is it?' Raymond shook his now quite fuzzy head. 'So Jupiter has life upon it too.'

'It did when we played there last week.'

'And you play all the planets?'

'All there are to play we do, which is all of them that be.'

'So there's life on every single planet?'

'Well there wouldn't be much point in there being a planet, if there was no-one to live on it, would there?' The professor laughed once more. But Raymond didn't.

'Play Venus a lot then, do you?' he asked.

The coldness of his tone was lost on the professor, who nodded with his chin and said, 'We do.'

'Nice for you.' Raymond put down his glass rather heavily. It tipped upon his plate and spilt out its precious contents. Raymond suddenly became aware of just how drunk he had become. And just how angry. And when you're drunk and angry at the same time . . . well . . .

'Bloody nice,' said Raymond rising in his chair, but sinking down again. 'Lots of bloody nice food on Venus, I'll bet. Though, of course, you don't eat the "George", do you? Not like those bastards do. Not like how they sell human beings there for food. I wonder if they bring a packed lunch when they come to your shows.'

'Raymondo, please.'

'My name's not Raymondo and it's not George. It's Raymond.'

'Raymond then, please. Calm yourself do.'

'I don't want to calm myself,' said Raymond, who didn't.

'Well, have another drink then.'

'I don't want another drink. I just want to be heard.' As Raymond's voice was now a very loud voice and the only voice now speaking, it was a reasonable assumption that it was being heard. 'All right!' he continued. 'Tell me how it works! Tell me why it works! Tell me why you can swan around between the planets in your magic boat, while people like me – What are *we* then, part of the food chain?'

'Have you quite finished?' the professor asked.

'No,' said Raymond. 'Yes,' said Raymond. 'I don't know,' said Raymond. 'Tell me what is going on.'

'Quite so.' The professor poured Raymond another drink.

'I don't want that,' said Raymond.

'We'll see.' Professor Merlin poured another for himself. 'Firstly,' he said, 'this banquet was laid on specially for you. It was a sort of test.'

'Which I've failed,' said Raymond with a sneer.

'Which you have passed,' said the professor, 'with full marks. I gave it all to you. Everything you'd ever dreamed of. That suit, the woman of your longings, this feast. Most men would have snatched it all without a second thought, looking out for number one and damn the rest. But you couldn't do it, could you?'

'No,' said Raymond. 'I could not.'

'You could not. Your outrage at what goes on on Venus was too much for you to contain. Your sense of moral justice—'

'Don't lay it on too thick,' said Raymond.

'Bravo. Modest also. I knew that we'd finally found the right man.'

Raymond scratched once more at his head. But with the pointy end of the fork this time and nearly took his eye out. 'What if I'd been the wrong man?' he ventured.

'We'd have had to let you go.'

'What?' Raymond made a worried face. 'Over the side, into space?'

'No. Of course not. I would have let you go home. Back to Earth. You could have kept the suit and Zephyr said she liked the look of you and was prepared to go also.'

'*What?*' Raymond fell back in his chair. 'That's what I would have got for failing?'

'Exactly. The trinkets of trivia. The baubles of boloney.'

'So what do I get for *passing* the test?'

Professor Merlin rose, as did all else about the great table. He doffed his wig and bowed from the waist. 'You get the opportunity to join us upon a perilous mission. To take up arms against an evil adversary. To fight for the cause of justice. To give your life for all that is true and honourable. Raymond, we salute you.'

The professor flung his wig into the air and the air was swallowed up by frenzied applause.

Strangely no record exists of exactly what Raymond said next.

9

> Ahriman Boy
> Lucifer Lad
> Seven Seals
> Millennium Choice

Simon was the first in the queue outside the bank that morning. When it opened at nine-thirty he went in and drew out all of his savings. Precisely one hundred pounds. Then he set off for the bookies, where he placed his now legendary four-horse accumulator bet.

He would have whistled, if it hadn't been for the hangover. How come he'd neglected to mention the hangover to the writer of Raymond's biography? If he had mentioned it, then he'd have known in advance not to drink so much last night. And so he wouldn't have the hangover now, and there'd be no mention of it in the book. Which there wasn't, although he *did* have the hangover.

Simon knew well enough why the hangover hadn't been mentioned. Because he had no wish for the doings of last night to be given to posterity. That's why!

It all began for him just after he'd made up his mind to tell the truth, the whole truth and nothing but the truth, to the future writer of Raymond's biography; and then formulated the ingenious (though bastardly) plan for winning on the horses. The winning horses were listed just where he would ask the writer to list them. In a little box above the chapter that began, *Simon was the first in the queue*.

Simon had copied the names of the winning horses

onto the envelope of his precious 'doctor's note', carefully hidden the book from the future, taken a shower, put on clean clothes and gone out for the evening.

It was a big mistake.

He should never have gone to The Jolly Gardeners. But he did.

Andy met his arrival with a face like thunder. He had certain things he wished to say to Simon.

These things concerned the unpleasantness which had occurred after Simon's rapid departure from The Jolly on the previous night. Things which Andy held Simon responsible for by default. Things concerning Simon's girlfriend Liza.

Liza, said Andy, had kicked Dick Godolphin's lurcher, and when Dick protested, Liza had kicked Dick. Long Bob the chicken farmer, who employed Dick on a part-time basis, had stepped in to bring order and had then received a kicking of his own.

Andy, as everyone knew, had strict rules regarding kickings in his bar and Liza had been barred for life.

Simon brightened upon hearing this. For it meant that he could drink here in the future, without always having to look over his shoulder. But his brightening soon dulled down as Andy went on to say that, after it had taken three members of Roman Candle to forcibly eject the kicker from the bar. The kicker in question had then employed the deadly martial art of Dimac upon his pub sign. Leaping twelve feet into the air and kicking it from its single hinge. And, as Liza was now barred, Simon was going to have to pay for the reparation, which Dick (who had a part-time cleaning job at The Jolly) had agreed to take on, for fifteen quid.

Andy added that, as he considered himself a fair man, Simon could, if he wished, choose not to pay, and opt instead for lifelong banishment.

'I will pay you on the morrow.' Simon said. Re-brightening to the thought that when the morrow came and his horses won, he would have enough money to buy The Jolly Gardeners outright if he wished.

'A pint of the usual,' he continued. 'And put it on Raymond's slate, which naturally I cannot borrow from to pay you, it not being *my* money.'

Andy mulled that one over, found it all too confusing to argue about and set to the pulling of Simon's pint.

'Oh, and a bag of nuts if you will. And take one for yourself.'

Andy took a bag of nuts for himself.

It was early yet and the bar was far from crowded. It was empty but for Simon. But it smelt a bit odd. Not of fish, more of sulphur. And Simon really should have noticed this. And the half-drunk glass of Guinness at the end of the counter.

But he didn't.

So he really wasn't prepared when the door to the gents' bog opened and Mr Hilsavise ducked his big bald head, with its distinctive pentagram tattoo, beneath the-beam-that-strangers-always-bang-their-skulls-on-when-they-come-out-of-the-Gents.

'Well well well,' went the far from jolly gardener. 'What do we have here then? An apprentice in a new hat who's taken the afternoon off.'

Simon looked the big man up and down. He recalled reading this article about how dog owners came, after a while, to resemble their dogs. Apparently, the pet owner loving the dog, subconsciously wanted to be 'as the dog' and the dog, returning its owner's love, yearned to be 'as the owner'. They both tuned into this biological frequency and gradually exchanged elements of their appearance. Exactly what this biological frequency was and how it functioned, had not been fully explained. And Simon had had severe doubts about the whole business.

But now, as he sat, somewhat upon the edge of his stool, he realized that it must be true. For the proof stood right there before him.

Not that Mr Hilsavise owned a dog. He didn't. Nor a cat. Mr Hilsavise was in love with his work.

And Simon supposed, his work must be in love with him.

It was all there. The pumpkin head. The cauliflower ear. The eyes of beetroot red. The hands were two bunches of bananas. And a whole lot more. But it all looked as it always looked . . .

Full of menace.

If this man wasn't in league with the devil, then it was purely due to an oversight on the part of the Prince of Darkness.

The gardener's apprentice smiled his winning smile. But it didn't come up a winner this time.

'Where is my flat-back?' asked Mr Hilsavise.

'I took it home to give it a clean,' Simon lied.

'Oh I am so terribly sorry,' said the apple-barrel-chested giant. 'I had no idea.'

'No idea of what?' was not the question Simon should have asked.

'No idea that your home was now the car-park behind the supermarket. Been evicted, have you?'

'Er no, ha ha ha.' Simon tried really hard to make it sound like laughter. 'The flat-back's there for safety's sake. Perhaps you noticed the wheel clamp *I* put on it. That should keep the joyriders at bay, eh?'

'These would be the joyriders who have driven off on my Allen Scythe, I suppose.'

'It's in the garage, having an oil change. At my own expense, naturally.'

'Naturally.' Mr Hilsavise came slowly along the bar. The sulphurous smell preceeded him. Brimstone, that's what they used to call sulphur. Mr Hilsavise loomed above Simon.

'The horse field at the bottom of the-lane-that-dare-not-speak-its-name, nine-thirty tomorrow. I will be there. You will be there. My flat-back will be there. My Allen Scythe will be there. Do I make myself absolutely clear?'

Simon's head bobbed up and down. His teeth were trying very hard to smile. Between the chattering.

'Because if you're not. And they're not . . .' Mr Hilsavise leaned hideously near and whispered certain explicit details into Simon's ear. Simon's legs and eyes crossed simultaneously.

'Good lad.' Hell's horticulturist patted Simon's trembling shoulder. Returned to his Guinness. Drank it down and left the bar.

Andy, who had been maintaining a low profile throughout the foregoing, now presented Simon with his beer and nibbles.

'Dry roasted nuts?' he enquired.

'Your hearing's most acute,' said Simon.

And that was the start of it.

Simon should just have drunk up and gone home. Kept a clear head for his day of destiny.

But he didn't.

He finished his pint and he ordered another. He would buy out Mr Hilsavise. He would buy out the whole village. Set himself up as the squire. Things of that nature.

By eight the bar was busy and Simon was in high spirits. The Scribe was at the bar to Simon's left. Here on one of his non-scribing evenings he was, as ever, bitterly bewailing his lot. To whit that scribes of far less talent than himself were earning millions, whilst he was forced to live upon a pittance, made bearable only by the consumption of large quantities of alcohol.

Simon really wasn't all that interested. His interests lay with the tall young woman seated to his right. She was something of a looker and had come in by herself. Out of politeness Simon had engaged her in conversation.

'It's called short-term memory loss,' he explained.

The looker nodded her striking profile. 'Must make life very difficult for you,' she said with a yawn.

'It has up until now,' replied Simon, who always liked a challenge. 'But I have a substantial inheritance due tomorrow which will make me a man of independent means.'

'Really?' said the looker. 'And when did you learn of this?'

Now a lesser fellow would have fallen into that and said 'Why just this afternoon', but not Simon. After all, he was playing on the home ground, as it were.

'It was bequeathed to me when I was a child. Would you care for another drink?'

'A Bloody Mary would be nice. I love your teeth, by the way.'

And that was the start of the next bit of it.

The looker had another Bloody Mary and another. Simon could see Raymond's line of credit growing shorter and shorter. But he could also see the looker growing more and more 'relaxed'.

She wasn't much of a talker for a looker. But Simon, being the professional that he was, coaxed her along with subtle flattery towards the wit and wisdom of her words.

Presently she asked him, 'Do you have a car outside?'

Simon made the pretence of consulting certain notes in his wallet. 'It appears that I have one of my firm's executive demonstration vehicles on hold in the car-park behind the supermarket. Why do you ask?'

'Well, I just thought it might be nice to go and have a screw in it.'

And that was the start of the last bit of it.

Simon got a carry-out with all that remained of Raymond's credit line, then he and the looker left the pub. They walked arm in arm to the car-park behind the supermarket. The looker was giggling a lot. And so was Simon, who had drunk very much more than he meant to. By the time they had crossed the car-park and climbed into the flat-back, they were carrying each other's clothes.

And then it was rocking flat-back time. With Simon in the driver's seat.

'Yes yes yes,' went the looker, doing the sexual pogo

and striking her head repeatedly on the underside of the roof. 'Yes yes yes, oh ow wow wow.'

'Yes,' went Simon. 'Book shanka boom.'

And of course it went on for hours. They stopped at intervals and changed positions. They finished the carry-out, opened the windows and smoked cigarettes. And then they went at it again.

'You won't forget me when you're rich?' asked the looker during a moment when she didn't have her mouth full.

'No no no.' Simon kept the rhythm going. 'Meet me to-mor-row.'

'When when when?'

Simon took a breath. 'Three-thirty, in the high street. I pick up the money then. It's all in cash. I'll take you out for something to eat. Something *else* to eat. Don't stop. Don't stop. Don't stop. Boom Shanka Booooooom!'

Quite unforgivable!

And that was the end of the last bit of it. Because the next thing Simon knew, he was waking up alone, naked in the flat-back at nine o'clock in the morning with a lot of lady shoppers looking in.

And this terrible hangover.

So now he went into the bookies.

'Good-morning, Simon,' said Mr Jones the Welsh turf accountant. 'Lost, is it are you? Like the new hat.'

'I have come to place a bet,' said Simon, clutching his hatless but hangovered head.

'A bet, you say? the bookie looked aghast. 'But you don't bet at all. Never heard of such a thing, I haven't.'

'Well you have now. I had this dream you see.'

'Ah,' went the bookie, 'dream, is it? Well, I would strongly recommend against that. Go along off to work would be my advice to you. Pay off the wheel clamp and reclaim the Allen Scythe from Long Bob who stole it, so he did. There's words of wisdom for you. Take them and leave.'

'I'll just place the bet for now, if you don't mind.'

'It's a dreadful mistake you're making.'

'Listen,' said Simon, 'I appreciate what you're saying. But I am determined on this. I will place the bet and that is that.'

'Be it upon your own head then.'

'Be it so.' Simon took out his envelope and read off the horses' names.'

'And you dreamed these four horses would win?'

'Yes,' said Simon, as this was the lie he had decided upon.

'They're all rank outsiders.'

'So much the better when they come in.'

'I shall never forgive myself when they don't,' said Mr Jones.

'Here is my money,' said Simon. 'Now write me out my betting slip.'

'*That's one hundred pounds, boy!*' Mr Jones fell backwards from his seat. Happily his wife, Mrs Jones, was at the mop and bucket to his rear and caught him.

'You naughty boy, Simon,' said herself, as she applied eau-de-Cologne to her husband's wrists. 'Frightening him with one hundred pounds all at once like that. And him Bramfield's token ethnic minority and everything. Racial harassment so it is.'

'Look, just get him back into his chair and make him fill out my betting slip. *Please.*'

Mrs Jones fussed her husband into his chair. She placed a Biro between his fingers and soothed his fevered brow.

'Will you be paying the tax?' asked Jones in a quavery wavery voice.

'Bugger the tax,' said Simon.

Mrs Jones crossed herself. 'Blessed saints and chapel hat pegs, whatever will become of us?'

'Oh deary deary me.' Mr Jones shook his head dismally and filled in Simon's betting slip. He pushed it under the security glass and accepted the two fifty-pound notes. 'How do you ring up one hundred pounds on the cash register?' he asked his wife.

Simon left the premises. He had a spring in his step. Mrs Jones watched him through the venetian blinds. 'So long, sucker,' she said.

And Mr Jones was out of his chair. He was jumping up and down with a clenched fist in the air and going 'Yes!' over and over again.

Simon had enough small change to purchase some sandwiches, a bottle of Lucozade and a packet of cigarettes. And having done so, Simon left the village.

He felt it prudent to seek haven in a neutral port until his ship of fortune dropped anchor in the high-street harbour. As it were.

There was a long-abandoned game keeper's hut that he knew of. It had a comfy mattress on the floor. This mattress had two deep depressions in it. They were just the size of Simon's knees. Perhaps he went there to pray, who can say.

He was certainly praying in it today though. Praying and waiting and worrying. What if it didn't work? What if the horses didn't win? One hundred pounds he's paid out. *One hundred pounds!* But it had to work. He knew it had to work. And he knew that shortly he'd be *very* rich.

But that was hours away. Hours and hours and hours.

By ten o'clock Simon had finished his sandwiches and by eleven his cigarettes too. He really wished he'd splashed out on some aspirins instead.

He tried to get some sleep. But he couldn't. He tried counting seconds. He tried counting slats in the hut walls. He tried counting nails in the slats. He did press-ups. He did jumping on the spot. The he did holding his poor sick head and sitting very still for a while.

About a million years later he did getting up to leave.

As it was early-closing day, the high street was deserted. So no-one noticed Simon as he sidled on his way. But it didn't ease his tension and by the time he'd reached the betting shop, Simon's heart was trying to punch its way out of his chest, his mouth was as dry as a skeleton's bum. And his head still ached.

The betting shop had undergone a subtle change of atmosphere.

No. 'Subtle' is *not* the word.

Mr Jones was on the telephone. He was shouting things in Welsh. Things were being shouted back at him. A selection of village oldsters loafed about. They wore tweedy caps and those cardigans that you get given for Christmas when you reach a certain age. Two of them applauded when Simon came in. Another doffed his cap, tugged at the place where his forelock used to be and said, 'Gawd bless you, guvnor.'

'YES!' went Simon inwardly.

Mr Jones slammed down the phone, turned around and saw the gardener's apprentice.

'Aaaaaagh!' went Mr Jones.

'Good-afternoon, Mr Jones,' said Simon. 'Mrs Jones.'

'Aaaaaagh!' went Mrs Jones, clinging to her husband's arm.

'Something troubling you?' asked Simon.

Mr Jones was lost for words.

'You bloody bastard!' said his wife.

'Excuse me please?' Simon flashed his dentalware.

'Ruination!' Mr Jones found words again. 'You've bloody ruined me, boy.'

'You mean I won?' Simon displayed the surprise he'd been rehearsing.

'Won? Bloody won? You've cleaned us out. Thousands and thousands and—'

'Thousands? Simon asked. 'My word. I trust you have enough to pay me with.'

'A whole week's takings,' mumbled Mr Jones. Which Simon overheard.

'Sorry, I didn't quite catch that.'

'I will pay you your winnings. The bastards at head office say I must.'

'Bastards? Simon shook his head. 'What is all this talk of bastards?'

'Bastards like you,' said Mr Jones. 'Rich bastards!'

'I find this change of attitude surprising.' Simon didn't. 'Earlier today you seemed so concerned that I would lose my money. I thought you would rejoice in my good fortune.'

Mr Jones' lip was all of a quiver.

Simon began to pat at his pockets. 'Now what did I do with that betting slip?'

'What?' went Mr Jones.

'I put it somewhere.' Simon began to pat himself all over. 'Oh no, my wallet. My wallet?'

'Lost, is it?' Mr Jones began to rub his hands together.

'It's been stolen!' Simon's face was the old grey mask of horror.

'Oh what a terrible shame.' Jones began to bob up and down on his chair. 'Can't pay out without the ticket. Oh what a terrible shame.' He and his wife began to laugh.

'Just my little joke.' Simon produced his wallet. 'Knew it would make you smile.'

'You bloody—'

'Now now now.' Simon waggled a finger. 'Let's have no more of that.' He took out the betting slip and placed it upon the counter beneath the security glass. The hand of Jones moved towards it.

'Naturally a witnessed photocopy is lodged with my solicitor.'

'Naturally,' said Jones, snatching the slip.

'And I worked out the sum of my winnings down to two decimal places. I do hope no disparity will exist between my computation and your own.'

The bookie made clenched fists.

'Just pay the bastard out,' said Mrs Jones.

'YES!'

Simon's bank was only six shops along from the

bookies. And even with the two heavy carrier bags cutting rings into his fingers, a pretty short jog.

Well, no-one about. Early closing day. *Early closing day!*

The half-a-million-dollar man stared at the big locked door of the bank. 'Bugger,' he said. 'Oh bugger.'

And then he said, 'Oh shit!'

To the accompaniment of that distinctive wheel-screeching sound which always screams 'Big Trouble', a car swerved out from its parking place across the road. It was an old car, one of those Jags so beloved of the criminal fraternity in shows like *The Sweeney*.

It didn't half shift. It was over the road and up on to the pavement before you could say 'shit' (again).

Simon ran like a mad thing.

But what sort of chance did he have? Not a lot. Unless the Jag suddenly ran out of petrol, of course. Which it didn't. Of course.

It swept along the pavement, knocking down the new litter bin which had been erected by public subscription, and mangling the postmaster's bike. Simon's shoes burned rubber.

Now it could have been one hell of a chase. Down side roads and leafy lanes. Across fields. There could have been lots of gates getting burst through, chickens fluttering, near collisions with oncoming tractors. That kind of thing.

But real life's not like that. Simon didn't get five yards. The Jag brought him down in the locked entrance way of the supermarket. Not fatally. Just a clip. But sufficient to get the job done. Professional.

Car doors flew open. Masked men leapt out. Three masked men and big chaps all. With sticks.

And one woman.

She wasn't wearing a mask.

And even from where Simon now lay, with three right boots pressing down on his chest, she looked like a looker.

She looked like *the* looker.

She *was* the looker!

'Aw shit,' Simon gasped. 'Aw shit shit shit.'

The looker looked down. She was smiling. 'Remember me?' she asked.

'Aw shit,' said Simon once again.

'Just take the money,' said the looker. 'Don't hurt him, it would be a waste. The money's all we want.'

'No,' wailed Simon. 'No no no.'

'Yes,' said the looker. 'Yes yes yes.' And she wasn't pogoing this time. Just standing still. And smiling.

The three masked men took their feet from Simon's chest and prised the carrier bags from his still so tightly gripping fingers.

'Who are you?' blubbered Simon. 'The IRA, is it?'

'IRA?' The looker laughed. 'Not the IRA. Something more than that. Not that you would understand. This money is needed to help fund a perilous mission. To take up arms against an evil adversary. To fight for the cause of justice. You are giving up your money for something that is true and honourable. Simon, B.E.A.S.T. salutes you.'

The masked men clapped. One of them said, 'Nice one, mate.'

Strangely no record exists of exactly what Simon said next.

IO

Now, time passes differently in space, and Raymond was still at the feast in the grand salon of the *SS Salamander*. Only moments having elapsed since he'd spoken those words, of which strangely no record exists.

The banqueters had done with their applause and returned to their banqueting. Professor Merlin poured Raymond another drink.

'Pin back your lugholes, Raymond,' said the showman, 'for I must lay some deep do-do on your doorstep.'

Raymond replied with an inebriated, 'Eh?'

'Things that you must know. True things, all true. The gold brick and untarnished. What you hear may not be to your taste and you may wish to dismiss it. This will not, however, disenfranchise it of its verisimilitude.'

'Eh?' went Raymond once again.

'Firstly, I must regretfully inform you that you are *not* drunk.'

'I am.' Raymond giggled foolishly. 'I'm pissed as a puddle, me.'

'Sadly no. You see all the drinks served at this table are of a non-alcoholic nature.' The professor waited while this 'sank in'.

Raymond refocused his eyes and steadied his spinning head. 'Oh,' said he, in a sober tone. 'Just fancy that.'

'Just fancy that indeed.' Professor Merlin toasted Raymond with his glass. 'But you will not, I fancy, fancy what I have next to tell you.'

'Now that I find surprising.' Raymond took up his own glass, sniffed at its contents, sighed and returned it to the table.

'Are you sitting comfortably?'

Raymond nodded mournfully.

'Then cop your whack for this, our kid. To begin somewhere near the beginning. Do you know of *Symmes' Theory of Concentric Spheres and Polar Voids*?'

'Of course I do,' said Raymond. 'Doesn't everyone?'

The professor raised his tattooed eyebrow. 'Is that intended to be an ironic retort? Or was it just a plain old lie?'

Raymond shrugged. 'Just a plain old lie, I'm afraid.'

'Fiddle-de fiddle-dum.' Professor Merlin frowned and Raymond was fascinated to see the way the tip of his chin touched the end of his nose. 'I shall try to keep this as short as possible. To spare us both the agony.'

Raymond popped another sweetmeat into his mouth. If he couldn't get drunk, then at least he could get really fat.

'Captain John Cleves Symmes was a philosopher,' said the showman, 'and he had a theory concerning the composition of the Earth. He believed that the planet consisted of a number of concentric spheres, one inside another, open at the poles to allow access between them. Are you following this?'

Raymond munched and nodded. 'The hollow Earth theory. My pal Simon had a book on the subject. The theory has been around for centuries, that there may be another race living inside the Earth.'

'And you do not believe this theory.'

Raymond shook his head. 'I certainly don't.'

'And why would that be, do you think?'

'Because it's a load of old cobblers.' And here Raymond winked. 'Although I'll tell you this. Apparently there were these Russian scientists. And they were doing this experiment in Siberia. And they drilled down twenty-three miles. And their drill broke into a kind of a cavern. And they lowered down a microphone on a very long lead. And you'll never guess what they heard.'

'Was it the sound of millions of souls, screaming in eternal agony?'

'Aw, you've heard it.'

'I have. And a horrible noise it is too.'

'Eh?'

'But let us return to Symmes' theory. What if I were to tell you that the planet Earth consists of two concentric spheres, one inside the other. And that both have intelligent life on their outer surfaces?'

'I would say it were cobblers,' said Raymond.

'But nevertheless it is true.'

'Oh no it's not.'

'Oh yes it is.'

'Not,' said Raymond. 'Not not not. Believe me, Professor. If there was another race living beneath the Earth, we would have discovered them by now. And the polar openings. There is no other world beneath the one I live on.'

'You are correct and true as Peter Pure.' Professor Merlin smiled once more. 'Because it is *above* the one you live on.'

'Come again?'

'It is you who live *inside* the Earth. Another world exists above your head. About ten miles above it, in fact.'

'No no no.' Raymond shook the head that had no other world above it. 'That is serious cobblers. Listen, if I stand in my garden and look up. I don't see the underside of some other world above. I see the sky.'

'An illusion of sky.'

'I've got the sun in the morning and the moon at night.' Raymond whistled the refrain, but he couldn't remember who sang it. 'I've seen the sun and the moon and the stars,' said he.

'Oh no you haven't.'

'Oh yes I have.'

'Oh no you haven't.'

'Have too,' and Raymond stuck his tongue out.

'Now just you listen!' Professor Merlin threw up his

hands and grew just a little bit fierce. 'I am going to explain this to you just the one time. And when I have spoken, you will be permitted to ask questions. Do you savvy? Comprehendo? Are we firing on all pistons? Do you *understand* me?'

Raymond nodded. 'No need to shout,' he said.

'Righty-right.' The showman straightened his waist-coat and rearranged his watch chains into a pleasing composition. 'A brief lecture entitled "The True History of Mankind", delivered by Professor Prometheus Merlin.'

'Prometheus?'

'Shut it!'

'Sorry.'

'"The True History of Mankind". As follows. Pay close attention if you will.' Raymond sat up straight. 'Intelligent life on Earth began on the *outer* shell of the planet, a very very long time ago. A race evolved, as races often do, formed into a society, mapped the planet. And discovered the holes in the poles. Early explorers descended through the northern polar opening in hot air balloons and found the world within. A twilight world, ruled by monsters of the deep. Dinosaurs. The world which later *you* would be brought up on, Raymond. Of course then it was dark and dank and not really suitable to support human life. There just wasn't enough light coming in through the pole-holes. It needed proper lighting.

'Of course it was many centuries later that the tech-nology came into being, capable of developing the artificial sun, miniature moon, planetary and starry sky effects you see today. The "topsiders" wanted to create a real Garden of Eden down there and they wanted to reproduce a perfect facsimile of the heavens. It's a true masterpiece of engineering, I'm sure you will agree. Most convincing.'

Raymond sighed and rolled his eyes. 'So how does it work?' he asked.

Professor Merlin shrugged. 'I don't know. *But it does.*'

'Cobblers,' said Raymond (who wouldn't let it lie).

'Shut it!'

'Sorry.'

'So. And so. The world below is now ready for colonization. The government of the day has all but bankrupted itself constructing the artificial sun, etcetera, but is expecting to make a vast fortune from the millions of eager bodies wanting to buy land down there. But, oh deary me. To their surprise, no-one wants to move below. Because, when you think about it, who would really want to live *inside* a planet? Bits of the outer planet might fall down on your head. Which, of course, they do. You call them meteorites. And the artificial sun might break down once in a while and plunge you into darkness . . .'

'Which we no doubt call solar eclipses,' said Raymond in a most sarcastic tone.

'Shut it once more.'

'So sorry.'

'So what can the government do?'

Raymond put up his hand.

'What is it?' the professor asked.

'Let me guess what they did. They did just what we did when we shipped our convicts off to Australia. They dumped all their criminals down onto the inner world.'

'You are the personification of exactitude, me old cock sparra. That is precisely what they did. The inner world was rich in mineral resources and so it was speculators who snapped it up and took the criminals for slave labour in the mines and cultivating the land and whatnot.'

Raymond rolled his eyes once more.

'Now, as you can imagine, these early "settlers" were something of a rough old bunch and not exactly given over to conservation issues when it came to the indigenous wildlife and so—'

'Me me!' Raymond's hand was once more in the air.

'Go on,' said the professor wearily.

'They hunted the dinosaurs to extinction. I'll just bet they did.'

'Punctiliously pukka. They did just that. From then on you will find that the history of mankind on the inner world is pretty much as you read it in your books. The exception being that all references to the world above have long since been deleted.'

'Hold on, hold on.' Raymond flapped his hands about. 'I spy a flaw or two in all this.'

'You do?' The professor *was* surprised.

'I do. For one thing, how come no-one today knows of the existence of the outer world?'

'But they do, my dear Raymond, they do. Those in charge know. Those whose job it is to maintain the myth that space above is an airless void. Those who control the population. Those who oversee and profit from the interworld transportation of "George". Those who keep mankind in ignorance.'

'What, you mean like prime ministers and presidents and people like that?'

'It's an inner-world-wide conspiracy.'

'Nah.' Raymond shook his head. 'If these people in power knew there was a world above, they'd all want to go up and live there.'

'And they do, young Raymond. They do all the time.'

'Nah.' Raymond gave his head another shake. 'You don't hear of the US president vanishing away for months on end every year.'

'What, *this* president, do you mean?' Professor Merlin pointed. And where Zephyr had been sitting—

'Mr President,' said Raymond. 'How did *you* get here? Oh I see! You're not! I mean. Oh bloody hell!'

'To my own knowledge,' the showman counted on his wonderful fingers, 'the present president has so far been played by no less than four topsiders, working shifts. No-one down below can tell the difference, because outwardly there is no difference.'

'They walk among us,' Raymond said.

'And they sell us for food and have been doing so for centuries, since they began to trade with the other planets. Uranus holds the current franchise.'

'Abdullah, the *lying* starfish.'

'Abdullah, is a pirate. More unscrupulous than most.'

Raymond took to the scratching of his head. The big question was, and it was a big question, was any of this really true? The Abdullah bit was certainly true. And the replaceable presidents? That *could* be done. But that the world he had grown up upon was actually inside another world? It still seemed a little far-fetched.

'Could I see it?' Raymond asked.

'See what, me old fruitcake?'

'The Earth. From the outside. With its outer shell and its holes in the poles. Through a telescope, or something?'

'Of a surety you may.' Professor Merlin produced a slim brass telescope from his top pocket. 'I thought you might enquire. Thrust it through yonder porthole.'

'Which one where?'

'That one there.' Professor Merlin gestured and Raymond spied out the porthole in question. It had been incorporated into the erotic wall fresco in a manner which, although amusing, was immodest to say the least.

Raymond excused himself from the banqueting table and took himself over to the saucy porthole, raised the telescope to his eye, focused it and then said, 'Shiva's sheep! There's a big blue planet out here with a hole in the top.'

'Now he gets the picture,' Professor Merlin said.

And Raymond returned to the table. He returned the telescope to the professor and his well-tailored bum to its chair.

'There's a hole in my planet,' said Raymond, said Raymond.

'There's a hole in my planet,' said Raymond. 'A hole.'

'Must come as a bit of a shock to you.'

'*A bit of a shock?*' Raymond buried his face in his hands.

'Perhaps you have other questions you would care to ask.'

'Other questions?' Raymond unburied his face. 'Yes I do have one or two.'

'Then ask on, O guest at my table.'

'Right then,' said Raymond. 'Assuming that I believe what I just saw, and I think I probably do, tell me one thing. Which Earth are *you* from? The inside one or the outside one?'

'From the inside, as yourself. My circus and I were kidnapped on the whim of a certain very Far Eastern potentate. We would have ended our days in the pot had it not been for the fair Zephyr.' Professor Merlin bowed his head to the beauty in question. 'We "appropriated" this vessel and made good our escape. Now we travel between the planets on forged papers, posing as topsiders and affecting rescues where we can. Gathering recruits to our noble cause.'

'This cause being that you intend to wage war against the topsiders?'

'We must. The trade in human beings must cease. And the plans that the topsiders are presently formulating must not be allowed to proceed.'

'And what plans are these?'

'Plans to deal with the pollution.'

'I am lost once more,' said Raymond.

'Pollution.' Professor Merlin plucked at his nose. 'From the inner Earth. Our Earth. All that smoke and gas and what-have-you. Where do you think it all goes to?'

'Well, I always thought it went into the atmosphere and just sort of hung about there. I'd be wrong on that I suppose.'

'As wrong as can be. It pours out of the polar openings and contaminates the world above. And the world above has had enough of it. Their ruler, an evil despot, has decided upon a drastic course of action:

that the inner world be environmentally deprioritized.'

'Environmentally what?'

'Deprioritized. The plan is to switch off the artificial sun and plug up the holes in the poles. Concrete them over. Seal them. Airtight!'

'*What?*' Raymond fell back in his chair. 'But if they did that, then it would mean . . .'

'It would mean that the last man alive on the inner Earth would be the one who could hold his breath the longest. Probably a pearl diver, would be my guess.'

'That's *not* funny!' Raymond smote the table with his fists.

'It wasn't meant to be funny. Pearl divers really can hold their breath for a long time. I used to have one with the circus. Did the now legendary Houdini's water tank escape. Used to hold his breath and drink his way out. Got too fat to perform in the end, if I recall.'

'Stop it!' Raymond's raised voice was once more the only one to be heard. 'We must act at once. Do decisive things. Lead your army against the evil topsiders. Blow up all their cement works for a kick off. I will be honoured to serve in this noble cause.'

'Knew you would, good sir. Just knew you would.'

'But to take on a whole planet. That is some challenge. How many thousand men do you have so far?'

Professor Merlin diddled at his chin. 'How many *thousand*, did you say?'

'You do have several thousand men?'

'Not several thousand, no.'

'One thousand then?'

Professor Merlin shook his head. 'Not as such.'

'Several *hundred* then?'

Professor Merlin made the 'so so' gesticulation. 'Not as such,' he said again.

'How many men *do* you have in your army?' Raymond demanded to be told.

'Just you,' said the professor. 'You are it.'

'*I am it?*' Raymond, who in the heat of things had risen

from his chair, now fell back into it. '*I* am it? But you said you were affecting rescues. Gathering recruits to the cause.'

'We are, dear fellow-me-lad. But you're the first who's actually passed the entrance exam. Do you think perhaps that I've been setting too high a standard? Perhaps I should just get them to fill in a form or something, rather than go to all the expense of the banquet each time?'

Raymond once more buried his face in his hands. And this time he began to weep.

'Is something wrong, my boy?'

'Oh no,' Raymond blubbed. 'How could anything be wrong? My world is about to have its airholes paved over and the army of deliverance amounts to myself alone. How could anything possibly be wrong?'

II

Simon limped home and kicked his cat. Not specifically, but just in passing. The way you would. All things considered.

It wasn't a particularly interesting cat. Just one of those tabby jobs, that slide round your legs like a silken pervert whenever they want feeding, and pointedly ignore you the rest of the time. Simon rarely remembered to feed it, but cats being far less intelligent than their doting owners give them credit for, this one turned up again and again on the off-chance of a free lunch. It wasn't getting one today though.

But there was no love lost. The cat did not resemble Simon in the very least and he in turn looked like it not at all.

Simon kicked his cat. The cat bit Simon's leg. Simon swore at his cat, pushed open his front door, went inside and limped upstairs.

He was not best pleased about the way things had turned out this day. Having pushed the dresser aside, he tore up the loose floor board, dragged out *The Greatest Show Off Earth*, threw it into the air and head-butted it across the room.

Then he screamed, slumped down onto his bed and clutched once more at his poor aching head. It now appeared to ache in stereo.

'You rotten sods,' he complained to the world. 'You dirty rotten sods.'

When the double vision had cleared, Simon crawled across the floor and retrieved Raymond's biography. 'Stitched up,' he snarled. 'Done. Robbed blind. All my winnings and my one hundred pounds also.'

The man of sorrows returned to his bed of pain and spread the book before him on his lap. Boldly going where no man had gone before, well at least not him, Simon turned straight to the back of the book. Did it have an index? Yes it did. Was he mentioned in it? Yes he was. Not a lot of entries though. Considering it was such a thick book. In fact, the final entry appeared to be on page ninety-four.

'Hold on there.' Simon leafed violently back to the page in question. Yes, here he was, leaving the bookie's with his winnings. Simon skimmed down the page. There was no mention of any car knocking him down, or B.E.A.S.T. terrorists stealing all his money. Why was that, eh?

'I'll tell you why.' Simon made a bitter face. 'Because bloody B.E.A.S.T. wrote this book and they are hardly going to admit that *they* stole all my winnings. What *do* they say?'

He read aloud from the book,

> In a sudden and quite unexpected
> gesture of goodwill and public
> spiritedness, Simon donated all
> of his winnings to a local charity.
> And on which selfless note, plays
> no further part in our narrative.

'*What?*' Simon gawped at the book. '*No further part in our narrative?* You set me up you . . .'

The old couple next door were both deaf. So they didn't hear the word BASTARDS! Although they felt the wall vibrate and saw their framed picture of The Queen Mother (Gawd bless you, ma'am) fall down into the coal scuttle. Which was quite upsetting.

'You can't do this to me.' Simon shook his fist at the offending page. 'I won't let you. I'll . . . I'll . . .' He really didn't know what he would do. 'I *do* know what I will

125

do,' he went on. 'I will lie. That's what I'll do. When I'm interviewed for this book I'll lie. I'll give the names of the wrong horses. So then I won't win the money. Let's see how they like that. The bastards.'

He flicked back a few pages. The same names of the winning horses were still there in their little box at the top of chapter nine.

'Damn,' said Simon. 'Damn damn damn. I don't understand any of this.'

And now there came a knocking on Simon's front door.

Simon looked up in alarm. And then he looked down at the book.

It had nothing to tell him.

'Damn.' Simon flung it once more to the floor, rose from his bed, slouched over to the bedroom window and peered down.

Three men were standing below. Two wore police helmets, the third had an Arthur Scargill comb-over job.

'*Police!*' Simon flattened himself against the bedroom wall. What did they want him for? He hadn't done anything. He was an innocent man. He *was* an innocent man. 'I *am* an innocent man,' said Simon. 'In fact . . .'

A small dot with the word HOPE written on it suddenly appeared on the otherwise bleak horizon that was Simon's future. The word HOPE was in purple. To match the prose. It grew and it grew.

'Of course,' said Simon. 'I know what must have happened. Someone must have seen me being robbed in the high street, telephoned the police with a description of the Jag. The police then intercepted the vehicle and after a hair-raising chase, down side roads and leafy lanes and across fields, with lots of gates getting burst through and chickens fluttering and near collisions with oncoming tractors, there was a shoot-out and all the B.E.A.S.T. terrorists were killed (HOPEfully) and now the officers of the law wish me to come down to the police station and identify my winnings. That has to be it.'

It takes a certain kind of mind, doesn't it?

'Coming,' called Simon.

Now, the constables knew Simon. And Simon knew the constables. They'd all been at the village school together. Simon could recall no past animosities. Although he felt sure that one of the constables had a younger sister whom he'd once . . .

'Good-afternoon, officers of the law,' said Simon brightly. 'How might I help you?'

'Mr—?' The Arthur Scargill spoke Simon's surname.

'Not so loud.' Simon flapped his hands about. 'Yes, that's me.'

'Mr—.'

'Simon, please, just Simon.'

'I'll call you "sir" if you don't mind.'

'*Sir?* Have I been awarded a knighthood then?'

'No, er, sir. But as servants of the public, we are obliged to speak to that public in a respectful and polite manner. It's a tradition. Or an old charter. Or something. My name is Inspector D'Eath. And I wonder if I might just ask you a few questions, sir?'

'I'm easy,' said Simon.

'So I've heard,' muttered one of the constables. The one with the sister, Simon supposed.

'Thank you, Constable. Perhaps if I might just step inside for a minute or two, sir.'

'Do you have a search warrant?' Simon asked.

'No, sir, why do you ask?'

'I've always wanted to know what they look like.'

'I saw one once,' said the other constable. 'They're not all that special. Just typed paper really.'

'Thank you, Constable.' Inspector D'Eath pushed past Simon. 'This way, is it, sir?'

'You chaps coming in?' Simon asked.

'No.' The constable with the sister shook his head. 'We are going to guard your front door.'

'Why? Do you think someone might try to steal it?'

'No. We are going to guard the front door so that you don't get out through it.'

'But I don't want to get out through it. I live here.'

'You might do a runner. It has been known.'

Simon shrugged. 'Well, if I do, I'll be sure to do it through the back door, so as not to disturb you in the course of your duties.'

'Thank you, sir.'

'No, hang about,' said the constable who didn't have a sister, but had once seen a search warrant. 'Could I come through and guard your back door?'

'Be my guest.'

The constable went through and stood beside Simon's back door. Simon followed Inspector D'Eath into the front sitter.

'So,' said Simon. 'I trust it's good news. Have you made an arrest then?'

The inspector shook his head. A hamstring of greasy hair slipped down across his right ear. 'We are expecting to very shortly,' he said.

'It will be a great weight off my mind,' said Simon.

'Good, sir, good.' Inspector D'Eath took out a regulation police-issue notebook, withdrew a slim pencil from its spine, licked the tip and made a jotting. 'Good,' said he once again. 'It makes things so much easier all round. I'm sure you understand.'

Simon nodded. 'No,' he said.

'So. If we might just clear up a few small details.' The inspector displayed a coloured photograph. 'Have you seen this boy?' he asked, which rang a bell somewhere.

Simon took the photograph. 'Raymond,' he said. For it was he.

'Then you would say that it's a good likeness of the deceased?'

'*Deceased?*' Simon returned the photograph. 'What do you mean, deceased?'

'Missing then. But as you must know, today's "missing", is so often tomorrow's torso case.'

'Torso case? What's a torso case?'

'Well, I am referring in this instance to a criminal case involving the discovery of a human torso. As opposed to, say, a specially designed sharkskin case with a hand-tooled lid, in which a torso might be kept.'

'Thanks for clearing that up for me.'

'So, sir. When did you last see the "missing person"?'

'Ah.' Simon made a thinking face. The correct answer to this question was, of course, 'The night before last, on the allotments. He was being sucked into the belly of a flying starfish from Uranus.' But, just because this was the *correct* answer, did it necessarily make it the *best* answer to give? Simon concluded that definitely it did *not*.

'I can't remember exactly,' Simon said. 'About a week ago, perhaps.'

'About a week ago.' The inspector made a note of this. 'And what about this lady?' He took out another photograph and held it before Simon's nose.

Simon gave it the once over. Then the twice over. It was the looker.

'*That's her!*' It was a fair old shriek. In next door's front parlour, Britain's favourite grandmother found herself back in the coal scuttle.

'That's her. That's the woman. Did you get the money?'

'Did *I* get the money, sir? Which money would this be?'

'*My* money.'

'*Your* money?'

'Don't mess around. You know what I'm talking about.'

'I think I do, sir, yes.' Inspector D'Eath dictated a further jotting. 'The suspect asked whether I'd got the money he'd sent me.'

'I didn't say that. *Suspect?* What do you mean *suspect?*'

'This woman has been missing since last night, sir.

She was not at her regular place of work and her bed had not been slept in. That's two in a single week, sir. And you in the frame each time.'

'Frame? I'm not in any frame.'

The inspector flicked back through his notebook. 'Would I be correct that you suffer from "short-term memory loss"?'

'No, you would not. Look, who is this woman?'

'The Boston Strangler.'

'That's never the Boston Strangler. The Boston Strangler looked like Tony Curtis.'

'Short-term memory loss,' said the inspector. 'The Boston Strangler had it too. Murdered seven women and never remembered a thing about it.'

'I do not suffer from short-term memory loss.'

'That's not what the vicar's wife says, sir.'

'My memory is perfect,' said Simon. Although he *had* forgotten about the vicar's wife. 'I have total recall.'

'But you cannot totally recall when you last saw the missing gentleman in the photograph.'

'No.'

'Then perhaps I can help.' The inspector was once more at his notebook. 'Ah yes. According to one Long Bob, chicken farmer and long-standing member of the local chamber of commerce, it was around eight-thirty p.m., the night before last, on the allotments. I quote from his statement, "Simon was behaving in a highly suspicious manner with Raymond. I believe he might have been on the magic mushrooms again."'

'The bastard!' said Simon.

'All coming back to you now, is it, sir?'

'Listen, all right I was with Raymond the night before last. But Raymond is not important. Let's forget about Raymond. Let's talk about the woman.'

'You want to own up to the woman then, do you, sir?' The inspector licked the tip of his pencil once more. 'Do you have a pencil sharpener I might borrow?'

'No I don't!'

'I'm sorry. Was that you don't want to own up to the woman, or you don't have a pencil sharpener?'

'Just tell me the woman's name,' Simon pleaded. 'That's all I want to know.'

'You mean you never asked her her name? Yet you spent an entire evening in her company.' More page flicking. 'According to Andy the barman at The Jolly Gardeners, "He homed right in on her. He was spending Raymond's money. He got her very drunk and then they left together. That was the last time I saw her alive." Then I have the testimonies of no fewer than five late-night dog walkers, who state that they saw you and the young woman "taking tea with the parson" in the cab of Mr Hilsavise's flat-back. Is that where you did her in, sir? Like you did with all the others?'

'All what others?'

'Come now, sir. Why not make a clean breast of it? I've a stack of unsolved missing persons files on my desk, going back years. Where did you bury all the bodies, sir? Was it on the allotments?'

'I didn't bury any bodies.' Simon was starting to get a bit of a sweat on.

'We'll find them all eventually, you know. You were a bit too heavy-handed this time, ploughing over the entire area.'

Ploughing over the entire area? The grey men cleaning up! 'Stop,' said Simon. 'Stop please and listen. I have not killed anyone, nor have I buried any bodies. You are making a terrible mistake. Raymond is alive and well. Shit, I could tell you exactly where he is at this very moment. I'd only have to look him up.'

'Did you say *dig* him up, sir?' The pencil, though blunt, was back at work.

'I said *look* him up. You heard me quite clearly.'

'So you admit that you keep a record of your slayings in a special book.' The inspector consulted *his* book. 'Is this because of the short-term memory loss, like the Boston Strangler?'

'I do not have short-term memory loss.' Simon shook his fists.

'I must warn you, sir, that I know how to use this pencil.'

'All right!' Simon pocketed his fists.

'So might I have a look at this book of yours?'

'No,' said Simon. 'Absolutely not.'

'Oh dear, oh dear, oh dear.' The inspector shook his head and further horrid hair-strands draped over his right ear. 'And I thought you were going to make it easy. Recall when I told you that we were going to make the arrest and you said, and I quote, "It will be a great weight off my mind . . ."'

'Yes,' said Simon, 'but I didn't mean . . .'

'Oh you do remember saying that, do you? So you've been lying all along about the short-term memory loss?'

'*I* never said I had short-term memory loss.'

'According to the vicar's wife you carry a doctor's note to this effect in your wallet. Might I ask you to turn out your pockets, so we can clear this matter up once and for all?'

'Not without a search warrant you bloody well can't.'

'Simon—,' the inspector spoke the surname, 'I am arresting you on suspicion of multiple murder. You do not have to say anything. But anything you do say will—'

'No!' Simon threw up his hands.

'Beware the pencil, sir.'

'No. Stop. I am innocent of all these charges. I have a book upstairs that will prove I'm telling the truth. I didn't want you to see it. I didn't want anyone to see it—'

'Bit grisly, is it, sir? Not bound in human skin, or anything like that, I suppose?'

'Of course it's not.' Simon buried his face in his hands.

'Pity. But go on anyway. The book will prove you innocent, you were saying. Might I enquire who wrote this book, by the way? Was it you? Or was it God perhaps? Do you get the voices, sir? Does God make you do it?'

'God,' said Simon. 'Without a doubt. Now, if you'll just let me go and get it, you can read it all for yourself. Perhaps you're even in it. I certainly hope you are.'

'Er, sir?'

Simon was at the door by now. 'Yes?' he said.

'Sir, are you suggesting that *I*, an officer of the law, should let *you*, an all but self-confessed serial killer, whom the Press will no doubt soon be referring to as The Butcher of Bramfield, go upstairs on your own and fetch down a book which you claim was dictated to you by God?'

'It will only take a moment,' said Simon. 'And you do have a constable guarding the back door.'

'Go on then, sir. Fetch down your book.'

'Thank you. I will.' Simon went upstairs to his bedroom, put on his jacket, snatched up Raymond's biography and tucked it under his arm. Then he tip-toed across the landing and into the bathroom, climbed out of the window, shinned quietly down the drainpipe, took to his heels and once more fled.

12

'Right,' said Raymond, pouring out a vodka, downing this and pouring out some more. 'Right right right.' He raised his glass to the professor. 'Right,' he said again.

'Why does he keep saying "right"?' Professor Merlin asked Zephyr.

The beautiful woman shrugged Shirley from the shoe shop's shoulders. Which was easier to do than to say really.

'Right.' Professor Merlin grinned at Raymond. 'Right, eh?'

'I mean, right. All right. I'll do it. I mean, OK. So there's just me. Not good odds against an entire planet that I know nothing whatever about. Not any odds at all really. But it's a start.'

'Bravo, mon Armani.' The professor twirled his moustachios. 'It *is* a start. Regrettably it is also a finish. But, a beard well lathered is half shaved, as I always say.'

'What do you mean, it's a finish?'

'Tempus fugg-it I'm afraid. We have no planets left to play but Saturn. From there we must return to Earth at very much the hurry up. Toot sweety, abracadabra, double time and don't dilly dally on the way.'

'It's true.' Zephyr offered Raymond a smile, which he took for what it was worth. 'The topsiders intend to start sealing up the polar openings within the week. If we hope to stop them we must get there within the next two days.'

'Two days to travel from Saturn to Earth?' Raymond raised his eyebrows along with his glass. 'Now that *is* nonsense. What do you take me for, some kind of schm—'

'Schmecker?' the professor asked. 'Schmo? Schmoozer?'

'Schmuck. But you can't travel from Saturn to Earth in two days.'

'Really?' Professor Merlin plucked a grape from his plate, poked it up his left nostril and then produced it from his right ear. 'Would this be the same as, you can't fly a steamship through space?'

'Same sort of thing, yes. That is a really disgusting trick by the way.'

'You think it would be less disgusting if I poked it in my ear and it came out of my nose then?' Professor Merlin swallowed the grape.

Raymond swallowed some more vodka. 'We had best get moving, hadn't we? Full steam ahead for Earth.'

'One thing at a time, dear boy. We have a show to play on Saturn.'

'Stuff Saturn,' said Raymond.

'What, and let down my public?'

'Stuff your public also.'

'So you don't think we should play Saturn then?'

'No,' said Raymond. 'I do not.'

'What a pity. But I suppose you know best.'

'I do in this case. We must go at once to Earth.'

'You don't think we should rescue the two hundred kidnapped people who are bubbled up on Saturn first then?'

'*What?*' went Raymond. 'What what what?'

'That's why we're here, you see. The final consignment before the paving over. They arrived last night. I thought it might be nice of us to give them a lift. As we're going in their direction, as it were.'

'Two hundred people?' Raymond whistled.

'That's a really annoying whistle you have there,' the professor remarked. 'But two hundred it is none the less. Those of the beating heart and still this side of the cold meat counter. Bubbled up and awaiting distribution. Shame to leave them behind. But if you've made up your mind.'

'No,' said Raymond. 'I haven't. Two hundred people. We must save them, of course. How many men in a regiment, do you think?'

The professor had no idea. 'Exactly two hundred,' said he. 'Two hundred and one counting yourself. You'd be the general, of course.'

'Well then.' Raymond rubbed his hands together. 'We must formulate a plan of campaign. Synchronize watches. Things of that nature. Do you have maps?'

'No,' said professor Merlin. 'It's just the way my trousers hang.'

The banqueters erupted into mirth.

'Most humorous,' said Raymond. 'But I refer, of course, to maps of Saturn. Street plans and the like, showing where you will be playing and where the kidnapped people are being held. Do you have such maps?'

'Piles,' said the professor, nudging Raymond in the ribs.

'Careful of the suit please.'

'Sorry pardon. Send me the dry-cleaning bill. Maps we do have, Raymond, and aplenty.'

'And what about weapons?'

'I have my trusty sword.' Professor Merlin drew this from its shining scabbard, flourished it grandly and made thrustings and parryings amongst the pies and puddings. 'All who meet it do so at their peril.'

Raymond ducked the rapier as it swept past his head, nearly taking his ear off. 'I'll bet they do,' he said.

'They do.' Professor Merlin examined the selection of cheeses he had shish kebabbed. 'Anyone for afters?'

'What about guns?' Raymond enquired. 'Do you have any big guns?'

'Big guns? Siege cannons, do you mean?' Professor Merlin tucked into cheese and biscuits.

'I was thinking more about General Electric mini-guns, as it happens.'

'Ah,' said the professor. 'You mean those really

amazing rotary machine-guns, like the one Blaine had in *Predator.*'

Raymond nodded enthusiastically.

'No we don't.'

'Yes we do,' said Zephyr.

'Do we?' The professor spat bicky.

'If that's what Raymond wants. Then that's what Raymond must have.'

'Yes, of course he must. So it's all settled then.'

'Sorry,' said Raymond. 'Did I miss something? What is all settled?'

'The plan of campaign.'

'I did miss something.' Raymond scratched at his head. 'What plan of campaign?'

'Fiddle-de fiddle-dum.' The professor dusted biscuit crumbs from his chin. 'The one you wanted the maps for. I assume it is your intention that, whilst my circus plays to a packed house and much acclaim, you rescue all the people and sneak them back to the ship.'

'Oh, *that* plan of campaign.' Raymond nodded slowly.

'It's not the way I'd do it,' said the professor. 'But I'm sure you know your own job best. A dwarf on a giant's shoulders sees the further of the two, as I always say.'

'You always say that, do you?'

'Always. Except when I'm saying something else. So, now that all that's settled, shall I introduce you to my artistes?'

Raymond looked along the rows of eager smiling faces. 'Why not?' said he. 'Now that all that's settled.'

'Jolly good.' Professor Merlin took up the vodka bottle to pour himself a drink. But it was empty. 'Jolly good,' he said again.

Jolly good!

The words recalled to Raymond a certain pub back home in Bramfield. And he really truly wished that he was in it.

*   *   *

And, coincidentally enough, at this precise moment . . .

The saloon-bar door of The Jolly Gardeners swung upon its hinge and Raymond's best friend Simon sidled in.

He'd had a rough day, had Simon, and he really needed a quick drink before he fled the country. Like you would.

Paul the part-time barman sat at the far end of the unpatronized counter. He was filling in *The Times* crossword. He didn't look up. 'Evening, Simon,' he said. 'New hat?'

'No!' Simon stalked across to his favourite stool, mounted it and glared down the length of the counter. 'It is not a new hat, because I never wear a hat. I never have worn a hat and I never will wear a hat.'

'No need to be snappy,' said Paul, his eyes firmly fixed upon five across. Alice's teatime host. 3.6. 'Thank you.'

'It's not even funny. It's pathetic, that's what it is.'

'Had a bad day, have you?' Nine down, Horrific, ten letters.

'Horrendous.'

'Thank you.' Paul filled it in.

'Where is Andy?' Simon asked.

'Night off. What did you want him for?'

'Nothing important. Did he mention to you that I might be in?'

Paul shrugged out a no and returned to his crossword, without asking Simon what he wanted to drink.

Simon gazed around the otherwise empty bar. He knew perfectly well that it was Andy's night off, otherwise he would never have dared to put his head inside the door. But he hadn't known whether Andy had said anything to Paul about the statement he'd made to Inspector D'Eath. Obviously he hadn't. Perhaps this was briefly a safe haven for the man on the run.

'Any chance of a drink?' Simon asked. 'Desperate man here.'

Paul clicked his Biro and folded his newspaper. And made his way sedately up the bar. 'A pint of the usual?'

'A large Scotch.'

'Indeed.' Paul took a glass to the optic and drew off a double measure in a slow and deliberate manner. Simon liked Paul. Most of the Jolly's patrons liked Paul. Except for those who didn't, of course. They didn't like him at all. But Simon did.

Paul was 'all right'. Paul was tall, a thirty-something with own teeth and hair and waistline. One marriage down, girlfriend with new baby, old Lotus he could never quite afford to do up. Easy going was Paul. Unharassed. Unhurried. Marched to the beat of a different drum. That kind of thing.

'Quid and a half,' said Paul, placing Simon's drink before him.

'I have an arrangement with Andy. It's on Raymond's account.'

'Fair enough. I'll keep a mental note of what you drink. Save all the paperwork. Will there by anything else?'

Simon made that 'hhhhhhhh' noise that you make after you've just drunk down a double Scotch in a single go and said, 'Same again please.'

'I thought that might be the case.' Paul returned once more to the optic. 'What's the book?' he asked over his shoulder.

'Book?'

'The one you're incubating under your armpit.'

'Science fiction, I think.'

'Not some of that crap the Scribe writes?'

'Does he write science fiction?'

'Apparently.' Paul presented Simon with another double Scotch. 'Says he's written dozens of books. Not that I've ever seen any in the shops. Let's have a look then.'

'Ah, no.' Simon kept his elbow tight at his side. 'First edition. Musn't get the pages creased. Sorry.'

'Please yourself. Are you going to want another, or can I get back to my crossword?'

'I'm fine with this one. I have to be going in a minute. And I—' The sound of the saloon-bar door opening caused Simon to falter in his speech and turn suddenly upon his stool. This really *wasn't* the place for him to be. There were just too many potentially dangerous pub-door openers in this village. The men in grey. The boys in blue. The horticulturalist from hell. The B.E.A.S.T. terrorists from God knows where. Simon prepared himself for some more heel-taking-to.

But it was only the Scribe.

'What a coincidence,' said Paul. 'We were just discussing your work.'

'In glowing terms, I have no doubt.' The Scribe laboured his way across to the counter. A ponderous fellow was the Scribe. In fact, one to make Paul seem positively frenetic by comparison. This early evening he was rigged out in his full-scribing apparel.

The country tweeds, the riding boots, the watch chain, the velvet cravat. A lot of pretentious bits and bobs. Middle forties, baldy front and pony-tail behind. Spreading about the waist and slightly broken about the nose. And very tight about the pocket.

The scribe yawned. A lot of fillings from too much sweet eating.

'I've been looking for you, Simon,' he said. 'Where are you going?' he continued.

'Toilet,' said Simon, making for the door.

'Well, don't be too long. I wanted to buy you a drink.'

'Ah,' said Simon. 'The toilet will keep then.'

'Death-by-Cider for me, Paul, and whatever Simon was having.'

Simon returned to his stool and watched the scribe watching Paul drawing off a double Scotch. 'That's what you were having, was it?'

The Scribe's lip had a bit of a quiver. 'Not your usual?'

'Cheers,' said Simon.

Paul pulled the Scribe his pint.

'Cheers,' said Paul.

'Cheers,' said the Scribe, worrying his wallet. 'Cheers it is.'

Money changed hands and the Scribe carefully counted his change.   Paul returned to his crossword. Simon flashed his teeth.

'So,' said the Scribe, settling himself down upon a bar stool.

'So?' asked Simon, with one eye on the door.

'I am writing this book you see,' said the Scribe. 'It's a sort of a fantasy, but to give it a sense of reality I have set it here in Bramfield. The publishers' idea actually. They'd done some research apparently and decided that this was the ideal place. In fact, they even gave me a list of local people they wanted me to put in it. It's not the way I usually work, but they're paying, er, just enough for me to scrape by on, so I have to do it their way.'

'This is all most fascinating,' said Simon, now halfway through his latest double. 'But I really must be leaving.'

'I won't keep you long. It's just that I wanted your advice.'

'Why mine?'

'Because *you're* in the book.'

'What?' went Simon.

'Starring role.'

'*What?*'

'I wasn't supposed to tell you. In fact, it's all very hush-hush. No idea why, it's only fiction after all. But I've got to this sticky bit in the plot and I don't know where to take it next and I thought that if I asked you what you might do if it was in real life, well, that would give it an extra touch of authenticity.'

'*WHAT?*'

'I've got "what" thank you,' called Paul along the bar. 'It was three down, "used with a noun in requesting the identity of something". I'm on three across now. Unit of power equal to one joule per second.'

'What?' went Simon again.

'Oh WATT. I see thanks.' Paul applied his Biro.

'Extra touch of authenticity,' said the Scribe. 'Are you a bit deaf, or *what*?'

'Not,' said Simon. 'But just let me get this straight. *You* are writing a fantasy set in Bramfield.'

'Partly in Bramfield.'

'In which *I* have the starring role.'

'One of two starring roles.'

'And who has the other, might I ask?'

'You'll never guess.'

'Won't I though?'

'Raymond,' whispered the Scribe.

'Raymond. I see.' Simon stroked at his chin and it must be said, the beginnings of a wry smile began to play about his lips. As it were and like they would. 'Might I enquire,' said Simon, 'the name you have in mind for this book?'

'Why do you want to know that?'

'No particular reason,' Simon lied. 'Except, of course, so I can look out for it in the bookshops and buy lots of copies.'

'Well,' said the Scribe, 'I'm not supposed to mention anything about any of this to anyone really.'

'Yes, but you have now. And I would be *very* willing to help you out. In fact, it would be a real honour to feel that I had in some way helped to, how shall I put it, guide the plot in the right direction. In the strictest confidence, of course.'

'The strictest confidence, yes.'

'The title?' Simon shone his smile upon the Scribe.

'*The Greatest Show off Earth,*' came the reply.

'The Greatest Show off Earth.' Professor Merlin bowed and curtsied, as he made the introductions to his guest.

Raymond shook hands and returned smiles, and he wondered all the while of it. His first impressions of the banqueters had been of big broad-shouldered men and wild exotic women. But these impressions did not hold up to closer scrutiny. The 'artistes' all looked, well, a bit hollow-eyed and haggard.

And they were queer fish all. Raymond had never met Siamese triplets before. Nor did he thrill to the professor's lurid description of Aquaphagus the Human Aquarium's speciality act. This certainly wasn't your everyday circus.

But then your everyday circus did not commute between the planets in a Victorian steam ship.

Raymond met Disecto the Living Jigsaw, who could detach his limbs at will and rearrange them into whimsical compositions; Billy Balloon, who performed feats of inflatability which involved the employment of a high-pressure airpipe and had a novel method of playing the penny whistle; Phoenix the Fireproof Fan Dancer.

He exchanged pleasantries with walkers upon wires and swallowers of swords. Politely declined the outstretched hand of Dr Bacteria, trainer of germs, who claimed himself capable of displaying the outward signs of any terminal disease Raymond cared to mention; and received a kiss on the cheek from Lady Alostrael, whose star turn apparently consisted of summoning up the spirits of the dead whilst riding a unicycle, or was it a unicorn?

It was all very confusing. But to Raymond, who was now making a career of confusion, it was just about 'par for the course'.

'Oh yea and verily-do,' crooned the professor. 'And finally, Raymond, you must meet this fellow. A performer of peerless precision. A master of pedestrian presti-digitation. The one, the only. I give you, Monsieur LaRoche.'

'Monsieur LaRoche?' Raymond now found himself being pecked upon both cheeks by a small and sallow chappie, with a tiny waxed moustache and a wandering wig.

'*Mon* pleasure,' said this man, clicking his heels together and offering a salute.

And, 'How about that?' said Raymond. 'Professor, you'll never guess what.'

'I would if the clue were, "used with a noun in requesting the identity of something".'

'Yes, I mean, no. I mean, Monsieur LaRoche. When I escaped on Venus, it was because I remembered my chum Simon telling me about a Victorian circus performer called LaRoche. He invented this act where he got inside a metal ball and rolled up this spiral track. How about that, eh?' Raymond beamed down at the little Frenchman and shook him warmly by the hand. 'I'm very pleased to meet you,' he said. 'Are you related to the original LaRoche? Was he an ancestor, your great great grandfather or something?'

LaRoche looked Raymond up and down. 'I am LaRoche,' quoth he. 'I am ze original LaRoche. Inventor of ze internally perambulated sphere. I am ze Sisyphus of Circusdom.'

'You mean the original act is still in the family. Brilliant.'

'I mean I am *the* LaRoche.'

'Yes, but not the real one. The real one performed over one hundred years ago.'

'Not ze real one?'

'Let us move on,' said the professor. 'I don't believe you've met—'

'Not ze *real* one?' The Frenchman stamped his foot. 'He is saying that I'm not ze real LaRoche.'

'Well, you're not,' said Raymond.

'Pooh poohs.' LaRoche pulled a kid glove from his pocket and slapped Raymond across the face with it.

'Slap!' it went.

'I say,' said Raymond.

'*You* say?' cried the Sisyphus of Circusdom. 'You say? You say I am not ze original LaRoche. That is what you say.'

'I do,' said Raymond.

'He does!' The Frenchman stamped the other foot. 'He spit upon my good name. He drag my reputation through ze horse's manure.'

'Now you're being silly,' Raymond said.

'Silly! Now he say I stone bonker.'

'Slap,' went the glove again.

'Stop that,' said Raymond. 'I only said.'

'I hear what you say. You say my sister do it for money with ze sailor boys.'

'I never said any such thing.'

'Slap,' went the glove for a third time.

'I'm warning you,' said Raymond.

'Oh yeah?' said Monsieur LaRoche.

'Gentlemen, gentlemen,' said Professor Merlin, stepping into the verbiage with some of his own. 'Let us have no ambivalence here. Contrariety leads to contradistinction. Dispute to discord and discord to inharmonious circumstance.'

'This pig start it,' LaRoche protested. 'He insult me. He wee wee upon my shoes and do a jobby in my wife's handbag.'

'I never did.'

'Slap,' went the glove.

'Right,' said Raymond, taking off his jacket and handing it to Professor Merlin. 'One more slap and you're—'

'What am I?' LaRoche made a continental gesture.

'You're a dead frog,' said Raymond.

'*Frog!*' LaRoche threw up his hands. 'Frog he call me. He use ze "F" word in front of ze ladies. My honour, she must be satisfied.'

'Look,' said Raymond, rather loudly, 'I'm sorry. But you can't be the original LaRoche. The original LaRoche was born in 1857. I've seen pictures.'

'Hear him?' The little Frenchman appealed to his fellow artistes. 'Now he say he have photographs of my mother giving birth to me. Filthy pervert. My pistols someone. Now take that.'

And with no further words spoken, Monsieur LaRoche kicked Raymond in the ankle.

'Ouch!' went Raymond, clutching at his leg and hopping wildly about.

And, 'Ouch!' went Dr Bacteria, as Raymond hopped heavily on to his foot.

And, 'Eeeeeek!' went Lady Alostrael, as Dr Bacteria fell backwards off his chair, dragging a section of table-cloth with him and dislodging a bowl of punch into her lap.

And, 'Oooooh!' went Billy Balloon, as Lady Alostrael elbowed him in the face, while trying to duck the avalanche of food that was careening after the punch bowl.

And, 'My suit!' cried Raymond, as cakes and ale went all down his trousers.

And, 'Urgh!' went Professor Merlin, as Raymond took a mighty swing at LaRoche, missed and brought *him* down instead.

And then things got somewhat confused.

They're a tight-knit bunch are circus folk. Have to be. It's a very hard life on the road. So they all look after each other. And they live by a code. Which to the outsider means, offend one and you offend all.

But they're only human. And within such a closed community rivalries occur. And jealousies. And passions that ferment like mildewed Bramleys in a Death-by-Cider barrel.

And once in a while they boil over. And get stains all over the mat.

History does not record who threw the first custard pie. Nor at whom it was deliberately thrown. But it struck one of the Siamese triplets. The one who had this grudge against Phoenix the Fireproof Fan Dancer. And it was she who flung the plate. And Disecto who caught it on the ear. And it was while *he* was thrashing about in search of his fallen head, that someone tipped the soup tureen into the lap of one of the sword swallowers. And the soup was hot.

The other sword swallower hit one of the high-wire walkers and this man fell on top of Raymond, who was trying to help the professor up. And Raymond lashed out at the high-wire walker and hit Mr Aquaphagus by mistake. And Mr Aquaphagus drew his sword. And was promptly set upon by three dwarves, two clowns, Hercules the circus strongman, Polly, of Polly's Performing Poodles, Leonora the lion taming lady and Puff the Magic Dragon, all of whom were really miffed about not getting a mention sooner.

And then, at exactly this moment, the police burst in.

13

'Right, my lad, you're nicked!' The police who had done the bursting in were looking pretty good. They wore those really spiffing riot helmets with the plexiglass visors and those bullet-proof vests that make you look like Mr Michelin. All in those tasteful tones of metropolitan blue.

Very nice.

The one who shouted 'Right, my lad, you're nicked!' wasn't wearing a helmet. Which was a shame, because he had one of those awful Arthur Scargill comb-over jobs and he'd have looked a good five years younger with the helmet on.

But he wasn't wearing one. So there you go.

But he *was* carrying the gun.

'You're . . .' He turned this gun a full muzzle-sweeping three hundred and sixty degrees of the bar. 'Nicked?'

Paul looked up from his newspaper. 'You've missed him,' he said. 'He left ten minutes ago.'

'Ten minutes ago?' Inspector D'Eath stalked up to the counter. 'I told you to keep him talking. When you phoned me, I said, "Keep him talking."'

'Do you think that I'm mad?' asked Paul. 'According to you, the man is a suspected serial killer. I waited until he'd left the premises before I telephoned. I was thinking of you.'

'Thinking of me?'

'All the extra paperwork. If I'd tried to keep him talking, which I couldn't have done anyway, because he'd left before I phoned you, but say I had tried to keep him talking, and he'd got suspicious and maybe brought out a chainsaw or something and it had turned into a siege situation and maybe innocent victims got in the line of fire and the pub got burned down and—'

'Yes yes yes. I get the picture. The paperwork.'

'Exactly. But I have this.' Paul brought out something wrapped in a handkerchief. He placed it carefully on the counter and teased away the wrappings.

'It's a whisky glass,' said Inspector D'Eath.

'It's *his* whisky glass,' said Paul.

'So?'

'So you can take fingerprints from it.'

Inspector D'Eath shook his head, releasing all those nasty strands again. 'Why should I want to take fingerprints from it? We've been to his house. His fingerprints are all over that.'

'You'll be able to get a match then. You did say fifty quid for a verifiable sighting, didn't you?'

'Nice try.' The inspector smiled. 'What I actually said was, fifty quid for information leading to an arrest.'

'Semantics,' said Paul. 'Same thing.'

'It's not the same thing at all. I have to know where the suspect is at this very moment.'

'Fifty quid,' said Paul. 'For the information. Fifty quid.'

Inspector D'Eath made an exasperated sighing sound. '*Do* you know where the suspect is now?'

'Fifty quid,' said Paul.

'You *do* know.'

'Fifty quid.'

'Constable, pay this man fifty pounds and get a receipt for it.'

The constable with the sister said, 'who me?'

'Who me, *sir*,' said Inspector D'Eath.

'Thank God,' said the constable. 'I thought you meant me.'

'I did mean you, lad. Pay this man fifty pounds.'

'I don't have fifty pounds, *sir*.' The constable saluted. 'My wallet is at home in my sports jacket.'

'Sports jacket?' Paul shook his head. 'I'll bet he's got slippers too.'

'He has,' said the constable who didn't have a sister, but had once seen a search warrant. 'I've seen them. And I've seen a search warrant as well.'

'Constable pay this man fifty pounds now.'

The constable with the taste for casual leisurewear shook his head fiercely. 'I haven't got fifty pounds, sir. But Derek has.'

'I never have,' protested the constable without the sister, whose name was Derek. (The constable's name was Derek, that is, not the sister that he didn't have (her name was Doris).)

'He does, sir. He's saving up for a motor scooter.'

'A motor scooter?' Paul shook his head once more.

'A motor scooter, and he always carries his money with him.'

'I bloody don't.'

'You bloody do.'

'*Shut up!*' Inspector D'Eath slammed his gun down on to the counter. There was quite a devastating bang as it went off. A lot of smoke too.

The constables dived into each other's arms and from there to the floor where they huddled in a gibbering heap.

Paul didn't even get a shake on. Not a twitch. He looked from the now shattered whisky optic to the now sweating face of Inspector D'Eath and from there to his paper. 'Discharge,' he said.

'Discharge?' Inspector D'Eath sniffed the smoking pistol.

'Ten down, "as in fire from a gun". Discharge. Thank you.'

'My pleasure. Constables, get up off that floor and pay this man fifty pounds. *At once!*'

'Yes, sir.'

'All right,' said the inspector, as he watched Paul counting coinage into his trouser pocket. 'Where is the suspect, *now*?'

'He's at the Scribe's house. Forty-nine, fifty, thank you.'

'And where does the scribe live?'

'Search me,' said Paul.

Inspector D'Eath cocked his pistol.

'Try the phonebook.' Paul produced one from beneath the counter. 'His name's Sprout. Kilgore Sprout.'

'So what do you think, Mr Sprout?'

Simon had his feet up on the Scribe's sofa.

It was a knackered old sofa, all draped over by those dreadful woollen multicoloured shawl things that cat owners delight in to cover up the claw marks on the furniture and make the place look 'homely'.

The Scribe's house was right at the bottom of the-lane-that-dare-not-speak-its-name. Tucked down behind that of the mad old major. It had a big high hedge around it. And Simon, who had lived all his life in the village, and thought to have crept around every inch of it, had not until now known that a house was even there.

It was 'homely' within.

The sitting-room had that middle-class, professional-country-person-who-earns-his-money-in-the-City look to it. Stacks of glossy magazines, with matching spines. And in date order. One of those computer contrivances that you hear so much about, the ones that look like an electric typewriter with a little television set screwed on the top. *Word Procurers* they're called. An inglenook fireplace, where you could burn logs on a wintry day to heat the sky up.

Not exactly Simon's cup of meat.

'What do I think?' The Scribe sipped a sweet sherry. He'd brought in the three-quarter-finished bottle from the kitchen. The one he kept for guests who 'weren't staying long'. 'Kindly take me through it one more time, if you will.'

'It's very simple.' Simon took a small sip from his full glass and found it now to be an empty glass. 'From what you've told me about the character you've based on me, he's a bit of a bastard, yes? But with a heart of gold. A lovable rogue.'

'Well, I had him down as just the bit of a bastard actually. All bastard, in fact. But continue, none the less.'

'He should do something big and exciting.' Simon put down his minuscule glass and reached for the sherry bottle. The Scribe drew it beyond his reach. 'I'm not just saying this because you've based the character on me. But because, if it *was* me, I'd do something big and exciting. You wanted my advice, didn't you?'

'Yes, but the kind of advice you're giving me, is not quite what I'd had in mind.'

'Of course not. That's why you've got to the sticky bit in the plot and you need some fresh input.'

'Well it's very exciting, this new scenario you've come up with. Where your character doesn't give his winnings to charity, but, in fact, has them stolen from him by these urban terrorists. And he goes after them and steals the money back. Do you think he'd really be brave enough to do that though?'

'You bet I, er, *he* would. That giving the money to charity business is too far fetched. That's where the plot's gone wrong.'

'I could rewrite it so he never wins the money in the first place.'

'No, don't do that . . . He wins the money, has it stolen and then steals it *all* back.'

'I think you're right,' said the Scribe, pouring Simon half a glass. 'I never liked the giving-it-to-charity bit. It was the publishers' idea that I put that in.'

'Damn right it was,' muttered Simon. 'Who did you say the publishers were, by the way?' As if he didn't know.

'They're called B.E.A.S.T. Although I don't know what it stands for. Have you ever heard of them?'

'Never.' Simon shook his head.

'All right,' said the Scribe. 'So he goes after these terrorists that you've invented. But how does he know where to find them?'

How indeed? thought Simon. 'That's the clever bit,' he said. 'You've been writing this so far. And you're about halfway through it, right? So you don't want to go introducing too many new characters, do you? They'd have to be holed up with some character that you've written about already.'

'Yes,' said the Scribe. 'But which one?'

That's what I want *you* to tell *me*, you stupid sod, thought Simon. 'Well, you tell me. If you were going to write about a secret terrorist group based in the village. Where would *you* base them?'

The Scribe scratched at his bald spot.

Simon made free with a dental dazzle.

'There's an abandoned gamekeeper's hut just outside the village.'

'Too small,' said Simon.

'You know it?'

'Know *of* it. They'd be with some local character.'

'The vicar?'

Simon shook his head once more. This particular gambit had seemed so straightforward, when it had come to him in The Jolly Gardeners. His line of thinking had run thus: If the Scribe is the one who has been commissioned to write Raymond's future biography, and is actually writing it now, without knowing that he's really writing truth instead of fiction; then, if Simon could persuade him to bump up the part *he* was playing, by getting back the money, for one thing, well, that would be the kiddie, wouldn't it? And once more the possibilities would be endless, for the man who knew the future before it arrived. And that man would be he, Simon.

Bastard!

'I have it,' said the Scribe.

'You have?' asked Simon.

'I have. It was staring me right in the face. Long Bob's chicken farm.'

'Ah,' said Simon thoughtfully. 'Why?'

'Well, he's up to something, isn't he? Remember I told you the bit about how your character sees him trying to train his chickens?'

'I think you mentioned it.' The Scribe hadn't.

'Well. He's behind it all. He's a crazy, right? And he's breeding this new strain of chicken. Planning to take over the world. That kind of thing.'

'I like it,' said Simon. 'What else?'

'Well. He needs the money for this diabolical project. The terrorists are in his pay. Yes, I see it all. It's a religious cult. An End Times religion.'

'Steady on,' said Simon. 'That's a bit over the top, isn't it?'

'Messianic.' The Scribe reached for his exercise book. 'This is the kind of stuff I like to write. I'm not going to do the publishers' stuff any more. I'm going to write it my way.'

'Bravo,' said Simon. 'I hope that will work.'

'What do you mean?'

'Nothing. Never mind. Right then. Well, I think I'll *go home now. Get an early night.*'

'Not in my book, you won't.' said the Scribe, scribbling away. 'In my book you'll be off to Long Bob's to steal back your money. Oh yes indeed.'

'Would that life was like fiction, eh?' Simon gathered himself up from the sofa and disentangled himself from one of the dreadful woollen multicoloured shawl things. 'But in real life, I shall be going home to bed. In case anyone might ask.'

'I can't imagine why they would.' The Scribe was busy a-scribbling.

'Fair enough. Goodbye then.'

'Goodbye.' The Scribe didn't look up, so Simon snatched away the sherry bottle and tucked it into his pocket.

'Goodbye to you,' he said.

Simon took his leave along the abandoned railway track, which led down behind Raymond's house to the lower end of the village.

It was a wise choice. Because before he had gone but a hundred yards, he heard the distinctive wail of police car sirens. And the distinctive crunching sounds, as the cars bumped in and out of the-holes-that-no-one-takes-responsibility-for, in the-lane-that-dare-not-speak-its-name.

Simon put a bit of spring into his step and set out, not for home, but for the chicken farm of one Long Bob.

As it was now reasonably clear that the police had, in fact, burst into The Jolly Gardeners, rather than the grand salon of the *SS Salamander*, it follows that the punch up there was still in full swing.

And it was.

Someone in sequins flew over the table, smashed to the floor and came up again fighting. A lot of crockery was getting broken and a lot of priceless glassware done to bits. And in the middle of all the shouts and yells and screams and shrieks and whatnots, a great voice suddenly boomed, 'So this is The Greatest Show off Earth!'

Raymond, who now sheltered beneath the table, beheld a pair of golden boots and a portion of exclusive-looking trouser-work.

The clashing of swords and the breaking of bits came suddenly to a most conclusive conclusion. Well, at least for a tinkle or two.

The professor clubbed at the dwarf who was clinging to his breeches. Billy Balloon said, 'Blow me down.' And one of Polly's Performing Poodles growled in the key of B sharp.

'The Greatest Show off Earth? Ha ha.' It was a curious voice. Raymond did not recognize the accent. And it had a fussy nasal tone to it. The words seemed almost to be coughed out, rather than spoken.

Raymond didn't like the voice. It made him feel uncomfortable. He felt reasonably sure that he was really going to hate the owner. And he wondered just what he might look like. Because it sounded like a *he*, you see.

So Raymond lifted the torn length of table cloth that shielded him from view and took an upward peep.

And when he had done so, he let the cloth fall again, crouched down upon his knees and said, 'Oh shit!'

He *had* just seen what he thought he'd just seen, hadn't he?

Raymond took a tiny little second peep.

He *had*.

But it wasn't real, was it?

No, it just couldn't be.

Oh yes it *could*.

Raymond took a third peep. And this is what he saw.

From the golden boots, Chisel-toed and Cuban-heeled, to the swish trouser-wear, tailored, fitted, black satin, chic, to the matching jacket, clenched in at the waist, golden buttons in two rising rows, golden belt with elaborate boss, a winged disc with profiled supplicants. Epauletted shoulders, scarab cartouche on left breast pocket. Ornamented cuffs, from beneath which showed delicate human hands, manicured and pampered.

So far so swell and hoity-toity.

The problem was the head.

It wasn't a human head.

It was an animal's head.

It was the head of a wolf. No, not a wolf. Raymond did furtive perusals. One of those animals that sneak around after the carrion that lions leave behind. A jackal. It was the head of a jackal. And it wasn't some carnival head. This was a living breathing job and a really magnificent specimen. The way the nostrils flared, the black lips curled, the yellow eyes, with their slitted pupils, blink blink blinked.

Very impressive indeed. And the way he carried himself. Almost . . . Raymond paused. Almost.

'Blimey.' whispered Raymond. 'It's *him*. It's that god. The Egyptian one. Off the tomb paintings. Thingy . . . er . . . Anubis. It's Anubis.

'Perhaps it is a mutiny.' This was a new voice. A very strange voice. High and piping. Almost a whistle. The user of this voice stepped forward and Raymond copped an eyeful.

About the same height (which was tall). About the same build (which was lean and athletic). About the same outfit, a detail of difference. But not the same head.

This was his mate. The fellow with the bird's head. The head of the sacred ibis. He looked amazing also. The feathers were black, with the rainbow sheen of starlings. The eyes bright red points of light. The beak was a dazzling yellow.

Set. That's who it was. Set. Or Thoth, he had a bird's head as well. Raymond weighed it up. Set, he decided. Thoth was far too hard to pronounce.

It was Set. And no mistake about it.

'Blimey,' whispered Raymond again and settled down hard on his bum. Two Egyptian gods, and both in a single day. This was some surprise.

But then.

Raymond considered the kind of day he'd had today.

It had started with him waking up and thinking he was at home, only to discover that he was actually on board a Victorian liner in orbit around Saturn. And floating in air. Because space was full of air. Then there had been Zephyr the dream woman and Giorgio the dream suit. A dream suit now thoroughly besmirched and destroyed. And the revelation that the world Raymond had grown up on was, in fact, inside another world. And that the folk on the outer world, fed up with all the pollution wafting up from the inner world, had decided to plug up the polar openings and thereby suffocate everyone down there.

Wipe out mankind. Just like that.

Then there had been the matter of him passing the special recruitment test set by Professor Merlin. The passing of this had offered Raymond the prospect of almost certain death, as it put him in the unenviable position of being the only soldier in an army fighting to prevent the topsiders carrying out their pole-plugging plans.

Oh yes, and before he got stuck into that, would it be all right if he rescued two hundred inner-Earth people who just happened to be held captive upon Saturn?

Yes.

And he'd just got into a punch up with a Frenchman who claimed he was more than a century old.

That was the kind of day he'd had today.

The arrival of two Egyptian gods really shouldn't have come as that much of a surprise. He would just have to learn to take this sort of thing in his stride.

But what to do for the best now?

Should he bow? Out of politeness? He was C. of E. himself, of course. In fact, more so in the last two days than ever before.

But it was always respectful to show a courteous regard towards the gods of other religions.

Especially when you met them in the flesh.

'Bow I think,' whispered Raymond. 'I expect that's what everyone else is doing.'

Raymond bowed beneath the table.

Professor Merlin cleared his throat.

Prayer coming, thought Raymond, putting his hands together.

Professor Merlin spoke. 'Bugger off my ship, you dog-faced gremlin,' were the words he chose to use.

Beneath the table Raymond gnawed upon his knuckles.

Above the table great Anubis gazed about the grand salon. A grand salon no longer quite so grand. Chairs all broken, plates all smashed. Food all over the floor. Food all over the banqueters. And here a black eye and there a bloody nose. And there a fellow searching for his head. Gorgeous clothes all ripped and torn, wigs awry and all forlorn. And fractured glass and fine wines spilled. 'Oh dear, oh dear,' he said.

'I told you to bugger off,' Professor Merlin made shooing-away motions with his fabulous fingers. 'I will have someone accompany you up onto the deck and toss a stick for you to fetch. How will that suit you?'

Raymond flinched.

Set said, 'Perhaps we shall have you all immediately executed for crimes of violence committed within Saturnian territorial jurisdiction. How will that suit *you*?'

Professor Merlin gave the god a haughty look. 'Are you talking to me, or whistling *Dixie*? Try to enunciate more clearly, do.'

Turn it in, thought Raymond. Are you completely insane?

'I don't recall hearing you being piped aboard.' Professor Merlin addressed the two gods. 'I fear you crept on unannounced.'

'You have cream cake on your chin,' said Set.

'Is that a chin?' asked Anubis. 'I thought it was a hammock with a pig at rest therein.'

Professor Merlin fanned at his nose. 'Dog-breath,' said he, 'and Bird-brain. Off my ship now, before I take a whip to the one and have the other plucked and stuffed and cooked for my pussycat's tea.'

Anubis curled his lip at this and showed a row of teeth. Set did a sort of 'pecking the eyes out' mime with his beak.

'You both know where the door is. Kindly hop or bound back through it, as the fancy takes you.' Professor Merlin licked the cream from his chin with a quite considerable tongue. 'Woof quack.'

'Papers!' barked Anubis.

'At once!' whistled Set. 'Or it's in with the execution squad and death to the men of violence.'

'Zephyr,' called Professor Merlin. 'Pray take a letter, if you will.'

Zephyr smiled, turned a chair upright to sit upon. Sat upon it. Produced pen and pad from nowhere and said, 'Ready for dictation.'

'So kind. Address it please to, His Royal Highness Grand Duke Fogerty, The Palace of Celestial Pleasure, Number One, The Big Posh Road, City of Fogerty, Saturn.

'Dear Binky.'

'Binky?' went Anubis. Set shook his beak.

'Dear Binky. It is with very great regret that I regret most greatly being unable to attend the celebration of your birthday today. I know you so wanted to see my circus perform again, and, of course, as we have been such close friends for so many years now, it is always a pleasure beyond price to share your hospitality and your wives.

'Sadly, however, it cannot be. I was interrupted halfway through the full dress rehearsal of the special novelty food fight number you choreographed for the entertainment of your poor sick son Colin, in the hope that it might raise his spirits and possibly turn the tide of his illness, by two louts who burst in unannounced and threatened my company with death . . .'

The professor paused. Set and Anubis were backing quietly towards the door.

'Off so soon?' the professor asked. 'I was hoping you might entertain us with a jump or two through a flaming hoop, or that thing that budgies do when they run up and down the little ladder and ring their bell. No?'

But now he was speaking only to the empty open doorway of the not so grand salon.

A moment's pause. Then laughter filled the air.

Raymond crawled slowly out from under the table. He was shaking his head in despair. And most of his body in fear.

'I wondered where you were hiding yourself,' said the professor. 'Very wise, keeping out of the way like that to avoid identification later. Smart move, me old Scarlet Pimpernel.'

Raymond's head was still shaking and his jaw was going up and down in a foolish manner. 'You . . . you . . .' he went.

'I I I?' queried the professor, brushing crumbs and cake and bits and bobs from around and about himself. 'What is this I I I?'

'You. Those gods. You insulted those gods.'

'I did?' There was a pause. And then there was a lot more good loud laughter and it of a raucous kind.

'Anubis and Set. I saw them. I heard them. I heard *you*.'

'Ah.' Professor Merlin plucked something fruity from his peruke and popped it into his mouth. 'You did not approve?'

'It was outrageous. Blasphemous.'

'Good,' said the professor.

'Good?'

'Good. Raymond, if I had behaved in any other way, shown any respect whatsoever, shown any politeness, any deference, shown anything but complete arrogance, total self-confidence and absolute bloody-mindedness, they would have seen through me in a twinkling. I told you we pose as topsiders. And that is how topsiders behave.'

'But to gods?'

'Oh no, I doubt that even topsiders would dare behave like that to gods.'

'But you just did.'

'No, Raymond, I just behaved like that to a couple of snotty Saturnian customs and excise men. Fido and Tweety, I think their names are. Though I can't recall which is which. But, hold the horse, Tonto, you didn't really think that—'

'Of course not.' Raymond scraped at something crusty on his strides.

'You thought they they . . .' Professor Merlin turned a smirk to his battered artistes. 'Raymond thought that they . . .' The artistes began to titter. 'He thought that those two twats were—'

'I did *not*.' Raymond shook his head fiercely, showering the professor with cake.

'No, of course you didn't.' Professor Merlin winked and patted Raymond on the back. 'That they . . .' he made thumbings toward the door.

'Stop it!' Raymond stamped his foot. 'And look at the state of my suit. It's ruined, ruined. My beautiful suit.'

The professor sniffed at Raymond's devastated dresswear. 'It is a mite cakky.'

'My beautiful suit!' Raymond raised fists in the air.

'I'll pay for the dry-cleaning bill.'

'It's *his* fault.' Raymond pointed at the little Frenchman, who was struggling to his feet.'

'You started eet,' shrieked LaRoche, 'defiler of my old brown *chien*.'

'*You* started it, you lying frog.'

'The "F" word again, my pistols someone.'

'Do calm down.' The professor raised his hands and his fingers elongated to the rudely frescoed dome, where they tickled the bum of a cherub. It certainly calmed down Raymond.

'English peeg,' said LaRoche.

'Lying Frog,' said Raymond.

'He's not lying,' said Zephyr, whom alone had avoided any soilage and looked wonderful as ever. 'He's telling the truth, Raymond. He is the original LaRoche.'

'But that would make him . . .'

'One hundred and fifty-three,' said the Frenchman, clicking his heels. 'And twice ze man you'll never be.'

'That's very old,' said Raymond.

'How dare you! I am ze youngest member of ze circus.'

'What?'

'It's a pity you don't believe in magic,' said Professor

162

Merlin. 'Or I'd tell you how it's done. But now, enough is enough for today I think.'

'Hm,' went Raymond and then brightening considerably and glancing at his 'wife', he said, 'Yes, we really should be turning in. Early start tomorrow, which way is the Bridal Suite?'

'Bridal Suite?' Professor Merlin laughed. 'Nice try, me old Casanova, but bedding will have to wait, I'm afraid. We landed upon Saturn twenty minutes ago. The circus parade begins in half an hour and our first performance an hour after that. So if you want to synchronize watches, we had best do it now. Then you can tell me exactly what time I can expect you to return with the two hundred people you will have rescued. Well?'

'Well,' said Raymond. 'Well indeed.'

14

Simon sat in the hideaway bush that he'd all but forgotten about. A lot of good times had been spent in that bush. Innocent times. Childhood times. When he and Raymond had bunked off school, painted their faces with clay, taken up bows and arrows and sworn great and secret oaths.

Happy times indeed they'd been, but now the bush was gloomy with their recollection.

Simon was still too young a man to miss his childhood. He was glad to see the back of it. But it now occurred to him that he might just be missing Raymond. After all, Raymond was his bestest friend and since he'd been gone, things hadn't been quite the same in the village.

To say the very least of it.

Simon sighed and twiddled a twig. They'd had some laughs in this bush. That was for sure. Remember the time when . . . Simon paused, sighed, twiddled and sniffed.

'Bloody Raymond,' he said. 'This is all his fault.'

And Simon scratched at his head. His hangover was gone, which was something. It was quite remarkable how the simple application of three double Scotches and a couple of mouthfuls of sweet sherry could sort out a hangover that had been plaguing you all day. It was a pity that he hadn't brought any crisps with him though. He'd hardly eaten a thing in the last twelve hours. And he was really hungry now.

'Bloody Raymond.'

The sun was sliding down beyond the village. It did picturesque things to the fine old meadow oaks that bordered the allotments. But these were lost on Simon. Simon heard the discordant sounds that rang from the church, where Bramfield's inept bellringers practised. He could smell the reek of slurry pits and Long Bob's chicken farm. A dog barked in the distance. A heavy lorry rattled windows in the high street.

Sunset? What sunset?

Simon poked his head out of the hideaway bush and stole a shifty glance down the hill to the chicken farm. He had a good view from up here. The only trouble was that there was nothing to see. The chickens were all inside. Long Bob's Land Rover wasn't there. The place was deserted.

'Come on,' muttered Simon. 'Hurry up.'

He'd been sitting here for hours in this damp little bush. Risking the onset of haemorrhoids and waiting for something to happen. Anything to happen. He had considered it all for the best to wait until nightfall, before slipping down for a good nose around. But he'd hoped to see a bit of action in the meanwhile. Suspicious men carrying suspicious-looking crates about and going 'mumble mumble secret plans, mumble mumble tonight is the night mumble mumble mumble', the way they should be doing. But they weren't. No-one was doing anything. It was all very disappointing really.

The Greatest Show off Earth lay before him in the dirt. He couldn't bring himself to take a peep inside. If nothing had changed in it and it did not now contain the Scribe's rewrite, Simon was in big trouble. Written out and wanted for murder. Not what he had in mind for himself at all. There was, of course, the strong possibility that B.E.A.S.T. would simply edit out any changes the Scribe made. But Simon being Simon thought they would not. He reasoned that if he was able to steal back his winnings, then he would effectively change the true history that was to be published in the future.

Effectively change the future in fact and the role that

B.E.A.S.T. played in it. It was some kind of a theory, but not much of one. And Simon did have it in mind that, should he be able to steal back his winnings, the best course of action he could take would be to get as far away from Bramfield as he could. Passport or no passport. Thank you and goodbye.

Simon shook the Scribe's sherry bottle about. It was still empty and he was still hungry. And now he needed the toilet.

'If it's not one thing, it's another.' Simon climbed carefully out of the bush. Stretched, grumbled, skulked around to the back and relieved himself. And he was just zipping up when a flash of blue caught his eye. Not from his trouser regions, but somewhat off to his left across the fields. From a little spinney, or was it a thicket, it's often so hard to tell.

'Policemen.' Simon dropped down into the grass. The wet steamy grass. 'Oh damn,' he complained.

The flash of blue flashed again. It was a hiker in an anorak, or was it a cagoule, it's often hard to tell.

'Pull yourself together, Simon.' Simon crept back around his bush. And there . . . 'Oh yes indeed.'

Long Bob's deserted farmyard was no longer deserted. The chicken farmer's Land Rover was drawing in at the gate and behind it, one of those old Jags, so beloved of the criminal fraternity in shows like *The Sweeney*. It was the same Jag.

And now the cars were pulling up and folk were getting out. Long Bob from the Land Rover, and who was that with him? Black three-piece suit, crewcut, glasses. Military Dave. And who else? Flurry of auburn hair. Nice figure in tight blue jeans and Led Zeppelin T-shirt. Simon's Led Zeppelin T-shirt. *Liza!* What?

The Jag's doors were opening. The B.E.A.S.T. terrorists were climbing out. The looker and her cohorts. Simon strained his eyes to see. Did she have his carrier bags? She *did* have his carrier bags.

'Boom Shanka,' said Simon. 'But Liza?'

He cocked an ear. Sounds of conversation drifted up to him from the farmyard.

'Mumble mumble,' they went. 'Mumble mumble secret plans, mumble mumble tonight is the night mumble mumble mumble.' And then they all marched off to the farmhouse, went inside and were gone.

Simon sat in his bush for a moment wondering what to do next. What was Liza doing with them? Was she a B.E.A.S.T. terrorist too? That didn't seem very likely. There was only one way to find out.

The sun was hitting the skyline and the shadows beginning to lengthen. Simon slid out of his hideaway bush, onto his stomach and crawled off down the hill. Bound for Long Bob's chicken farm and *An Appointment with Fear*.[1]

'Frankly,' said Raymond to Zephyr, 'I'm scared.' They stood upon the foredeck of the *SS Salamander*. The ship lay at berth in the harbour. The harbour was on Saturn. The sky was blue. The quayside crowded. Zephyr was beautiful. Raymond was scared.

'Look at them all,' he whispered. 'I don't like the way they're looking at me.'

'They're not looking at you, don't be silly.'

'I'm not being silly. They're staring. It's my suit. They can see all the stains. I told you lemon juice wouldn't get red wine out. I can't go through with this. We'll have to call it off. At least until the damp patches dry out.'

'Raymond, they are not staring at *you*. They're staring at the ship. They've never seen anything quite like it before.'

'But this isn't the first time you've played Saturn.'

'No, but it's the first time we've brought the ship down with us. We usually leave it in space and come down in unmarked lifeboats. It's safer that way.'

[1] A Lazlo Woodbine thriller. Though not one that belongs in this book.

'Safer?' A note of greater alarm entered Raymond's voice.

'This is a stolen ship remember.'

'So why bring it down this time?'

Zephyr sighed. 'Because of the two hundred new passengers you're hoping to bring on board.'

'Ah yes, those.' Raymond chewed upon a knuckle and peered down at the crowds. Egyptian gods to a man. Or a woman. Or a child. Big ones and small ones. Hawk heads and jackal heads and ibises and eagles. Colourful dressers. It did look a lot like a carnival. Although to Raymond it looked more like hell.

Nice day for it though. And lovely setting.

From beyond the dock the city rose up like a hymn to Ra.

Marble obelisks flanked avenues which led toward pale palaces.

And pyramids crowned off with golden cones.

Triumphal arches, nobly hewn.

With bas-reliefs of star and moon.

To praise the rising Sun God on his throne.

Or;

It was Memphis.

But not Tennessee.

This was Egypt.

Four thousand BC

'Is it pretty, do you think?' asked Zephyr. 'Is that what pretty is?'

'It's incredible.' Raymond said. 'And it scares the life out of me. But I get this, you know. This makes sense to me now.'

'Does it?'

'It does. My chum Simon told me once about a book he'd read. It was called *Royalties of the Gods*, or something like that. Written by this German chap, who'd figured out that all the gods of ancient Earth were, in fact, astronauts from outer space. And this proves it. Ancient Egypt on Earth was just a copy of this city.'

'It's good,' said Zephyr. 'But it's not the one. Ancient Egypt on Earth *was* a copy of this city. But it was the topsiders who built it. It was intended to be a theme park, an interplanetary tourist resort. Saturn World, it was called. But unfortunately nobody wanted to come and it went broke. A sort of forerunner to Euro Disney, I suppose. After it went broke, the slave workers who'd built it, moved in to live there. But as they hadn't built it very well, it soon fell down, so they had to move out. I think they all went off across the Red Sea and sort of got lost in the end. I don't really know that much about the history of the inner Earth.'

'Nor apparently do I.' Raymond shook his head. 'Is the big circus parade about to start?'

'In five minutes or so. I have to go with it Raymond.'

'I know.' Raymond chanced an arm around her shoulder. She drew herself close to him and for the first time he realized just how marvellous she smelt. It made him go numb from the nostrils down. 'I don't want you to go with the parade,' he told her. 'I need you to stay with me.'

'But I can't.'

'You can and you must. I can't do this all on my own. I wouldn't last five minute down there amongst that lot on the dock. But with you and your remarkable powers to help me, then I could do it. I know that I could.'

'But the professor needs me with the parade.'

'The professor can manage without you this once. And let's face it, if *we* can free the kidnapped people and we all escape in this ship I don't think the circus is going to be welcome back here anyway. Do you?'

Zephyr smiled her beautiful smile. 'All right. I'll go with you. So, tell me all about your plan.'

'Ah that.' Raymond leaned upon the ship's rail with his free arm and made a thoughtful face. 'So far it appears to consist of watches being synchronized and us all meeting back here in three hours.'

'And?'

'And then making our escape, I suppose.'

'And would you call this a fool-proof plan?'

'Proof against fools possibly. As for the rest, I couldn't say.'

'You really don't have any plan at all, do you?'

'No,' Raymond grinned. 'But then I never said that I did. Because with you to help me I don't need any plan. I just need two other things.'

'Courage and good fortune?' Zephyr asked.

'No,' said Raymond.

'Determination and the will to survive?'

'No,' said Raymond.

'Fortitude and dedication to a just and noble cause?'

'No,' said Raymond. 'No no no. Although all those things would come in handy. This is more, how shall I put it, an image kind of thing. If you're going to save the world, there's only one way to do it.'

'And that is?'

'Wearing black leather and riding on a Harley David-son.'

Courage and good fortune, determination and the will to survive, fortitude and dedication to a just and noble cause.

Given the choice of these, Simon would have gone for good fortune and the will to survive. And the black leather outfit and the Harley Davidson, of course. Because these two particular fashion accessories figured quite high up on the list of necessary purchases he meant to make as soon as he had reacquired his winnings.

And he meant to reacquire them very soon. The sun was down now and the stars were out and it was growing cold. No fun.

Simon wrapped his jacket round himself and crept forward on his elbows as commandos do. Light welled from the farmhouse windows, the yard seemed empty and safe. The chickens in their sheds were restless though. And Simon smelt a smell.

He was just at the perimeter fence. And as he raised his head up he could smell the smell. Above the normal reek of chicken pooh. A strange smell, queer to him. Uncomfortable. Disquieting. Plain odd. Simon sniffed this smell and shook his head. He had no time for strange smells, he had things to do.

As with Raymond, Simon didn't have a plan.

But unlike Raymond, Simon *did* have the market cornered when it came to low cunning and the ability to 'think on his feet'.

And though he didn't know it now, both of these would soon be tried and tested to their limits and beyond.

It was a reasonably short scuttle across the farmyard to the house. Just a swift shin over the fence and don't trip up on the rusting iron or the plastic bags or the sundry junk all around. Simon climbed to his feet, dusted himself down and prepared to do the shinning over.

He was just reaching out for the wire when two sounds caught his wary ear. Unrelated first they seemed. But significant.

One of them was a wolf-like growl, the other a clock-like tick.

The countryman in Simon knew them both. The first even a towny would have got. *Guard dog.* Easy that one. The other . . . Simon's hand eased back from the wire. *Electrified fence.* Not quite so easy that one. Something you have to learn about through painful experience, that one.

Now it must be said that the combination of these two sounds need not have signalled any fear at all in Simon. Had, for example, the dog's growl come from the other side of the electrified fence. That would have been quite acceptable. But it didn't. The electrified fence lay before Simon, the dog's growl came from behind.

'Grrrrrrrrrr,' it went.

Simon turned slowly. From the darkness two evil yellow eyes glared at him. The low growl became a low-to-medium growl.

Simon pondered his predicament.

He recalled reading once in Liza's Dimac martial arts manual, that a guard dog could be easily disabled by a single hard sharp whack upon the tip of the nose. Speed and accuracy were stressed as being quite important factors when attempting this. The dire consequence of an ill-considered blow being an arm down the dog's throat.

Counte Dante, who composed the now legendary manual added that, 'should this occur, the student is advised to reach down deeply into the dog and tear out its still beating heart with a single brisk upward movement.' This, the count wrote, 'rarely fails to show the dog you mean business'.

The evil eyes drew nearer. The evil growl grew louder. And Simon's heart began to beat a little faster. He made a fist. He stood his ground. He took up a Bruce Lee pose.

Then the special chemical in his brain kicked in and Simon ran for his life.

Along the fence he ran in leaps and bounds, the beast upon his heels. It was a big one by the sound of it. A Pit Bull, or one of those Japanese killer jobs the size of a Shetland pony.

As Simon ran he wondered in his terror, Could a man outrun such a dog?

Possibly a fit man could. A man in regular training. A sprinter say, or a hurdler. A hurdler could outrun such a dog and vault the fence for an encore.

But what of a man who wasn't quite so fit? A man who hadn't eaten for a while? A man who had been recently run down by a Jaguar? A man with several large Scotches underneath his belt?

Could such a man outrun such a dog?

No! Such a man could not.

Simon fell, the hound of hell upon him. Fangs and paws and growls and howls.

The howls were Simon's. 'Help!' he shrieked, protecting groin and face as best he could. 'Down, boy, good boy, sit.'

He didn't have a chance and what a death. Savaged to pieces, eaten alive, alone in the dark, without help.

What a hideous way to go.

Simon kicked out, lashed and thrashed, he'd go down fighting at least. The beast bayed for blood and went for his leg.

The evil snarling baying beastly brute was tearing into him. It's acrid breath seared Simon's nostrils, choking up his lungs. The fiendish eyes blazed yellow fury and a dark demonic stiffy humped his leg.

'Hold on a minute there!' Simon ceased his struggles. 'Dark demonic what?'

Hump hump hump, went Dick Godolphin's lurcher, hump hump hump hump hump.

'Hump,' went the TV commentator. '*Humph*rey Gogmagog here.'

(Is that a cunning link or not? *Not?* Well please yourselves then!) 'Reporting live,' went Hump, 'from the dockside in the sun-soaked city of Fogerty. Here to welcome the arrival of Professor Merlin and his interplanetary circus. They're here to perform at the celebrations of his Royal Highness the Grand Duke's birthday. The gangway is down upon this magnificent vessel, gracing the harbour here with its awesome presence and in just a moment now the circus parade will begin. It promises to be a show you'll long remember, so don't touch that dial and we'll be right back after this commercial break.'

The dockside crowds took to cheering, as the strains of *The March of the Gladiators* burst forth from the *SS Salamander's* rusty, yet serviceable, public-address system.

At home, the viewing public of Fogerty, who were enjoying the public holiday, settled down in their armchairs, while an onscreen actress, with the head of a hawk and a nice line in surgically adjusted breasts, extolled the virtues of boil-in-the-bag George.

Professor Merlin rode upon an elephant. It was a very old elephant, by the look of it, and somewhat shaky on its feet. Its rouged cheeks and feathered crown could not disguise this fact. And those who knew the fate awaiting pachyderms who've passed their big-top prime, spoke one unto another saying, 'Lo, here comes five piano keyboards, four umbrella stands, three complete sets of matching grey luggage, two pervert's purses, and one ton of pussycat food.'

'Gee up, Jumbo,' went Professor Merlin. 'Show them what you're made of.'

He looked good, the professor. All in white satin this time. The full ringmaster's rig-out. Top hat, bow tie, tailcoat, jodhpurs, white kid riding boots. He had the whip and this he cracked into the sunlit air.

Jumbo trod the gangway with a dowager's dignity. At each uncertain step, a brave asthmatic trumpet and a bowing of the head.

Behind him came the big parade.

Clowns capered into the crowd. Pierrots and harlequins, Coxcomb and Pantaloon. Tossing favours. Juggling with balls and coloured clubs. A bandaged limb or two was evident.

And all in black upon a black-wheeled chariot, drawn by two jet-coloured mares. All high steps and ostrich plumes. Dr Bacteria, perched like a crow upon the buggy-board and raising a pitch-dark stovepipe hat, exposing a large Elastoplast dressing fastened across his forehead.

Phoenix the Fireproof Fan Dancer, naked neath the two asbestos fans? The males in the crowd crane forward, hoping for a flash of something pink. Fire-eaters breathe their flames upon her as she dances, baring nought, and thick dark smoke wreathes up into the sky.

And put your hands together and gape up. For drifting through this smoke comes Billy Balloon, blown up to a quite preposterous proportion. It's done with helium they say. What a crowd-pleaser! Moored by ropes and playing on a small guitar.

A dwarf now on a giant's shoulders (seeing furthest of the two). The Lady Alostrael upon a unicycle. And about her, twist and turn, half seen, half imagined, what? A throng of sprites? The fairy folk? Can this thing be, and how, sir, is it done?

Roll up, roll up.

Oh no. Four horses now and a fine wide wagon, open to the sides. On this a mighty tank of glass filled up with water, splish and splash. A man within swims underneath the surface. His name is Aquaphagus and around him dart a shoal of silver fish. He's all in gold. His jaws are wide, his teeth flash . . .

But let's pass on.

The Siamese triplets, pretty girls, though one a little bruised of cheek, another black of eye, blow kisses to the crowd and wave small flags. And ride upon three ostriches. In tandem.

Onward goes the big parade.

Poodles on their hindlegs. Lions in a cage. Roaring, rather fierce they seem, though somewhat taken with the moth.

More clowns. A strongman bearing weights. A man whose head revolves upon his shoulders, and a metal sphere revolving on its own accord. How is *that* done?

Some fireworks pop. The streamers stream. Confetti falls. A lone dwarf with a painted smile is last and bows and bows again.

The big parade moves on. The crowd falls in behind it, cheering. Laughing.

Merriment.

The sun shines.

And now the dock, deserted.

Just for a moment there, the magic came and sparkled, now it's gone, into the distance. You can follow it if you want to. But you'll have to run.

Here. Streamers and rose petals. Trinkets and confetti. Dust and dreams and echoes.

All gone now. The circus.

Shame.

Shame indeed!

Because now the public-address system crackles back into life. A hissing as a needle descends on to a black vinyl disc.

Let's Rock 'n' Roll. And deep bass chords boom out across the dock. A rich dark voice sings out.

'Bad to the bone,' it goes. *'B-b-b-b-bad to the bone.'*

The throaty roar of twin pipes, as a gloved hand drums the throttle and out of the belly of the ship it rolls. Low and mean with long extended chrome-dipped forks. It's customized.

And it's a Harley D'.

And who is this a-cruising on it?
All black leather head to toe?
Is this Raymond, young schmuck Raymond?
Someone say it isn't so.

It isn't so. It's Zephyr.

Raymond had always meant to learn how to ride a motor cycle. It had always been one of his ambitions. But, as he'd never had enough money to buy one, and he didn't have any friends silly enough to let him practise on their's . . .

He was now riding pillion.

He was all in black leather though. Which was something.

And he was labouring under the considerable weight of a 7.62mm M134 General Electric mini-gun.

Which was something else again.

So Raymond sang. He gave his lip up to an Elvis curl and sang along to the song.

'Bad to the bone,' he went. 'B-b-b-b-bad to the bone.'

15

'Get off my leg, you flea-pecked mangy crud.'

Simon limped along beside the electrified fence and entered the fortified farmyard by the unfortified open gate. 'Will you get off me *please*?'

The dog would not. It felt passionately for Simon's leg and it would not be moved.

It wasn't worth the struggle. At least the beast had stopped growling now and was just breathing heavily. And as no-one had come out of the farmhouse to answer Simon's cries for help, he felt reasonably assured that they wouldn't hear the heavy breathing either. So he limped on with a will.

He reached the Jag and peeped in through an open window. A shaft of moonlight twinkled on the ignition keys. Handy. Simon reach in, drew them out and slipped them into the pocket of his non-dog-bearing trouser leg. Labouring on to Long Bob's Land Rover, he took a peep into that. No keys. Well, there wouldn't be, would there? Long Bob would have taken out the keys to open his front door. Fair enough.

Simon carefully stooped down and let the air out of the two off-side tyres. Then he limped on towards the house.

Sounds of jollity issued from within. A bit of a party, was it?

Simon eased his way to the kitchen window and put his eye to the unwashed pane. Then drew it back, then looked again, and then cursed bitterly beneath his breath.

A bit of a party was right!

There they all were, ranged about the kitchen table.

The looker, with her back to the window.

Her terrorist chums. Now maskless and revealed to be none other than the members of Roman Candle (the parachute accident not the firework).

And there was Long Bob, at the bottom of the table, drawing the glasses of cider.

And there was Military Dave, toasting Long Bob.

And there was Liza, Simon's girlfriend.

And Liza was sitting on Military Dave's knee, with her arms around his neck.

'Bastards,' said Simon.

And, oh yes, there was all Simon's winnings, piled up neat and nice in the middle of the table.

'Bastards bastards bastards,' whispered Simon. 'This calls for action.'

Lurching with the lurcher, he returned to Long Bob's Land Rover. The kind of action this called for, he decided, was drastic action. Confrontation was out of the question, there were too many of them. So distraction was the best kind of action. Something to distract their attention and get them all out of the kitchen, so that he could nip in and retrieve his winnings.

'And,' whispered Simon, as he dragged his way to the back of the Land Rover and unstrapped the big petrol can, 'there is nothing like a good big fire to cause a bit of distraction.'

Now arson is a pretty heinous crime. And not one Simon had ever dreamed of committing before. But he was angry now. Very angry indeed. And the only question in his mind was, what was the best thing to set on fire?

The Land Rover? No, that was too close to the Jag in which he intended to make his escape. Something else. Something on the far side of the farmyard, well away from the gate. Something that would go up with a really big whoosh. What?

Beyond the farmhouse, silver tinged with moonlight, stood the chicken sheds.

'Perfect,' said Simon.

Perfect? What was he saying?

'Perfect. Naturally I shall release all the chickens.'

Thank God for that. Some spark of decency at least.

'They should add considerably to the confusion.'

No spark of decency at all!

Simon glared down at the lurcher on his leg. 'Haven't you finished yet?'

The lurcher had not.

'Perhaps a chicken dinner might persuade you.'

The chicken sheds were wide and wooden, windowless and wretched. They looked near to collapse anyway. Simon might well have convinced himself that he was doing Long Bob a favour by burning them down. At least he could then claim the insurance money and get some new ones built. But such false justifications for the appalling act he was about to commit did not enter Simon's mind at all.

'The biggest one would be favourite,' he said, as he trudged on, burdened heavily by dog and petrol can.

The chickens were a-clucking. It's a horrid noise that chickens make. Like the babbling of the insane.

Simon didn't care for chickens. Pigs he liked, except for their eyelashes, which were far too human-looking. But chickens, no. Stupid brainless things were chickens.

The door to the big shed wasn't locked. Just bolted. Simon drew the bolt. The plan was straightforward. Nip in, shut the door, switch on the light. The sheds had no windows, it wouldn't be seen. Splash the petrol all about. Throw open the door, shoo out the chickens. Light blue touch paper and retire to a safe distance. Simple.

'I'm gonna burn your hen house down,' sang Simon, to the tune of an old Paul Young song.

Now, it was dark in there. And the first thing Simon noticed was the smell. It was that smell that he had smelt earlier. The weird one, above and beyond the one of chicken pooh. It was really strong in here.

'What a wang, now where's that switch?'

The second thing he noticed was the noise. Or rather the sudden lack of it. The chickens had ceased all their cluckings, which was strange, considering that a strange man with a dog on his leg had unexpectedly entered their shed.

Simon's searching fingers found the light switch and he thumbed it down. Neon tubes fizzed and popped and came alive to bathe the shed with a harsh and unforgiving glare.

Simon blinked, and as his eyes adjusted to the light, a small but significant gasp of surprise escaped his open mouth.

The outward appearance of the chicken shed certainly belied what lay concealed within. This was *not* your average run-down Bramfield chicken house. This was more like some animal research establishment, or something.

It was clean. It was clinically clean. The floor was spotless, white linoleum, scrubbed. Along the newly painted walls, polished aluminium racks supported hundreds of glass-sided nesting boxes. Four tiers of them to each side and running the length of the shed. At the far end, a hospital screen concealed something. Now more than a little intrigued, Simon put down the petrol can and stiff-legged the lurcher, to see just what.

Three steps along and he stopped. Something wasn't right in here. And that something, or part of it anyway, was the chickens.

Simon glanced about at them. They all sat very still and they were all staring intently at him. And though chickens can never look friendly, these birds looked decidedly – what? Evil, thought Simon, decidedly evil. And *that* wasn't right with chickens.

Simon gave a shiver. It was cold in here too. Colder than outside, it seemed. His breath steamed before his face. Was this place refrigerated. *That* wasn't right, was it?

Simon swung his lurcher leg and found it lurcher-free. The dog was now cowering at his side. Its hackles were up, its lips were drawn back, its eyes were fixed on the hospital screen.

'What is going on here?' Simon considered the dog and the chickens and his steamy breath and the hospital screen. 'Right. Let's have a look.'

Simon sidled forward in the way that only he could do. Chickens to the right of him and chickens to the left of him shifted and grumbled. Every little beady eye upon him. 'Bugger this.'

And as each step took him nearer to the screen, the smell grew stronger. Simon still didn't know what it was, but at least he knew now where it was coming from.

The chickens were becoming more and more agitated, and as Simon put his hand out to the screen, their voices rose to one horrible compelling shriek.

And then stopped. Fell silent, all as one. Which put the wind up Simon something wicked.

'Let's get this done and get out.' Simon swung the screen aside.

The smell was overpowering, but it wasn't this that caused him to lurch back and gag into his hands.

It was what he *saw* that did that!

Revealed was a steel table, supporting a large, glass-sided incubator, linked to a refrigeration unit and lit from above by a row of white neon tubes.

Within the incubator something lay on a red velvet cushion.

Something naked and new-born-baby sized. Something vile.

Much of it was human, much was not. The chest and stomach were covered by a soft feathery down. The plump little arms and legs terminated in unappealing chicken claws. The tiny head was bald, but for a Mohawk crest of jet-black feathers.

Simon looked on in horror, as the head turned slowly towards him. Human eyes of piercing green, but where the nose and mouth should have been, a cruel beak.

The eyes glared at Simon, the cruel beak moved, a long black tongue lolled out. Demonic, hellish, cold dark evil.

'Dear God.' Simon stood for a moment trembling.

Then the special chemical inside his head conveyed to him a very explicit set of instructions. 'Put things back as you found them and run for your life,' they were.

With a wobbly hand Simon rolled the screen back into place and backed down the shed with growing acceleration. As he neared the door he turned to run, tripped over the petrol can and fell flat on his face.

'Torch it.' Simon struggled to his feet. 'I don't know what you are,' he whispered as he wrenched the cap from the petrol can, but you're evil and you're gonna burn.'

'Oh no he ain't, you know.' Simon heard the voice and felt the cold hard touch of steel against his neck. A cold hard touch which he correctly deduced to be that of a shotgun barrel.

'Oh dear,' Simon said.

B-b-b-b-bad to the bone. The Harley cruised along the thoroughfares of Fogerty. They were certainly handsome. A bit like the set from D.W. Griffith's *Intolerance*, or was it *The Birth of a Nation*? The one with those huge sort of Babylonian steps and the statuettes of the elephants on vast pillars. *Intolerance*, it was definitely *Intolerance*.

But not in the original black and white. This was in glorious *Technicolor*.

'There's nobody much about, is there?' Raymond called to Zephyr.

'All gone to the circus,' Zephyr called back.

'So where are the kidnapped people being held?'

'At the auction house. Marked on your map.'

'Marked on my map?' said Raymond thoughtfully. Now I wonder exactly which map that might be? he thought, even more thoughtfully.

'The one I tucked into your jacket as we were leaving the ship,' called Zephyr the Miraculous.

'Ah, that one, got it, thank you.'

Naturally it was in English, as were the street signs of Saturn's capital city. Many things would eventually be made clear to Raymond. Eventually, but not now.

For now he would just have to content himself with cruising along behind this marvellous being, on the bike she had conjured from thin air, wearing the clothes she had conjured from thin air, and carrying the preposterous gun she had likewise conjured from that same thin, yet apparently quite malleable air. It was all quite impossible, of course, but it was one hell of an adventure.

'I can't hold on to this ridiculous gun and read the map at the same time,' called Raymond. 'Some things really *are* impossible. Could you stop the bike for a moment please?'

Zephyr pulled the Harley over to the side of the road, switched off the engine and swung the heavy machine effortlessly back on to its stand. Then she climbed from the saddle.

'You really look great in that outfit,' said Raymond.

'Thank you.' Zephyr did a little bow. 'Now show me that map please, because we really don't have a lot of time. And I don't think we've stopped in a particularly nice neighbourhood.'

Raymond glanced about. It wasn't very nice at all. They had somehow wandered off the main thoroughfare and now, rather than being in Uptown Memphis, they were in Downtown Cairo. It had that certain look about it which says 'stranger beware'. Raymond hated it without a second thought.

Now, there are many things that can be guaranteed to draw a crowd on the street. An accident will do it, or two woman fighting, or sometimes even a man on a soapbox. A Harley Davidson always draws one. And a Harley Davidson accompanied by a beautiful woman dressed head to toe in black leather. That will draw one. Check it out.

Zephyr unfolded the map.

'Having a spot of bother?' asked a passing jackal-head, in a loud check suit. He put Raymond instantly in mind of Lon Chaney snr. in his now legendary performance as *The Wolf Man*. Or was it *The Werewolf*?

Or was it Warner Oland in the 1935 production of *Werewolf of London*? And did it really matter anyway?

'Perhaps I might be of assistance?' asked wolfman in a greasy, if well-educated tone.

Zephyr ignored him.

'Tourist, are you?' Wolfman did admiring lookings at both girl and bike, while pointedly ignoring Raymond. 'Let me guess, you're from Eden, aren't you?'

Zephyr turned away. Raymond pondered 'Eden'. Was that how the outer Earth was known, Eden?

'Lovely planet.' Wolfman flicked imaginary dust from an ample lapel and grinned over Zephyr's shoulder. 'Went there for my hols last year. Pongs a bit though, don't it? Be all the better once they've plugged those holes in the poles up, eh, doncha think?'

'Think?' Zephyr gave the jackal-head a haughty once-over. '*I* think, therefore I am from Eden. Hub of knowledge and racial purity. Go and foul a footpath, will you?'

Seemingly oblivious to insult, or perhaps just like Simon, in revelling a worthy challenge, wolfman continued without pause on his line of chat.

Raymond was growing uneasy and the arrival on the scene of two more Saturnians, with an eye for a Harley Davidson and a woman in black leather, did nothing to halt the growth of this unease.

A pair of falcon-headed fellow-me-lads in sportswear and trainers.

'Don't touch the bike,' said Raymond, as one reached out an inquisitive hand.

'Say,' said falcon-head. 'This is a really nice bike.'

'Piss off,' replied Raymond, right off the cuff.

A pair of sparsely clad hawk-faced females, who had lately appeared from what was very probably a house of ill repute, tittered at this.

'And you,' said Raymond.

'What's happening here?' asked an ibis lady in a straw hat. 'Has there been an accident?'

'There will be in a minute.' Raymond made meaningful motions with his great big gun.

'That's never real,' sneered the young falcon fellow-me-lad. 'Hey, Zip, come over here and show the man *your* gun.'

'Zephyr, I think we really should be going now.'

'Give us a ride on your motor bike,' said the ibis lady in the straw hat. 'Just once round the block.'

'Leave the bike alone please. Zephyr, come on.'

Now, it probably wasn't the wolfman who pinched Zephyr's bottom. It was probably the big-shouldered hawkman with the broad-brimmed hat, who ran the house of ill repute and had just come out to see what his girls were up to. It was the wolfman Zephyr turned and hit though. Right on the tip of the nose. A single hard sharp whack. Counte Dante would have loved it. The growing crowd were not best pleased.

Zip drew out his gun. It was a Saturnday-night special (sorry).

Raymond tried to fire his into the air, but as he had no idea how the thing actually worked, he swung it instead at the gun-toting falcon, missed and carried by the mini-gun's considerable weight, fell off the back of the bike.

Things now happened fast.

Zip leapt astride the fallen Raymond, the other falcon leapt astride the bike. Hawkman grabbed Zephyr around the waist and hoisted her into the air. The ibis lady in the straw hat tried to drag away the mini-gun and the young falcon tried to get the Harley started.

'No!' shouted Raymond.

Zip pulled the trigger upon him.

There was a blinding flash, a very loud bang and then there was screaming and shouting.

Raymond, whose eyes had been tightly shut, awaiting the arrival of Zip's bullet, now opened them again. He was still in the land of the living. But now this land had gone mad.

Zip was sprawled several yards away. A swordfish saw

protruded from his chest. The rest of the fish flapped
behind him in the gutter.

'Aaaaagh!' went Raymond.

The young falcon was screaming, but not for the loss
of his friend. The Harley he'd been sitting on was now a
tiger. He held it by the ears, it turned its head and—

'Aaaaagh!' went Raymond once again.

Hawkman too was screaming. Big and burley though
he was, he was never a match for the bear he now held.
The bear with the claws that went—

'Aaaaagh!' Raymond covered his eyes.

And it was, Aaaaagh! all over the place. The ibis lady
with the straw hat fought with what was no longer a
mini-gun, but a snake with a bad attitude. Wolfman was
down and out, a hyena at his throat. A storm of bats was
going for the running, screaming rest.

'Take me home,' wailed Raymond, adopting the foetal
position. 'Take me home, I don't want any more.'

'Be calm now.' Zephyr's voice was at his ear. 'Get back
on to the bike.'

'The bike?' Raymond opened an eye. The bike was
back. Standing there amongst the bodies and the blood.

'The bike. Get on. We're out of here, as they say.'

'Out of here,' said the man with the shotgun. 'Out of here
now, I say.'

'I was just cleaning up,' explained shivering Simon.
'Long Bob employs me to keep the place clean. I was
just getting some stains off the floor with this can of
methylated spirits. All done now, I'll be off home then.'

'You're a lying bastard, ain't ya?' said Dick Godolphin, for indeed it was he. 'But full marks for trying.
Get a move on now or I'll shoot you dead.'

Simon's knees wouldn't work properly. They kept
knocking together when he walked. His teeth were
chattering too. And all the further lies he told Dick the
poacher, as that man prodded him across the farmyard,
sounded hollow, even to Simon himself.

Because Simon now was really truly scared.

'Stuck your nose in the wrong place this time,' Dick told him. 'Now you gotta speak to the man.'

'I'll give you lots of money,' Simon pleaded.

'We got all your money already,' said Dick. 'Now we got you too.'

Simon wrung his hands and made a face of great despair. 'Your bloody dog is up my leg again.'

Happily the farmhouse door was only on the latch. Happily, that is, for Simon, whose head it was that bashed it open, as Dick Godolphin clubbed him with his gun.

Simon fell directly into the kitchen, stirring the jollifiers from their jollifying. Liza spilled from the lap of Military Dave. 'Simon,' she said, adjusting her bra through her T-shirt. Through *Simon's* T-shirt. 'What a surprise this is.'

'What a surprise indeed.' Long Bob put down the jam jar he had been drinking from. 'Anybody with him?' he asked Dick.

The poacher shook his head. 'The bastard's all on his own. He was about to torch the chicken house. His Majesty—'

Long Bob put his finger to his lips. 'You really are a nuisance,' he said to the fellow on the floor with the lurcher up his leg.

Simon clutched at his skull. The headache was back. 'This man is mad,' he declared, pointing at the poacher. 'I was taking an evening stroll when he pounced on me with his gun. He should be arrested. Kindly allow me the use of your phone and I'll call the police.'

'You have to give him full marks for trying,' said Military Dave.

'I already did,' said Dick. 'I give him a good clout with my gun too.'

'Where is the book?' asked Long Bob. 'Does he have the book?'

'Book?' went Simon. 'What book is this?'

Dick kicked Simon in the ribs.

'Ouch,' went Simon doubling up.

Dick bent down and rooted through Simon's pockets. 'He don't have the book,' said Dick.

And Simon didn't. Because Simon had left the book in the hideaway bush. Which seemed to him as good a hideaway for it as any.

'Where is it, Simon?' Long Bob loomed above. 'We know you've got it, otherwise you could never have won on the horses. We need that book very badly. It wasn't intended for you. Where is it?'

Long Bob took a kick at the cowerer. The cowerer rolled nimbly aside, dragging Dick's dog with him.

'The Scribe's got it,' Simon lied. 'I was round at his place just now. He's had it all along. It was him that told me which horses to back.'

'The Scribe told you?' Long Bob stroked at his big full beard. It was not a beard that had been previously mentioned, but it was a beard he had about him nonetheless. And he stroked it now.

'Dick,' said Long Bob, 'go and see the Scribe. Tell him what Simon's just told us. Bring the book back to us.'

'I'll go with you,' said Simon. 'In fact, if you like, I'll go for you.'

'You'll stay right here,' said Long Bob. 'Let us all pray that he does not return with disappointing news.'

Let us pray he does not return at all, prayed Simon. 'Oi, Dick, you scumbag, don't forget your dog.'

The farmhouse door closed upon one man and his dog and Simon climbed most painfully to his feet. 'Any chance of a drink?' he asked.

'Sit down and shut up.'

'Absolutely, Bob, yes.' Simon dropped into the one vacant chair and smiled a sickly smile about the table. As no positive response was forthcoming, Simon hunched up and peeped at his winnings. Oh so near, yet oh so far away.

Long Bob placed a jar of cider between Simon and his dreams.

'You're in a bit of shit here, aren't you?' said the chicken farmer.

'Shit? Me? Simon flashed his teeth as best he could. 'I am a tad confused, as it happens. What exactly is going on around here?'

'You saw for yourself in the shed.'

'I didn't see anything.'

Long Bob sniffed at Simon. 'I can smell him on you. I can smell your fear as well.'

'I don't know what you mean.' Simon took the jar up in a shaky hand and gulped away its contents in a single go.

'You know, but you don't understand.' Long Bob patted Simon on the shoulder. 'No need to cringe,' he said. 'Not just yet anyhow.'

'What *is* going on?'

Long Bob drew Simon off another glass and passed it to him. 'What is going on, eh? Well, I shall tell you. After all, it won't go beyond these four walls, will it?'

'Positively not.' Simon crossed his heart and swigged his cider.

'Because *you* won't be going beyond these four walls, ever again.'

'Oh,' said Liza. 'That seems a shame.'

'Thank you, Liza darling,' said Simon. 'I love you as I always have.'

'His Majesty requires a sacrifice,' declared Long Bob. 'I nominate Simon. All in favour please say aye.'

'Aye,' said all in favour, all but Simon. All including Liza.

'I nominate Dick's dog,' said Simon. 'Come on now, a joke's a joke. A sacrifice indeed. Could I use your toilet, by the way?'

'Sit still.' Long Bob fixed Simon with a most unsettling stare. 'Sit still and shut up and I'll tell you everything.'

Simon sat still and shut up and quaked very quietly in his boots.

'Now is the special hour,' intoned Long Bob. 'Now is the time as no time's been before.'

189

Simon knocked back his cider. Bad stuff's a-comin', thought he.

'The End Times,' quoth Long Bob.

Oh dear, thought Simon.

'The End Times draw near. Ominous signs and portents fill the heavens. Omens of the coming of Ragnarok.

'Of Gotterdammerung,' cried Military Dave.

'Quite so,' said Long Bob, 'quite so. And unto us a child is born. Unto us a king is given. As the sky grows dark and the sun falls from its orbit.'

Orbit? thought Simon. Oh dear, oh dear.

'As the air grows rank and the soil crops wither and the beasts of the Earth crawl upon their bellies, gasping, gasping,' Long Bob did dramatic throat-clutching mimes. 'Then *he* shall rise to save us. He who is rising even now. He whom you have seen. The new born one. The born again.'

'Praise be unto him,' called out the looker.

'Praise be unto him,' agreed the members of Roman Candle, in a three-part harmony.

'Praise be unto him,' sang out the other praise-be-untoers.

Simon somehow dared to ask. 'Please, praise be on to *who*?'

'His Majesty . . .' Long Bob flung his arms aloft, then bowed down to the table. 'His majesty whose time is now. His Majesty Lord Satan.'

'S . . . S . . . S . . . Satan?' said Simon.

'Satan,' said Long Bob. 'Or, as we correctly pronounce his sacred name . . . SATE-HEN.'

16

'What happened back there?' Raymond clung to Zephyr as she sped the bike along. 'Those people dead. It was horrible. Horrible.'

He no longer carried the big mini-gun. He had just seen what death looked like up close. He did not wish to see it again. 'Thank you,' he said.

'Thank you?' Zephyr smiled over her shoulder.

'For saving my life. Could you stop the Harley now, I'm going to be sick.'

'We don't have time I'm afraid. But you'll be all right. Just hang on tight, I know where we're going now.'

And so Raymond hung on tight. The Harley took a left and then a right and he hung on.

'There'll be trouble about that back there, won't there?' he called to Zephyr.

'Lots of trouble, I should think. So just hang on, we're almost there.'

And there they almost were.

Ahead loomed a serious pyramid. It looked like marble, but it wasn't. It was plastic. The auction house logo flashed from the golden cone on the top. In neon.

'Is this it?'

'This is it. Now let's be swift.'

'Be swift?'

'Act like an Edenite. You know how it's done.'

'Act like an Edenite. And that's what the upper world is called then, is it? Eden? As in the Garden of Eden?'

'Later.' Zephyr swung the big bike into an elegant avenue. Lines of obelisks (plastic), fruit trees (plastic) and nice clipped hedges (plastic as well, but they all looked very impressive to Raymond).

'I hate this planet,' he said.

'Remember,' called Zephyr, 'bullshit baffles brains. You can do it. And if you can't well then I'll—'

'No!' That swordfish saw was still fresh in his mind. 'I'll handle it.'

Before the hulking pyramid there was a grand-looking gateway. This had one of those lifty-up barriers and one of those little security guard's huts. You know the ones. They have them at the gates of car-parks and factories and things like that.

They're always the same and they always contain a hook to hang your coat on, a miniature television set, an electric fire for winter, an electric fan for summer, an electric kettle for the rest of the year and for boiling up water for tea, a seat with a personal cushion and a selection of 'harmless girlie magazines' which, when brought forward as evidence by the prosecution, are generally referred to as 'hardcore pornography of the most debased and sordid kind'.

They always have the same sort of smell inside them, these huts. A musty, organic kind of smell. Best not dwelt upon.

As Raymond and Zephyr approached, a large dark hawk-head appeared from the hut. He had a neat blue uniform. He was carrying a clipboard.

Raymond did not give him the benefit of the doubt. He simply hated him on sight.

Zephyr drew the Harley to a halt. Raymond climbed down from the pillion and made a fuss of his jacket and trousers, straightening lapels, dusting out creases. He quiffed out his hair at the front.

'Can I help you?' asked the guard, when he could stand no more of it.

Raymond glanced in his direction, as if noticing him for the first time. 'Raise the barrier at once,' he sniffed. 'I wish to go inside.'

'Nature of business?' The guard took up Raymond's haughty sniff.

'Export representatives from Eden. Get a move on now and let us pass.'

'I don't think so. Do you have an appointment?'

'We do not require one. Stand aside upon the instant.'

The hawk-head shook his hawk-like head and consulted his clipboard. 'You will require not only an appointment, but official government clearance, entry permits stamped with today's date, positive proof of identity, and I will need to see your interworld passports, your visas and your vaccination certificates.'

'Pah!' said Raymond.

'And it will be necessary for me to give the young woman an intimate body search.'

'*Why?*' went an outraged Raymond.

'Are you kidding?' asked the guard.

'Stand aside, you odious lout.' Raymond took a step forward. The guard before the barrier barred his way. Tough-looking hawk-head, the guard.

Raymond puffed out his chest. 'I demand that you let us pass this minute. We are here to inspect the latest consignment of "George".'

'Sorry, pal. It's more than my job's worth. Back the way you came and have a nice day now, won't you.'

Zephyr made urgent tongue-clicking sounds.

'I can handle this,' said Raymond. 'Now just you see here,' he told the guard. 'I am acting under direct instructions from my good friend Binky.'

'Binky? Do you mean—'

'His Royal Majesty the Grand Duke. Yes.'

'You are a personal friend of His Royal Majesty?'

'I am.' Raymond preened at his hair. 'A personal friend.'

The guard looked Raymond up and down. 'And my arse smells of snowdrops from a curate's garden. Take a hike.'

'Take a letter, Ms Zephyr,' said Raymond.

The pencil and the notepad materialized once more in Zephyr's hands. 'Certainly, sir,' she said.

'To His Royal Highness Grand Duke Fogarty, The Palace of Celestial Pleasure, Number One, The Big Posh Road, City of Fogerty. Dear Binky. Following your explicit instructions, I proceeded with great urgency to the auction house to inspect the consignment of "George" to be served tonight at the special state dinner in honour of your poor sick son Colin.

'However, when I explained the nature of this royal mission, to whit, that contaminated specimens were possibly being held for sale, which, if served, would likely poison yourself, your royal household, poor sick son Colin included, I was denied access.

'It is therefore my recommendation that in the interests of health and hygiene, the entire auction house complex be razed to the ground and the would-be assassins brought in for interrogation, trial and execution. The gatekeeper will, I have no doubt, offer up the names of his fellow conspirators, when put to the rigours of extreme torture for a week or so. His full name is . . . ' Raymond paused. 'What is your full name, by the way?' he asked the guard.

But the guard was already lifting the barrier. 'Go straight on through,' he said politely. 'And *do* have a nice day.'

'That was very good,' called Zephyr, as they swept into the pyramid.

'Thanks,' Raymond grinned. 'But I just copied the professor, of course.'

'Yes, but you did it your way.'

'Well, not really. I did it Simon's way, as it happens.'

'This would be the Simon you mention about every five minutes?'

'He's my best friend.' Raymond clung on as Zephyr did some nifty cornering. 'I tried to pretend I was him, you see. Use his nerve. Use his bullshit to baffle brains.

He's really good at that kind of thing. Simon can always talk his way out of trouble.'

'Sounds a most interesting man this Simon.'

'Oh he is.' Raymond laughed. 'I'll tell you what. I can't imagine there ever being a situation that he couldn't talk his way out of. Cool as they come is Simon. Cool as they come.'

Simon had a sweat on. 'S . . . S . . . S . . . Sate-Hen?' he stammered. 'You can't be saying this.'

'It's in the bird.' Long Bob did fluttering bird-like finger motions. 'I never knew it, you see. I thought that chickens were just chickens. But they're not. They know. And now *we* know.'

'We know,' chorused the table sitters. 'We of B.E.A.S.T. know all.'

Simon knew he shouldn't really ask, but he really had to know. 'What does B.E.A.S.T. stand for?' was the question.

'B.E.A.S.T.?' Long Bob leaned closer to Simon. Simon shrank back in his chair. 'B.E.A.S.T.,' said the chicken farmer, 'stands for Bramfielders Eagerly Awaiting Satanic Transmogrification, of course.'

'Oh yes, of course.' Simon grinned painfully. 'I thought that was probably it. Satanic Transmogrification, right.'

'We are the chosen ones, you see. For He is hatched unto us. Thousands of generations of fowl, billions and billions of chickens, all leading towards Him. I had a dream, you see. A vision. They opened my eyes. They spoke unto me.'

'The chickens?' asked Simon.

'The chickens,' said Long Bob.

Oh dear, oh dear, oh dear, thought Simon.

'I was drunk,' said Long Bob.

'I wish I was,' said Simon.

'I fell down. In the chicken shed. And they spoke

unto me. They can speak, you know, chickens. If they want to. They spoke to me. They told me that they had chosen me.'

Simon didn't speak.

'Chosen me to be the father of The Born Again.'

Simon didn't speak once more.

'And so I gave my seed unto the great mother hen.'

Simon did speak now. 'You shagged a frigging chicken?' he said.

Long Bob's hands caught Simon by the throat and dragged him from his chair. 'Hold your blasphemous tongue!' roared the father of Sate-Hen.

'All right, I'm sorry.' Simon's hands were now in amongst the money. It felt *so* good. And he *really* wanted it back. But with the money, or without the money, his first priority was immediate escape. His second to call in the Army to nuke out the *Horror in the Henhouse*.[1]

Simon recalled that brigadier who ran U.N.I.T. in *Doctor Who*. He'd be the fellow to phone. U.N.I.T. versus B.E.A.S.T. That sounded about right.

So. It was time to be off.

'Right, that's enough.' Simon jerked free of the chicken farmer's grip. 'That is *quite* enough. You're doing it all wrong. I just knew that you would. It's lucky I arrived when I did.'

'Is he pissed?' asked Military Dave. 'Or what?'

'*You* are not even supposed to be here.' Simon told Dave. '*You* are supposed to be at home, awaiting an important phone call.'

'What is he talking about?' Dave looked bewildered.

'And you three.' Simon turned to the men of Roman Candle. 'You should all be at The Jolly Gardeners for the fight.'

'Fight?' asked a Candle called Kevin. 'What fight.'

'The one you have with Paul the barman.'

'Why?' It was Kevin's turn to look bewildered.

[1] A Kilgore Sprout tale of terror.

'I can't tell you that.' Simon turned to Long Bob. 'I can't tell him that, can I?'

'Can't you?' Long Bob looked a little bewildered. But mostly he just looked barking mad. 'What *are* you talking about?'

'The book.' Simon gave Long Bob a wink of an eye and a flash of some teeth. 'The book from the future. The book you so desperately want. The book that *I* have.'

'Aha!' cried Bob. 'Aha!'

'And the one that I've read. All the way through, from cover to cover.'

'He's lying.' The looker curled her most attractive lip. 'Don't believe a word he says.'

'That's good coming from her.' Simon directed all his remarks towards Long Bob. Experience told him that if you start having three-way conversations, you can get easily side-tracked.

'Why is it good coming from her?' Long Bob asked.

'Because of the stroke she tries to pull with all the money I win tomorrow.'

'Tomorrow?' asked Military Dave.

'Are you still here? You'll miss that phone call.'

'Thanks.' Military Dave got up to leave.

'Sit down, Dave,' ordered Long Bob.

Dave sat down again.

'What *do* you know, Simon?' asked the chicken farmer.

'All of it really. That's why I'm telling you you're doing it all wrong. You were not supposed to rough me up and threaten me. You are supposed to be winning me over to the cause. That's how it's written in the book. I join B.E.A.S.T. and I take all this money and I put it all on an accumulator tomorrow. And I win us millions and millions. That's how you can afford to build the fortress and buy the TV station for His Majesty. Cor, there's a bit in chapter thirty-two, where the TV station gets surrounded by this military taskforce, U.N.I.T. I think they're called. And I save His Majesty by—'

'Stop!' Long Bob rammed his fists over his ears. 'You're not supposed to be telling it all to us now. We're not supposed to know it all yet. That's not how it works.'

'Hang about.' The looker pointed an accusing finger at Simon. 'He can't know all this, he's got—'

'Short-term memory loss,' said Simon hurriedly. 'That's why the book came to me, I suppose. Tomorrow I won't remember any of this. Anything I read in the book. Anything I've seen here tonight. I think I must have been chosen by some great power, to be a humble, but significant, pawn in a mighty cosmic game.'

'He's lying,' said the looker. 'Don't you see, he's making it all up.'

'Well you would say that, wouldn't you? And you do, it's in the book.'

'Long Bob, tell him . . .'

'Shut up!' Long Bob waved his hands about. 'Shut up! I have to think about this.'

'He does,' said Simon, adding for good measure. 'Except when he does it in the book, he's supposed to be wearing this special uniform. Very elegant, it is.'

'Aha!' went Long Bob again. 'Describe this uniform to me. In precise detail.'

'Certainly,' agreed Simon, who could recall in precise detail the weird uniform he'd secretly observed Long Bob wearing on the morning before last when Simon had come to take the big Allen Scythe over the bottom field beneath the chicken farm. Actually, Simon wondered whether now might be the time to broach the subject of the stolen Allen Scythe. Probably not, he considered. '. . . and with a pair of chicken wings fastened to the helmet,' he concluded.

All present, Simon included, were now all staring at Long Bob.

'It's true,' said that man. 'In every detail. I was going to put it on later to show you all.'

Handy, thought Simon. 'My fault,' he said. 'I think I must have arrived too early. Shall I go out and come back in again?'

'No,' said the chicken farmer. 'I want to see this book. And I want to see it now.'

'Not a chance,' said Simon. 'That might really screw things up. You'll just have to trust me on this.'

'Bugger that,' said the looker.

'Let him finish,' said Long Bob.

'You see,' said Simon momentarily lapsing into the truth, 'there is no mention of B.E.A.S.T. at all in the book. In fact, the book says that I gave my winnings to charity.'

'Ah.' said Long Bob.

'Ring a bell?' asked Simon.

'That's what we agreed to put in the book, yes.'

'And that's why you'll have to trust me. The book won't work for you because you have to put lies like that in it to keep this operation secret. It will only work for me. Because I'm in it all the way, through and through, just a pawn, you need me to make everything work out.' The truth that Simon had momentarily lapsed into, had now lapsed away. He was growing in confidence. Lying was really what Simon did best. Well, lying and sex. And looking after number one. They sort of tied for first place.

'I must act on my own, according to what is decreed in the book. You will just have to trust me. And now I really must be going before the police arrive.'

'Police?' The cry was a communal cry.

'The police who are currently after me for the suspected murder of Raymond and that traitorous woman there.' Simon returned the finger of accusation. 'They'll be arriving at any moment now. So I'd best get this money safely out of here and be gone. You'd better meet them at the gate and tell them you haven't seen me, Bob. You don't want them searching the chicken sheds, do you?'

'No, I er . . .' Long Bob got all in a dither.

'He's lying,' said the looker.

'He's not,' said Liza. 'I met Paul earlier. He was stacking crates outside The Jolly Gardeners. He told me the police were on their way to the Scribe's in search of Simon.'

'And the Scribe knows I've come here,' said Simon.

'I er . . .' went Long Bob.

'We must go and give this Paul a kicking,' said Kevin.

'Now you get it,' said Simon. 'So. Do I take my leave now, or what?'

Long Bob looked at Simon. Simon looked at Long Bob. The Roman Candles looked at one another. The looker looked at Liza.

Liza looked at Military Dave. Military Dave looked at his watch. 'I'll miss that important phone call,' he said.

'Go,' Long Bob told Simon. 'But—'

'But?' asked Simon, who was already stuffing his well-won-back-winnings into his pockets.

'If you play us false, by even a tenth of a degree then . . .'

'I know,' said Simon. 'I do not recall the exact words in the book, but I think there was a reference to a car battery, a set of jump leads and certain tender parts of my anatomy.'

'Uncanny,' said Long Bob, who really didn't have that kind of mind. 'Exactly what I was going to say. So be warned.'

'I consider myself warned. So, give me ten minutes' start, then do what you're supposed to do. Tell the police when they arrive that you are just locking up for the night and that you've seen no-one.'

'Hold on,' cried the looker. 'You can't let him get away like this.'

'Oh yes,' said Simon. 'And when you jump me outside the bookies tomorrow to steal all the money back, keep an eye on her.'

'I will,' said Long Bob. 'And thanks, Simon.'

'Only doing my bit for the cause. Hail Sate-Hen and farewell.'

'Hail Sate-Hen and farewell.'

Simon left the farmhouse at the trot. He ducked across the moonlit yard, threw open the door of the Jag and leapt inside.

And *'Yes!'* he went as he fumbled the keys into the ignition. 'I beat you all, you bastards. Beat you all.'

He turned the key, the engine roared. He gave the lights full beam. And with another *Yes!* and a small punch in the air, Simon drove the car full pelt out of the farmyard and away into the safety of the night.

He'd done it. He'd actually done it. Escaped from those lunatics and with his money and everything. He'd telephone U.N.I.T. from the first call box he came to. Well, perhaps not the first. The first one in the next town. Or the town after that. Or perhaps from onboard the cross channel ferry. Or from France.

'Boom shanka,' said Simon. 'Boom shanka boom boom boom.'

'Boom boom boom,' echoed a voice from the seat behind. It was the voice of Police Inspector D'Eath.

'Aaaagh!' went Simon, steering all over the place.

'Easy does it, sir.' The inspector's Scargill crown rose from behind Simon's seat. 'We don't want to go running over any innocent pedestrians, do we? Is that drink I smell on your breath, by the way? And are you the rightful owner of this car?'

'I,' said Simon. 'I . . . I . . . I . . .'

'If you'd be so kind as to just pull up at the police road block ahead, sir. I think we can consider you good and nicked this time.'

17

'I think we're here,' said Raymond. And they were. At the pyramid's heart. In the stockyard.

It was huge. A soccer pitch and a half of it. High ceilinged. Concrete. Not a nice place to be. The air smelt rank and the ambience really sucked. A terrible Dachau gloom made the hairs on Raymond's neck stand up and his spirits fall down low.

There were pens and cages, but these were thankfully unoccupied. There was a lorry park, with big spanking new lorries parked in it. There were some cranes, some fork-lift trucks and little sort of jeep things for getting about in. All were very Earth-like in design.

And there were racks. Long aluminium racks. A bit like egg racks from fridge doors. But magnified. And these supported the bubbles. Two hundred bubbles. Each containing its pitiful cargo. A single crouched-up, sleeping, naked human being.

'Aw God!' Raymond shuddered. 'This is sick. This is really sick. I can't deal with this.'

'Perk up.' Zephyr climbed from the Harley. 'You've come this far. You can do the rest.'

'I can't, you know,' said Raymond, faintly and with pathos.

'Of course you can. So. What do you want to do? Smash all the bubbles and set the people free?'

'NO!' Raymond threw up his hands and fell off the back of the bike. 'Not here. Two hundred naked people in a state of shock. Don't even think about it. We must let them sleep on and somehow get them back to the ship as they are now. Release them there. Carefully. One by one.'

'You're a real humanitarian, Raymond.'

'Thank you.' Raymond picked himself up from the floor and dusted at his leathers. 'Go on then,' he said.

'Go on, what?'

'Do your magic,' said Raymond. 'Turn yourself into a helicopter or something and transport all the people back to the ship.'

'I can't do that.'

'My turn to say, of course you can. You magicked up the Harley, didn't you?'

'Yes, I did, but—'

'So you can magic up a big lorry, or something. Why not magic up one like,' Raymond pointed, 'that one over there. It's got a special rack on the top for transporting the bubbles and everything.'

Zephyr looked at Raymond and Raymond looked at Zephyr.

'Yes?' said Raymond. 'What?'

Zephyr shook her beautiful head. 'Can you drive a big lorry?'

'Actually I can.' Raymond folded his arms.

'Like for instance the one you just pointed at?'

'If it's the same in the cab as an Earth lorry, yes.'

'Well, why don't you just drive that one over here and we'll use that?'

'Oh,' said Raymond. 'I see. Yes, right, OK.'

There was nobody about. All off enjoying the national holiday, Raymond supposed, at the circus or watching it on TV. Raymond climbed into the cab of the big spanking new lorry with the special rack on the top for transporting the bubbles and everything.

It looked just like any other lorry cab that Raymond had ever seen. Why was that?

Raymond perused the steering wheel. On the glossy boss at the wheel's centre were printed the words ACME Big Truck Company, Eden.

'Well, that explains that, doesn't it?' The keys were in the dash, Raymond started the engine and drove the big truck over to Zephyr. 'Piece of cake,' he said, climbing down. 'Piece of cake.'

'Later,' said Zephyr. 'Let's hurry now and load these people.'

'And carefully. Be sure not to cover the little airholes under the seats.'

'A real humanitarian.'

'Thank you once more.'

'So, go on then,' said Zephyr.

'Go on then, me? What do you mean?'

'I mean, Raymond, go and get us some help. It will take hours for just the two of us.'

'But there's no-one around,' Raymond said.

'Well go and see the guard on the gate. Demand assistance, you know the kind of thing.'

'OK.'

Raymond marched back towards the entrance of the pyramid. He turned once or twice to watch Zephyr. She really was so wonderful, rolling bubbles carefully on to the lorry. So strong. So assured. But *what* was she really? She was certainly not human. Magic, was she? Some conjuration of magic? Raymond had no idea.

He marched on.

The guard was sitting in his little hut. Raymond could see the back of his head through the rear window. The guard's feet were up. He was watching a portable TV. And as Raymond drew closer, Raymond could see just what the guard was watching.

He was watching Professor Merlin's circus.

Raymond stopped before the window and peeped over the guard's shoulder. The professor was in his full ringmaster's rig-out. The white topper. The spangled tailcoat. The riding boots. The whole caboodle. He was cracking his whip. Polly's Performing Poodles were going through their paces. Theirs was a most bizarre act, by the look of it. They wore little costumes. Dames and dandies. Plumed hats and tiny swords. They pranced on their hind legs. Danced the minuet. Bowed and curtsied.

And surely the ones playing the harpsichord and the cello, were *actually* playing the instruments.

'Whacky stuff,' whispered Raymond. 'Hello, what's this?'

The screen suddenly blanked. Then the shoulders and the jackal-head of an announcer appeared.

'We interrupt this programme,' said Humphrey Gogmagog, for it was he, 'to bring you a special news bulletin. Twenty minutes ago our flying eye picked up a multiple killing in progress on the lower east side of the city. Images have now been run through the central computer system and, once again, first with the news, this station now broadcasts the fully enhanced images of the two mass murderers.'

The screen flashed up two pictures, side by side. They were very clear pictures and in full colour. One was of Raymond. The other Zephyr.

The guard jerked up in his seat.

Raymond didn't know what to do.

The guard reached out for his telephone.

Raymond chewed upon a knuckle.

The guard began to dial.

Raymond rushed around to the side of the hut and threw open the door. The guard looked up at him in horror. Raymond looked down at the guard in horror. Then Raymond snatched the telephone receiver from the guard's hand and hit him with it. Again and again and again and again.

'Don't hit me again.' Simon flinched and covered his head. He was in the interview room of the Bramfield police station.

It was an unpleasant room, too brightly lit – they always are, it makes them more intimidating. Simon cowered behind a nasty Formica-topped table. It had a big full ashtray on it. They always do. It's a tradition, or an old charter, or something. Or perhaps they'd just cut back on the cleaning staff.

The constable with the sister, lounged against one wall. He had his riot gear off. He was smoking a cigarette.

Inspector D'Eath, who had been cuffing Simon about the head, sat down before the nasty Formica-topped table and pushed the full ashtray aside. He wasn't smoking. He'd given it up.

It was the current fashion amongst police inspectors, to have given up smoking. Something to do with it not being politically correct for authority figures to be seen puffing fags.

Simon recalled reading an article to this effect. But the article had also said that the police inspector should ideally be played by a woman. Helen Mirren, wherever possible.

And hitting the prime suspect was right out of the question.

'Leave me alone,' wailed Simon. 'I demand a woman.'

'Make a note of that, Constable,' said the inspector. 'Even though in custody, the suspect's appetite for female flesh was in no way diminished.'

'What?' went Simon.

'Right, now then, Simon,' said the inspector.

'Simon?' said Simon. 'What happened to "sir", then?' And 'Ouch,' he continued as the inspector cuffed him once again.

'I'm sure you get the picture, *Simon*.'

'Yes, indeed I do.'

'And so, shall we go through your statement once again?'

'Oh yes please. Hearing it all for the sixth time would bring me no end of joy.'

'Sir,' said the constable with the sister.

'Constable?' replied the sir in question.

'Should I pencil in, "the suspect slipped and banged his head on the radiator"?'

The inspector raised an eyebrow to Simon.

'I should be delighted to go through my statement

once again,' said Simon. 'If it will help you with the course of your enquiries.'

'Good boy. So.' Inspector D'Eath shuffled papers before him. 'Ah yes,' he said. 'The chicken house. Tell me again about the chicken house.'

'There's a thing in it. A horrible demonic thing. It's Satan. Sate-Hen, they call it.'

'Sate-Hen.' The inspector underlined the word on Simon's statement. 'Half man, half chicken, you say.'

The constable with the sister sniggered. 'Half man, half chicken, half a pint of lager and a packet of crisps, eh guv?'

'Thank you, Constable. And less of the "guv".'

'But, sir, it's always "guv" on the telly.'

'In moderation then. And put that bloody cigarette out.'

'Yes, sir. Sorry, guv.'

'Come on,' said Simon. 'This is really important. They were talking about the end of the world and this thing taking over and all kinds of crazy stuff. It's a big conspiracy. Pull them all in. I'll help you make them talk.'

'This conspiracy. This would be the B.E.A.S.T. conspiracy, would it? The terrorists who stole your money. Which was why you went to Long Bob's?'

'Bramfielders Eagerly Awaiting Satanic Transmogrification. Look, I've told you all I know. You have to get back there now.'

'And arrest a half man, half chicken?'

'No, destroy it. Blow it up. Burn it.'

'Which was what you were going to do with the can of petrol.'

'Yes,' said Simon.

'You were going to burn down the chicken sheds.'

'Yes,' said Simon.

'And God told you to do it.'

'What?' said Simon.

'God. Surely you haven't forgotten about God. The

God you told me dictated that book to you. The book you were going upstairs to fetch when you chose instead to make a run for it.'

'That God, that book. Ah,' said Simon.

'Ah,' said the inspector. 'And this God told you that the devil was a chicken and so you should burn the chicken sheds down.'

'I never said anything of the kind.'

'Yes you did.' The inspector showed Simon his statement. 'Just there, see.'

Simon gaped at the statement. 'You've just pencilled that in. You've crossed what I said out.'

'You won't be able to tell the difference once it's typed up.'

'What?' went Simon again.

'Shall we talk about the Jaguar?' asked the inspector. 'The Jaguar which I caught you joy riding in, when over the legal limit?'

'Belongs to the woman you think I murdered.'

'Did you catch all that?' The inspector asked his constable.

'Yes, guv. The suspect replied, "It belongs to the woman I murdered."'

'I never did.' Simon drummed his fists on the nasty Formica table.

'Why won't you just come clean, Simon? You're banged to rights and you know it.'

'I'm innocent. And *you* know it. And you won't make me sign these false statements. Free the Bramfield One, say I.' Simon folded his arms and made a firm face.

'Shall I pencil in the "slipped and banged his head on the radiator" bit now, guv?'

'I think so, Constable. And you'd better put "he then struck his head repeatedly on the table, breaking several of his front teeth".'

'No!' shrieked Simon. 'Not the teeth. Anything but the teeth.'

'Then let's be having you, lad. I want the full

confession. And I want it in sounds bites. "God told me to do it, says Butcher of Bramfield." Shall we start with a clean sheet of paper, or do you just want to sign the statement I composed in your absence earlier in the day? I've already had photocopies done to hand out to the Press.'

'Listen,' said Simon, 'please. I swear to you I have murdered nobody. The book will explain everything. It's all in the book.'

'God's book?'

'Not God's book. The book from the future. The one that Long Bob and his looneys are after. It's all in the book. If you want to give the Press a story, just wait until you read this book.'

'And this is the book that you say is in,' the inspector consulted Simon's statement, 'the hideaway bush at the top of the hill overlooking Long Bob's farm.'

'You haven't pencilled that bit out then?'

'Not as yet. I've despatched an officer to search for this book. He should be back at any moment now.'

'Good,' said Simon. 'Good. Then you'll know. Then you'll see.'

'I very much hope so. Because if I don't,' the inspector pointed towards Simon's dental glory, 'the world will henceforth know you by the nickname, "Gummy".'

Simon cringed.

A knock came at the door.

'The tooth fairy,' said Inspector D'Eath. 'Enter,' he called.

It was the constable who didn't have a sister, but had once seen a search warrant. Derek, wasn't it? Or was the other one Derek? It doesn't really matter.

'Well, Constable,' the inspector rose from the unsightly table. 'Did you find this magic book?'

Constable Derek, for that *was* his name, took out a book of his own. An official Metropolitan police-issue notebook. And this he read from. Aloud. 'Acting upon instructions from Police Inspector Death—'

'Too late,' said the inspector.

'Too late, sir? What for, sir?'

'Gags about my name, Constable. If you're going to have a running gag about someone's name, it has to be done from right at the start and carried on through.'

'Like the one about my surname,' said Simon helpfully. 'And my hat.'

'Exactly,' said the inspector. 'You can't just slip it in like that, it doesn't work at all. It's not funny.'

'Oh,' said the constable who didn't have a sister but had once seen a search warrant (which was probably a running gag, but not a very good one). 'Should I start again then?'

'If you wouldn't mind.'

'Right, sir,' the constable cleared his throat. 'Acting upon instructions from Police Inspector D'Eath, I proceeded in an orderly fashion to the aforedescribed-to-me "hideaway bush" at the top of the hill overlooking the chicken farm of one Robert Bum-poo—'

'Hold it!' cried Inspector D'Eath. 'Robert what?'

'Bum-poo, sir.'

'You just made that up, Constable. It isn't funny. It's childish.'

'It's quite funny,' said Simon. 'I used to go to school with him. Not that I ever made any rude remarks about his name.'

'Well you wouldn't,' said the inspector. 'Not with yours being—'

'Quite so,' said Simon. 'Do you think the constable could continue? I am growing rather anxious.'

'Continue please, Constable.'

'Yes, sir,' the constable continued. 'Having located the aforedescribed-to-me "hideway bush" I instigated a search for the book alluded to by the suspect in his statement. During the course of my search I turned up an empty sherry bottle answering to the description of that stolen from Mr Kilgore Sprout, whom we had formally interviewed in connection with the present whereabouts of the suspect.'

'Very good, Constable. We'll add that to the charge sheet.'

'Thank you, sir. The bottle is now with forensic. I'm sure we'll get a match on the fingerprints.'

'Excellent, so, continue.'

'Continue, sir?'

'The book, lad, did you find the book?'

'No, sir.'

'No, sir?'

'No, sir. There wasn't any book.'

'*What?*' It was Simon's *what* once again.

'There was no sign of any book, sir. Just a lot of chicken feathers and this really horrible smell.'

If auras have smells, then Raymond's now smelt really horrible. He staggered back to Zephyr, who was struggling with the bubbles. She saw the look on his face, and being whatever she was, she smelt his aura also.

'What has happened?' she asked.

'I think I just killed the guard.'

'Why did you do that?'

Raymond's lip began to quiver. 'He saw us on the television. Our faces were on the screen. They want us for murder.'

'We'd better get a move on then. Come and give me a hand.'

'Zephyr. I think I just killed the guard.'

'So you said. Now come on and help.'

'Zephyr, please.'

Zephyr came forward and took Raymond in her arms. The touch of her flesh. The smell of her perfume. She kissed him. 'Did you look in his lunch box?' she asked.

'His lunch box? Well no I did not.'

'Perhaps you should have. I expect he had "George" in his sandwiches.'

'Oh God,' said Raymond, getting a good blub going.

'These people will all die if you don't save them. Are you going to blub, or are you going to help load?'

'Both,' said Raymond.

'Good,' said Zephyr. 'Then let's get it done.'

And get it done, they did.

They would probably have got it done quicker, had it not been for Raymond's blubbings, which were interspersed with 'useful suggestions' for speeding up the loading process. When Zephyr finally tired of both, she gave Raymond a smack and made him sit in the lorry until she had finished.

'And that's it.' Zephyr secured the final bubble on to the special rack and joined Raymond in the cab.

'All better now?' asked Zephyr.

'Yes,' said Raymond sniffily.

'Then let us get back to the ship.' Zephyr didn't wear a watch, but, as she glanced at her wrist, one obligingly appeared. 'We have twenty minutes.'

'Then we can do it.' Raymond gave the ignition key a tweak, thrummed the engine and applied full wellie to the accelerator pedal.

'Slowly,' said Zephyr.

'Of course, slowly. I just wanted to hear the engine roar, that's all.'

'Drive,' she said.

And Raymond drove. As they passed the guard's hut, Raymond craned his neck in the hope of seeing movement. There was none.

'Damn it,' said Raymond. 'Damn, damn, damn it.'

'Left at the top here.'

'Right surely.'

'Left, Raymond.'

'Are you certain? I'm for turning right, me.'

'Turn left or I will smack you again.'

Raymond turned left. 'I'm not altogether sure that I approve of this new disciplinary element which has entered our relationship.'

'Turn right at the bottom here.'

'No more smacking me.' Raymond turned right at the bottom there.

'Then behave yourself.'

Raymond frowned and drove on. He managed the big truck really quite well. Smooth gear changes. Easy on the air brakes. After one or two near-death experiences, he even got the hang of which side of the road he should be driving on. 'How are we doing for time?' he asked.

'We have about ten minutes.'

'Will the professor be back in the ship on time?'

'To the minute. He's a professional.'

'Hey look, the dock's up ahead. I think we're actually going to make it.'

'Red light, Raymond. Red light!'

'I saw it, I saw it.' The big truck juddered painfully to a halt at the red traffic light.

'You didn't see it.'

'I did too see it.' Raymond wound down his window, leaned out his arm and did nonchalant finger drummings on the door. Inside he was quaking with fear. It had been building up and up and now that they were *so* close to the ship. Raymond began to sway gently in the driving seat. The street went slowly in and out of focus.

'We're going to make it, aren't we?' he asked, in a quavery wavery voice.

'Of course we are,' said Zephyr. 'There's nothing can stop us now.'

They were stopped, as chance would have it, outside a corner café. It was a weird café, as a matter of fact. Very wide doorway, big high ceiling. It catered for the more exotic off-worlder. Non-bipedal. Not of the genus *Homo sapiens*. Or any derivatives there from.

It was a bit like that bar in *Star Wars*, where those strange aliens played those improbable instruments. But not much.

Actually here Faith No More played on the jukebox and rival sportswear cultists had at one another with the Saturnian equivalent of the snooker cue. The one designed 'with the tentacle in mind'.

One doubtful-looking off-worlder lay spread across three window seats, watching the traffic go by. His name was Abdullah and he was a flying starfish from Uranus.

And Abdullah spied out the spanking new auction house lorry. And likewise did he spy out the cargo it was carrying. And Abdullah waxed most sorely vexatious and did cry aloud unto the heavens, or at least the ceiling, 'Some bastard is nicking my George!'

And lo he did gaze upon the driver of the stolen vehicle and further words did flee his unsightly aural orifice. 'Tis the schmuck from Bramfield, currently wanted on Venus with a big price on his head. How did he get here?'

Abdullah extended a really frightful pseudopodium with rotational optic accessory, out through the letterbox of the café, across the pavement and up the side of the big spanking new lorry, to follow the direction of Raymond's now ever so fixed stare.

'Lo and behold,' quoth big Abdullah. 'I spy with my little eye something beginning with S. Can this be the very ship stolen from my most magnificent ruler The Sultan of Uranus some one hundred and some years ago? Or does my frightful pseudopodium with rotational optic accessory deceive me? Nope! It's the bleeding *Salamander* all right. *Waitress!*'

'Yeah, wotcha want?' The waitress was for the most part formless protozoa. But she wore the apron and the bleached blond wig, chewed gum and spoke in that nasal Brooklyn accent that waitresses in American movies always do. 'Yeah, wotcha want?' she said again. 'Asshole,' she added, for good measure.

'Telephone,' said big Abdullah.

'It's in the back.'

Abdullah rose obscenely and drifted into the back of the café. With a most revolting appendage he lifted the overlarge receiver (designed with the tentacle in mind) and put it to the part of him that answered for an ear.

'Number ple-ase,' came the voice of the operator.

'E.T. phone home,' said the flying starfish. 'Uranus and quick. I have to speak to the Sultan.

'The police and quick. I have to speak to the police.'

It was the guard at the auction house. Somewhat bruised about the head region, but still this side of the graveyard. 'Yes, police, hello. The two psychos wanted for the multiple killings. They were here. The man and the woman, yes. They—'

'Stole our last consignment of George,' said the auction house relief guard, who had just come on duty. 'I saw them drive by. I recognized the woman too. She came with the circus, she was on the big ship that docked earlier at the harbour.'

'Did you catch all that?' asked the guard with the bruised head.

'Assume we did,' came the helpful reply. 'An armed response team is being despatched directly to the dock. Pop on over yourself if you're feeling up to it.'

'Thanks a lot,' said the guard. 'I will.'

'Thanks a lot,' said Inspector D'Eath. 'And if you would just sign this one and this one and this one too.'

'I'll retract them all in court,' said Simon as he signed the false confessions.

'Of course you will. They always do.'

'I shall tell them that you threatened to break my teeth if I didn't sign.'

'I expect you will, yes. Sign this one too, if you please.'

Simon signed that one too. 'You just don't get it, do you?' he asked. 'That thing is out there in the chicken house. It has to be destroyed.'

'Of course it does. And it's all in God's book. Except that God's taken it home with him. Keep signing.'

Simon kept signing. '*They've* got the book. The smell in the hideaway bush, that was the smell of the thing. You've got to do something.'

'I am doing something. I am processing the statements of a self-confessed serial killer. Sign that one as well.'

Simon signed that one, as well. 'You'll regret this. I shall get myself a really good barrister. A lady one. One who looks like Helen Mirren.'

'On legal aid? I shouldn't think so. Sign that.'

'What's that?'

'My autograph book. You're the first serial killer I've ever arrested.'

'Fair enough.' Simon signed. 'And what do you mean, legal aid? I don't need legal aid. I can afford the best.'

'On a gardener's salary? You have to be joking.' Inspector D'Eath pocketed his autograph book.

'Forget about my salary.' Simon returned the inspector's pen. 'You know what I'm worth. You counted my winnings when you searched me upstairs. That's *my* money you now have locked in your safe. Legitimately won. There's two kinds of justice in this country – one for the rich and one for the poor. I can now afford rich man's justice.'

Simon flashed his pearly whites. 'So there.'

'Really?' Inspector D'Eath rearranged greasy strings of hair above his forehead. 'Well, this is most curious. I don't remember Simon having any money on him when he was searched. Do you, Constable?'

'No, sir guv.' The constable with the sister shook his head. 'I don't remember any money at all.'

'What?' went Simon.

'Constable without the sister, but who once saw a search warrant,' asked Inspector D'Eath, 'do you remember us putting a small fortune in twenty-pound notes into the safe upstairs?'

'No, sir.' This constable also shook his head. 'I recall we found a knackered old wallet on the suspect, which contained a doctor's note that you told us was an important piece of evidence. But money? No, sir. I would certainly recall if the suspect was carrying a large amount of money, all in twenty-pound notes stuffed into his pockets, much of which we had to prise from his fingers during the search, Sir.'

'*What?*' went Simon once again.

'So there you have it.' Inspector D'Eath turned up his hands. 'Or in your case, there you don't have it. There is *no* money.'

'*What?*' went Simon in a higher register than ever. 'No money? What?'

'Of course, you *were* drunk when I brought you in. You failed the breath test, don't you remember? No, you probably don't, do you? Not with the short-term memory loss and everything.'

'*What? What?*' Simon began to flap his hands about in a demented fashion and bob up and down in his chair. 'This isn't happening. You can't do this to me. You can't just steal all my money, bully me into signing a false confession, ignore everything I've told you. You can't do this. You can't.'

'But I can.' Inspector D'Eath smiled hideously. 'I can do anything I want to. You're a homicidal maniac. No-one is going to care what happens to you and no-one is going to believe your word instead of mine.'

'No,' shrieked Simon. 'No no no.'

'He's getting a bit uppity, sir guv,' said a constable who was planning to spend some of his new-found wealth on a motor scooter. 'Shall I give him a smack with my truncheon?'

'No need for that.' The inspector continued to smile. 'Tell you what. Why not go and fetch the police doctor. Tell him we have a lively one here and why doesn't he bring his big hypodermic.'

'No,' whimpered Simon.

'Yes, sir guv,' said the constable. 'And shall I ask him to bring the strait-jacket too?'

'Good idea, Constable.'

'And what about the leather mask with the little bars over the mouth hole?'

'No!' screamed Simon. 'No no no.'

'A very good idea too. Now hurry along, Constable
The Butcher of Bramfield is getting a bit foamy around
the jaws. The sooner he's put under heavy restraint and
pumped full of phenobarbitones, the safer we'll all sleep
in our beds.'

'Noooooooooooooooooooooooooooooooooooooooooooo
oooooooo!' went Simon.

'Baaaaaaaaaaaaaaaaaaaaaaaaaaaaaaaaaaaaaaaaarp.' The red
light changed to green and the traffic began hooting.

Raymond fumbled with the gears on the big spanking
new auction house lorry.

'Get a move on,' Zephyr said. 'We have a deadline to
keep with the professor. We have to get off this planet as
quickly as possible.'

Raymond pulled himself together, changed the gears
and rolled the big truck forwards.

'There's a guard on the dock gate,' said Raymond,
spying same. 'And he's got a clipboard.'

'No time for that now. Run him over.'

'I will not.'

'Yes you will.' Zephyr grabbed the steering wheel and
the lorry veered towards the guard on the dock gate.

As the guard ran for his life, the lorry mashed down
his little guard's hut. Electric kettle, bar fire, fan, TV set,
smutty mags, the lot.

'Bastards,' swore the guard, pulling out his portable
telephone.

'Get me the police.'

Woo Woo Woo Woo, came the sound of police car
sirens.

'That's what I like about Saturn,' said the guard.
'There's always a policeman around when you need
one.'

'I hear police cars,' moaned Raymond. 'Will the ship's
gangway take the weight of this huge lorry, do you think?'

'No,' Zephyr said. 'But keep driving.' And she was
there and then she wasn't. Raymond drove on towards a

gangway now miraculously reinforced by mighty girders of steel.

I wonder how she does that, Raymond wondered, as he shifted gear, made the big truck's horn go 'Baaarp!' and steered very carefully up the gangway and into the bowels of the SS Salamander.

Cogs meshed, hydraulics shifted. The gangway rose and closed into the side of the ship.

A piece of cake.

Raymond switched off the engine. Climbed from the cab. Shinned up various stairways and finally joined Zephyr, who was standing on the deck.

'We did it, eh?' Raymond raised fists to the sky, flung his arms about the miraculous one and kissed her. 'We did it.'

'*We* did.' Zephyr extracted herself from Raymond's fond embrace. 'But look out there.'

Raymond looked. All along the dock there was now what is known as a police presence. A dozen Earth-like American black and whites. Officers running to and fro. Guns being hefted. Shouting and jostling. A distant whirr of copter-blades announced the imminent arrival of three gunships.

'Bloody hell,' said Raymond. 'Let's get out of here. Engage the space drive, say the magic words. Let's have lift off.'

Zephyr shook her head. 'We can't.'

'We can't? What are you saying?'

'I'm saying we can't leave the planet.'

'I hate to contradict you on this. But I really must insist. Where is the professor?'

'Out there,' Zephyr pointed beyond the dock towards the city. 'Out there somewhere, with the circus. They haven't come back, Raymond. Something dreadful must have happened.'

18

The Sultan of Uranus was a nasty piece of work. He wasn't a flying starfish. The flying starfish were part of the indigenous population, subjugated centuries before the Edenites. The Sultan was an Edenite. A big fat one. Very old, but still very fit. And very bad tempered.

He was one of three brothers, who, although hating each other in the manner that only brothers can, and having not exchanged a single word in over two hundred years, still wielded between them a considerable amount of interplanetary clout.

Now, much time could be spent describing the sultan and the wonders of his palace. But not here.

The big fat old, fit, bad-tempered man shouted things into his telephone receiver. Angry things. Things like. 'Bring me their heads' and 'get my ship back' and 'do it now or know the wrath of my displeasure'. Things like that.

'To hear is to obey,' said big Abdullah, putting down the phone.

'To hear is to obey.' Professor Merlin stood in the middle of the sawdust ring at the palace of celestial pleasures and bowed once more to His Royal Highness the Grand Duke Binky. 'Another full performance coming up.'

His Royal Highness the Grand Duke was a nasty piece of work. He wasn't a Saturnian dog-head or anything like that. The indigenous population of Saturn had been subjugated centuries before.

By the Edenites. The Grand Duke was an Edenite.

A big fat one. Very old, but very fit. And very bad tempered.

One of three brothers.

Much time could, of course, be spent in describing the Grand Duke and the wonders of his palace. But happily this will not be necessary. Because he looked just like his brother the sultan. And their palaces were virtually identical.

Phew!

'A moment to refresh ourselves, Your Majesty, and then we shall play for you once more.' Professor Merlin bowed himself from the circus ring and limped away on worn-out legs towards the dressing-rooms.

Here sat his artistes, in a state of major collapse. Having each been forced to perform their routines at least twice, all were now exhausted.

'We cannot go on again.' Monsieur LaRoche spied out the professor's approaching legs from the doubled-up position in which he was crouched. 'My back, she is gone. A buggeration to Binky and a plague of boils upon his poor sick son.'

'The Black Death be on him,' agreed Dr Bacteria. 'Three times the little shit demands to see me die of malaria. Three times. I refuse to do it again.'

Similar moans and complaints filled the air. The professor raised his marvellous fingers. 'I have implored him a moment's respite. The man is clearly a stone bonker and we are late. We return at once to the ship.'

'He won't like that.' Aquaphagus coughed up a small trout. 'Ah, I wondered what I'd done with that. The Grand Duke will hunt us down.'

'Be that as it may, we are leaving. Take only what you cannot live without and follow me.'

'What are we going to do?' Raymond tried to make himself heard. The deafening clap of the copter-blades as the gunships circled above, made any kind of communication, save possibly that of mime, rather difficult.

'I have to find the circus and bring it safely back,' Zephyr shouted.

'*What?*'

'You stay here. Leave it to me.'

'*What?*'

'Stay here, I'll fetch the professor.'

'No!' Raymond tugged Zephyr into the nearest cabin and slammed shut the door. 'No.'

'Yes, Raymond. I can get off the ship undetected and return the same way with the professor and the rest. No-one will see us.'

'No,' said Raymond once again. 'You might get yourself killed.'

'I can't be killed.'

'Oh,' Raymond wondered at that one. 'Well *I* can. What if they storm the ship while you're gone?'

'We can't leave without the professor, and I'm the only one who can bring him through the lines of police.'

'Fly the ship,' said Raymond.

'What?' said Zephyr.

'Fly the ship. Let's go and pick the professor up.'

'That's a very good idea, Raymond.'

'Do you think so? I thought it was a rather obvious thing to do really. Of course, it would depend on those helicopters backing away.'

'*Attention SS Salamander.*' It was one of those police loud hailers and it could be heard because the helicopters had moved away to allow for the loud hailing bit which always comes just before the big shoot-out bit. '*There is no escape for you. Give yourselves up now or we open fire.*' (That bit.)

'Now would be the ideal time,' said Raymond.

'All right. You go up to the wheelhouse and get the ship moving. I'll distract the police.'

'No,' said Raymond.

'What do you mean, no?'

'I mean, I don't know how to fly the ship. So let me bullshit the police. Then if I get shot, at least you'll still have a chance to escape with the kidnapped people and pick up the circus.'

'That's very brave of you.'

'Is it?'

'Yes, it is. I'll help you as best I can.'

'Come out on deck or we open fire.'

'Let's go,' said Raymond. But Zephyr had already gone.

'Hey hey hey.' Raymond strolled out on to the deck and waved gunless hands at the police marksmen. 'No need for any of this.'

A shot whistled past him and went thud into a lifebelt.

'Hold your fire,' called the policeman with the loud hailer.

'Best to,' Raymond plucked at the crotch of his leather trews. Still dry, but for how much longer? 'You wouldn't want to turn this city into a smoking ruin, now would you?' he called out.

'Eh?'

'One shot in the wrong direction and we'll all be dead.'

'Eh?'

'The ship's space drive system.'

'What about it?'

'Very unstable. It functions on the transperambulation of pseudo-cosmic anti-matter.'

'Get away.'

'No kidding. And if one of your bullets interrupted the cross polarization of the beta-particle flow. Poof.'

'Who are you calling a poof?'

'The city will go poof. This whole city. All of it. Gone. Just gone.'

'Gone?'

'All of it.'

'All of it?'

'All,' said Raymond.

'Yeah? And my arse smells of snowdrops from a curate's garden.'

'Haven't we met?' asked Raymond.

223

'No, but you duffed up my brother the security guard at the auction house.'

'Just duffed up? You mean he's not dead then?'

'No, he's fine. Got a bit of a headache though.'

'Well send him my best wishes and say I hope he gets well soon.'

'OK, I will. So now are you coming down, or do we shoot you dead?'

Raymond scratched at his head and wondered what Simon might say next, the unstable space-drive-system ploy having proved a real no-mark. 'I have diplomatic immunity,' called Raymond. 'I am the new official ambassador from Eden. Shoot me and you'll have an interplanetary incident on your hands.'

'You're a lying git,' called the police officer who had the brother that Raymond had duffed up but not killed. 'I'm going to count up to ten and if you don't come down then we shoot you dead and storm the ship.'

Oh for the General Electric mini-gun, thought Raymond. And 'Oh,' he continued as it materialized as if by magic in his hands.

This time the firing button had a big sticker on it which read 'Press here for bullets and hold on tight'.

'Back off!' shouted Raymond. 'Or I fire. I know how to use this thing.'

'That's not a real gun.'

'Oh yes it is.'

'Oh not it isn't.'

'Please yourself then.' Raymond angled the six rotational barrels in the general direction of the police presence and pressed the firing button.

To lovers of high-velocity firepower, those sad individuals who buy gun magazines and partworks about *Nam*, the General Electric mini-gun stands in a class of its own. Tried and tested upon many an innocent farming community in the Mekong Delta, it dispenses its six-thousand-round-a-minute payload in a wide body

224

format, offering maximum tissue penetration and optimum soft-target takedown.

It didn't half go some. Raymond held on with a will as the recoil adaptors took up the kick and bullets strafed along the dockside.

Fogerty's finest fled as police-car tyres shredded, bonnets were torn asunder and petrol tanks exploded. Plumes of smoke bowled into the sky, confusing the pilots of the gunships, who simply gave the open fire order and steered around in faulty circles.

Mayhem!

Raymond had his eyes firmly closed, if he was doing any soft-target takedowns he didn't want to see it. He had his legs crossed also. This was all very much, too much.

What a lot of smoke!

If you're actually firing six thousand rounds a minute, it doesn't take long to use up all your ammunition. Unless, of course, you have a great deal of ammunition. Raymond didn't seem to lack for it. The big gun's barrels whizzed around. Smoke and flames and chaos.

Very gratuitous. But if you *are* one of those sad individuals who buy gun mags and the *Nam* partworks, right up your street really.

What a lot of smoke.

Raymond couldn't see a thing. He dropped the gun and clung to the ship's rail. Because things were shaking all around him. Bursting shells. Smoke and flames. The snapping of cables and chains.

More mayhem.

Further chaos.

And then the clear blue open sky.

Raymond blinked. The ship was rising. The great liner was moving upwards. The smoke was all below. A black shroud covering the dockyard. Copter-blades whacked under the hull. Struck the hull. A helicopter gunship cartwheeled down into the harbour.

Raymond covered his face and then did what so many

shipboard passengers had done before him, though for far less dramatic reasons. He threw up over the side.

The SS *Salamander* turned about in the sky. Majestic and magical. And dizzying too. Raymond toppled to the deck. Clung to a steamer chair. Slid along the deck clinging to a steamer chair. Then levitated through the open door of the wheelhouse.

'All right?' asked Zephyr.

'Oh yeah, never better.'

'Then hold on tight. It's going to be a bumpy ride.'

'Your Majesty.' A cringing menial with an ibis head and a natty line in scarlet livery spoke at the Grand Duke's regal ear. 'Professor Merlin has just left the building.'

'Without my permission?' The big fat fellow rose in his royal box, dislodging his poor sick son Colin from his knee. 'Call out the guards. Get after him. My boy wants to see the malaria man again.'

'But the guards all have the day off, Your Majesty. You declared it a national holiday.'

'Oaf! Buffoon! Bring back the circus. And pick up my son.'

'To hear is to obey.'

'Too bloody right it is. Now get a move on.'

'Get a move on, Jumbo, do.' Professor Merlin put spur to his flagging pachyderm.

'Less of the spurs. I'm going as fast as I can.'

'You can talk. By Jimmy, you can talk.'

'Of course I can talk. I just never wanted to before.'

'Is that an Indian accent?'

'I'm an Indian elephant. You expected Yiddish perhaps?'

'No, I . . . well. Fiddle-de. Why now, my old muck-a-muck? Why do you wish to talk now?'

'Just exercising my prerogative,' said the elephant in the unconvincing Indian accent. 'Now are the End Times come and all the beasts of the field will speak out.'

'All?' asked the professor.

'All,' said Jumbo. 'The lion and the lamb. The chimp and the chicken. Especially the chicken.'

'What about the fish?' asked Mr Aquaphagus, who was hanging on behind.

'Don't be a schmuck,' replied the elephant. 'A talking fish? My life already. Oi vey.'

'After that elephant,' cried the cringing menial.

'Who *me*?' The solitary guard in the little hut by the palace gate shook his head. It was the head of a mullet. 'It's more than my job's worth to leave this hut.'

'Call the police then.'

'No point. They're all at the dock shooting at the big ship that brought the circus in. Look, it's live.' He pointed to his portable TV. 'Humphrey Gogmagog's doing the commentary.'

'Oh, I like him. Turn the sound up.'

'Shall I put the kettle on for a cup of tea?'

'Well,' the cringing menial stroked his beak, 'I really should be chasing after the circus.'

'Why bother? Tell you what you do: phone the police at the dock, get them to arrest the circus when it tries to get back on the ship.'

'Can I use your phone?'

'Sure. Ask for my brother Charlie, he's in charge of the loud hailer.'

'Nice one,' said the cringing menial. 'Where do you keep your phone?'

'Down there, by the dirty mags.'

'Down here?'

'Down there.'

'Down there! Down there!' Raymond pointed down there. 'It's the professor on the elephant. In fact, it's everyone on the elephant.'

'Then hold on tight, we're going down.'

227

Chop chop chop, came the sound of helicopter gunship blades.

'Over there,' cried the pilot. 'The ship's going down to pick up the circus. Open fire. Shoot everything and everybody.'

'Up there!' Lady Alostrael did the pointing. 'The *Salamader*.'

The circus folk began to wave and cheer.

Raymond looked into the ship's rear-view mirror. 'Helicopters are coming up behind us. What are we going to do now?'

'Take the wheel please, Raymond, and steer us down.'

'Me take the wheel? Just like that?'

'Just like that. Hurry now.'

'You have something in mind then?' Raymond took the wheel and once again found Zephyr wasn't there. 'She gets around, that woman.'

Whoosh went an air-to-air missile. It sailed along the deck, clearing the wheelhouse by inches, dipped away into the distance and fell upon the guard's hut at the palace gate, destroying it utterly. Hardly fair, but there you go.

'It's very exciting this,' said Raymond. 'Although quite frightening when you're personally involved.' He turned the wheel and the ship took a quite frightening dip to the port side.

'Whoops,' said Raymond.

Down in the hold, the big spanking new auction house lorry, whose handbrake Raymond had thoughtlessly neglected to put on, rolled forward and bashed into a bulkhead (whatever that is).

'Down here,' waved the circus folk.

Raymond waved back at them. How does this work? he wondered. This way, or the other? He yanked the wheel to the starboard side with most alarming consequences.

The big spanking new auction house lorry rolled back across the cargo hold and ground its rear end into an upright wall-like partition of the vessel (a bulkhead).

228

Chop chop chop, went gunship copter-blades.

Ratatatatatatat, went their armaments.

'Take cover behind the elephant,' yelled Mr Aquaphagus, as shells racked over the street.

'Take cover behind the elephant, he says.' Jumbo threw up his trunk in disgust. 'This goy thinks I'm a sandbag already. Such a shemozzle I never have seen.'

Chop chop chop.

Ratatatatatatat.

Swerve, went Raymond, pulling hard on the wheel.

Crash and bang went the big spanking new auction house lorry overturning violently and spilling off its load.

'Something's shifted.' Raymond fell forward over the ship's wheel. The *SS Salamander* took a rapid descent.

'Wheel back! Wheel back! cried Professor Merlin, as the great ship blotted out the better part of his sky.

'Wheel back, I think.' Raymond dragged the wheel back as far as it would go. The ship shuddered to a halt in mid air and the first of the two oncoming gunships struck the stern and exploded.

'Oh dear,' said Raymond.

The second gunship came about and shot up the front of the wheelhouse.

'Dear oh dear,' mumbled Raymond from the safety of the floor.

'Oooh, aaagh, eeeek and so on,' went the circus folk, as flaming shards of the first gunship rained down over the street.

'I'm just not getting this right,' Raymond sighed. 'Let's try forward a bit and left a tad.'

Forward a bit and left a tad.

The big ship swung around in a forward, leftish arc.

'Back away, back away,' cried the gunship pilot. 'He's trying to ram us, back away.'

'Or I could try back a bit and right a tad.'

Back a bit and right a tad.

'Take evasive tactics, he's coming right for us again.'

'Or. Down a bit, left a bit, up a tad and—'

'I'm bailing out,' cried the pilot of the gunship, as the *SS Salamander* struck it down a bit, left a bit, up a tad and double top.

A considerable second explosion.

No more second gunship.

'Up and down and around and about. There's a knack to this, I know it.' Raymond rolled the wheel to the left and right. The ocean liner dipped and turned and settled.

It was such a very large ship though and it could have come down just a tad slower. Two tads actually. And a bit.

And another tad.

'Stand clear of the doors.' Raymond clung to the wheel. 'All ashore that's going ashore. Oh my goodness me.'

The way it took out the entire parade of shops.

That was something to see.

Dust and falling rubble.

Sparking electrical cables.

Fleeing circus folk.

More mayhem.

Further chaos.

Then that terrible groaning, as the ship's hull ground its way into the dirt.

Several further explosions.

More chaos.

A whole lot of silence.

And then . . .

'My God,' croaked Raymond, as he collapsed in an unconscious heap. 'I think I just sank the ship.'

19

Simon awoke without his usual natural sense of optimism for the day ahead. He had, amongst other things, a terrible headache. Far worse than any he had previously experienced. Due, he supposed, to the massive dose of barbituates shot into him the night before.

The final hours of that night had been unhappy ones for Simon. Violent hands had been laid upon his sensitive person. Cruelly had the strait-jacket been strapped about him. Evilly the leather mask upon his face. And then, oh then, the hypodermic needle.

And then. Oh then, oh then, oh then.

The hideous and unthinkable bit.

The-being-flung-into-the-police-cell bit.

Not utterly hideous and unthinkable, you might think. After all, we've all been thrown into a police cell at one time or another, haven't we? Indeed we have. But it was the occupants of the cell and what they had done to Simon.

Yes! THAT!

Simon recalled the final vindictive words of Inspector D'Eath. 'We've got a mate of yours in here for you to have a chat to. Caught him skulking around outside the Scribe's house with an unlicensed shotgun in his possession. Couldn't get the vet up at this time of night, *so we've had to put his dog in there with him.*'

And then Simon, sinking into narcotic oblivion, had been cast into the cell. All jacketed up and helpless to face the untender mercies of Dick Godolphin and his lurcher.

'Aaaaaaaaaaaaaaaaaaaaaagh!'

Simon struggled in his strait-jacket. Say it wasn't true. Say he'd only dreamt it. Say they hadn't done THAT to him.

Anything but THAT.

But they had.

Simon stared up at the high barred window.

> Upon that little tent of blue
> Which prisoners call the sky.

That was Oscar Wilde, wasn't it? Oscar Wilde . . .

'Aaaaaaaaaaaaaaaaaagh!' went Simon again.

The nasty little steel shutter on the cell door shot open and the mouth of Constable Derek said, 'Shut your bloody gob in there.'

'Let me out,' screamed Simon. 'I have to take a shower. I have to see a doctor. I probably need rabies shots. I'm tainted. Let me out.'

'Just keep it quiet.' The nasty little steel shutter shut.

Simon's wild eyes took in the rest of the cell. He was all alone. The poacher and his dog had been released. Dick had probably been given his bus fare home by Inspector D'Eath. God, perhaps the policeman had actually looked on while Dick and his dog . . .

Simon managed another 'Aaaaaaaaaaaaaaagh!' But 'Aaaaaaaaaaaaaaaaaaghs!' weren't going to help him in here. 'Aaaaaaaaaaaaaaaaaaaaghs!' were the general unit of currency in a place like this.

Nothing was going to get him out of this place but himself. *He* had to get out of here. Right now. Right at once.

He had to escape. Escape and make good.

Because Simon had finally come to realize that the mess he was in was all of his own making.

He had witnessed his best friend being sucked into space by a flying starfish from another world. He had met up with the men in grey and learned that human beings are snatched away from Earth on a regular basis, that they are treated as a trade commodity. And that a huge conspiracy exists to cover this up.

He had learned this awful secret and then into his hands had come the book from the future. *The Greatest Show off Earth*. A book which, had he used it wisely, could have helped him to expose this dreadful business and save the lives of innocent victims.

But what had he done with it?

What had *he*, Simon the bastard, done with it? Why, he'd used it to seek personal gain. To enrich himself. And where had this greed got him? It had got him right here, that's where!

His greed had led him to encounter Sate-Hen, spawn of the bottomless pit himself. His greed had led him into the clutches of Long Bob and his satanic loonies. And now he had lost the lot. The book. The money. His girlfriend. THE OTHER THING!

And here he was. Lying on the floor of a police cell, in a strait-jacket and a leather mask, bullied into making a false confession that he was a serial killer and branded The Butcher of Bramfield.

Friendless, hopeless, damned. And all his own fault.

He really *did* have to get out of here. Get out. Make good. Right now.

Somehow.

But how?

Simon recalled a book he had once read about the great Houdini, and how that now legendary fellow could find his way out of a locked safe with little more than a cat's whisker and a piece of crystal to aid him. Or was that something entirely different?

And strait-jackets? Houdini scoffed at strait-jackets. Pooh-poohed them, he did. Held them to ridicule.

Simon struggled in his strait-jacket. It clenched him very firmly. Scoffed at, it would not be. Pooh-poohed? I think not.

Simon ceased his struggles. It was probable that the design of strait-jackets had been improved since the days of the great escapologist. And where could he get a cat's whisker from at this time of the day?

No, if he was going to get out of here he needed just the one thing.

A miracle.

Not easy to come by, you might think.

But this is Simon we're dealing with here.

Simon closed his eyes. 'Dear God,' he prayed. 'I'm terribly sorry to bother you. I've never done it before and I know I should be doing it kneeling down. But as you can see, if you happen to be looking, I'm just a mite immobilized at present.

'The reason I'm intruding on your valuable time is because I came face to face with the devil last night. And if he's here in the flesh, then I suppose that what Long Bob said about the End Times having come, must be right.

'So I would like to offer my help. I know I've been a sinner in the past, but I'd really appreciate it if you could see your way clear to letting me make good and do the right thing for once.

'So. With your kind permission, I am volunteering to take up the sword of righteousness against the powers of darkness and go forth to do battle with the Evil One.

'There'll just be me on my own, I'm afraid. Because I don't know who else I can possibly trust in this village.

'Anyway. I hope you've been listening and if you have and you'd like me to help, then just say the word and I'm your man.

'For ever and ever. Amen. Love Simon.'

And with that said, Simon lay back and prepared himself to wait. You didn't chivvy up the Almighty, everyone knew that. If God in His infinite wisdom decided to enlist you to his holy cause, then He got around to it in His own sweet omniscient time. That was how He did business.

The nasty little steel shutter on the door flew rapidly open.

'You've got a visitor,' said Constable Derek.

'Praise the Lord,' said Simon. 'Praise the Lord.'

'That sounds about right pal. It's a nun.'

It's a none too big bump on ze head,' said Monsieur LaRoche. 'Ze mad dog Englishman will survive I think.'

'A gallon of cold water is the thing,' said Aquaphagus. 'Shall I up-chuck on his head?'

'No no, I'm quite all right.' Raymond struggled to get up from the wheelhouse floor. 'Where are we?'

Beyond the broken wheelhouse windows the sky was black as night. Blacker. And with more stars.

'We are back in space.' Professor Merlin helped Raymond to his feet. 'We have escaped the planet Saturn and are on course for Earth.'

'Phew,' said Raymond. 'We did it then.'

'*You* did it, my boy. A hero, so you are.'

'*We* did it. In fact, Zephyr did most of it. Where is she?'

Professor Merlin shook his head. Dusty, battered artistes looked from one to another of themselves and said nothing.

'Where is she?' Raymond asked again.

Professor Merlin turned up his hands. 'Regretfully she is gone from us.'

'You mean we've left her behind on the planet? We must return at once to find her.'

'She will not be found, Raymond. She is gone.'

'Dead? You mean she's dead? She's not dead. She told me she couldn't be killed.'

'She is lost, Raymond. Remember her fondly.'

'No,' said Raymond. 'No no no. She can't just be gone. No.'

'Raymond, I'm sorry.'

'No,' Raymond found tears swelling up in his eyes. 'She can't have just ceased to exist.'

Professor Merlin nodded gravely.

'No.' Raymond plucked at his leather suit. 'See this

outfit? She magicked it up for me. *She* did. If she doesn't exist any more then this . . . ' he paused. The leather suit was crumbling from his shoulders. It fluttered down in flakes of dust to vanish on the floor. Leaving him alone once more. A poor cold naked schmuck.

'Noooooooooooooooooooo!'

'Let me find something for you to wear.' Professor Merlin put a hand about Raymond's shaking shoulder. The artistes turned their faces from his nakedness and nursed sorrows of their own.

'Come with me now and we will speak of this.'

Professor Merlin led Raymond to a sumptuous suite. The furnishings were lavish, ornate, marvellous. Over-stuffed settees. Fine Persian rugs. Walnut tallboys. Pale gilded whatnots.

Their antique splendours meant nothing to the broken man who slumped down into a settee, a paisley quilt about his sagging shoulders.

Professor Merlin handed him a crystal glass containing something alcoholic. 'She wasn't real, you know,' he said.

'She was real to me.' Raymond slurped at his drink.

'She looked as you wanted her to look. She felt how you imagined she might feel.'

'What else could any man dream of?'

'She was just a dream. Our dream.'

Raymond knocked back his drink and slammed down his glass. 'Then let us dream again. If she was your magic, bring her back to me.'

'I cannot. I helped to bring her into being, but now her time is passed.'

'I don't understand any of this. If you brought her into being, how did you do it? Tell me how.'

'We prayed for her.'

'What?'

'When the circus was captured so many years ago and taken to Uranus. It was the cooking pot for us. For my wonderful artistes. This is no ordinary circus,

236

Raymond, you have no doubt come to realize this. The feats my artistes perform are feats which simply cannot be performed. You had read of Monsieur LaRoche, many have tried to duplicate his act. None can. Because without magic, real magic, it cannot be done.'

'So you're all black magicians, is that it?'

'Hardly black. A little grey at the temples perhaps. Each of my artistes is unique. The gift that each possesses is unique. Precious. Unrepeatable. We put our talents together in a time of great mutual crisis and she came to us. Zephyr came to us. Freed us. And now she is gone. Her time is passed. Now is your time.'

'My time? Don't look at me. I don't have any magical powers. I don't have anything.' Raymond sank lower in his gloom.

'But you have. You are of the now. My time, the time of my circus, that time is passed. We have all grown weary. Our world is weary of us. It is weary of the circus. It is weary of magic.'

'Huh,' said Raymond.

'But it is. You yourself, to fight the foe and free the people, you called up a motor bike and a fearsome gun. I would have called up a snow-white charger and a shining sword.'

'The police would have shot you then.'

'And perhaps a magic shield,' said the professor. 'But you get my point. *We* have had our time. That time is done. Now is your time. Our magic fades. I do not think my circus will play again.'

The plaintive tone in the old man's voice made Raymond look up at him. 'Of course you will play again.'

'There is no planet now that we may play on. None but Earth, and I fear not even there.'

'You'll play again,' said Raymond. 'And on Earth.'

'The Earth is doomed I fear.'

'Is it, be buggered.'

'Sorry?'

'All right.' Raymond smacked his naked knees. 'Your sorrow is no less great than my own. But we cannot give up, can we? There's billions of people on Earth, our sorrow is somewhat less than theirs will be when the Edenites fill up the polar openings and suffocate the lot of them. I've got a family down there. I'd like you to meet them.'

'I would be most honoured.' The professor bowed.

'So we'll have to save them, won't we?'

'Then *you* will . . .'

'*I* will do everything I can, though without Zephyr . . .' Raymond shrugged sadly.

'I knew I had not misjudged you.' Professor Merlin poured Raymond another large drink. And one for himself as well. 'Your very good health,' said he.

'To Earth and to magic and to the circus.' Raymond paused. 'And to Zephyr.'

'I will drink to that.' Professor Merlin drained his glass. 'Now tell me, Raymond, what is a Millwall supporter?'

'What?' Raymond spluttered into his glass, sending something alcoholic up his nose. 'Whatever makes you ask me a question like that, at a time like this?'

'Well,' the professor gave his moustachios a pluck, 'it would appear that we have two hundred of them running riot in the hold.'

'Well bless my soul,' said the nun, in that Irish accent that nuns always have in American movies, well, in all movies really.

'If you'd be after closing the cell door on your way out, young man.'

'No way.' Constable Derek shook his head fiercely. 'I can't leave you alone with this maniac.'

'Sure and he looks pretty harmless to me. All trussed up like a Christmas turkey.'

'He's evil,' said the constable.

'I shall call you if I need you, go with God's blessing.'

'Well, all right then.' Constable Derek left the cell. But

not before giving Simon a passing kick in the ribs. As you would. 'Yell out if you need me, I'll be just down the corridor.'

Slam went the door and clunk went the key in the lock.

The nun looked down at Simon. 'Will you look at yourself?' she said. 'You're a sight to be seen, so you are.'

'Get these straps off,' whispered the lad on the deck. 'Set me free.'

'Set you free, is it?' The nun swung her foot and kicked Simon viciously between the legs.

'Aaaaaaaaaaaaaaaaaaagh!' went Simon.

'Shut your gob in there,' came the voice of Constable Derek from just down the corridor.

The nun kicked Simon again. She had a fine kick on her for a nun. A fine young kick. From a fine young foot. Set, where Simon always considered a fine young foot should be set, if it was a female one, inside a white, winklepickered shoe, with a three-inch stiletto heel.

'Liza,' wailed Simon. 'It's you. Stop kicking me.'

'You bastard.' Liza kicked him again. 'Get up on your feet.'

'So you can head butt me? No thanks.'

'So I can set you free.'

'Oh right. Yes please.'

Liza helped the battered one to his feet and plucked at the buckles on the strait-jacket.

'So, you saw the light, did you?' Simon asked.

'What are you babbling about?' Liza undid the straps.

'The light of the Lord.'

'Are you taking the piss, or what?'

'Why have you come here?' Simon asked.

'Long Bob sent me, of course.'

'Long Bob?' Simon tore off the strait-jacket and flung it to the floor.

'You look a right prat in that mask.'

Simon ripped it away from his face and checked his teeth. Intact. But they could do with a brush. 'So Long Bob sent you.'

'Of course he did. Dick turned up at the farm at about three in the morning. He told us the police had arrested you. I don't know what was up with him though, he couldn't keep a straight face. And his dog looked really shagged out.'

Simon flinched. 'Did you bring a gun or something?'

'Are you crazy?' Long Bob's going to blow the side wall off the police station.'

'Is he?' Simon nursed his tender parts. Most of his parts were tender.

'What do you mean, is he? You've read the book from the future, haven't you? You know what's going to happen next.'

'Ah yes.' Simon put his brain into gear. 'Of course I do.'

'Yeah, well. But what Long Bob wants to know is, how come, if you knew the police were coming, you let yourself get captured?'

'I'll bet he does.'

'Well?'

'Well,' Simon paused. 'Because that's what it says in the book. That's why. But I couldn't tell Long Bob that. Like I said at his farmhouse, he isn't supposed to know. Only me. That's how it works.'

'That makes sense,' said Liza.

Then you're a bigger fool than I took you for, thought Simon. But he was now extremely puzzled. Where was the book? Who had it? The constable who had gone searching had said that it wasn't in the hideaway bush, but that the bush was covered in feathers and stank of a horrible smell. So Simon had assumed the Sate-Hen and his acolytes now had the book. But obviously they didn't.

So who the hell did?

Simon adjusted his hair and made a puzzled face.

'You're acting bloody strange for a man who's supposed to know what's going to happen in the future,' said Liza.

Simon looked her up and down. She'd been a real disappointment to him, this woman. Joining the satanic loonies. Taking up with Military Dave. A real disappointment. God would permit a small act of justified revenge, surely?

'Actually,' said Simon, 'I am just a little disorientated. You see it says specifically in the book, and I quote, "Simon and Liza were making love in the police cell when Long Bob sprung him," and I do not have a watch on me. How soon might we expect him?'

'About five minutes from now.'

'Then quick, take off all your clothes.'

'It's called a *habit*,' said Liza.

To which Simon didn't reply.

20

'Two hundred Millwall supporters?' Raymond slumped back on his seat. 'Rioting in the hold?'

'And chanting,' said the professor.

'Chanting?'

'Oh lay oh-lay-oh-lay-oh-lay ooooh-lay ooooh-lay.'

'Oh dear,' said Raymond. 'Oh dear, oh dear, oh dear.'

'Warriors though.' Professor Merlin offered a salute. 'Most martial.'

'And are they all still naked?' Raymond didn't much fancy the thought.

'They were.'

'But you clothed them?'

'They clothed themselves, so to speak.'

'With what?'

'With the big spanking new auction house lorry. They stripped it to pieces and they've made themselves suits of armour.'

'Yes, I suppose they would.'

'Most enterprising young men. Interesting tattoos. But somewhat turbulent. I felt it wise to keep all the hatchways to the hold locked and barred for the time being.'

'I think that would be for the best, yes.'

'But they seem intent on breaking out. They're taking it in turns to head butt the doors. I wonder if perhaps you might go down and have a word with them. Explain things, as it were.'

'Have you tried?'

'I did.' The professor stroked at his mobile chin. 'I waved to them through one of the little windows in the doors. They didn't seem too pleased to make my acquaintance.'

'What did they say?'

'They chanted. Old iron old-iron-old-iron-old-iron, Ooooold-iron, Oooooold-iron. What does that mean exactly?'

'It's Cockney rhyming slang. Iron hoof, it means—'

'Aha!' Professor Merlin raised a wonderful finger. 'Rhyming slang. Iron hoof rhymes with, what *aloof*? Some say that of me, without cause, I might add. Or would it be, *proof*? A mis-spelling of prof?'

'Something like that probably.'

'Well, blessed be for that. I thought they were calling me a poof.'

Raymond spluttered once more into his drink.

'So you will go and have a word with them.'

'I will. But I'll need some clothes to wear. Do you have anything in blue and white?'

'I have a rather spiffing frocked coat, with quilted lapels, slashed sleeves and lace ruffles down the front and that's about all I think.'

'Oh dear,' said Raymond once again. 'Oh dear, oh dear, oh dear.'

'Oh,' went Liza. 'Oh oh oh.'

'Boom,' went Simon. 'Boom shanka boom.'

'Oi!' went Constable Derek. 'What's going on in there?'

Then, 'Oh my God!' he continued, as he peered through the nasty little shutter hole in the door. 'Now he's raping a nun, the bastard.'

Constable Derek fumbled his key into the lock and thrust the cell door open. 'Just stop doing that. Oh, you have. Where are you?'

'I'm here.'

The constable turned. Simon swung the cell door hard at him. Clunk it went against the constable's forehead.

243

'Oh,' went the constable, sinking down in a heap on the floor.

'Good one,' said Liza, adjusting her habit. 'Now let's go.'

'Ah no.' Simon gripped her by the arm. 'Not you.'

'What are you doing?' Liza struggled. Simon twisted her arms behind her back and secured them with her string of rosary beads. (Strong string.)

'Don't do that now. You know I only like it with the fur manacles and the pony harness.'

'Sorry.' Simon dodged the kicking feet and gagged her with that sort of bib thing that nuns wear around their necks. 'I have to go now. But you're not going with me.'

'Grmmmph mmmph mmm,' went Liza.

'That's easy for you to say.' Simon took a moment to admire his handiwork. Nuns in bondage. It had a certain something. Perhaps at some future time, with the girl who worked at the costume hire shop in Brighton. Some future time.

'If I have a future time.' Simon left the cell, locked the door behind him and sidled along the corridor and up a flight of steps.

At the front desk, a single constable was on duty. He sat with his feet up, reading the day's copy of *The Bramfield Mercury*.

He was not a constable that Simon had seen before.

So it followed that . . .

'Good-morning, Constable,' said Simon marching up. 'Having a bit of a rest, are you?'

The constable threw down his paper and jumped to his feet. 'Who are you?'

'Are you familiar with Inspector D'Eath?'

'No. I've just been transferred here. This very morning. I don't know him at all.'

'Well, you're looking at him now. So do up that button and look alert.'

'Yes . . . I . . .' The constable did up his button. 'Aren't you a bit young to be an inspector?'

'*Sir*,' said Simon. 'A bit young to be an inspector, · *sir*.'

'*Sir*,' said the constable.

'No,' said Simon. 'Do you have the keys to the safe?'

'Yes, sir.'

'Then open it up, lad.'

'Could I see your warrant card, sir?'

'Very thorough of you, lad. We'll make a policeman of you yet.'

'So could I see it, sir?'

'It's in the safe, lad. I have been interviewing a very dangerous criminal. All my personal possessions are locked in the safe. Warrant card. *Money.*'

'Yes, sir, right.'

'Then get a move on, lad. I've had a rough night.'

'Yes, sir.' The new constable took his keys from his pocket, went over to the safe and fumbled one into the lock.

Simon watched the seconds tick by on the big clock above the desk. 'Get a move on.'

'I am, sir. There.' The constable swung open the safe door.

The safe was empty.

'Shit,' said Simon. 'Shit, shit, shit.'

'Sir, please, I don't understand. No hang about.' The constable nipped past Simon and snatched up his newspaper. There on the front was a big banner headline. POLICE ARREST BUTCHER OF BRAMFIELD.

And beneath this there was a photograph of Simon. A bit fuzzy perhaps, but quite recognizable. Blown up from a group shot of The Jolly Gardeners' cup-winning darts team. The editor of *The Bramfield Mercury* had paid Andy one hundred pounds for it.

'You!' went the young constable. 'You're him.'

'Aw shit.' Simon leapt over the desk.

The young policeman drew his truncheon.

Simon made for the door.

The constable made after him.

And then there was an almighty BOOM and they both fell down.

The cringing menial fell down on his knees. 'Your Majesty,' he cringed.

His Royal Majesty the Grand Duke looked down upon him (in every sense of the word). 'You're not the same cringing menial I sent out earlier. What happened to him?'

'He got blown up, Your Majesty.'

'By the mad professor?'

'No, sire, by one of your helicopters.'

'Bring me the heads of the crew then.'

'The crew got blown up, sire. By the mad professor.'

'Outrageous. And where are the police?'

'Mostly in hospital, sire. There was a lot of smoke on the dock and in the confusion they all seem to have shot one another.'

'Anything else you'd like to tell me?'

'Well, a large amount of the city is now on fire. The fire spread from the row of shops the professor's ship hit when it landed to pick him up.'

'And where are the firemen?'

'They have the day off, sire. You declared it a national holiday.'

The Grand Duke wrung his big fat bejewelled fingers. 'Do we still have an airforce?' he enquired.

'When they come back tomorrow after their day off, we do.'

'Ye gods!' The Grand Duke wrung the neck of the cringing menial. 'I do not *believe* it. The professor decimates my police force, burns down my city—'

'Steals all your "George", sire.'

'*What?*'

'The two hundred bubbles of George. The ones you were really looking forward to eating.'

'*WHAT?*'

'Stolen from the auction house and loaded on to his ship.'

'Right!' The Grand Duke struggled to his big fat feet, dumping Colin to the deck once more. 'He will pay for this. His circus will pay for this. All the bloody Edenites of Eden will pay for this. Get on the telephone. Call Humphrey Gogmagog. Tell him I wish, no, I demand, to make a royal speech to the nation, to the entire planet, in half an hour's time. Got that?'

'Yes, sire,' cringed the cringer.

'Well, bugger off then.'

'There's just one more thing, sire.'

'What is it?'

'There's an elephant outside.'

'Circus elephant? Jumbo the circus elephant?'

'Yes, sire. It seems that the circus folk ran off without their animals. They're all still inside the palace. Except for the elephant. He's outside.'

'Well, that's something at least. Have my chef slaughter all the animals and cook them up for dinner. Poodles for starters, I think.'

'That's what the elephant wants to talk to you about, sire.'

'*Talk to me? What are you saying?*'

'He can talk, sire. Really, I heard him. And he wants you to set all the other animals free.'

'*He does what?*'

'Set them free. He says his name's not Jumbo any more, it's Moses. And to tell you, "Let my people go".'

'Oh let Oh-let-my-people-go, Leeet-go, Leeet-go.'

The chant greeted Raymond as he came down the steps leading to the cargo hold. The little window in the door, through which the Millwall supporters had chanted their considered opinion of Professor Merlin was now broken. But the hands that craned through it were unable to reach the outside bolts.

Raymond adjusted his silk cravat and smoothed down the knees of his velvet pantaloons. It wasn't going to be easy this. For one thing he had a bit of an image problem. For another, he had no idea just what he should say to these people. 'Hello, lads, you'll never guess what, but you were kidnapped by a flying starfish, flown to Saturn to be sold as food, rescued and are now on a Victorian steamship travelling through space on its way to do battle against the people of another Earth which surrounds the one you live on.' How would they take that? Raymond wondered.

Probably not well.

On a bulkhead near the hold door there hung a speaking tube arrangement. Raymond deduced (quite correctly as luck would have it) that here was a means of communicating with the warriors in the hold.

He took down the speaking end and blew into it.

A piercing whistle blasted through the cargo hold.

'Ahem,' went Raymond, wondering just what to say.

The professor had told him that, from his 'intelligence network', he had gleaned the information that the Millwall supporters had been travelling in three coaches to an away match against Manchester United when the alien abduction had occurred.

Raymond had seen a very obvious flaw in this. But he hoped no-one else would.

'Ahem.' Raymond cleared his throat once more. He had to tell them something. How would Simon deal with a situation like this?

Perhaps in this manner.

'Ahem. Good-afternoon. This is captain Raymond of the Sealink Line welcoming you aboard the cross channel ferry *Salamander*. We hope you are enjoying your journey, but regret that due to a forecast of rough seas ahead, we must keep the hold doors firmly locked.

'You may be experiencing a slight sense of disorientation and wondering just how you came to be here and why you didn't have any clothes on.' Raymond paused in search of a spurious explanation suitable to the occasion. 'You were drugged,' said Raymond, 'that's what it was. While you were on the coaches on your way to Manchester, rival fans laced your lager with LSD. Or your beer, if you were drinking beer. Or your cigarettes.' Raymond considered the unlikely possibility that one of the Millwall supporters had not been either drinking or smoking on the way to the match. 'Or it was fed through the air conditioning in the coaches.

'So you were all on this really bad acid trip and the manager of Millwall, Mr . . .' Raymond had no idea whatsoever who the manager of Millwall was. 'Mr . . .' he made the sound of static crackling, 'has sent you on this trip to France at the club's expense to let you recuperate.

'Your clothes, which were removed for decontamination of toxins, will shortly be returned to you. The company doctor advises against further head-butting of the doors, as this may induce toxic shock and permanent brain damage. Food and drink will soon be served and we hope you will enjoy your all-expenses-paid holiday in France. Thank you.'

Raymond hung up the speaking tube and put his ear to the bulkhead.

There was a temporary silence.

There always is before a really violent storm explodes.

The explosion at the police station rocked the better part of Bramfield. The not quite so good part of Bramfield, on the other side of the high street, didn't get rocked at all.

There was a lot of smoke and dust and falling masonry and fire alarms going off and chaos and confusion.

Armed men in stocking masks stormed the police station. One with a lurcher clinging to his leg.

The young police constable rising from the rubble was cruelly clubbed down by a rifle butt. The armed men kicked open doors, rushed along corridors, shouted Simon's name.

But Simon didn't answer them. He was no longer in the police station, having made a break for freedom through a side window leading to the car-park.

Here stood an impounded vehicle. It was one of those old Jags, so beloved of the criminal fraternity in TV cop shows like *The Sweeney*. And Simon had the keys.

How?

Well . . . er . . . he snatched them from the keyboard in the police station just before he leapt out of the window. That's how!

Simon peeped into the car. Just to make sure there were no back-seat drivers this time. There were none. So he leapt inside, keyed the ignition and made good his escape.

But to where?

Simon had one place in mind. A house hidden away at the bottom of the-lane-that-dare-not-speak-its-name.

The house of the Scribe.

A few startled souls were stirring as Simon drove up the high street, but not many. He kept his speed down and cruised past the shops and storefronts which now held evil memories for him.

The Bramfield Arms, where he had first encountered the men in grey. The bookies where he had won his fortune. The bank which had been closed against the banking of his fortune. The stretch of pavement he had raced along with his fortune. The supermarket doorway where he had been knocked down and relieved of his fortune.

Simon shuddered, what a nightmare. But he must put all that behind him now. It would have been nice if the money had been in the police safe. But that was asking rather a lot of God.

And as he was a soldier of the Lord now, bound upon a sacred mission, he must rise above such matters.

For now.

The soldier of the Lord drove carefully around the mini roundabout that everyone drives straight across, turned right at the big house that's always being done up, down King Neptune Road, past The Jolly Gardeners and left at the top of the hill.

The jag bumped in and out of the potholes that no-one wants to take responsibility for and as Simon passed Raymond's house he kept his head down, just in case Raymond's mum might be looking out of the window, awaiting the prodigal's return.

At the bottom of the lane Simon parked the car beside the abandoned railway track. He pocketed the keys and left the driver's door unlocked, in case a speedy escape was required.

Then he sidled along beside the high hedge sheltering the Scribe's house. Would there be a policeman on guard outside? Simon didn't think so. And there wasn't.

In through the gate and up the garden path.

The milkman had been and the paperboy. Simon removed the copy of *The Bramfield Mercury* from the letterbox and flung it back over the hedge. And then he knocked boldly at the door.

A moment's silence, then the shuffling of feet.

'Who's there?' called the voice of the scribe.

'Postman,' the voice of the postman replied. 'Package to be signed for. Registered mail. Money, I think.'

'Oh jolly good.' The sound of bolts being drawn. The door opened on the chain. They eye of the Scribe appeared in the crack.

'Oh no!' went the Scribe.

'Oh yes.' There was a bit of a struggle, but Simon's foot was firmly in the door.

'I have a gun,' shouted the Scribe, retreating in search of it.

Simon took three paces back and shoulder-charged the front door. The fact that this never works in real life meant nothing to him. The security chain shattered and Simon burst into the hall. Having now added a severely bruised shoulder to his already overstocked catalogue of superficial wounds.

'Stand back or I shoot you.' The Scribe stood in his PJs, dressing-gown and slippers. And he really did have a gun.

How come, Simon wondered, everybody in this bloody village has a gun except me?

'I just don't have time for that.' Simon kicked the gun from the Scribe's hands, stooped, retrieved it from the floor and pointed it at the now squirming author. 'Stick 'em up.'

'No,' said the Scribe. 'I won't.'

'Why?'

'Because the gun's not loaded.'

'Fair enough.' Simon raised the gun, club fashion. 'Stick 'em up, or I will beat you severely. The Scribe stuck 'em up. 'Into the living-room.'

Simon followed the stuck-up one into the living-room.

It was a shambles. Tables overturned. Papers everywhere. The stacks of glossy magazines with the matching spines were all over the place, out of date order. The word procurer lay upside down on the carpet.

'What happened here?'

'I had a visit from the police.'

'You and me both. But why did you do it? I told you, if anyone comes asking for me, tell them I've gone home to bed. I said it several times. And what do you do? You tell them I've gone to Long Bob's. Why?'

The Scribe looked puzzled. 'I told them you'd gone home. But that Inspector Death—'

'D'Eath,' said Simon. 'It was decided not to bother with a running gag about his name.'

'Nobody told me.'

'Never mind, carry on.'

'Well, Inspector D'Eath didn't believe me when I told him you'd gone home. He got very unpleasant. So as I was just writing that you were going to Long Bob's farm, I told him that. And he left. What were you doing at Long Bob's farm anyway?'

'Never mind.' Simon sat down on the sofa with the dreadful woollen multicoloured shawl thing on it. 'So why did he wreck your room?'

'He didn't. It was the other police who arrived later. The plain-clothed ones.'

'What plain-clothed ones?' Now Simon looked puzzled.

'They said they were a special unit. I didn't like the look of them one bit. All dressed in grey they were. Pinched faces. Even had grey sunglasses.'

'Oh no,' Simon sank into the sofa.

'You know them? Can I put my hands down now please?'

'I know them. And yes of course you can. Why did you try to stop me getting in?'

'Inspector D'Eath told me you were a psychotic.'

'Well I'm not.'

'So why have you come here?'

'I need to see the manuscript you're working on. I have to know what happens next. It's very very important.'

'I don't have it,' said the Scribe.

'Why not?'

'The special unit men took it with them.'

'*What?* You let the men in grey walk off with it? How could you do that?'

'They said they needed it for evidence.'

'But you know who they really are.'

'I don't know what you're talking about.'

'You bloody do.' Simon rose from his seat and made menacing moves towards the Scribe. 'You wrote about them in the bloody book. You know exactly who they are and what they do.'

'In my book?' The Scribe backed away. 'Come off it. Are you trying to tell me that the men in grey who were here last night are the same men in grey I wrote about? My book's just a fantasy. Are you mad?'

'Very.' Simon showed his fine set of teeth as a snarl

and advanced on the Scribe. 'You're lying to me.'

'I am not.' The Scribe took a step back and nearly fell into the inglenook. 'Leave me alone.'

'I want to see that manuscript.' Simon drew back his shirtcuffs and knotted his fists. 'And I want to see it now.'

'I don't have it. Uuurgh!'

Simon gripped the Scribe's throat in one hand and raised the other up to strike. 'I am going to beat you up now,' he said. 'When you feel like telling me all the truth and all about your involvement in all of this, just say the word and I will stop. Do I make myself clear? Do I make myself clear?'

But the Scribe didn't seem to be listening. His eyes were fixed upon a point somewhere beyond Simon's left shoulder. And his eyes were starting from their sockets.

'Do I make myself . . .' Simon paused. A most unpleasant smell had entered the living-room. A smell that Simon had smelt before. And a terrible coldness had entered with it.

Simon loosened his grip and slowly turned to follow the direction of the Scribe's socket-starters.

There, half shadowed in the doorway, something stood. It was a big something. A very big something indeed. Big and broad-shouldered and covered in feathers. And it stank like the devil himself.

This terrible something raised a gory-looking claw and displayed a large and glossy, if somewhat dog-eared, book. 'I think you are looking for this,' it said, in a dark Sate-Henic tone.

21

'You told them what?' Professor Merlin asked.

'Well, I had to tell them something.' Raymond dropped onto an over-stuffed settee. 'They'll be great if we have to go into battle. But for now we can't have them smashing up the ship. You'll have to get food sent down to them. And whatever drink you happen to have. Lower it down on a rope or something.'

'Fiddle-de fiddle-dum.' The old man lifted his wig and brushed dust from his head. 'So to work. We are full steam ahead toward Eden. Speak to me now of your plan.'

'Of my plan.' Raymond sighed. 'This would be my plan to stop the Edenites paving over the polar openings to Earth, I suppose.'

'*Alethic,* my dear pot noodle. "As relating to such philosophical concepts as truth, necessity, possibility and contingency. Lay that plan upon me, bro".'

'I don't have a plan,' said Raymond, 'as you know full well. I know nothing about Eden and I don't have the faintest idea how we might stop them proceeding with their evil schemes.'

'This is most dispiriting news.' The professor made a most dispirited face. 'I had hoped that we might just synchronize watches like we did the last time.'

'I think not.' Raymond shook his head in a manner which left no room for doubt regarding his opinion of this. 'My suggestion is, that we get all your unique artistes around a table and, as this is once more a time of great mutual crisis, we attempt to conjure up a plan, much as you conjured Zephyr.' Her name made

Raymond sad, but a man's gotta do what a man's gotta do, and macho stuff like that.

Professor Merlin pulled upon his chin. 'There is wisdom in your words, but my artistes are weary.'

'*I'm* weary,' said Raymond. 'And sick at heart. But I'm prepared to try my best. I'm only a plumber from Bramfield, you know. And did you ever hear of a plumber saving the world?'

'Mario,' said the professor. 'And his brother Luigi.'

'I shall pretend I didn't hear that.'

'Sorry. So.' Professor Merlin leapt to his feet to rock upon creaking knees. 'All right. So be it. Yea verily thus and so. We shall call a council of war. I will have the nosh sent down to the warriors, get a J-cloth taken across the grand salon and we'll all meet there in half an hour. How does that sounds to you?'

'Sounds good,' said Raymond. 'Let's go for it.'

'Counting down,' said the director. 'Five four three two one. Let's go for it.'

'Good-afternoon and hi there.' The jackal-head with the swish tuxedo grinned twin rows of teeth. 'Humphrey Gogmagog here, live at The Palace of Celestial Pleasure. Where it is with a sense of great honour and humility that I am privileged to introduce you to a man who needs no introduction from me. Our benevolent ruler, the man we worship and adore, his magnificence, his handsomeness, the birthday boy himself, let's hear it for the Grand Duke . . .'

Clap clap clap, went the canned-laughter machine, clap clap clap and cheer.

Those people of Fogerty, who had not been driven from their homes by the raging inferno sweeping through the city, but were enjoying it live on the telly, rose to switch off and make tea.

'Don't touch that dial,' cried Humphrey. 'This is a broadcast of worldwide importance and affects *you* personally. His Royal Highness—'

'Thank you, Humphrey.' The big fat fellow's fat face filled the screen. 'Good people all,' he smiled. 'I speak to you this day, this special holiday, which I have given you in celebration of my birthday, not to thank you for the thousands of cards and messages of good will bestowed upon me—'

'Because the fat bastard never got any,' whispered Humphrey to the cameraman.

'—but with sadness, to declare that a state of world-wide emergency now exists. Today our capital city was viciously attacked and set ablaze. You will have seen it yourselves on your TV screens.

'Our gallant fire fighters have not been able to bring the blaze under control—'

'Because you gave them all the day off, you prat,' whispered Humph.

'Thousands flee in terror, homes destroyed, businesses ruined. A tragedy. A tragedy.' Small tubes, cunningly concealed on the Grand Duke's temples, dispensed 'teardrops' which trickled down his cheeks. 'Sniff sniff,' went the Grand Duke. 'My heart is breaking.'

'Not,' whispered Humph.

'It is the nightmare we have all secretly dreaded. An unprovoked attack by the Edenites. That warlike and tyrannical race under whose yoke we have laboured for too long.'

'That's good coming from you.'

'I myself,' said the Grand Duke, 'hail from Eden. But I am not as they. I am one of you. And I have struggled ceaselessly to bring independence to Saturn. But here, as indeed upon Uranus and Mars, the insidious Edenites have spread their culture, their products and their language.'

A pity that Raymond wasn't here to hear this. It would have explained a lot to him.

'We import their products, they dominate our economy and now they seek to destroy us. Shall we stand idly by and let them do it? Will we watch helplessly while our beautiful cities burn? Or shall we strike back? Take up arms against the evil tyrant and smash him utterly?'

'Could this just be the excuse he's been waiting for for years to have a pop at his hated brother?' Humphrey whispered. 'Or am I just being cynical?'

'My own brother.' The Grand Duke shed more tears. 'My own triplet twin, King Eddie of Eden. How, you may ask, can a peace-loving, merciful teddy bear of a man such as I, stir the hand of war against my own flesh and blood? With great sorrow, that's how. But he has used and abused us and we shall stand no more. I am ordering full mobilization. I want the army upon red alert and the airforce made ready to attack. We move against Eden. We are at war.'

'Hail Saturn,' the Grand Duke raised a fat fist. 'I thank you.'

'Cut,' said the director. 'Roll the national anthem.'

The big fat Grand Duke mopped the bogus tears from his face. 'I think that went rather well. What do you think, Humphrey?'

If you like irony, thought the jackal-head. 'Stirring stuff, sire,' he said, hurrying over and bowing low. 'I hope you will permit me the honour of being the exclusive war correspondent throughout the conflict.'

The Grand Duke stroked his big fat chin. 'I don't think so, Humphrey.'

'No, sire?'

'No, Humphrey. You see, during my long long reign as monarch of this planet, I have become quite adept at overhearing all the little snide remarks made by my subjects when they think they're out of earshot. So I think I'll just have your head chopped off, you smart-arsed dog-faced bastard.'

'Oh,' said Humphrey. 'What a bummer.'

The cameraman tittered into his hands.

'And watch *your* step too,' said the Grand Duke. 'Or you're dead, you stinker.'

* * *

Simon held his nose against the stink. The monstrosity stood, filling the doorway and blocking the only exit. The Scribe's eyes turned up into his head and he fainted dead away into the inglenook.

Thanks for your help, thought Simon. Oh bloody hell!

The thing took a step into the room and raised once more its terrible claw. 'The book.'

No words came to Simon. His throat was dry, his heart was doing step aerobics and his legs, although wanting to run, had grown somewhat weak at the knees. This was serious stuff. You couldn't fight a thing like this. You wouldn't stand a chance.

Another step.

The horror.

Simon did something so singularly pathetic that if God had been watching, He would no doubt have turned away His face and gone, 'Oh my God.'

Simon put his two forefingers together to make a cross and said, 'Back, I command you in the name of the Lord.'

'The book.' The thing lurched forward at him, stumbled and collapsed in a heap on the floor at his feet.

'Blimey,' said Simon, examining his fingers. 'This stuff really works.'

He stared down at the monster. The thing. Sate-Hen.

It wasn't Sate-Hen.

Simon gaped at the tattooed pentagram on the blood-bespattered head. It wasn't Sate-Hen.

It was Mr Hilsavise!

Simon stooped and with difficulty turned the big man over. He was in a really terrible shape. Covered in feathers and V-shaped cuts and lots and lots of blood. This man had been in a battle. And he had lost, by the looks of it.

'Are you all right?' Simon shook his head. Why do people always ask that stupid question to people who are quite obviously not all right? Simon didn't know. 'Sorry,' he said. 'Are you still alive then?'

'Only just,' Mr Hilsavise gripped Simon's shoulder, cutting off the circulation and dislocating a couple of bones. 'Get me a drink, will you.'

Pleased to and one for myself, I think. Simon made off to the Scribe's kitchen. It was a very posh-looking kitchen. He opened the refrigerator. Champagne. Two dozen bottles of Champagne.

'Bastard.' Simon drew out a bottle and returned to the living-room, drawing the cork also as he did. So to speak.

'Here you go.' He put the bottle to his employer's lips.

'Thank you.' Mr Hilsavise did big swiggings. 'That's enough.'

'Good, I'll have some too.' Simon wiped the neck of the bottle on his cuff (dental hygiene) and took a swig of his own. There was nothing left in the bottle.

'Help me up.' Simon helped the injured man onto the sofa.

'What happened to you?' Simon asked.

'Chickens. Bloody chickens. Stinking bloody chickens. They went at me like vultures.'

'You got the book.' Simon took it up from the carpet. 'I don't understand.'

'I saw you.' Mr Hilsavise was coming to a bit. 'I was walking my dog last night and I saw you. Taking a piss on the hill above Long Bob's farm.'

Simon recalled the hiker in the blue anorak, or was it a cagoule?

'So I went up there to dry roast your bloody nuts for getting my truck wheel-clamped, losing my Allen Scythe and quitting the job without telling me.'

'Ah,' went Simon.

'But you'd gone. I heard the dog growl and you howl and I found the book. I thought you'd come back for it, so I sat down to wait. And while I waited, I read it.'

'Ah,' said Simon again.

'And I watched all the rest. You letting Long Bob's tyres down, taking the petrol to the chicken sheds, Dick Godolphin—'

'You need not continue,' said Simon. 'I recall it all well enough.'

'Did I mention that I liked your new hat?' asked Mr Hilsavise.

'We've dropped the new hat gag,' said Simon. 'No-one understood it and it wasn't very funny.'

'Oh, fair enough. So later I see you drive away in the Jag. But the thing is, I'm reading it, in the book. The same thing, you driving away in the Jag.'

'Then I'm back.' A toothy smile broadened across Simon's face. 'I'm back in the book. It worked.'

'I need another drink,' said Mr H. 'Get another bottle, Simon, I'm parched.'

'Oh yes.' Simon got more champagne. Two bottles. He returned and popped the corks from both. The Scribe awoke from his faint, saw this occur and fainted dead away once more.

'So.' Mr Hilsavise took one bottle and Simon drank from the other. 'So, I'm reading this and thinking, This can't be true. And I'm flicking back and forwards and I read this bit that says, "Mr Hilsavise was sitting in the hideaway bush, reading the book, when the chickens sniffed him out and attacked." And I go, What? and the next thing I know—'

'Yeah,' Simon said. 'I get the picture. I don't want to hear about it.'

'Those things nearly killed me. I bit a few heads off though.'

'That's enough,' Simon said. 'I get the picture.'

'But this is bad, Simon. This is really bad.'

'I know, I'm up to my neck in it.'

'According to the book, you've found the Lord.'

'Yes I have.' Simon suddenly drew back. 'But you . . . I thought . . .'

Mr Hilsavise raised a hairless, blood-specked eyebrow. 'You never were too bright, Simon,' said he, pointing to the pentagram on his head. 'It's point-upwards. I'm not a satanist. I'm of the old religion. A white witch, if you like. Although I prefer the term, white warlock.'

'Oh,' said Simon. 'And do you have a coven then?'

The warlock nodded. 'There's many of the old religion in Bramfield. This *is* a country village, after all.'

'And do you' Simon paused, 'how shall I put this. Do you dance around with young women in their bare scuddies? You know, by the light of the moon?'

'Most Wednesday nights, yes.'

'And you've never asked *me* to join?' Simon made a most offended face.

'Would *you* ask you to join?'

'Hmmph,' went Simon. 'But well, glory be, so we're on the same side, anyway.'

'But I'll still dry roast your nuts if you don't get back my Allen Scythe.'

'Long Bob has it.'

'Is that the truth?'

'Cross my heart and hope to die.' Simon crossed his heart and hoped not to. 'How are you feeling now?'

'Pretty wretched, I need a bath. But I think I can summon up enough strength to do what must be done.'

'Fight Sate-Hen and his followers.'

'Destroy Sate-Hen and scatter his followers.'

'Bravo,' said Simon. 'Naturally I have a pretty foolproof plan of my own for dealing with them, but; he paused in his lie, 'I should be grateful to learn what you have in mind.'

'I'll bet you would.' Mr Hilsavise smiled. Something Simon had never seen before. It was most unsettling. 'If you're going to destroy the devil in a chicken house and save mankind,' he said, 'there's only one way to do it.'

'And that's wearing black leather and riding on a Harley Davidson.'

'No,' said Mr H. 'That's by marching up there at night, with a whole lot of villagers carrying flaming torches. Don't you ever go to the pictures?'

'Not the same ones you go to, obviously.'

'So. I shall make some phone calls. You tie up the

illy bugger in the fireplace and get some breakfast on.'

'Right,' said Simon. 'No, wrong,' said Simon. 'I mean, isn't the silly bugger supposed to be writing what happens next in the book?'

'From what I can make out, he *did* write it, up until the time the men in grey took his manuscript away. I think *you* probably wrote the rest.'

'*Yes!*' Simon threw up a fist. 'Then, tie the silly bugger up it is and get the breakfast on. For later shall we hasten forth to war.'

Before we hasten forth to war,' said Raymond, sitting at the table's head, I am wondering if it might be better for us to hasten forth in peace instead.'

The artistes of Professor Merlin's circus sat once more about the wonderful table in the grand salon. It has been *-clothed, spruced up and again spread with a most marvellous feast. Nobody seemed particularly hungry though. The performers were weary. Their shoulders down, their make-up flaking. Raymond looked from one unto another of the dismal throng. 'Peace anybody?' he asked.

No-one replied.

'Perhaps we could reason with the Edenites.'

Monsieur LaRoche replied, 'Forget it, *mon ami*. We are nothing to them. George for their tables, that's all.'

'But if we told them the game is up. If we informed the people of Earth about what was going on and told the Edenites that they knew.'

Professor Merlin shook his head. 'The Edenite shape-shifters hold the power on the inner Earth. They would see that none down there believed you. And that even if they did, nothing would be done.'

'Tell me about these shape-shifters. Are the Edenites possessed of magical powers, or what?'

'Possessed of technology is all. Somewhat in advance of that on the inner Earth.'

'Like holograms, do you mean?'

'A more advanced principle. I had a hoarding of m
own once. But somebody broke it.'

'Quite so,' Raymond said. 'But let me get this straigh'
The presidents and prime ministers and so forth of Eart'
have been replaced by these advanced holograms, is tha
what you're saying?'

'In a word. Nutshell. You will recall how Presiden
Reagan got shot through the heart and yet lived. Ho\
no-one is allowed to touch the Queen of England
How heads of state only shake hands with other head
of state.'

Raymond ignored the gaping holes in this theory. 'S\
how is it done?' .

'Projections from above, dear boy. An actor, playin
the part of the president let us say, acts in a specia
studio on Eden. A holographic image of him, compute
modelled to resemble the president is beamed down
His movements become the president's movements or
Earth.'

Raymond scratched at his nose. 'I don't see how tha'
could actually function. What about when the president'
in a moving car, or on an aeroplane. How could tha'
work?'

'I don't know. *But it does.*'

Raymond shook his head. 'So what would happen i
we could somehow switch off the holograms on Eden?'

'Chaos on Earth.' Professor Merlin threw up his hands,
caught them again and thrust them into his pockets. 'All
the world's leaders, vanished in a flash.'

'I quite like the sound of that. But chaos on Earth
wouldn't stop the paving over.'

'There is only one way to stop it,' said Dr Bacteria
darkly (and with menace). 'Kill the king. That's all.'

'That sounds like war to me.'

'I could do it with a handshake. Anthrax, I think, or
cholera.'

'Quite so.' Raymond leaned back in his chair. 'But
where would that get us? Even if we killed him, and I'm

not keen on killing anyone, another king would probably take his place. It won't solve the problem. No. Hang about. It might.'

'He has an idea.' Professor Merlin clapped his hands. 'See that. I told you all he would. Speak on, my sweet boy. I'll synchronize my watch.'

'It's just a thought. But if these super-dooper holograms fool people on Earth, would they fool the people of Eden, do you think?'

'Fool anyone I suppose. As long as you don't touch.'

'And nobody touches a king?'

'Nobody.'

'Well,' Raymond said.

'Well?' Professor Merlin asked.

'Aw come on.'

'Sorry?'

Raymond sighed. 'Say we could get to Eden and quietly bump off this king, or kidnap him, or something. Then we replace him with a hologram. And then this hologram tells his people, "Let us not pave over the polar holes, let us instead live at peace with our brothers of the inner Earth. Let us begin a new golden age of love and understanding. Let us share our knowledge and—"'

'Pardon me while I up-chuck,' said Mr Aquaphagus. 'Anyone for sushi?'

Professor Merlin grinned from ear to ear and nose to navel. 'No, by Gadfry, Raymond's right. His plan is most inspired.'

'But we still have to get to this king.'

Professor Merlin gave this some thought. 'You could go in alone by night,' he suggested.

'No,' said Raymond.

'Take Dr Bacteria with you then.'

'No,' said Dr Bacteria.

'The two hundred warriors then.'

'No,' said Raymond once again. 'But I think I know a way.'

'This doesn't surprise me one bit.'

'You could put on a show.'

'I could put on a what?'

'A show. Like you did for the Grand Duke. You coul offer to put on a show for the king.' Raymond laughed 'I don't suppose it happens to be the king's birthday too does it?'

'Ah,' said the professor, mournfully.

22

There was a lot of busyness in Bramfield. It was ten-thirty now and the pubs were open.

The Jolly Gardeners was packed. Not with the usual morning wastrels today, but with the nation's Press. Andy was going great guns behind the counter and the words, 'Jolly good', were rarely far from his mouth. The fact that an as yet unidentified terrorist force had freed the Butcher of Bramfield had spiced things up no end. And our moral representatives were eager to interview anyone with an inkling into the psyche of the psycho.

Their numbers were swelled by a coterie of coquettes, who, having read of chequebook journalism, were anxious to sell their exclusive stories. *The Simon I knew, by the fiancée who loved him,* being a popular exclusive.

Glasses rose and fell, the pump handles went back and forwards and the cash register went in and out.

'Alone in the bar, we were,' said Paul to a reporter with a notebook. 'Just me and the Butcher. You could have cut the atmosphere with a razor. It was me who passed on the information of his whereabouts to the police. I suppose I can take much of the credit for his capture. Do you know the bloke who sets the crosswords, by the way?'

'Oh yes,' said a bandaged Constable Derek to another reporter with a notebook. 'Six armed men. No, not men with six arms. Six men, armed, I fought them off as best I could, but they knocked me unconscious and released him. Commendation for bravery? There has been some talk of that, yes. Reports of a nun seen running away with the terrorists? *No,* I certainly didn't see any nun.'

*   *   *

In The Bramfield Arms the atmosphere was quieter. But as it *was* the atmosphere of The Bramfield Arms, it was still one best tested first with a miner's canary, or whatever the sub-marine equivalent might be.

Black Jack Wooler lurked behind his counter and, in a far and fetid corner, two men in grey sat over a pile of typed paper.

'Told you,' said grey man number two. 'I knew that bastard was lying about his short-term memory loss. We were right to keep him under surveillance. He's been writing his bloody memoirs, by the look of it.'

Grey man number three ground his grey teeth. 'According to this he was on the allotment when Abdullah snatched up the other schmuck. Here, I like this bit where he kicks you out of his house.'

'He did *not* kick me out of his house. That bit is a lie.'

'Yeah. But what about the rest? What about this Raymond's adventures? That has to be fiction, doesn't it?'

Grey man number two looked doubtful. 'But it's all there. About Eden and everything. You're not going to tell me he just made *that* up. And what about the Edenites sealing up the polar openings? What if that's true? What about *us*?'

'Shut up!' said grey man number three. 'That fat bastard's listening.'

'Well I don't like it. We haven't been paid and I don't want to be left down here to die.'

'Shut up. We'll soon know what's what. Grey man number one's phoning the guvnor on Eden. He'll find out the truth.'

'*Grey man number one?* Doesn't he have a name?'

Grey man number three flicked through the pages of the Scribe's manuscript. 'Apparently not. But look, here he comes now.'

Grey man number one appeared through the murk and sat down with his nameless companions.

'What's to do?' asked grey man number two.

'I don't know. I couldn't get through to the guvnor. The answer-phone was on. So I left a message for him to call us back here.'

'I don't like it.' Grey man number two didn't like it. 'I think we're being stitched up. Deserted. That's what I think.'

'No.' Grey man number one shook his head of grey. 'The Edenites wouldn't do that to us. We have their respect. We're loyal workers. We shall continue with our work. Take care of this Simon.'

'And Mr Kilgore Sprout?'

'He's not important. The fellow with the teeth is the smoking pistol. Snuff him out and our job here's done.'

'Yeah but—'

'Trust me,' said grey man number one. 'The Edenites will look after us. Or my name's not grey man number two.'

'My name is Moses,' said the elephant. 'And I say, let my people go.'

'Look, I've told his Highness that,' replied the cringing menial. 'But he's very busy right now. He's got a war to organize. Why don't you call back later?'

'Tell the Pharoah,' quoth Moses, 'and if thou refuse to let them go, behold I will smite all thy borders with frogs, Exodus 8.2.'

'Frogs?' said the cringing menial.

'Frogs,' said Moses.

'Right. Well I'll pass that on to him. But I don't think he'll be happy.'

Inspector D'Eath was not a happy man. Having turned in the previous night, in the knowledge that he had not only nabbed a serial killer and secured for himself a good chance of promotion, but also he had nabbed the serial killer's money and secured for himself the opportunity to buy a little country pub somewhere, when he took an early retirement. The rude awakening that masked gunmen had blown up the police station and snatched away Simon, took the edge from this contentment.

And with half the police station reduced to smoking ruination there was now the matter of where to set up a task force headquarters, to coordinate the massive operation that would have to be set in motion.

The village hall had the spring flower show on and the youth club, where they play the loud music on Mondays, was closed pending structural repairs to its foundations. The only decent-sized room available in the whole of Bramfield was the 'reception suite' above the saloon bar of The Jolly Gardeners.

Andy had been most pleased to rent out the musty cob-webbed chamber. And Inspector D'Eath, in no position to argue, had been forced to pay a daily rate, something in access of twice The Jolly Gardeners' average weekly takings.

And so now the inspector sat and seethed behind a trestle table, whilst fellow officers scurried to and fro, setting up telephones, linking computer terminals, sharpening pencils and giving up smoking. Word was out that a chief inspector was on the way from Scotland Yard to take overall control. Word was also out that this chief inspector was a woman. And that she looked just like Helen Mirren.

Inspector D'Eath had a pistol in his pocket. And he would *not* be pleased to see her.

'Please, sire. Please, sire. There's something you have to see.' A cringing lacky (as opposed to a menial, the distinction is subtle, but nonetheless valid) burst unannounced into the bed chamber of the Sultan of Uranus.

The sultan was celebrating his birthday with his concubines and one was just being lowered down in the revolving split-cane basket. It wasn't the time for interruptions.'

'Get out of my bedroom,' shrieked the sultan.

The cringing lacky flung himself face down upon the floor. 'It's your brother, sire, the Grand Duke of Saturn.'

'My brother here? Well don't cower around on ceremony. Get his head chopped off at once.'

'No, sire, not here. On satellite TV.'

'*What?*' The sultan arose and swung aside his dangling lovely (which you can take as you will). 'You burst in here to tell me that my no-good brother's on TV?'

'He's declared war, sire.'

'What? On us?'

'No, sire. On Eden. On your other brother. King Eddie.'

'That shitbag!'

'You're not what you'd call tight knit, for triplets, are you, sire?'

'A Pox upon your impudence. Kiss my toe at once.'

The cringing lacky kissed the sultan's toe. 'I'd rather kiss your dangling lovely,' he said beneath his breath.

'That's enough toe work. Why has the one shitbag declared war on the other shitbag?'

'It's to do with your ship, sire. The one Abdullah phoned home about. The ship has left Saturn and the Grand Duke is sending his airforce to destroy it.'

'*Destroy my ship?*' The sultan kicked his lacky in the ear.

'And wage war on Eden.' The cringing lacky rubbed his ear.

'Stuff Eden. I want my ship back. Call out the special marines. Send out a strike force. Smash the Saturnians and bring back my ship.'

'But—'

'*But?*' roared the sultan.

'But you've given them all the day off to celebrate your birthday.'

'Rrrrrrrrrgh!' went the sultan. 'And where is Abdullah?'

And where was Abdullah indeed?

'And where is Simon and where is all our money?' Long Bob made a most fierce face across his kitchen table.

'I don't know.' Liza struggled. She was still in the nun suit and still tied up. Nuns in bondage. It did have a certain something. Long Bob could go for it.

'Let me free.' Liza struggled again. 'Simon knocked out the constable, tied me up and ran off.'

'She's covering for him,' said the looker. 'The two of them are in it together. Probably planning to split the money. And he nicked my car.'

'It looks bad for you,' Long Bob told Liza. 'His Majesty was deprived of his sacrifice last night. He's a growing boy. He must have his grub.'

'What?' went Liza. '*What?*'

'I'm afraid so. Unless,' Long Bob glanced around the room at the other members of B.E.A.S.T., 'any of you would rather stand in for Liza.'

The heads were shaking. The 'nos' had it.

'No!' screamed Liza. 'You can't do that to me.'

'You should look upon it as an honour.'

'Let me go, you raving loon.'

'Tut tut tut.' Long Bob shook his long head. 'Dick,' said he, 'gag this woman, take her over to the tool shed and lock her in.'

The poacher's dog began to wag its tail.

'It will be our pleasure,' said Dick.

'"*It will be our pleasure,*" said Dick!' Simon slammed down *The Greatest Show off Earth*. 'Those maniacs are going to sacrifice Liza. Jesus Christ! Oh pardon me. But, the bastards.'

'If it's not one thing, it's another.' Mr Hilsavise, now bathed, bandaged and squeezed into the Scribe's best suit, slammed down that fellow's telephone. 'I can't get through to anyone. The GPO have cut off half the lines in the village to link them up with the police operations room at The Jolly Gardeners.'

'We have to do something now,' said Simon. 'This very minute.'

'Not without the villagers and the flaming torches we won't.'

'Sod the villagers.' Simon snatched up the book. 'I'm going to flick forward and see what happens next.'

'I don't think you should do that, Simon.'

'Well *I* do.'

'I don't think you're really supposed to know what happens next.'

'I don't care. I'm going to look anyway.'

'Don't do it, Simon.'

'So who's going to stop me?'

Mr Hilsavise sighed. Then swung a fist the size of a prize-winning turnip straight at Simon's chin.

The seeker after future knowledge collapsed in a limp and unconscious heap onto the sofa with the dreadful woollen multicoloured shawl thing on it.

The warlock gazed up towards the ceiling. 'I'm sorry about that, Lord,' he said, 'but if he'd read about what he has to do, there's no telling what he might actually do. If you know what I mean, and I'm sure that you do. So I think we should best let him sleep and cut this chapter short, so we can get into the build up for the big exciting climax at the end. If that's OK with you.'

The Lord did not reply to this, as he rarely does that sort of thing. But as the chapter came to an abrupt end at this very moment, it's safe to assume that he agreed.

23

'Shiva's sheep!' said Raymond. 'Would you look at that down there?'

The circus folk were on the deck of the *SS Salamander*, which now turned in orbit above the northern hemisphere of Eden.

Pretty swift journey from Saturn?

And who's been steering the ship?

Good points. But moving right along.

It looked just like Earth only bigger. And with a dirty great hole where the north pole should be.

'It's very beautiful,' said Raymond, admiring the view. 'The colours are so vivid.'

'It is Eden.' Professor Merlin clamped a pair of darkly tinted pince-nez across the bridge of his shark's fin hooter. 'Cradle of mankind. Earthly paradise and things of that nature. Or once was, at least. Do you see the fug?'

Raymond saw the fug. Drifting out of the dirty great hole where the north pole should be. 'What a shame.'

'And do you see the moons?'

Raymond searched the black sky for moons. 'I see two.'

'An observational *tour de force* on your part, me old Galileo. Two small moons, newly captured into orbit and soon to be drawn down to plug up the holes in the poles.'

Raymond shrugged. He had been expecting something unlikely when it came to the matter of how the holes in the poles were going to be blocked up. Not perhaps quite as unlikely as this. But something close.

'So,' said Professor Merlin, without enthusiasm. 'I suppose I should get on the blower and give Eden a call.'

'And what are you proposing to say?'

'Well.' Professor Merlin preened at his natty lapels. 'Actually I have come up with a rather inspired idea of my own.'

'Oh yes?' said Raymond doubtfully.

'Oh yes indeedy do. As you are now aware, today is King Eddie's birthday also. Thus I will let it be known that we are a Saturnian circus, sent as a special birthday surprise by his dear brother the Grand Duke.'

'You don't think that the king might get on the old inter-planetary telephone and call up his brother to check our credentials?'

'Why ever should he do that?'

Raymond shrugged again. 'It was just a thought.'

'Well dismiss it from your mercurial mind.' The professor smiled hugely. 'You see, Raymond, it isn't just you who can hit upon a really good idea.'

'Who hit me?' Simon awoke to a violent application of cold water. '*You* did. Why?'

'I tripped,' said Mr Hilsavise. 'Sorry.'

Simon clutched at his grazed chin. And worried at his teeth. 'I think you've loosened a cap.'

'Forget about your damned teeth for once. We have to go.'

'Good, I told you there was no time to lose.' Simon climbed shakily to his feet and stretched. Beyond the living-room windows all was dark. 'It's night already, how long have I been out?'

'I thought the rest would do you good.'

'But Liza—'

'She'll be all right. But we have to go now.'

'Are the villagers with the torches here then?'

'Ah those.' Mr Hilsavise did sickly grinnings.

'What do you mean, ah those?'

'Things are a bit difficult,' Mr H. explained. 'You see since you've been, er, sleeping, Bramfield has been put under curfew. All the roads leading out of the village have been blocked and a special police weapons unit is combing the area. F.A.R.T.'

'Excuse me if I don't.'

'F.A.R.T. The FireArms Response Team. A rather gung-ho bunch, by the sound of it.'

'Typical,' said Simon. 'All it takes is a few armed terrorists blowing up a police station to free a serial killer and you get that kind of knee-jerk reaction.'

'Quite. So I haven't been able to raise as many torch-bearers as I had wished.'

'But you got a couple of hundred?'

'Well . . .'

'*One* hundred?'

'Well . . .'

'Fifty?'

Mr Hilsavise scratched his shaven head. 'Did you read that bit in *The Greatest Show off Earth* where Raymond asks the professor how many soldiers he's already recruited to the cause?'

'Of course,' said Simon, who had only ever read the bits that he personally was in. 'How many did he say, again?'

Mr Hilsavise handed Simon a stick with an oily rag tied to the end. 'He said, *Just you. You're it.*'

'He said we can come on down.' Professor Merlin returned to the deck. Raymond stood all alone. He had been doing something over the side that he shouldn't.

'Who said?' Raymond hastily buttoned his fly.

'My good friend King Eddie.'

'Your *good friend?*'

'Charming fellow. We had a long conversation. He's a big admirer of the circus. Funny thing. It was almost as if he was expecting us. Charming man.'

'This would be the same charming man who intends

o stuff moons into the polar openings and extinguish all life on Earth.'

'Fiddle-de fiddle-dum.'

'And fiddle de de. Can you muster up much of a show, Professor? Most of everything was left behind on Saturn.'

'The show must go on. And where are my artistes, by the by?'

'Gone to get changed, I think. They all do look pretty knackered. Perhaps this is a big mistake.'

'They are troupers. If it is to be our final performance, we shall give it our all.'

'Fair enough. Just one thing, Professor. Could I ask you a favour?'

'No need to ask. If it is within my power to grant it, you can consider it granted.'

'Thanks a lot,' Raymond said as he made off along the deck towards the wheelhouse. 'I just wanted to steer the ship down to Eden by myself.'

'I just want to deal with this by myself.' Inspector D'Eath squared up to the well-dressed woman who stood before him in the operations room above The Jolly Gardeners.

She wore a waisted blue woollen suit, white blouse, black stockings, shoes just high enough at the heels to turn heads. And she bore an uncanny resemblance to a certain Helen Mirren.

'Chief Inspector Jenny Lestrade, but you can call me ma'am.'

'Can I call you guv, ma'am?' asked Constable Derek.

'Of course you can, Constable. So, Inspector, what do we have?'

Inspector D'Eath chewed upon his lip and regrouped some breakaway hair strands that had made it as far as his chin. With a rictus smile he displayed the large map of the area, which had been blu-tacked to the wall by the window. 'We have road blocks set up here, here, here, here, here and here.'

'There?' Chief Inspector Lestrade pointed.

'There,' said D'Eath. 'And there and there and ther
and there.'

'And there?'

'*And* there.'

'What about there?'

'There too.'

'And there?'

Inspector D'Eath examined the map. 'That's The Jolly
Gardeners, where we are now.'

'Just testing. Well, you seem to have road blocks pretty
much everywhere.'

'Yes,' said the inspector proudly.

'Then let's just hope he doesn't choose to simply hike
across the fields to freedom.'

'He won't do that.'

'Oh.' The chief inspector took a packet of cigarettes
from her handbag, stared at them wistfully and then put
them back.

'Given it up?' asked D'Eath, with more than the merest
hint of malice.

'Just today.' The chief inspector peered at the map.
'Do you have any specific reason to believe that the
killer will still be in the area?'

'I've got half a million of them actually.'

Constable Derek coughed nervously.

'Please explain,' said Lestrade.

'I know this psycho, ma'am. Know the way he thinks.
He's somewhere close and I'll have him.'

The chief inspector pointed once more to the map.
'What is this big area here that doesn't have any road
blocks around it at all?'

'Ah that.' Inspector D'Eath smiled. 'That's just a
chicken farm. It belongs to a prominent member of the
local chamber of commerce. Town councillor. Robert
Bum-Poo his name is.'

'Did you say Bum-Poo?'

'I did, but it's not particularly funny.'

'I wonder.'

278

'No really. It's not funny at all.'

'It makes me laugh,' said Constable Derek.

'Shut up, Constable.'

'No,' said the chief inspector. 'It makes me wonder if t could be the same Bum-Poo.'

Constable Derek sniggered and nudged Inspector D'Eath. 'One Bum-Poo's much the same as another. Unless you've had an "Indian", eh, guv?'

'Constable, shut up.'

'Yes, sir guv.'

'The same Bum-Poo as who, ma'am?'

'There was a doctor, Robard Bum-Poo, genetic engineer, worked for the ministry of agriculture. Brilliant scientist. But he went off the rails, tried to create a new strain of chicken using human hormones. There were some rumours that he was actually, you know, *doing it* with the birds.'

Inspector D'Eath groaned.

'Questions were asked in the House and the project was abandoned. Bum-Poo slipped out of sight.'

'Down the toilet?' Constable Derek collapsed in laughter.

'I'm warning you, Constable.'

'Sorry, sir.'

'I heard that he's opened some kind of wildlife sanctuary or something.' The chief inspector ignored the convulsing constable. 'ANIMAL, I think it was called. No, BEAST, that's what it was.'

Inspector D'Eath groaned again.

'Still, I can't see what that would have to do with the man we're looking for, or the terrorists who released him.'

'Oh dear,' said D'Eath. 'I think *I* can. It's the same Bum-Poo, ma'am, and he's the brains behind the entire operation. Constable.'

Constable Derek was clutching at his stomach with one hand and dabbing tears of mirth from his eyes with the other. 'Yes, sir,' he managed.

'Pull yourself together, you stupid boy. Get on the telephone and call the special police weapons unit that is combing the area.'

'Special police weapons unit, sir?'

'The FireArms Response Team. F.A.R.T.'

'What?' The constable's eyes started from his head.

'F.A.R.T., you idiot. F.A.R.T. If Bum-Poo's up to what I think he's up to, then only F.A.R.T. can stop him.'

'Only F.A.R.T. can stop Bum-Poo?' The constable collapsed on to the floor, where he lay writhing with laughter and kicking his legs in the air.

Inspector D'Eath made the call himself.

'See, I told you I could do it by myself.' Raymond stood at the wheel.

'We're not down yet, do take care.' Professor Merlin hid his face.

'Piece of cake,' said Raymond. 'I have the hang of it now. What really makes this ship fly, Professor?'

'It's engine, Raymond.'

'Yes, but how does its engine work?'

'I don't know.'

'*But it does.* Never mind. Hold on tight, we're going in.'

The great Victorian ship dropped down towards Eden. Oceans passed beneath, continents took shape, mountains ranged and rivers meandered. Forests and plains, hamlets and more seas.

'Take a left here, Raymond.'

Raymond took a left.

'Just a tad,' said the professor.

'That was a tad.'

'It was more like a bit than a tad.'

'Ah,' said Raymond. 'I see where I've been going wrong.'

Ahead a great city arose upon the coast.

'Eutopia,' said Professor Merlin.

'Eutopia? They named their capital city Eutopia?'

'They're a high-minded people.'

'They're a pack of bastards and I hate them.'

If Fogerty was Memphis, Egypt, then Eutopia was not. It had a flavour of New York about it. But a New York designed by the architect who worked on the Tower of Babel.

The scale was daunting. Tier upon tier of yellow stone, rising to meet the clouds.

'Ziggurats,' said the professor. 'Thousands of years old. All mod cons within, of course. Up there,' the ancient pointed towards the mother of all ziggurats, 'the king's palace.'

'Should I land in his back garden?'

'No, Raymond. I think we should observe protocol. Land in the harbour.'

'Okey-doke.' Raymond pushed on the wheel. 'Down a half tad and here we go.'

Now a harbour's a harbour's a harbour (though a good cigar is a smoke), and the harbour and docks of Eutopia looked much the same as those of Fogerty.

Some splendid-looking vessels lay at anchor, they resembled the galleys of ancient Rome, although they appeared to be newly constructed. Elaborately painted they were, with double rows of oars on each side.

'Slave ships?' Raymond asked.

'Not every "George" goes into the pot.'

'What?' Raymond knotted his fists.

'Both hands on the wheel please, helmsman.'

'Bastards!' said Raymond.

'Quite so. Right a tad and down two bits.'

The dock was lined with people. Gaily dressed and cheering. And human. Well, of the same root race. As Raymond brought the great ship gently down, the professor waved to the people who were waving up at him. 'A reception committee,' he crooned. 'You see, Raymond, wherever the circus of Professor Merlin goes, folk tip their hats and greet us with a merry wave. Tra-la-tra-la-tra-la-tra-le.'

Raymond raised an eyebrow. The old man seemed to have conquered his 'weariness'. Remarkable what a cheering crowd can do for a sagging ego.

Beneath his breath Raymond whispered, 'Cannibal bastards,' gave the ship's wheel a violent tad and a half back and pulled on the hand brake. The *SS Salamander* belly-flopped into the harbour, raising a fair old wave, that slapped against the dock and drenched the feet of the reception committee.

'Sorry,' said Raymond, who was anything but.

'Fiddle-de fiddle-dum,' said Professor Merlin.

Raymond found the button that made the anchor drop and gave it a press. And on the dock a band began to play.

'Shall we synchronize our watches now?' Professor Merlin asked.

Elsewhere other watches were being synchronized. Those on the steely-thewed wrists of the special police weapons unit F.A.R.T. for a dirty half dozen. These were manly men. Several had even been thrown out of the SAS for being too manly. They wore black body armour, black trews and great big boots. Their faces were boot-blacked and so hard and tough and manly were they, that they boot-blacked their eyeballs also. They carried high-calibre assault rifles, with infra-red image-intensifying night sights and had Desert Eagles stuck in their belts.

They were not the kind of men you would wish to meet on a dark night. Or at any other time really.

Three men in grey were synchronizing their watches.

They were still in The Bramfield Arms. And although grey man number one (who had erroneously referred to himself earlier as grey man number two) had made repeated phone calls to his guvnor on Eden and made more and more urgent pleas into the answerphone, his calls had not been returned and so now the three grey men were getting up to leave.

'Where are we going to?' asked grey man number two.

'Bum-Poo's,' said grey man number one.

'Oh, I went before I came out, actually.'

'Bum-Poo's chicken farm. Trust me, I know what I'm doing.'

And on Bum-Poo's chicken farm, Long Bob, who didn't have a wrist watch, synchronized his kitchen clock. 'Shall we put on our robes?' he asked.

'Robes?' Military Dave, who now had the looker sitting on his knee, said, 'I didn't know we were going to have robes.'

'I ran them up myself.' Long Bob opened the kitchen cupboard, rooted them out and handed them round.

The looker sniffed at hers disdainfully. 'They're just old feed sacks, stitched together and dyed black.'

Long Bob indicated the feathered pentagram chest motifs. 'I sprayed these on with luminous paint. You each have a winged helmet too.'

The Roman Candles looked at each other. 'Fab,' they said.

'Where's Dick?' asked Long Bob. 'I've done one for him as well and a little one for his dog.'

'I think he's still in the tool shed,' said a Candle called Kevin.

'Well go out and get him. He's supposed to be laying out the bleachers for the chickens to sit on during the service. Tonight the blood sacrifice will be made and the new world order will begin. Hail Sate-Hen.'

'Hail Sate-Hen,' they all went.

Barking mad the lot of 'em.

The lot of 'em on the dock were still cheering. Somewhat soggy of footwear, but still cheering. They wouldn't get the big parade though. The knackered speaker system crackled out 'The March of the Gladiators' and the artistes trooped down the passenger gangway from the deck.

Raymond watched them sadly. They looked so very frail, as if they might crumble to the slightest touch. Perhaps this was all a bad idea. But it had to be done. And the artistes were strutting. They were troupers and they trooped.

From his eyrie in the wheelhouse, Raymond could see the band below struggling to fall in with 'The March of the Gladiators' and the cheering crowd that engulfed the circus folk as they reached the dock.

And then he saw the soldiers.

A dozen of them, dressed in uniforms of red and white.

They sprang up from nowhere and suddenly seemed to be everywhere. They had vicious-looking weapons and these they pointed at Professor Merlin and his troupers.

The cheering stopped, the band ceased to play. The ship's speaker system, as if taking its cue, faltered, the needle got stuck on the record, three bars of music repeated again and again and again.

And then died.

'Oh my God.' Raymond cowered on the wheelhouse floor. All alone once more. Clothes on this time, though not his own, but all alone again. 'Oh my God, what shall I do?'

He crawled over to the port-side door and peeped from its broken window. The once-cheering crowd was melting away. Soldiers were marching the circus folk into the distance. Others had taken up guard positions at the foot of the gangway.

'What to do?'

Raymond crawled over to the starboard wheelhouse door, opened it quietly and slipped out on to the deck. Dive over the side and swim ashore? Raymond didn't think so. He could hardly swim. Drowning was a particular nightmare of his. Creep along to the stern and try to jump down on to the dock? Big ship. Too high to jump from.

Raymond ducked behind a steamer chair and peeped once more at the tragic scene. He heard a soldier's voice hout, 'Hurry up,' and he saw the rifle butt as it struck he professor between his jagged shoulder-blades.

Raymond turned his face away and bit upon a knuckle.

He would have to do something. And something right now.

There was nothing else for it. Raymond took down an aged lifebelt and crept back to the starboard side of the ship.

It was a long way down. The water was probably very cold and very very deep. And he couldn't swim much. And he was just about as scared as it is possible to be.

Raymond slipped the lifebelt around his middle, took a great big breath, offered up a sailor's prayer for deliverance and leapt into the sea.

24

A lot of really hair-raising things seem to happen in slow motion. Car crashes, for instance, and being shot they say. Or, as in Raymond's case, leaping to almost certain death from the side of an ocean liner.

On the long journey down, much of Raymond's short life flashed before him. It seemed to consist of a catalogue of smallish mistakes, all leading inexorably towards this final very largish one. Just before he hit the water it occurred to Raymond that perhaps he should not have jumped at all. Perhaps he should have released the two hundred Millwall warriors instead. But it was rather too late for that now.

With a dull little splash that nobody heard, the sea received Raymond's body and covered it with water. It was a pretty clapped-out old lifebelt he was wearing and one which had long ago lost all of its buoyancy.

The waves lapped about the hull of the SS *Salamander*. Seagulls turned in the sky. The weather looked like staying nice.

The night was now pitch black in Bramfield, with the smell of a storm in the air. Simon shone the Scribe's electric torch along the abandoned railway track. He was saving the stick with the oily rag on the end for some moment he hoped might soon arrive.

'We need you villagers,' he whispered to Mr Hilsavise. 'Long Bob's bunch have got guns.'

'I saw you slip the Scribe's gun into your pocket.'

'It doesn't have any bullets.' Simon shivered. 'You

hould have let me look at the book. I'd have known what ·
o do then.'

'I've read the book,' whispered Mr H. 'And you don't
ave the book with you when you do what you do in it.
f you follow me.'

Simon made a face of desperation in the darkness. 'Do
ou get the feeling we're being watched?'

The warlock, who numbered night vision amongst
ertain uncanny powers which Simon knew nothing of,
aid, 'No, you're imagining it.' But kept a wary owl's
ye upon the figures he could clearly see, skulking from
ne bush to another along the ridge above the abandoned
rack. 'Just keep moving,' he whispered.

'ust keep moving.' Professor Merlin and his sorely
roubled circus folk had reached the palace of King
ddie.

Ziggurat. Yellow stone. Very large and no time for
urther details.

At the grand entrance there was one of those lifty-up
arriers and a little guard's hut. A large guard issued from
nis. He was carrying a clipboard. 'Halt who goes there?'
e said.

'The same soldiers who marched out of here about
alf an hour ago, you stupid jerk,' replied the officer in
harge.

'Ah, well, *I* didn't see that. I've only just come on
uty.'

'We are taking these prisoners to the king. Now, secure
nis gate and make sure no-one gets through.'

'Sure thing.' The guard drew his gun. 'Back off. None gets through.'

'No-one except us!'

'Sorry, I'm only following orders. Now back away.'

'Excuse me,' Professor Merlin raised his hand to speak,
out we don't do guard hut and clipboard gags. That's
eally Raymond's department.'

The guard consulted his clipboard. 'Ah yes, I have

some exposition here. You must be the circus folk that
the king is going to have tortured to death for starting
a war between Saturn and Eden. The announcement of
which the king picked up on satellite TV a few hours
ago.'

'Fiddle-de fiddle-dum,' said the professor.

'Pass friends,' said the guard. 'And have a nice day.'

It was still a nice day at the dock and Raymond, who still
had a good many things to do, including, of course, a
confrontation with the guard in the little hut, awoke from
drowning oblivion to find that he was no longer in it, but
had been washed up on a beach a short distance away.

It was rather a pleasant beach as it happened. Very
Miami. And very crowded too. Well, it was the king's
birthday and a national holiday had been declared.

The sun seekers stared at the frock-coated flotsam.
The flotsam stood up and wrung sea from its saturated
pantaloons.

'What are you lot looking at?' it asked fiercely.

The sun seekers returned to their seeking of sun.

Raymond plodded up the beach and up stone steps to
the promenade. Here he rested a moment to catch his
breath. He had to get to the palace, where he assumed
correctly enough, the circus folk had been taken. But
he didn't feel up to the walk. Well-dressed Edenites
paraded the prom. They raised their noses to Raymond
as they passed him by, but Raymond ignored them. He
needed transportation and his attention became drawn
to a knot of young folk gathered about something at the
kerb.

Raymond approached them and craned his neck above
their shoulders. An effete-looking young man, of about
Raymond's stamp and clad from head to foot in black
leather, sat idly revving a motor bike.

The motor bike was a Harley Davidson.

Raymond elbowed his way through the knot and
climbed on to the pillion of the Harley.

'Oh my,' said the effete young man, turning. 'You're
ll wet, you nasty man, get off my cycle do.'

Raymond stuck his right hand into the pocket of his
odden frock coat and thrust his finger into the small of
he young man's back.

'Say,' said he in a Hollywood tone, 'that's a really nice
ike,' adding, 'This is a gun, now get moving.'

There was movement in the palace of King Eddie. But
ot much of it came from the king. He was a nasty piece
f work was Eddie. Far nastier, in fact, than either of his
wo identical brothers. He was big and fat and old and
prightly and so on and he lolled upon a great big throne
n a great big hall which begged for description but didn't
eceive any. He stuck out a big fat bejewelled finger at the
ispirited, but far from done for, group that stood before
im and said, 'So you are the circus from Saturn, come
o entertain me. He he haw haw ho ho ha ha ha.'

It was one of those maniac laughs that, well, *maniacs*
lways have. A real bed-wetter. 'Come to provide me
vith entertainment. He he ho ho ha ha.'

The professor bowed low. 'If it is entertainment you
rave, sire, then none better than we shall supply it.
Might I introduce you to The Greatest Show off, er,
Saturn.'

'Oh do oh do,' said the king. 'It will pass a few minutes
vhile my cringing cat's-paw (as opposed to menial or
acky) fetches out the instruments of torture, upon which
ou will provide most excellent entertainment for myself
nd my court.'

'Your court?' The professor gazed around at the great
ig hall which begged for a description but didn't receive
ne. 'Which court might that be?'

'Actually they all have the day off. Although I think
have a dangling lovely upstairs. But do not worry, my
oldiers will cheer when I tell them to and I will clap and
augh. Like this.' He clapped. 'And ha ha ha ha ha. Ho.'

'If it please Your Majesty,' said Dr Bacteria, stepping

forward, 'might I be permitted to kiss the royal hand?'

'No you certainly may not.'

'Aw go on, just a little peck. No tongues.'

'You most revolting man. Something really horrible for you I think. The car battery and the jump leads perhaps. Tee he he. Where is my cringing cat's-paw?'

'I'm here, sire.' A cat's-paw in royal livery appeared, trundling a mobile rack piled high with whips, chains, manacles, ball-closure rings, flesh tunnels and Arab straps.

'Rooty toot,' said Professor Merlin approvingly. 'Reminds me of a weekend away I once had in Lourdes.'

'Frogs!' shrieked the Grand Duke's cringing menial. (Frogs-Frenchmen-Lourdes. Hardly a politically correct sort of link, but there you go.) 'Frogs all over the palace.'

'Frogs?' howled the Grand Duke, who, having recently waved off a hastily mustered, but quite substantial airforce, had, in keeping with his other brothers who really knew how to enjoy themselves on their birthdays, retired to his bedchamber with a dangling lovely of his own. 'What is with frogs? Have you gone completely mad?'

'They're everywhere, sire. Uuugh!' The cringing menial pulled a frog from his waistcoat and flung it to the floor. 'It's that Moses the elephant. He's cursed you with a plague of frogs.'

'How very thoughtful of him. Well gather them up and get them down to the kitchen. Frog's legs for tea, my favourite.'

'But, sire, frogs are only the first plague. He says there's worse to follow if you don't let his people go. Lice and flies and boils and blains.'

'What's a blain?'

'I think it's the big fellow in *Predator*. The one with the General Electric mini-gun.'

'Well, I'm not going to let the animals go. I'm going

o eat them. Invite this elephant of yours into the palace.
'll eat him as well.'

'Oh woe unto the house of Pharoah.' The cringing
nenial left the bedchamber.

'Now where was I?' asked the Grand Duke.

'Ribbiting your dangling lovely,' said the frog.

The Sultan of Uranus had left *his* lovely dangling. He
nad taken up residence aboard the four-masted flagship
of the Uranian navy and this was currently streaking
through air-filled space bound for Eden. Uranus is
nostly composed of water, you see, which explains the
navy and the flagship and the *SS Salamander*. And
he flying starfish too.

It all makes sense when you piece it all together.

'How long till we reach Eden, cringing lacky?'

'Not long.' The lacky consulted an unsynchronized
wrist-watch. 'Pretty soon. But the Grand Duke's mob
nave a head start.'

'But we have bigger ships.'

'Because they don't have any ships at all. They have
aircraft.'

'Does that give them an edge, do you think?'

'Haven't the foggiest idea, sire. I expect if they blast us
out of the sky, the answer would be yes.'

'Well see that they don't. And *where* is big Abdullah?'

Where, once again, *was* big Abdullah? Whither, whence
and what at?

And Raymond. What of he?

Raymond was riding a Harley Davidson. Not on the
pillion this time, but up front. And he was wearing black
leather.

The effete young man, who owned both bike and black
leather, sat in the gutter with a soggy frock coat around
his shoulders.

He was weeping dismally.

Raymond steered the big bike along quite well. He couldn't get it out of first gear, but you can go pretty fast on a Harley in first gear and it makes a really throaty twin-pipe roar when you do. Buggers the engine though.

Young Edenite women waved at Raymond, but Raymond, knowing their eating habits, did not wave back.

At very short length he arrived at the palace.

And the guard in the little guard's hut.

'Halt, who goes there?' asked the guard, holding up his clipboard. 'And whoever you are, you can't come in.'

Raymond revved the engine, drove straight into the guard, knocking him from his feet and then crashed through the lifty-up barrier.

Unsubtle? Unlikely? Unfunny?

Raymond didn't really care. He just roared up the drive towards the palace.

Within, the king was displaying his equipment (hm!).

'This one's really fiendish,' he said with a ha ha he. 'It stretches the limbs horrendously and then these little circular saw arrangements slice them right through. Gore everywhere. Lovely it is. Any volunteers?'

'I'll have a crack at that please,' said Disecto.

The front door of the palace was open. Raymond parked the bike and ducked inside.

He stood now in the grand vestibule. All mosaic floor, marble statuary, frescoed ceiling, panelled walls, Doric columns and that thing you find in the entrance hall of every palace you ever go into nowadays: The gift shop.

Raymond went over to the counter. 'Shop,' said he. But there was a closed sign on the counter. Raymond reached over and helped himself to an official guidebook and tour map. This he unfolded.

'Now let me see.' Raymond examined the map. 'Grand hall, royal bedchambers, kitchens, solarium, lounge, secret holographic broadcasting room. Ah yes,

e dungeons. Down the hall, first flight of steps and
·llow the signs. Right.'

Raymond strode away. The fine pair of motor cycle
oots he had borrowed from the effete young Edenite,
·ick-clacked gloriously on the marble floors.

First flight of steps and follow the signs.

Raymond hurried down the steps. It was here, he
·asoned, incorrectly this time, that Professor Merlin
·nd his circus were being held. Chained up and quite
·leased to see him.

The sign on the wall said, To the dungeons, and
·aymond followed its pointing arrow. Still nobody about,
·hich was handy.

A row of cell doors. Raymond slid back the nasty
·iding steel shutter on the first and peeped in.

In a not too distant corner of the tiny room, huddled
· figure. He was ragged and wretched. Long of hair and
·eard and wild of eye. He was talking to a cockroach.

'Hello,' said Raymond. 'Who are you?'

'I'm the Count of Monte Cristo,' said the captive.

'Ah,' said Raymond. 'Prisoner gags, is it? I suppose
·atrick McGoohan's in the next cell.'

'No, he's in number six.' The count tittered.

'Goodbye,' said Raymond.

'Goodbye,' said the count.

Raymond passed the prisoner of Zenda, the man in the
·on mask, the princes in the tower and some women in
·ell block H. He waved to a couple of British journalists,
·ho were awaiting their agents getting the contracts
·rawn up so they could go home and start work on
·eir bestsellers. Raymond gave Room 101 a miss.[1]

Finally he came to a big cell door at the end of the
·orridor.

'This has to be the one.' Raymond slid back the nasty
·ig sliding steel shutter and took a look inside.

---

[1] That room in *1984* where they do unspeakable things to
·ou.

A large group of people sat in what looked like
recreation room. It had a dartboard and a snooker tabl
and some video machines. But the group sat in armchair
watching TV.

The Birdman of Alcatraz was on.

Raymond sighed. 'Hello,' he called. 'Hello.'

Faces turned. But they weren't the faces of Professo
Merlin and his circus. But they were faces Raymon
recognized. Well, some of them he did. The presiden
of the United States, he recognized him. And the prim
minister of England. And the chairman fellow from
China. Although Raymond couldn't recall his name
And the Russian premier and a whole lot of others.

All very familiar.

'Hi there,' said the president. 'If you're a tourist, min
if we don't plead to be set free? The King's given us th
day off and we're watching TV.'

Again no exact record exists of what Raymond sai
next. But it was something to do with what Long Bob di
with chickens. Although this time applied to Raymond'
old brown dog.

25

And what of the chicken fancier himself? Oh what of Long Bob indeed?

Dick the poacher had the bleachers out, arranged on three sides of the farmyard facing the door to the big chicken shed. Strings of those horrid outdoor Christmasy lantern things, the ones that really annoying neighbours hang up to light their noisy evening barbecues that they don't invite you to, but *do* invite all these really attractive unattached women who take off all their clothes at the end of the evening and frolic around in the swimming-pool that he never got planning permission for and you nearly fall out of your bedroom window trying to get a look through your binoculars and someone else calls the police and he thinks you did and comes round the next day and punches you in the nose. Those lanterns. Strings of those lanterns illuminated the farmyard. And Long Bob's barbecue was well stoked up.

And what was that funny sound?

'What's that funny sound?' asked grey man number one. He and his grey companions were squeezed into the hideaway bush on the top of the hill. 'Does that sound like singing, or what?'

Grey man number two adjusted a pair of highly sophisticated night-vision binoculars, manufactured by the ACME Optical Instrument Company, Eden. 'The door of the big chicken shed's opening. Gawd, strike a light, look at that.'

Grey man number one put the binoculars to his squinty grey eyes and took a squinty grey look. And he too said, 'Gawd, strike a light.'

A procession was winding its way from the hen house. First came Long Bob in full regalia. Seed sack robes with luminous feathered pentagram chest motif, winged helmet. Swinging a censer.

He was chanting what might have been *Om Mani Padme Hen*. Or was possibly 'The Birdie Song'. And behind him came the chickens. In ranks of four. In perfect step. And singing.

Such dear little voices. Like a choir of cherubs. Not.

Long Bob paused beside the barbecue at the centre of the farmyard and the chickens filed past him, singing their little hearts out. They filed to the bleachers and in a fine rehearsed fashion, took their seats. No pushing or shoving, all very civilized. Very organized.

'With a little bit of this and a little bit of that and a little bit of,' Long Bob wiggled his bum and did finger peckings.

Barking mad. And lo . . .

From out of the farmhouse came the looker and Military Dave and the three Roman Candles (still the parachute accident and not the firework). Singing along and swinging their censers.

And where was God-awful Godolphin?

Ah, here he comes right now.

The tool shed door burst open and Dick emerged dragging a gagged nun in high heels.

'Nuns in bondage,' whispered grey man number one. 'I could go for that.'

A dog in a robe followed Dick, a tired looking dog indeed.

The gagged nun kicked and fought, but Dick dragged her along with a curse and a cowardly blow.

'What are they doing exactly?' asked Inspector D'Eath, who was dug into the long grass that Simon had missed during his Allen Scything. 'I can't make it out.'

'You're looking through the wrong end of the binoculars,' said Chief Inspector Lestrade, to the accompaniment of titters from Constable Derek.

Ah yes, I can see clearly now. But when are we going to make our move? I haven't heard a peep from F.A.R.T. about when they intend to flush Bum-Poo out.'

Constable Derek thrashed helplessly on the grass with his knuckle rammed into his mouth.

'Oh dearly beloved,' cried Long Bob, 'we are gathered here tonight as hallowed brethren and sister, to welcome the dawn of the new beginning. To honour and worship and make sacrifice to He who will deliver us when the light becomes darkness and the darkness covers the face of the Earth. Now as is prophesied, when moons shall fall from their orbits and the End Times will be upon us, let us praise the great one, let us praise and worship and generally toady up if we know what's good for us. So mote it be. Hail Sate-Hen.'

'Hail Sate-Hen,' agreed the censer swingers and the fellow who was getting his legs kicked.

'Hail Sate-Hen,' said that fellow's dog. 'Here, Dick mate, I can talk.'

'We shall sing,' Long Bob continued. 'Number three in the End Times Hymnal. "Old MacDonald Had a Farm", omitting the verses about ducks, cows, pigs, horses and plastic fertilizer bags. In the key of A.' Long Bob blew a pitch pipe.

'He's barking mad,' said Simon, who was lying under Long Bob's Land Rover.

'You're right,' agreed Mr H. 'The verse about the fertilizer bags is the best one. With a big pile here and a big pile there.'

'I have a plan,' whispered Simon. 'If I can just make it to . . .' He paused.

'The tool shed,' said Mr Hilsavise.

'Thank you,' said Simon. 'The tool shed it is then.'

'Are you tooled up?' asked the president of the USA. 'Are you holding? Packing heat?'

'No, Mr President, sorry.' Raymond was leading the

heads of state along the corridor. 'Handy the key being in the lock,' he said, before anyone could ask. 'We have to find Professor Merlin.'

'Is he packing heat?'

'No, but he has a great big ship for us to escape on.'

'I *wunt* to escape on the big ship,' said the British PM.

'And so you shall,' said Raymond. 'Let's try up here, I think I can hear something.'

'Oh ouch, oh dear, oh mercy me.' Disecto made unconvincing pain noises. 'Oh do have mercy please.'

'Shut up!' roared the king, without the maniac laughter. 'You've had your head cut off. You're not supposed to still be going, "Oh ouch, oh dear me." Die in agony like a man, for goodness sake.'

'Oh lummy,' said Disecto, 'I'm dead.'

'Oh no you're not.'

'Oh yes I am.'

'Oh no you're not.'

'Oh yes he is,' chorused the circus.

'Shut up, you lot. Lacky, stoke up the fiendishly hot roasting chair. Let's see who wants to sizzle.'

'I'd like a go at that please,' said Phoenix.

'Hee he he, ho ho ho, ha ha hoot,' went the King. 'And tittery tee hee too. The fiendishly hot roasting chair it is then.'

'Yes, it's definitely coming from in here,' Raymond pushed open the door.

'You might knock first,' said a dangling lovely.

'Sorry.' Red-faced Raymond closed the door.

'I *wunt* to see in there,' said the British PM.

'Best not,' said Raymond. 'Let's try up here.'

'Fry. Ha ha tee he he.'

'Oooooo!' went Phoenix, in mock agony. 'Oh shriek. Oh whimper.'

'It's not hot enough.' The big fat king put his finger on the chair. 'Oooooo!' he screamed. 'Oh shriek. Oh whimper.'

'Can I kiss that better?' asked Dr Bacteria.

'It's definitely in here,' said Raymond, pushing open another door. And it was. A dozen powerful-looking firearms turned upon him.

'Stick 'em up,' said the officer in charge.

'There,' said Raymond. 'I told you it was in here.'

'We are here,' cried Long Bob. 'Come unto us, oh magnificent one. Come unto us, Your Majesty.'

The door of the big chicken shed creaked open. A bright white light welled from within.

Made hazy about its edges by the glare, something hideous stepped forth. It was taller than Mr Hilsavise and much more powerfully built. It had certainly grown some since the evening before and as it made its ponderous way across the lantern-lit farmyard, the full enormity of its very-much-terribleness became apparent.

'Bugger my boots,' said grey man number one. 'Is that Bigfoot, or what?'

It certainly had big feet. Big chicken feet, with Velociraptor claws (Velociraptors! Spielberg must have made them up). These tore into the ground raising small clouds of dust.

The legs were finely muscled, dark featherage concealed whatever dangling unloveliness hung between them. The great chest was covered by a scaly network of silver-blue plumage and the shoulders were broad and muscular. A tall dark crest rose from the massive head, with its sickening eyes and very horrid beak.

'Hail Sate-Hen.' Long Bob and his followers fell to their knees. Seizing her opportunity, Liza made a break for it.

'Be still.' The voice which cried from the horrid beak echoed about the farmyard. Inspector D'Eath could scarce control a failing bladder, and it wiped the smile right off the face of Constable Derek.

'Be still.'

Liza's legs gave way beneath her and she sank to the ground.

'Bring me my sacrifice,' said Sate-Hen.

'Bring me the pillock in the black leather suit,' said King Eddie and the soldiers hastened to oblige. One clubbed Raymond down at the fat fellow's feet.

'That's a nice suit you have there,' crowed the king. 'I gave one just like that to my son Wilfred for his birthday. His had the royal logo on the collar, of course.'

The king stared down. '*Yours* has the royal logo on the collar as well.'

'Does your son drive a Harley Davidson?' Raymond asked.

'I *wunt* a Harley Davidson,' said the British PM.

'Silence! Where is my son Wilfred?'

Raymond climbed to his feet and went into 'Simon' mode. 'I have taken your son hostage,' he said. 'He's safe enough for now, but if I don't get back soon with the professor, his circus and all these heads of state, there's no telling what my mad brother, with the stammer and the thing about razor blades and eyeballs, might do to him.'

'Oh dear,' wailed the king. 'Oh dear, oh mercy me.'

'So we'll be going now.' Raymond smiled. 'If you'll just have your soldiers lay down their weapons.'

'Oh dear,' went the king. 'I don't know what to do.'

'I would strongly advise a weapon-drop scenario myself,' said Professor Merlin. 'Naturally I speak as an impartial observer.'

'Yes yes. Drop your weapons.'

The soldiers laid down their arms.

Let's go,' said Raymond.

'Daddy,' an effete young man in a soggy frock coat

burst in through a side door, 'a nasty boy stole my suit and my bike.'

'Weapons up,' shouted the king. 'And open fire indiscriminately. Although not in my direction.'

'We should open fire,' said Inspector D'Eath. 'Where is F—'

'No please,' Constable Derek held up his hand. 'Please don't say it again.'

'Should we shoot it?' asked grey man number three. The men in grey had some pretty snazzy hardware. From the ACME small arms factory, Eden.

'I'm not paid good money to take pot-shots at something like that,' said grey man number two. 'I'm for legging it, me.'

'Here,' said grey man number one, who had been looking through the special binoculars. 'Who are those blokes in black creeping around at the back of the farmyard?'

'Bring her to me,' roared Sate-Hen, and it was a most serious roar. 'Let me feast upon her. Bring her to me now.'

'Shoot them now,' the king shouted and the soldiers cocked their weapons.

'Sorry,' said Raymond to the professor. 'I think I've screwed this up.'

'Shoot them now.'

The soldiers squeezed upon their triggers. Then something whistled down from the sky, struck the palace and exploded most noisily.

'It's the bloody Saturnians!' The king, who had tumbled, rose to his feet. 'They shouldn't be here yet. My airforce is still on holiday, they haven't got back yet.'

Another explosion rocked the palace.

'Time to do something impressive,' said Professor Merlin. 'Are you up to it, Raymond?'

'Am I up to what?'

The professor shot out an extendible finger. It whipped across the great hall, poked the nearest soldier in the eye, hooked his weapon from his hands and flung it into those of Raymond.

'I should capture the king if I were you,' said Professor Merlin.

'Stick 'em up,' said Raymond, putting the muzzle to the king's big fat head. 'And tell your soldiers to drop their guns again.'

'Do as he says. Do as he says.'

The soldiers dropped their guns again and stood complaining.

Then yet another explosion occurred close at hand, so they ran.

'Come on,' said Raymond. 'There's still lots to do.'

Men in black took up positions.

Dick Godolphin prodded Liza in the back. 'To your master,' said he.

And in the tool shed Simon shone his torch around and asked, 'Just what am I doing in here?'

'In here,' said Raymond, prodding the king.

'Why in here?' asked the professor.

Raymond indicated the sign on the door. *Secret Holographic Broadcasting Room.*

'Aha!' the professor aha'd. 'Now isn't *that* convenient?'

'Very,' said Raymond. 'Now, quick, let's get this done.'

If you wanted a nice deserted beach to soak up some sun on, then the one where Raymond was washed ashore would now be it.

The sun seekers had fled.

Overhead Saturnian craft, dark aeroforms like winged

302

solar discs (in keeping with the ancient Egypt look) swung in circles and poured down fire upon Eutopia.

Shells burst into the sea, up the beach and along the prom. So perhaps it wasn't really the place to soak up some sun.

Yellow stone fractured. Ziggurats shook.

And now from above the circling craft came the ships of Uranus. Stirring craft, tall masted, with rows of gun ports.

The Sultan stood at the helm of the leading Man o' War. 'Bomb bays open, Mr Lacky.'

'Bomb bays open, sire.'

'Release consignment load.'

'Consignment load released, sire.'

And further bombs rained down.

'Switch it all off,' said Raymond to the king. They were in the Secret Holographic Broadcasting Room. 'Switch off all the holograms on Earth.'

'I *wunt* to do the switching off,' said the British PM.

'The king can manage,' said Raymond. 'Can't you, Your Majesty?'

'You don't know what you're doing.' King Eddie wrung his big fat fingers. You'll cause chaos down there.'

'Not for long, I intend to have all the heads of state back home very soon.'

'And we'll be making your existence well and truly known,' said the president.

'Oh dear oh dear. Whatever should I do?'

'Oh stand aside.' Raymond pushed the fat man out of the way, cocked his gun and shot the secret holographic broadcasting unit into a million fragments.

'There,' he said. 'That's done.'

'Ahem,' said Professor Merlin. 'A very thorough job. But do you not feel that this might compromise your plan to replace King Eddie with a hologram? You having destroyed the necessary equipment, and all.'

'Shit!' said Raymond.

Explode! went an explosion, bringing down a lot of ceiling.

'Back to the ship,' cried Raymond. 'Everyone back to the ship.' He turned his gun upon the king.

'Don't shoot me please.'

Raymond cocked the gun once more and put it to the big fat and now most sweaty forehead. 'Give me one good reason why I shouldn't.'

'Because . . . ' the king whimpered. 'Because . . .'

'Because he would be far better as a hostage,' said Professor Merlin. 'And because you're the good guy and good guys don't go shooting people in the head.'

Raymond put aside his weapon with some relief. 'That's two good reasons,' he said. 'I only needed one.'

26

'Come to me,' boomed the voice of Sate-Hen. And as the farmyard wasn't *that* big, Liza now stood before him, shaking in her habit and tottering on her toes. Sate-Hen tore off her gag.

'Kneel before me, girl. *Pray* to me.'

'*Pray?*' asked Inspector D'Eath. 'Isn't that a euphemism for—'

'Yes it is.' Jenny Lestrade snatched up her two-way radio. 'Open fire!' she ordered.

And the men of F.A.R.T. opened fire.

Indiscriminately. These were manly men after all and a soft target was a soft target, whether it was the soft target they were supposed to be shooting at or not.

The chickens arose in a frantic feathery cloud as shots raked across the farmyard, into the ground, overhead. Some even as far as the hideaway bush.

'We're under attack,' yelled grey man number one, flipping the safety catch from a small Howitzer affair. 'Return fire.'

'All I can see is bloody chickens,' yelled grey man number two.

'Then shoot the chickens.'

'This is the bit I really like,' and grey men all opened fire.

'Hostile fire on the hillside,' called a man with boot-blacked eyeballs. 'Take them out with mortars, wide radius.'

The men and women of B.E.A.S.T. were fighting their way through chickens to the farmhouse, where they kept their stock of weapons.

'I know I should help,' said Mr Hilsavise, beneath the Land Rover, 'but it says in the book that I stay here and wait for . . . ah yes.'

Along the abandoned railway track they came. The villagers. And they carried flaming torches.

'Pray to me,' crowed Sate-Hen, oblivious to the gunfire and the shouting and the chickens. 'The End Times come and so shall I.'

Now is that *evil*, or what?

'Run!' bawled Raymond. They were outside the palace now and chaos was king. Above, the warplanes of Saturn engaged in a mighty battle with the fleet of Uranus. Things kept falling out of the sky. Bombs, bits of plane, masts, people, more bombs.

'I cannot run,' said the professor. 'You must leave me here.'

Hercules the strong man, who hadn't had much of a part, scooped the old man up in his arms.

'We shall ride.' The Lady Alostrael spoke words of power. A wind arose and with it forms took shape. Horses. Great white horses, although somewhat fuzzy round the edges. 'Get on. Everyone. They will not last for long. Hurry now.'

'I *wunt* to ride on the motor cycle,' said the British PM.

'You *wunt* a clip round the ear,' said Raymond. 'Get on a horse at once.'

Now there's nothing quite like an all-out attack on your city to persuade enlisted men that perhaps they should be back on the job, rather than sitting about swigging tea and watching TV.

Soldiers in red and white poured from their barracks.

The strange cavalcade of semi-transparent horses, one with the king slung across the saddle, and lead by a fellow wearing the prince's leather suit and riding on his motor cycle, passed by these soldiers at close quarters.

The soldiers watched them, took stock of the situation, arrived at a joint decision and gave chase.

Simon backed away from the tool-shed door. He hadn't missed *anything* and he knew he had to do *something*. But he didn't know quite what. He shone the torch around in desperation. The shed was packed with stolen farm equipment, Long Bob must have been nicking stuff for years. But unless he also had a Sherman tank stashed away in here, none of it was going to help. Simon's torchlight flared across something in the corner, half concealed beneath several fertilizer bags.

It was the mighty Allen Scythe of Mr Hilsavise.

'Boom Shanka,' said Simon.

We're supposed to be shooting Simon, not these nutters in black.' Grey man number one let off another barrage.

'I've mostly just shot chickens,' said grey man number two.

'I just shot the poacher's dog,' said grey man number three.

Aw shame.

Tease tease, went Simon with the Allen Scythe.

Oh my God,' shouted Raymond. 'Look along the dock.'

'Soldiers,' cried Professor Merlin. 'What a lot of soldiers.'

'We'll never get past them.'

'Well we must surely try. *Charge!*'

The villagers with flaming torches had now reached the farm gate. But what with all the warfare and everything, Long Bob's brigade having opened up from the farmhouse and everything, and that monster that was about to make that nun . . . and everything . . .

And everything . . .

They felt somewhat disinclined to go any further.

'Come on,' said Mr Hilsavise. *'Charge!'*

'Into the jaws of death.' Professor Merlin drew his sword and spurred his fading charger.

The soldiers were now lined up before the *SS Salamander*. Two rows. Red and white. A bit like Rorke's Drift, but without Michael Caine. They raised their rifles and the officer in charge prepared to give the 'fire' order.

Raymond revved the Harley. He couldn't think of a better way to go. 'B.b.b . . . bad to the bone,' he shouted, as he let out the clutch.

'Charge!' Professor Merlin charged.

'Front rank fi—'

The missile whistled down, passed over the heads of the charging horsemen, over that of Raymond and close above those of the red-and-white riflemen.

And then it struck the side of the *SS Salamander*.

And then there was a bloody big explosion.

Raymond swerved the bike to a halt. 'Oh no,' he said.

The professor reined in his vanishing steed. 'My ship.'

Amid a lot of smoke and confusion the soldiers were climbing to their feet and picking up their weapons. 'Fire!' cried the officer in charge. And the soldiers raised their guns.

And then . . .

And then . . .

And then, through a large and gaping hole in the ship's side poured the Millwall supporters. Two hundred knights with home-made weapons and a bad attitude.

And the knights beheld the soldiers.

And the soldiers beheld the knights.

And lo, the soldiers were all clad in red and white.

The colours of Manchester United.

The men of F.A.R.T. shot at the men, and woman, of B.E.A.S.T. The men, and woman, of B.E.A.S.T. shot at the men of F.A.R.T. The grey men shot at the men of

F.A.R.T. and the men, and woman, of B.E.A.S.T. And when the men of F.A.R.T. and the men, and woman, of B.E.A.S.T. were not shooting at each other, they shot at the men in grey.

It was a shame that none of them chose to shoot at Sate-Hen, because he was just about to do the unspeakable to Liza.

'Get ready,' Mr H. told the torch bearers. 'It's going to happen any second now.'

And it did.

As the horrible claws of Sate-Hen closed about Liza's head, there came a great splintering of woodwork and a roaring of engine.

The mighty Allen Scythe erupted from the tool shed, with Simon clinging on behind. Its great solid wheels, with the nineteen fifties' racing-car tyres, ripped up the ground, scattering what chickens were left to be scattered and the huge hair-clipper grass-cutting attachment on the front rattled its razor-sharp teeth back and forwards. Very fast.

They minced through the bleachers as if they were balsa-wood, cascading chippings and sawdust to go with all the feathers and bite-sized chicken morsels.

And Simon held on.

'What is this?' The monster flung aside his kneeling sacrifice-to-be and raised his talons. Liza scrambled to her feet and fled. A certain chemical in Simon's head said 'kill it, buddy'.

'You're going to get yours,' yelled Simon as the Allen Scythe gathered speed.

'Torch bearers in,' cried Mr H. at the gate. And the villagers advanced at the trot.

'Back!' Sate-Hen's eyes flashed hell-fire and his beak hung open issuing suphureous smoke. What chickens remained rose screaming 'no no no' and flew at Simon's face.

The gardener's apprentice and soldier of the Lord kept his head down and the Allen Scythe ploughed towards Sate-Hen.

Sate-Hen stood his evil ground. 'Idolator!' he cried.

Simon rammed the throttle full on and let go.

The Allen Scythe caught Sate-Hen in the legs. Th[e] big blades cutting. Mincing. Horribly. The monste[r] screamed and kicked. A leg stump gouting blood. Th[e] big machine tore at him. Buffeted him down, ate int[o] him. Blood. Gore. Nastiness.

And quite right too.

And then came the villagers.

'Return to the pit from whence thou came.' M[r] Hilsavise had a flaming torch of his own. 'Burn i[n] Hades' fire where you belong.'

And the villagers flung their torches.

The creature took fire in a rush of blue flame. Stil[l] screaming and kicking. Flames licked up around th[e] Allen Scythe. Around its petrol tank.

'Run!' advised Mr Hilsavise. 'Run for your lives, I'v[e] read this bit.'

And the villagers ran.

And the men of F.A.R.T. and the men, and woman, o[f] B.E.A.S.T. and the grey men on the hill, all of whom ha[d] been holding their fire so as not to complicate the action[,] ducked their heads as the inevitable occurred.

It was a hell of a big explosion.

'Everyone back to the ship,' shouted Raymond, as furthe[r] explosions burst along the dock. 'Come on, get back o[n] board.'

The Millwall supporters were beating seven bells o[f] soccerdom out of the soldiers. And who could blam[e] them? They had a lot to get out of their systems.

'Come on.' Raymond shouted at them. 'There's a wa[r] going on here. Back to the ship and let's get home.'

'Isn't that Arnie?' asked a skinhead called Vinny wh[o] was putting the boot into a fallen soldier.

'Arnie Arn-ie-Arn-ie-Arn-ie Arrrrrnie Arrrrrnie.'

'Come on. Let's go.'

*   *   *

p above in the sky, the Sultan of Uranus was in a bit
a fix.

'We're on fire,' said his cringing lacky. 'I think this
oves that planes do have the edge on ships.'

'I'm fed up with you,' said the sultan, snatching the
cky by the seat of his pants and pitching him over the
de.

'Aaaaaaaaaaaaaaaaaaaaaagh!' went the lacky. Like you
ould.

'And bloody good riddance.' The Sultan swung the
ip's wheel in a plea to set a course for home. A
aturnian winged disc let free a barrage of missilery.

Wham bang.

And lovely left to hang.

The Sultan of Uranus was no more.

et's go. And I'm not kidding.'

The Millwall warriors, viewing the rather large con-
ngent of red-and-whites now pouring on to the dock,
ith the armoured vehicles and the half tracks and
verything, made a strategic withdrawal to the deck
f the *SS Salamander*, where they shouted abuse and
ooned at the oncoming troops.

'Will the ship still fly?' asked Raymond in the wheel-
ouse.

'Of course, my dear boy. Shall I be helmsman?'

'You have to be joking, Professor.'

'I *wunt* to be helmsman,' said the British PM.

Raymond turned around and did what an entire
neration of British youth have always wanted to do. He
id out the Prime Minister with a single blow to the chin.

'Now, let's go.'

'What about the aircraft and the space ships?'

Ground-based missiles now streaked into the sky. The
rcraft and the space ships that remained flew off to fight
nother day.

'Away to the North Pole,' said Professor Merlin. 'And
ep on it, by Jimminy.'

Around Long Bob's farm the gunfire had ceased. Me
with boot-blacked eyeballs searched the row of distraugl
B.E.A.S.T.ers, who now stood with their hands u
against the farmhouse wall. They had somehow lo
the will for further battle.

'You're all nicked,' said Inspector D'Eath. 'On mor
charges than I've got names for. And where do you thin
you're going, Simon?'

Simon, who, with his arm around Liza, was quiet
slipping away, said, 'Where indeed?'

'He's going to take his girlfriend home, I should think
said chief Inspector Lestrade.

'He's under arrest,' said D'Eath. 'He's a serial kille
that's what.'

'The woman I'm supposed to have murdered
standing over there with her hands up,' said Simor
'And I think we might expect Raymond home any tin
now. And you stole my winnings, you crook.'

Inspector D'Eath laughed. 'Stole your winning
indeed.'

'You did, sir,' said Constable Derek. 'I can't g
through with stealing his money. He did it, ma'ar
guv. He stole Simon's winnings. About half a millio
quid. It's hidden in his shed.'

Chief Inspector Lestrade smiled that little smile th
Helen Mirren does. 'I was sent here, not only to tak
charge of this task force, but to investigate claims
police corruption made against you, Inspector. I thin
we can say *you're* nicked, can't we?'

'I think we can say we did it.' Raymond sat at the head c
the table in the grand salon. The ship was on automati
pilot, or whatever it was. The circus folk crowded aroun
raising glasses. The heads of state of the inner Eartl
crowded around raising glasses. All except one, who la
unconscious on the wheelhouse floor.

And a king who was tied up in the hold, surrounded y two hundred guards.

'You have triumphed,' said Professor Merlin. 'Now all the inner Earth will know the truth about those who well above. With the king as hostage, the holograms estroyed and the heads of state returning to power, nowing what they now know, I think the Edenites will e persuaded to change their ways. And there are more ukes on Earth than on Eden. The threat of a few lobbed p through the polar openings might prove persuasive, hould they dither.'

'No more wars,' said Raymond. 'Let's have peace. ots of peace.' He raised his glass. 'To peace, lots of eace.'

'You'll have death, lots of death,' said a voice from on igh.

Raymond hadn't thought much about the strong nell of fish he had noticed in the grand salon. The ouillabaisse was on the turn, perhaps.

The eyes of all present gazed up.

In the great dome of the ceiling hung Abdullah the ying starfish from Uranus.

'Nice to get you all together in one place,' said bdullah. 'So I can snuff you out, all in one go.'

His hideous middle section bulged, extruded some-ing unseeable but solid. A transparent dome enclosed l beneath.

'And now,' said the odious one, 'I suck out the air and he lot of you croak, so you do.'

'No no no.' There was a whole lot of 'noing'. In any different tongues. And a whole lot of bashing at e dome. And screaming too.

'Say goodbye Abdullah.' The flying starfish took a eep breath.

The air left the transparent dome.

'Goodbye.'

Raymond clutched at his throat. Heads of state were

sinking to the floor, coughing and gagging. The profess
gripped his chest. The circus folk, grey faced and gaspin
tottered and fell.

'No,' Raymond fought for breath, but there was no a
left to breathe.

It was all over.

And so horribly unfair.

'Say goodbye,' laughed Abdullah.

'Goodbye, Abdullah.' Such a sweet voice. Raymon
half heard it and looking up he saw the sudden look
horror appear upon what Abdullah passed off as h
face.

A great swordfish saw plunged down from his midd
section, cleaving it open, spattering ichor onto the dom
And then the dome dissolved, air rushed in, Abdulla
crumpled in upon himself and collapsed in a big hea
all over the nicely spread table.

'Zephyr?' Raymond raised a smile, then parted com
pany with his senses.

27

There is always a loose end or two. Or three. Or possibly four. It's a tradition, or an old charter. Or something.

And folk can sometimes be left saying, 'What about *that*?' or 'Whatever happened to him?' or 'That bit was never explained at all.'

Hard to believe. But they do.

They might ask, for instance, what became of the men in grey? Well . . .

'I'm out of ammo,' said grey man number one.

'Me too,' said number two.

'I've got one shot left,' said grey man number three. 'And I've got Simon's head right in the cross hairs of this super-dooper telescopic sight.'

'Well shoot the sod and let's go home.'

The finger of grey man number three tightened on the trigger.

But then a big firm hand tightened upon his shoulder.

'I wouldn't do that if I were you, shithead.'

It was a big gruff voice. Real evil. We've heard it before somewhere. Ah yes.

'Put down the gun,' said Black Jack Wooler.

'Now just you see here—'

'Don't.' Black Jack raised his hand, his big Pit Bull terrier growled ominously. 'I heard you say you were heading this way. I've come to bring you a message.'

'Oh yes?' Grey men three looked up at the big man with the big dog.

'It's from your guvnor. His secretary called to say he

had the day off, for some king's birthday. But to tell yo[u]
that your services are no longer required. You're fired.'

Black Jack Wooler drew a sawn-off shotgun fro[m]
beneath his coat. 'Kill,' he told his dog.

And what about the Grand Duke? some folk might ask[.]
Surely he's got it coming to him.

Well . . .

'Dingle dangle,' said the Grand Duke to his lovel[y]
'All right, we may have lost the battle, but there's sti[ll]
a few hours of birthday left. So let us tarry a while, fai[r]
maiden, then I'll treat you to a slap-up supper. Poodle[s]
and frog's legs and heaven knows what. And *what* is tha[t]
infernal racket?'

The bedchamber door opened with a rush and th[e]
cringing menial bowled in to land in a heap. Behind hi[m]
came a whole lot of animals. Frogs included. Leading
them was an elephant.

'I can't talk for long,' said Moses. 'Because the End
Times have been postponed, so I'll have to shut up in a
minute. But *you*,' the elephant curled his trunk around
the Grand Duke's leg, 'you're dead, Jack.'

'My name's not Jack, it's Binky. Let me go.'

Moses dragged Binky from his bed and hefted him over
to the window.

They were about fourteen floors up.

'Say, Aaaaaaaaaaaaaaaaaaaaaaaaaaaaaagh!' said Moses.

'Aaaaaaaaaaaaaaaaaaaaaaagh!'

But what, and if there's one *big* what, what about that
book from the future?

Raymond and Zephyr stood on the deck of the *SS
Salamander*.

Down below, the heads of state, none the worse for
Abdullah, were tucking into the professor's grub and
carrying on like the good friends they had all become.

'I have to go away,' said Zephyr. 'Now is not my time
and I must go.'

316

'Oh please,' Raymond held her very close. 'You can't leave me again. You just can't.'

'I have to go Raymond. When I say that now is not my time, it's because I come from the future.'

Aha!

'Will I see you ever again?'

'Oh yes, in about a year from now. When the book comes out.'

'What book?'

'The one I'm writing about you. It's called *The Greatest Show off Earth*. A sort of unofficial biography.'

'Cor,' said Raymond.

'You see I run a little publishing house, in the future. It's called B.E.A.S.T. That's an acronym for Bolo Eolo Atolo Solo Tolo.'

'Which isn't English.'

'No. It's part of the new universal tongue which you create to bring peace and harmony between the planets. In the future. Roughly translated it means, the publishing company run by Raymond and his wife Zephyr.'

'Wow,' said Raymond.

'In the future. What is today's date, by the way?'

'The sixteenth, I think.'

'Then I must go. A copy of the book will arrive for you when you get home. Keep an eye out for the postman.'

'Zephyr, please don't go. I love you.'

'And I love you.' Zephyr kissed him. 'In a year from now,' she said. And then she vanished, just like that.

And Raymond was left all alone.

'A year,' Raymond sighed. 'A year from today. The sixteenth. No, hang about, it's not the sixteenth. It was the sixteenth when I got snatched away from the allotments. I wonder if that matters.'

There's a circus playing on Bramfield common nex
week.

It's well worth a visit. You'll not have seen anythin
quite like it before.

Raymond will be going. And his best friend Simon
And Simon's fiancée Liza.

They've booked seats at the front. In fact, they've
booked all the tickets for the first show. Simon's treating
the whole village.

It should be a show worth watching.

You won't miss it, will you?

It's The Greatest Show off Earth.

THE END